THE
NOBEL
CONSPIRACY

Robin Marshall

First published as a paperback in 2017 by Champagne Cat
First edition: December 2017

This is a work of fiction. Some real people who lived up to a century ago
are included and they only do what they would have done in life. Any
fictitious names, characters, businesses, places, events and incidents are
either the products of the author's imagination or used in a fictitious
manner. Any resemblance to actual persons, living or dead, or actual
events is purely coincidental. The author never encountered any
scientist who even remotely resembled his villain, who was created with
difficulty and with a need of much imagination.

ISBN 978-1-5498068-5-8

A CHAMPAGNE CAT PRODUCTION

Contents

Chapter 1

Stockholm 1934

There is a moment when the enormity of the deed comes home to the perpetrator. That moment arrived for Clive Blackmore on the 10th of December 1934, when he heard the King of Sweden speak his name. Blackmore gulped dryly as a succession of thoughts flashed across his mind. His Adam's apple rose, fell and scraped within his starched collar. He ran his finger slowly round the inside of the stiff cotton, stared blankly as the cloudy, translucent droplet lengthened on his finger tip and fell onto his starched bib, creating a dark spreading oval damp patch just below his bow tie. Blackmore snapped out of his dream and sat bolt upright. The heavy lights glinted on his forehead, a forehead so high that it started at his nose, continued over his head and finished at the nape of his neck. Blackmore was by no stretch of any imagination a handsome man. Even his mother had exclaimed, moments before dying in childbirth, that he looked like a frog. With protruding eyeballs and arched eyebrows, it was not hard to see why. He shuddered, feeling the sweat on his brow, his neck, his back, indeed, his whole body. His handshake, now to be offered to the King, felt at the best of times like a tree fungus on a dank February morning. Rubbing his hands down his trouser leg, a habit born of a lifetime of hyperhidrosis, did nothing, as always, to reduce the clamminess. What would the King of Sweden say? Panic seized Blackmore, unaware that the King had probably shaken the hands of thousands of frogs in his time.

Clive Blackmore had not a single redeeming feature; he did not even know whether or not he loved his wife. Yet sitting on the stage in the Concert Hall, under the gaze of thousands, he had suddenly felt the need for the succour of marital comfort. He had turned in his seat towards the close relatives' gallery, hoping for a reassuring smile from Brenda. Brenda alas, had her mind on other things and her husband saw only her face, set in the rictus that always perturbed him; her mouth was open like a black elongated figure of eight, wider at the edges than in the middle. Brenda was dreaming about the prize money.

1

Blackmore turned back sharply as he felt a soft nudge against his shoulder. Chuck Jordan, University of Houston joint prize-winner for physics with Blackmore, was waking him out of his trance. Jordan and Blackmore had both been shocked when told they had won the Nobel prize for physics; Jordan because he had won it, and Blackmore because he had to share.

'Go on Limey! It's y'all on now!'

Blackmore snatched up his lecture notes but immediately dropped them, the papers falling all over the floor. Jordan leaned over to help but Blackmore croaked noisily, causing more heads to turn.

'No, no, leave them, I'll do it!' Blackmore couldn't bear his papers being touched in case anyone spotted something they shouldn't.

'You don't need them now. Go on, I'll look after them for you.'

Blackmore also did not want them to become hopelessly out of order. The whole hall now craned to see what was happening, the flurry, the croaking, the stooping and the scooping. Blackmore in his panic, ran his hand over his dripping forehead, realised too late that it would become drenched, that he would be offering the King something more like a freshly culled squid than even a tree fungus. Blackmore, horrified and increasingly panic stricken, dropped his papers again. There were titters and Brenda Blackmore left her dreams of owning a vacuum cleaner and turned to see what the consternation was about. Over to her left, on the stage, she could see paper everywhere. Brenda scowled upon the farce and the usual words flashed through her mind: How could he do this to me? What will people say? Brenda turned away with a small choking cry. A flashbulb went off, blinding her. Clive jerked forward, propelled by the helpful Jordan. The King wore gloves, crisp and white. After a royal blink at the damp patch on Blackmore's bib, the handshake over, the gloves found their way into a small tub behind the flowers. The King then pulled on a second pair, a surgeon preparing for his next patient.

Blackmore snatched his medal and certificate, made as if to speak, but before he could, was drowned by the next prizewinner being announced to the sound of trumpets, as an equerry ushered him off.

Clive was re-united with Brenda for the short ride to the Stockholm City Hall where the new Nobel laureates, their wives, mistresses and relatives and hundreds of guests would gather for the banquet in the Golden Hall. They did not speak to each other. Brenda did not even ask to look at the gold medal. Clive did not want to show it to her. The silence continued all the way up to the Prince's Gallery where Clive once again offered a clammy grasp in return for royal congratulations. A trumpet fanfare on the stroke of seven announced that the banquet would begin and Clive took his seat opposite Chuck Jordan.

Clive was still pre-occupied with his lecture notes. He saw to his joy and relief that page one was at the top. He was, if nothing else, well organised. Nobel prize winners were always well organised. He quickly ruffled through the stack of his notes, becoming a schoolmaster handling miscreant schoolboys by the ear. He plucked out three pages and restored them to their rightful place in the stack. He had a lightning brain and analysed the sequence of the clearly written page numbers faster than his nimble fingers could move. But his brain was far too fast. As he flipped through the pile, page 16 flashed up and the crossed out name of Robert White punched him in the face. He had agonised on whether to mention White at all for his "pioneering" work. Protocol said he should. Fear, shame and conscience said he shouldn't. He had little shame and no conscience but fear had been enough. Now White was back at the front of his thoughts, back where he had been when the King had called out his name 'Professor Blackmore.' He had almost called out 'I'm not a professor.' but thought better of it. If he wasn't a professor by the time he got back to Cambridge, he would leave with his Nobel prize. The fracas with the dropped papers had pushed White out of his mind. But here he was, back again, just when he wasn't needed.

"Fuck you White." thought Blackmore. Then a froggy, rubbery smile spread over Blackmore's moist thick lips. He indulged in a few seconds recovery as he realised he already had.

'Those for tomorrow?'

Clive looked up puzzled at the smiling Jordan. 'Tomorrow? The lectures are now aren't they?'

'I hope not! I don't think we have the stamina for hours of lectures. We've come to dine. You've got your acceptance aphorism ready, haven't you? I guess you can memorise that.'

3

Clive had indeed thought he was giving his lecture at the dinner. 'Five minutes maximum is what I heard. Some people keep it to a single sentence. Somebody once went on for 10 minutes. I've timed mine at three minutes.'

Without Jordan, Clive would have been sunk. He had overlooked the fact that he needed to give a brief acceptance speech over dinner. All he could think of doing was to read out the first page of his lecture notes. That is exactly what he did.

'Your Majesty, your Royal Highness, Mr. President, Lord Mayor, Esteemed members of the Nobel Committee, Ladies and Gentlemen, it is a great and unexpected honour to be here today ...'

'Unexpected!' Blackmore was lying again, not for the first time. He had planned this moment for fifteen years with meticulous cunning. He could run rings round everyone in the department. He was the fox of physics and the faculty. The problem with lesser mortals was that they were all gentlemen of honour and that was where they failed, because Blackmore had no scruples. When you had perpetrated an enormous deed, a lie seemed nothing in comparison. Ten lies were not much more. What was a man's job and career worth, destroyed by a lie? If you had perpetrated a deed, then a simple career was a small fry to burn. They had all deserved it. White had deserved it for being too smart and too honest.

'The subject of my talk is the behaviour of electrons in semi-insulators or more properly called, semi-conductors. I believe that this will be a significant thread of the physics of the future and it is my privilege and honour to tell you about it now.'

Modesty was another trait, like a functional exocrinology, that through upbringing, training or genetics, had passed Blackmore by.

Talk? Worried looks were exchanged up and down the tables. The King leaned over to whisper to an equerry.

Brenda scowled. If there was one thing that upset her more than clammy cold superfluous foreplay, it was the sound of Clive's voice talking about physics. He never spoke to her or about her with such warmth and enthusiasm. A one hour physics lecture would turn Clive from a cold damp amphibian into a warm animated human being. It always worked like a prince's kiss and once again, she was intensely jealous. She despised physics almost as much as she despised Clive. But the vision of the Nobel Prize and fame flashed through her mind once again and she, herself, warmed a little towards Clive and his "lecture". Brenda was always slow to change her facial expression to match her thoughts and she was shaken from her scowl by a flashbulb as the official photographer took a picture of the row of accompanying women. The Nobel ladies. Wives, mothers, daughters and mistresses. They were all dressed in their finery, with uncomfortable identical and tight Stockholm perms, each one inflicted by the same hotel hairdresser who had started at seven o'clock in the morning to make sure he earned his kroner from all of them. Now they looked like a row of identical Hedda Gablers. Even the darkly attractive Countess of Alma, accompanying the American prize-winner Chuck Jordan had been made to look like one of the Marx brothers. Her normally shoulder length raven hair now circled her head in a tightly curled sphere. All were smiling, except Brenda, who was recorded for posterity in the deepest of deep scowls.

'What were you thinking of?' whined Clive when they received the official photographs a month later, in a thick, heavily and multiply stamped package from Stockholm. Brenda, with her hand on her new sleek upright vacuum cleaner, scowled even more fiercely than the startled angry face in the photograph, taken in the City Hall. And then another at the banquet in the Blue Hall, even more fierce. She started to explain but Clive was already concentrating on another letter, from the Vice Chancellor of Manchester University, warmly congratulating him of the recognition of the work he had done at the University and offering an honorary degree. Clive now felt uneasy going back to that place. It brought back too many dark memories. Even now, the letter brought them pouring back.

~   ~   ~

Chapter 2

Manchester 1912

T he day was grey, as close to black as it could be without being black. Manchester, Tuesday the 1st of October 1912. Grey drizzle fell from a grey sky onto grey slippery cobbles. The buildings were all black and magnificent, constructed from magnificent stones, now clad in a hermetic seal of soot. It was the sort of day that had provoked Mark Twain, visiting Manchester, to exclaim, 'I would like to live in Manchester, England. The transition between Manchester and death will be unnoticeable.'

Robert White, head bowed against the enveloping drizzle, made his way out of the Victoria and Exchange Station to find the tram. Although it was already nine o'clock in the morning, it was still dark. Not because the sun had not risen, but because its rays were absorbed by the usual Mancunian layer of soot laden clouds. At the stop, Robert was about to get on the number forty tram, when he became aware of the same extravagantly dressed, tall young lady who had got into his railway carriage at Burnley. She had been met off the train by a short, dark, fidgety, foreign looking man, dressed in dark foreign looking clothes. Robert had been struck by the mismatch between the two and felt a curious inexplicable pang of injustice at the sight of two complete strangers who did not seem to belong together. He stood aside and tipped his hat as she got on first. She almost imperceptibly tipped her head, which supported a glorious hat, which might have been a cottage garden covered with dew. With a trace of a smile, she swept on to the tram and sprayed Robert with a shower of Manchester drizzle as it flapped off her clothes. Without waiting to see if he was included in the courtesy, the short foreigner, as now he proclaimed himself by his action, swept past Robert onto the tram, giving Robert another cold shower as he flapped his long coat unnecessarily. Robert suppressed a gasp. He had been at the front of the queue, had done his duty to the lady and found his continued generosity put upon. No Englishmen would jump the queue. Not even in Manchester.

Fifteen minutes later, after clattering and swaying its way down Oxford Street and then Oxford Road, the tram paused briefly and noisily outside the main University buildings. Robert, Miss Extravagance and Mr. From-another-world all got off. Off the tram, and with hardly a glance left or right, Mary Ramsbottom swept across Oxford Road towards the entrance to Coupland Street. It reminded Robert of his visit to Liverpool Docks when a replica galleon swept in off the Mersey. She was followed closely by her companion, a tugboat, escorting her from three paces to the rear. Robert followed more cautiously. Half way across the road, Mary called out. It could have been more ladylike, but she had not yet learned how to hold back her expressions when things went wrong. Mary was waving arms in the air and tugging with her left leg.

'Chaim! Chaim! I'm stuck.'

Her shoe was firmly wedged in the groove of the tramlines. Both Robert and the now identified Chaim dashed forward from their respective positions. Chaim quickly reached the safety of the far pavement and Robert arrived in the middle of the road to find his damsel in distress.

'Let me help you.'

Mary's efforts only served to wedge the shoe more firmly. Robert looked anxiously up and down Oxford Road. He could see nothing, but then he could barely see a hundred yards.

'It's alright, there's nothing coming.'

'What am I going to do? It won't come out.'

'Steady on. Here, let's undo the straps and you get your foot out. Stand on this.'

Robert laid his suitcase flat on the cobbles and quickly unlaced the shoe, more a fancy boot than a shoe. With Mary's foot out of the shoe, it took a second to understand how the heel had swivelled after entering the groove, the heel becoming trapped under the tram rail. Robert swivelled it back and out it came.

'Let's get out of here before another tram comes. Here, take your shoe and lean on me till we get to the pavement. It's quicker.'

There was a distant clanging of a metal bell, the screeching of metal wheels on metal rails. Nothing was visible up or down the street but it could be a hundred yards away, 300 hundred feet, 30 miles per hour, that's 44 feet per second thought Robert, and that's about seven seconds. His calculations were done in a fraction of a second and five seconds later, Mary was safe on the pavement. Robert put down his case, took the shoe from Mary and placed it on the case. Twenty yards away, the tram heading for the city centre came to a halt. No actual danger, never an actual risk.

Chaim tried to seize control. 'That's all right now. I kept checking to see if anything was coming. You were always safe. I knew that.'

'Thank you, Chaim. I'll see you in the department in a few minutes. Would you be a sweetie and run ahead and get my specimens ready. I've got a lot to do today.'

Chaim scowled, was about to say something, opened his mouth in readiness, but nothing came out. He flounced away under the archway and into Coupland Street, a smart scarecrow flapping in a storm under a large homburg hat, lifting on one side as if hinged on the other, a gate-valve on the steam engine of his brain. It flapped up as if he needed something to leave or enter his head.

Robert turned his attention to Mary. 'I'm Robert. Robert White. If I may be so bold as to introduce myself.'

'You already have Sir! In style. I am Mary. Mary Ramsbottom.'

'May I escort you safely to where you are going?' Robert raised his hat.

'Your companion seems to have left you.'

'Oh, Chaim is all right. He's gone ahead to prepare the laboratory.'

'Laboratory?'

Robert did not know why his stomach churned. He was briefly transfixed by the intensity of the eyes that held him in their gaze. Blue and unblinking.

'Yes. In the chemistry building, down there and through the passage.'

'Ah, chemistry. I'm in physics.'

It was almost a lie from Robert. He had been in the department of physics as a student. He had graduated and this was the first day of his appointment as 1851 Exhibition Fellow. Technically, until he walked through the front door of the physics building, 25 yards down Coupland Street on the right, he wasn't 'in physics'. But he was pre-occupied with Chaim.

'Do you work with the gentleman? Chaim?'

'Chaim? He's doing his own thing but we sometimes help each other out. He's an intense person. Better with words than his hands. You could imagine him running his country if he had one. He is so passionate.'

'If he had one?' Robert was reduced to lamely repeating the last words he had heard as a question, to continue the conversation.

'He's Jewish. And all he can talk about is the new Jewish state.'

'The Jewish state? I didn't think there was one.'

'There isn't! Yet. Look, I must be off. Mondays are very busy.'

Mary had fully regained her composure and with an almost royal swirl of her clothes, she swept off down Coupland Street aiming to dock in the chemistry building. Two young men, in waistcoats, collar-less striped shirts and flat caps, carrying a piece of heavy equipment on a piece of wooden board like a corpse on a stretcher, swerved to one side to let her pass. One of the pair let go of the board with one hand to doff his cap, the stretcher swayed and the equipment slithered over the wet board trapping the other man's hand.

'Dibblee you oaf. For Mary's sake, do you have to do that every time you see her?' This was a reference to an equally virginal, but better known Mary.

'Can't help it, Alf. It's her fault. She shouldn't be allowed out. Women in the Yunivarsity!'

At that precise moment, Robert was also remarking 'Women in the University' to himself. 'What a woman.' He thanked under his breath the progressive style of Manchester University. Christian, Catholic, Baptist, Methodist, Jew, Muslim, male and female; if you wanted to study at Manchester, you did not have to swear an oath that you acknowledged only one Church, the Church of England. Robert shook his head clear for the ordeal ahead. It was almost time to meet his maker. Inside the doors of the physics building, he would meet the 'PROF'. Professor Ernest Rutherford, winner of the Nobel Prize for Chemistry in 1908. If Robert would become a physicist, Rutherford would make him.

Inside the physics building, Robert was greeted with a warm Mancunian welcome. 'Welcome back, Mr. White. It's a real pleasure to see you. Congratulations on the fellowship. We're all looking forward to what you're going to make of it.'

William Kay, laboratory steward, was Rutherford's prime assistant. He was everybody's assistant and on top of that, he prepared all the demonstrations for the lectures. If a lecturer needed a loud thermodynamic bang or a spectacular spark to illustrate an otherwise mundane chalk and blackboard lecture, Kay would provide it. Almost always, when such a request came in from a lecturer, who might wish to illustrate Maxwell's equations with real moving graphics, Kay would oblige and there would usually be an added bonus thrown in for good measure. Robert held out the letter of appointment to Kay, as if showing a passport. Kay brushed it aside.

'I'll take you upstairs, Sir, they're waiting for you.'

Upstairs, in the tea room, there was no one. Kay touched his forehead and left. Although he had been a student here, Robert had never been in the tea room. He had been at the door, seeing his tutor, not much unlike a visit to the Masters' common room at grammar school, where pupils, summoned to be told of a detention, or worse, could peer beyond the voluminous black gown and see schoolmasters, teachers, the high and even higher, lounging on frayed couches, surrounded by piles of books, exams papers, hockey sticks or rugby balls and clouds of tobacco smoke. From behind, and from the ceiling: 'You must be White. Hallo, I'm Fokker.' Robert turned and found himself looking at the buttons of a waistcoat. Upwards a neck, a moustache and finally, almost seven feet off the ground, the rest of the face - a smiling giant with a Dutch accent. 'Oh hello Sir, I don't . . .'

Robert was about to say he didn't remember a Fokker when he was a student but thought better of it. Just as well. Fokker, Big F as he was already known, had just arrived. Science and technology ran in the Fokker family.

'I'm Fokker. And you?'

'Oh, I think I have read about you in the paper. Do you make aeroplanes?'

'No. He's my cousin. But well spotted young man!'

'Welcome Mr. White.' This time the plummy voice came from a direction slightly to the right, but also from the ceiling. Robert turned to meet the gaze of a second friendly giant, perhaps half an inch smaller than Fokker.

'Darwin. Charles Darwin. You might have heard of my grandfather.'

Robert gulped. He knew that Charles Galton Darwin, expert mathematician, was working in Rutherford's group. He knew the line of hereditary, Erasmus Darwin, grandson Charles and now the great great grandson of Erasmus. Why were the alternate Darwins so relatively unknown? What made every alternate generation obscure? Robert raised his arm for the second time in a minute, like a Roman salute, and shook hands with a Darwin.

'My name's Robinson. Harold. But you can call me Roper.'

The voice came from a third giant. Robert already started to feel a strong sense of insecurity and inadequacy. He had striven to be six foot tall. He was five foot, eleven and three quarters of an inch tall and still hoped to grow a quarter of an inch. He had striven and had weekly plotted his own height, gauged with a wooden ruler flat across his head to touch the wall, held there as he lowered himself and then marked with pencil, the underside of the ruler. He had sworn. The pencil marks had not grown in line with his striving, but had jittered up and down around his official height of five feet, eleven and three quarters of an inch. Two of the pencil marks had exceeded six feet but Robert had been forced to conclude they were fluctuations of measurement. He was a scientist. Repeated measurements never gave quite the same answer. If they did, it usually meant unscientific enthusiasm or optimism on behalf of the measurer. He had accepted the truth but nevertheless had done some research. Pigeon meat, it was alleged, contained an ingredient to accelerate growth. Six months and 26 pigeons later he was still an eighth of an inch shy and decided to relegate the importance of the matter of height in favour of the more pressing matters of career and finding a soul mate. Salt was rubbed in the wounds.

'How tall are you then?' Robinson was almost taunting. 'We start counting at 72 inches here. That's defined to be zero.'

Robert flinched.

'Come on, you're a Manchester man. You can subtract 72 from your height in inches can't you?'

'Minus one eighth. With 95% probability.'

It was the second, unnecessary, but reflex remark that brought the laughter and with it, the realisation to the tall men that Robert carried a complex about his height.

'Well. What are we going to call you then? Lofty? Mr. not-quite-a-fathom?'

'How about Robert? That's my name.'

'Robert it is.' The new voice, shrill, came from Andrade who had entered the room. Ernest Neville da Costa Andrade pulled himself up to his full five feet one and a half inches and asserted his authority on the question of height.

'That'll do till Papa gets back. He usually likes to vet the nicknames.'

Papa was another pet name for the PROF. By mid afternoon, Robert had nothing to do. There wasn't much to arrange on his new desk once his pencils and notebook had been laid out, shuffled and put back the way they were. He was desperate to get started on his research, but until the PROF returned the next day, he would have to wait. The PROF was on important business, attending a meeting of the British Association. Just before four o'clock, another new face breezed up to Robert.

'Tea time!'

'Oh good. I'm ready for that, although I haven't earned it.'

'You will. Oh yes, you will in time. De Hevesy's the name.'

'Pleased to meet you. I'm White, Robert White.'

The physicists gathered in the tea room. Like all other rooms in the building, the walls were tiled, pale green, almost white and dark green. One hundred years later, in an 'enlightened' age, the building and its contents might be regarded as a death trap. Radioactive sources were handled, split and passed around with gay abandon. William Kay was becoming increasingly concerned. He knew of the burns that radioactive sources could cause. So did Arthur Schuster, the previous head of department, who had carried some radium back from Vienna in his pocket and got burned. But what the physicists did not know was that the tiles themselves were naturally radioactive. Uranium salt, dissolved in the glass during manufacture gave the distinctive green translucence. Their sole redeeming feature was that they reflected what little light came through the grimy windows.

In the tea zone, the physicists got together to exchange ideas and gossip. They made plans to visit the theatre and music halls. Robert nodded to those he had already met and mentally repeated their names to burn them into his memory. A tall dark-haired woman stood up, smiled and held out her hand.

'You must be Robert White. I'm Margaret. Margaret White actually – we've got the same name but I don't think we are related.'

'No, I don't think so. But you never know. We might get a surprise and find we are!'

Robert sat down next to Margaret and took the enamelled tin mug offered to him by Andrade. The edges were chipped and the black of the oxidised steel showed through.

'Don't forget to bring in your own mug tomorrow.' piped Andrade.

Margaret was keen to tell Robert about her research. It involved making meteorological measurements on Glossop Moor.

'Why don't you come up with us at the weekend? We're having an exciting time at the moment what with Ludwig trying out his new jet motors on the kite.'

'Ludwig?'

'Ah, he was a student in physics and engineering but went off to Cambridge last year. You probably won't know him. Ludwig Wittgenstein from Austria. He was in Berlin wanting to study with Boltzmann, who's also from Austria. Anyway, Boltzmann went and er, ended his own life, before he could start. So he came here. He's very intense.'

'Boltzmnann or Wittgenstein? They're both Ludwig.'

'Oh Ludwig Ludwig, I mean Wittgenstein! But he's all right when you get to know him. Although he does not suffer fools.'

"Ludwig, Chaim. This place is full of intense foreigners. I'm going to enjoy this." thought Robert.

A pair of heels snapped together in front of him and Robert looked up to see another imposing figure.

'Not another big Fokker!' Robert kept the thought to himself. 'But big enough.'

'I am the Geiger!'

Hans Geiger, new to the department and to English in England, had not yet totally mastered the art of introduction. The German form, literally translated 'I am the Herr Doctor Geiger' was too much and he knew that some of the words would have to go. But he was starting at the end and not at the beginning. Geiger was smart, well groomed and imposing. A small network of duelling scars traced across his left brow. It looked almost like irregular lace or a spider's web.

'I wish you a very happy and successful residence in the department.'

Geiger clicked his heels again. By now Robert was on his feet, shaking the offered hand and wishing Geiger similar success. William Kay had entered the tea zone carrying a small package, gift wrapped. Everyone turned to stare, wondering who it was for. The physics department, Kay and wrapped gifts did not go together. Kay picked out Robert and walked over, relieved to be able to place the package on the table in front of him.

'Compliments of the lady, Mr. White. She asked me to deliver it at once.'

'Lady? What lady?'

'Don't know Sir, she didn't give a name. Though I dare say I have seen her once or twice in Coupland Street. You can't miss her. She must work close by.'

'Can't miss her?' Robert was playing for time. The description was enough to identify his vision. He knew who it was. He blushed, rushing out of control.

'You've gone a dashing shade of pink, young man.' This was Fokker, though how he could see Robert's face from his altitude was a mystery.

'She's left a note on the packet.' Said Kay, keen to move the uncomfortable moment on.

'Read the card!' Fokker was smiling hugely.

'Come on, put us out of our misery and find out who it is from.'

'I can't imagine who.' Robert's protest was lamentable. 'There's no signature, just a message.'

'Well, what does it say?' Andrade was almost squeaking.

'To the knight in shining armour, for saving my life.' Robert started to read it out but got no further than 'knight'. He took the card, folded it and put it in his pocket.

'To the night!' Fokker was roaring. 'You can't leave us in suspense like that! You get a present from a lady who starts dedicating them to a night. A night together? What have you been up to? The PROF is not going to approve of this at all, you know. Coming from your colonies he has very strict moral standards.' The Dutchman did not draw the Dutch colonies into the discussion.

Robert felt trapped and awkward. He took out the card, unfolded it and laid it on the table.

'There you are. I don't want to have any secrets. It's knight with a k actually.'

Margaret White leapt to her feet, took the card with a snap, folded it back and put it in Robert's top pocket.

'Stop prying you lot. You're always poking your noses into other people's business.'

Margaret herself had felt oppressed by the excessive, school-boyish interest shown by the group of male colleagues. She had only had a friendly chat with Walter Makower, perhaps more than one, and then when the PROF had returned from a visit to a conference in Australia, he had mentioned it to her in a slightly disapproving, albeit gentle and jovial way, as soon as he got back. He'd been away a month and could not possibly have known unless someone had told him. Had someone written? Was it that important? Not to her, it wasn't. She had known Walter was married but chose not to treat her male colleagues any differently from female.   There were virtually no women scientists in the department, just her and Natasha Bauer and if she couldn't speak to the men, married or not, she would work in almost total silence. Natasha was a feminist and thought that Margaret was not severe enough with the men. Margaret had told the PROF that whatever was in Walter's head, her head was as clear as a bell. It mattered not a jot whether Walter was married or not as far as talking to him was concerned.

'Thank you, Margaret.' Robert offered his thanks quietly but then raised his voice for others to hear. 'Actually, it doesn't amount to much. Crossing Oxford Road, a woman got her shoe jammed in the tram lines. Her companion, a Chaim chap, just stood and watched. All it needed was a bit of logic. It is easier to twist and manipulate a shoe without a woman in it.'

'It's also easier to twist and manipulate a woman without a shoe on her!' Young cheeky Dibblee had joined the group for his mug of tea. Dibblee looked like a boy, a scamp, yet wore the clothes of a man. They were handed down from his father who had fought at Rorke's Drift and in the Crimea. Dibblee carried a huge enamelled tin mug, tea leaves already in, three spoons piled with sugar and a helping of condensed milk which was held in a non decaying state by a brown crust of dried milk on the tin and the high sugar content of the milk. It was almost a meal in itself. Scalding water onto the mix and then a five minute wait to let it brew. Meanwhile, if only to put an end to the stares, Robert opened the package. It was a box of cigars.

'So these are a mere thank you. Nothing more than that.'

Robert sought out Kay and quietly set up the next move. 'I really ought to send a thank you for the cigars, shouldn't I, Sir?'

15

'Firstly, don't call me Sir. I'll call you Sir when necessary. Yes, a brief note will be order. Unless you never want to talk to her again.'

'But I don't know where to send it. Well, actually I do, to the chemistry building. But I can't address it to the tall beautiful lady with the large hat. She'd never get it.'

'Yes she would. There's only one tall pretty lady with a big hat in the chemistry building. There's only one lady in the chemistry building so you could address it to the short ugly lady with the silly hat and she'd still get it. On the other hand, from what I hear, she has a bit of zest and might send the note back if it was addressed in that way! Just write the note and leave it to me.'

Writing the note turned out to be more complex than Robert had imagined. He remembered the first name 'Mary' with ease, but for the life of him, could not remember her surname properly, even though he had been told it. Ramsbottom? Higginbotham? Rowbottom?

'Dear Mary, Firstly an apology since your surname has slipped my memory ...' That sounded awful. The first words were not only over-familiar but then admitted he had forgotten her name. In the end, he followed her example and left off the name in the greeting. He went back to the cigar box and glanced at the envelope from which he had taken her card. 'To Dr. Robert White.' In a neat hand.

'Oh God, she hadn't forgotten his full name and even knew his title.' What he did not know was that Kay had supplied the name and she had written it on the spot. Kay could not write his own name, let alone someone else's. Kay produced an envelope and clean sheet of paper, octavo.

'Here you are, Sir. This should be sufficient.'

The message itself was no problem. 'With sincere thanks for the nice cigars. To the lady in distress who was never in distress.'

He left the envelope unwritten and scuttled round to the chemistry building, home of the chemists. There was a counterpart to Kay in the cubicle in the foyer. For a moment, in the dark, with a shaft of light across the shoulder making the face appear even darker, Robert thought it was Kay, playing a trick on him. The voice was equally Mancunian but gruffer.

'Good afternoon Sir. What can we do you for?'

'Could you see that this gets to the lady who works here, the tall lady with the striking hat.'

'Which lady would that be, Sir?' Chemistry Kay was playing him along.

'I smoothed her passage through a difficulty on Oxford Road and she has thanked me to excess. I am not worthy.'

The whole chemistry department by now knew about the event on Oxford Road. But chemistry Kay was not going to make it that easy for Robert.

'Not worthy of what?' The voice was familiar and Robert, struck by immediate panic, could not understand why his throat had become sandpaper. He turned, only to find himself impaled on a penetrating gaze.

'Not worthy of your gift.' It was not Robert's voice, but it came via his tongue. 'I have come to deliver my thanks.' Robert held out the envelope. 'To deliver it myself.'

Mary looked down at the blank envelope.

'But it's not addressed to anyone. How were you going to ensure I got it if I had not been here by chance? I think you have forgotten my name already!'

The tone was light, smiling but with a hint of mockery. Robert recognised the jest but had experience enough from his elder sisters to know that women rarely joked, to men or about men, except among themselves. He had been frequently stunned to overhear his female siblings dissecting the males of the village.

'No I haven't, Mary. How could I forget it? And since you only told me and I didn't see it in writing, I wasn't sure if your surname would be spelt with th or tt, –otham or -ottam. Both are possible and the wrong one would have been worse than none.'

Robert had always known that a little crisis had the ability to provoke the right name, or some other little fact, from his memory where it needed a simple probe to poke it out. He also knew the crisis would provide him with the context in which to use it to advantage. The same thing had happened over and over again during his PhD research. He fed on it. Little facts that he had noted years before leapt out of his memory when he was faced with teasing a shred of understanding from some mysterious and reluctant data.

Mary was clearly impressed and the outcome was more to his advantage than if he had recalled her name correctly in the first place. An awkward silence followed. Two pairs of eyes were locked but both tongues were strapped down as if by laces in a boot. Chemistry Kay stood like a tennis spectator turning from one to the other, waiting on the next word. He knew he was witnessing the start of something and would drink out on it for weeks, months or even years.

'I hope, I wonder, perhaps ...' What he wanted to say would not easily come out. 'I hope I see you again on the road. But not like today of course.'

'Oh.' The disappointment could be touched. 'I thought it was all rather exciting – with hindsight.' Mary wanted to add 'romantic' to 'exciting', but she would save that for her diary.

'Yes, I thought so too. If you get stuck again, please make sure that you don't have just Chaim around.'

Clumsily, Robert took his leave and Mary came out onto Coupland Street and watched him all the way back to the physics building, 200 yards away, fading into the dirty haze, leaving her life. Before entering the building, Robert looked back and was stunned to see Mary still standing there. They exchanged small, synchronised waves. Once again a burst of adrenaline came to his aid. With less than a millisecond of hesitation, he turned, walked, nay ran, back to Mary.

'I'm sorry, but I just can't help it.' Was this the time for blurting? It was. 'I want to see you again if I may be so bold. And not just on Oxford Road.'

Mary flushed.

'Yes. Let's. Let's meet tomorrow lunchtime in the refectory,' said Mary, taking control. 'Twelve o'clock?'

'Yes please!' The please came out before he could stop it. He managed a strangled grin, turned and walked once more into the haze. Mary turned, head bowed and bumped into chemistry Kay who was standing in the doorway, beaming.

'What was all that about?' Chemistry Kay had an insatiable appetite for gossip especially where scientists were concerned. He knew all their private lives, almost better than they knew it themselves.

'Never you mind!' Mary switched to her stern mode.

Chemistry Kay beamed. He could wait. He'd go to the Nelson's Arm with his brother Bill after work and they would exchange notes over a pint of beer. Between the two of them, they would compare, examine, deduce and guess their way until they had the rest of Mary and Robert's lives mapped out in the finest detail, right down to the number of children.

'She sent him some cigars.'

'Yes, we know that. I didn't know your man's name, he's new, so I told her to see you at the front door.'

'But she did know his name. And he's not new, he was here already for five years as a student. She checked with me she had got it right and tried to get me to write the envelope for her. I told her he might recognise my writing and made her do it herself.'

Chemistry Kay guffawed and wiped pork pie jelly and beer froth off his lips with the back of his sleeve. A small piece of jelly remained stuck in his moustache. He would have it last thing before he went to bed.

'Oh Yeah, I guess he might recognise the style of your X one day. You and your mark.'

Physical Kay flinched at the jibe about his literary skills.

'What's PROF going to say? He'll want the new young man to concentrate on his physics at the start and not go gallivanting down to your chemistry building.' Kay always felt protective towards his "lads". 'His number will be up if he does. The youngsters only get one chance. If they don't deliver, they're out. A quiet word might be needed.'

'Aw, you're not going to spoil the fun and make him knuckle down are you?'

'Hrrmph. When it comes to the lads, I can't help it. I want them to succeed. It's so good to see it. I don't know what it was quite, but when young Mr. Geiger came, he did something with the PROF with them new fangled alpha particles and they turn out to be just that new chemistry stuff helium. But they did something very important and it showed that the Planck chap in Berlin, the one they've all been talking about, has got it dead right on Black Body radiation.'

Sometimes the Kay twins liked to speak about physics and chemistry in the pub in a loud voice. It made them sound as if they were on the inside of all the new scientific discoveries. It was almost as if they were doing it themselves. They had to be careful how far they went, although William took part in a lot of the measurements being made on atoms in the physics department. But if they strayed from men's talk too much, they would lose their undisputed popularity and respect as the two Kings of department stewards.

'Black body radiation! You mean that singer Flora at the Palace? Phwaah, she's a right one, she is.'

'I've told you about black body radiation before, Ben. It's what you get from red hot coals and things like that.'

'Oh yeah. Red hot coals are black bodies. I remember being struck how obvious that was. Your physics bods are a bit weird sometimes. Any road, I don't think your bloke will go gallivanting. He doesn't look the gallivanting type. She had to make all the running.' Chemistry Kay was not in the mood for physics today.

'Maybe he's not, but you're right, she did! I think we are going to witness gallivanting like we've never seen it before. I feel it in my water.' Kay liked to steal the PROF's expressions.

The main door of the pub opened, a gust of fog, Dibblee and a tall tweed clad figure entered in quick succession. The fog dispersed and mixed with the clouds of tobacco smoke in the pub, swirling upwards where a blanket of smoke hung from the ceiling. It had been years since anyone had seen how high the ceilings were. Dibblee went to the bar and the tall figure gestured to Physical Kay from the doorway.

'I thought I'd find you here.' Arthur Schuster coughed and removed the handkerchief from his mouth only long enough to speak. 'How can you breathe in here? It's dreadful. I can't see the other side of the room.'

'Ah Sir, Just like out on Oxford Road isn't it! Except in here it's good old fashioned, healthy tobacco smoke. It kills the germs. What can you say about that grimy stuff outside that you breathe in the evenings? You should have seen that gust you brought in with you from where we were sitting.'

'Kay, I'm meeting Professor Rutherford at London Road Station tomorrow. He will want to be briefed on what has been happening. I'll have 15 minutes with him before he goes into the Senate meeting and has to deal with the Vice Chancellor. I've not been well these last few days, so I need to know the progress on Mr. Geiger's work with the student Marsden. It sounded most unusual last week.'

Schuster coughed and expectorated into the handkerchief. A dredger on the Manchester Ship Canal discharging a scoop from the canal bed could not have done better.

'You shouldn't be out, Sir. This air is not good for sore throats. What time does the train get in? Do you have time in the morning? Mr. Geiger often comes in for a beer even though he says our stuff is not beer. How can you say that about "Thwaite's"? He can't even pronounce it. First time in here, he goes to the bar and asks for a tankard of "Twats".' Accidentally or otherwise, the noise of more pneumonic dredging from Schuster's lungs drowned the coarse end of Kay's sentence.

'Five past eleven sharp. It's the early one. Can I see you and Mr. Geiger in my office at 8 o'clock on the stroke?'

8 o'clock was early for Schuster, now retired. He had handed over to Rutherford as Director of the Laboratories five years ago but still came into the department more often than he should, hovering in Rutherford's background and sitting next to him in the group photographs. Kay had to stand at the back. Schuster tugged his deerstalker down a notch, pulled up the collar of his checked tweed overcoat and swirled away into the fog like someone out of a Sherlock Holmes story. Kay watched him disappear into the darkness and heard the clatter of hooves on the cobbles.

"Not got his automobile yet then." thought Kay. 'Even knowing Mr. Royce personally hadn't speeded it up.

Back inside, Dibblee walked over with half a pint of mild ale.

'How old are you young Dib?'

'Nineteen!' The response was almost aggressive. 'Sir.' The recognition was delayed by just an amount to rile Kay but not long enough to be an insult. The problem was that Dibblee looked no older than 12 and even the half pint glass looked huge in his tiny hands.

'We're just talking about Romeo and Juliet. Did you spot it?'

Dibblee frowned. His heart, stomach and throat lurched every time he saw or heard of the "Lady in the Hat". He now saw her about to disappear over the horizon, never having appreciated she had always been out of reach. The Kays knew of the hopeless infatuation. It was Dibblee's second. He had just got over Margaret White.

'Did you not see his Lady? Walking down Coupland singing?'

'Yer what?' Poor Dibblee was lost. Lost in unrequited love, he would not admit he spotted anything. 'Nowt important if you ask me. They say there were something happening out on Oxford

Road and she's grateful for her shoe being rescued. Anyone could have done it.'

'It's more than a shoe, I'll tell thee lad.'

Chemistry Kay thought it was high time Dibblee moved on to women of his own sort, if not women of his own size. Physics Kay, though gentler in his attitude to Dibblee, nodded.

'Well, you two would agree wouldn't you, blood brothers. It won't last. It won't even start. Look how the PROF scotched that business between Mr. Makower and Miss White.'

'Dr. Makower to you lad. And there was nothing between Dr. Makower and Miss White to be scotched.'

'That's because PROF got in there and nipped it out like a weed.'

'You've no proof of that Dibblee lad. Dr. Makower is married and he wouldn't, couldn't get involved with her.'

'They shouldn't let women into the department. I always said it would come to no good.'

'Just listen to the oracle, all 19 years of his lifetime's experience!'

'You're wrong any road. He was supposed to be giving her advice on flying her kites off Glossop Moor. But you don't need to go and spend three days on the moor with her to give her advice.'

'He did not spend three days with her on the moor. There were four of them, Peteval and Wittgenstein went along as well and they all stayed together at the Grouse Inn.'

''Ave you seen that place?' Dibblee had worked there briefly, setting up the kite winch. 'Bedroom windows have no glass in them. They do say that Witt'stein doesn't like women very much and Peteval's too old. That just leaves Mr. Makower and don't tell me she didn't need saving from the fog and the dew in the middle of the night, coming in through them open winders off Glossop Moor.'

Physical Kay grabbed his flat cap and cuffed Dibblee on the ear with it. 'Now look here lad. We only deal with facts. If you are going to join in while we sort out people's relations, you have to deal in facts and not guesswork.'

'It's not guesswork. Miss Wilkins were sorting the PROF's correspondence and it were all there in a letter from PROF to Dr. Schuster.'

Dibblee's use of rank was consistently erratic. Brenda Wilkins was a part time secretary hired by Rutherford out of his own pocket because the University did not believe in giving their professors a secretary. There had been a huge row when Schuster had bought a typewriter for the department out of his own pocket in 1882, the year Remington put the first machine on the market.

'But I'm paying for it myself.' Schuster had protested.

'If you get one, they'll all want one and they won't know you've bought it yourself.' The bursar did not like precious money being spent, even someone else's.

'Then I'll probably have to buy them one as well.' Schuster could always handle such illogic with skill.

'She's only supposed to file the papers, not read them!' Part of Kay's objection was that he himself could not read.

'How could she know where to file them if she doesn't know what they are about? Private. Equipment. Letters to foreigners.'

'Gossip filed under G.' Both Kays spoke in unison as they both held their head in their hands.

'And what did it say then?'

'Ahah, curiosity eh? PROF said they would need a word about Miss White in Makower's ear. He wouldn't say that if he didn't think something was going on.'

Physics Kay nodded, pursed his lips to conceal his delight as the importance of the new development sank in. Brenda Wilkins had the ear of Dibblee and the PROF's letters had her eyes. The implications were far reaching. There was only one snag. Dibblee was a most unreliable intermediary. He would distort the facts, blab about them, wreak havoc everywhere. The stability of the department was at stake. This had to be stopped, nay controlled. But the thought of that information flow was alluring. Dibblee's eyes and ears suddenly became extremely attractive.

'Dibblee lad, would you like a pint of mild?'

~   ~   ~

Robert returned from his dinner date with Mary at one o'clock sharp. Kay was fussing, imitating a hospital matron. The three giants, Fokker, Robinson and Darwin were towering above a curious stranger. Kay took Robert's arm and guided him to the group.

'Here you are, Mr. Blackmore. This is your colleague Mr. Robert White. You are sharing an office on the third floor.'

'Dr!'

'Beg your pardon.'

'Dr. Blackmore.'

'Ah. I'll remember that Mr. Blackmore. You're a doctor. You're due to see PROF in an hour to discuss what you are going to do. You'd better get yourself sorted before you go in.'

A thick lipped, salubrious face turned to Robert. The head was virtually bald. A nervous tongue lubricated the fringes of a mouth that opened and shut several times before words came out. The words, when they did emerge, were smooth and silky.

'Ah, White, pleased to meet you. I've made the arrangements to meet Professor Rutherford at two o'clock. Perhaps we should go up to the office and get our plans straight.'

'Plans?'

'Oh yes. Professor Rutherford likes plans. I've got some. Come on and I'll fill you in.'

In the shared office, Robert was astonished to find his desk had been moved so that it would be effectively concealed behind the door whenever anyone came into the room. Blackmore had set up a desk by the window.

'Hope you don't mind the furniture rearrangement old chap. I have a problem with my eyes and need full light. Of course, I should have asked you first but they told me they weren't aware of any eyesight problems you might have. They said you were a picture of health, you lucky chap!'

'Now look, we have to tell the Professor what we plan to do. He might not like it and tell us to do something else. It won't be good if we make a poor impression from the start.'

The liberal use of the word "we" was not lost on Robert. He felt no affinity for this amphibian. Indeed, he could not dispel the feeling of repulsion that had sprung up on first sight and which was threatening to seek a permanent refuge in his reflexes. In any case, when Robert had been interviewed by Rutherford for his fellowship, he had discussed his research path in great detail. There had been some resistance from Rutherford because it was outside the mainstream of the research being done in Manchester. Anything new might need new money, especially if apparatus needed to be built.

'We don't have the money, young man. Therefore, we have to think. Thinking about new apparatus is all very well but that's as far as it can go.'

Robert had never forgotten that phrase – "We don't have the money, therefore, we have to think". If he would do one thing to impress the boss, he was going to have an idea that saved money. In the end, Robert had convinced Rutherford that all he needed was a variable number of volts and something with which to measure small currents of electricity. Volts were easy. There was a large battery of voltage cells in the basement, supervised and maintained by Geiger. Geiger was simultaneously maternal and bank-managerial about his battery of cells. He always wanted to lend out fewer cells than the borrower needed. He was worried about breakages and that lending out so many would mean that he couldn't keep them all charged up. In the end, Rutherford had agreed that the measurement of small electric currents was a significant problem in itself and if Robert did no more than develop a better device to do this, physics would be progressed. But he was less impressed with the notion of studying the electrical properties of materials like gas coke and silicon. 'They are so irregular Sir, there must be a reason.'

'Yes!' Rutherford had growled. 'It's because they are horribly complicated, messy structures, dug out of the ground and baked. They will tell you nothing. You must look for simplicity in the problem. I am a great believer in simplicity. I am a simple person myself.'

It was a sentiment that Rutherford often used to gain a laugh. Robert had almost scoffed aloud at the notion that Rutherford was a simple person. But it had set him thinking.

He had not been able to think for more than a second before Rutherford had boomed his objections so that they echoed round the room.

'Gas coke! It's twisted, amorphous and full of holes. It's mainly carbon, isn't it? With loads of muck built in. Why not just propose coal and be done with it?'

'I agree it's very irregular but I would get it under a microscope and slice out some uniform sections.' Robert rode the punches. No need for a row early on. 'I think the uniform parts will be a very pure form of carbon; almost a crystal of carbon, different from graphite. At one end of the scale, we have metals that

25

conduct electricity so easily and for which we have the law of Georges Ohm. At the other end, there are insulators, which hardly conduct electricity at all. I think it is those things in the middle, neither conductors nor insulators that will tell us the most. The nice thing is that it doesn't need a lot of expensive equipment. It just needs a lot of careful detailed measurements and even more careful thought.'

In the end, Rutherford had grudgingly given Robert six months to demonstrate progress. If there were none, he would have to join the alpha particle team.

'You'd enjoy alpha particles, my boy. They are simple and swift. What more do you want?'

"Swift", "simple", "epoch" were all words that regularly found a home in Rutherford's finger-tip-ready vocabulary. In Rutherford's eye, Robert's proposed line of research involved materials that were not swift, not simple and not likely to launch an epoch. Six months did not sound much to Robert, but to Rutherford, it was likely to be a lost epoch. Now, suddenly, an unpleasant frog was staring at him, eyes bulging and mouth opening and shutting as if Robert were an insect about to be dissolved by digestive juices.

'It won't be good if we make a poor impression from the start.' Blackmore was an expert in manipulation.

'I agree.' Robert, naïve was sucked into the web.

'So why don't you push your ideas past me and I'll give you my impressions?'

'But you don't think like the PROF. He has a special way of looking at things. He is the highest rank imaginable. We are way down.'

'Go on, it will give you practice anyway.'

Reluctantly, Robert "went on", and outlined his thoughts on studying materials half way between conductors and insulators.

'Sounds very messy. I can't see someone like the Professor Rutherford agreeing to that. What are you going to do if he turns you down? That wouldn't be a good start at all would it?'

Something held Robert back from explaining that his plans were already approved, albeit with reservations.

'So, what about you then? What are you aiming to do?'

'Oh, I'm going to start off gently. Back to basics. I'll take a Crookes tube with some radium at the cathode and see what they do when they are accelerated.'

Robert was stunned. The alpha particles came off radium with prodigious energies. "Swift" was the word Rutherford used to describe them and that was an understatement. It was almost certain that one would need millions of volts to get them to go as swiftly as they came out of radium if one was starting from scratch in a Crookes tube with alpha particles at rest. But the alpha particles that came out of radium were already swift, so there seemed to be something in radium that was equivalent to millions of volts, shooting them out. Sticking a few hundred volts on a Crookes tube with an alpha particle in it, was akin to puffing on an express train as it hurtled through a station in an attempt to speed it up or slow it down.

'Gosh. I know Dr. Geiger has a big battery but I didn't think he had that many cells.'

The frog blinked, swallowed and looked away, puzzled, looking for another insect. He did not know what he was talking about. He had not been good in the laboratory at Cambridge, having excelled in theory. His grasp of practical things like volts and electrons was tenuous. He thought it was just a matter of connecting a battery across the Crookes tube and off you go. He thought his idea of sticking a radioactive source in the tube was brilliant.

'I have been working on the details in Cambridge all summer. J.J. has been helping me.' "J.J." was Professor J J Thomson, former student at Manchester in the 1870s, who had gone to Cambridge to study more physics and had stunned the world of physics firstly by being appointed Cavendish Professor of Physics at the age of 28, and secondly by discovering the electron and thirdly, by being the second Englishman to win a Nobel Prize. Now it was Robert's turn to blink. Either he was missing something rather fundamental or the frog was talking absolute rubbish, even as far as implicating Thomson in his bizarre ideas. Robert decided to put Blackmore on probation. He was convinced that the PROF would.

Rutherford did not just put Blackmore on probation, he blasted him out the room with such ferocity that everyone in the building heard it, like a rumble of distant artillery fire, although no one could make out the words. What surprised Robert, when Clive later told the story, was that it took ten minutes. He had already been surprised when Blackmore had said he was going in first, alone, at two o'clock. But Robert could hardly argue and felt pangs of guilt at the stolen hour with Mary. He had sneaked off with a woman for lunch, a chemist even, and had probably been absent when the PROF came looking for him. Now he was paying the price by being second in the queue to Clive. It hurt. He did not know that Clive himself had gone to Rutherford's office and arranged the schedule, explaining that Robert was somehow nervous and he ought to come first and show him there was nothing to be frightened of. Rutherford had not liked that. Robert also did not know that Clive had spent the first ten minutes fruitlessly trying to convince the PROF that he should study semi-insulators, substances like carbon which were neither metallic conductors nor insulators. He had, so he asserted, spent the whole summer at Cambridge discussing it with Professor Thomson who had talked of little else.

'That's curious,' bellowed Rutherford. 'To start with, I've just spent a week at the British Association with Professor Thomson and he talked about anything but that. And for full measure, I am not having two idiots wasting their time on that subject. One is enough for six months.'

'So I can get started straight away can I?' Clive had misread the Rutherford's last utterance badly.

'No you damn well can't!' Damn was the worst word that Rutherford would allow himself to say when enraged. But it was not the power of the word that unhinged Clive, it was the sheer volume with which it was delivered, almost lifting Clive from his seat. 'What else have you got to say before I get you calculating alpha particle trajectories through gases? Have you any other ideas?'

'Oh yes, Sir. I'm glad you mentioned alphas. I thought I would stick some radium on the cathode of a Crookes tube and put some volts on.'

'Oh really? And how many volts do you think you need to stop an alpha particle coming from radium? Have you any idea?'

'Oh no Sir, I wasn't going to stop them, I was going to speed them up.' These were the words that led to Clive's premature ejection from Rutherford's office, sent home to reconsider his future. He was to report for work the next day, pencils sharpened, and check through Darwin's calculations on the energy loss by alpha particles as they passed through gases. Someone had to understand the empirical rule that was exhibited by the data recently measured by Hans Geiger and Jimmy Nuttall, a German from Neustadt and a Yorkshireman from Todmorden.

'You can get started on that tomorrow. If you get it right, it might be Blackmore's Law. Otherwise, they'll keep on calling it the Geiger-Nuttall law even though no one knows its origin. I don't believe in calling it anyone's law unless that person can explain it. NOW GET OUT.'

'ROBINSON!'

The Physical Laboratories in Manchester did not have internal telephones in 1912. But Rutherford never had a need of an internal telephone. Less than a minute after his roar, Harold 'Roper' Robinson, one of Rutherford's most trusted departmental staff, timidly poked his head round the door.

'Who in the name of thunder hired him? I thought I left you in charge.'

'You did Sir, but it was the Vice Chancellor. He came in one day while you were on your trip back to New Zealand and asked me to do a favour for his aunt and hire Blackmore. I reckon he was making sure of his inheritance. I did write to you, but it probably arrived in New Zealand after you set off back home.'

'Keep that nincompoop out of my hair in future, do you hear?'

'Yes, PROF!'

The thought of "Blackmore's Law" had spun through Clive's head for half an hour on the tram to Didsbury. It was banished spontaneously when his landlady had refused to let him in on the grounds that he was early and not due back until six o'clock. He had walked around the lanes of the village, his bald head becoming progressively colder by the minute. More thoughts of "Blackmore's law" had then returned to consume him. Two hours later, much chastened, he crept into his digs, only to find that it felt even colder inside than out. Mrs. Critchley was a great believer in fresh air. The air was indeed much fresher in Didsbury than the city and she kept the windows open with no fire even when it snowed. If people got cold, they could wear an army greatcoat, there were still plenty to be had cheap, left over from the Crimean war forty years ago. For any normal person, especially a budding scientist, Clive's first day in the physics department should have been the worst day of his life. But it wasn't. Clive was special and he gained nourishment from his inability to understand reality. His brain worked on a more devious level. It worked in such a devious way that it built on what would have been a humiliation for others. Clive could thrive where others would strive in vain.

When Clive had left the shared office for fifteen minutes of debacle with Rutherford, Robert had wasted no time in doing furniture removing of his own. He rotated Clive's desk to be side on to the window and then slid it over to the right. He then pushed his own so that it faced Clive's, parallel to it. The two desks were separated by a gap of two inches and his next move was to race to the workshop and have a word with Roy the carpenter. He had got to know Roy as a student. They came from the same village. He told Roy what he wanted and more importantly, why.

'How long will it take?'

'Aw, if you take your time and have a cup of tea on the way back, it might be done by the time you've finished.'

'You're a brick Roy, I won't forget this.'

Before Robert could leave the workshop, the rumble of cannons from Rutherford's office had swept through the building, heralding Clive's shortened first day. But Clive had left in such a hurry, that he failed to pass on the message that Robert should show up for his session at once. Robert sat and drank tea, and more tea. Kay stopped for a chat.

'How did it go then, Sir?'

'I'm still waiting, Dr. Blackmore is still in there. Must be having an interesting chat.'

'No he isn't. He left over half an hour ago. Almost ran out of the building he did.'

'What! Oh my gosh. He's probably waiting for me, wondering where I've got to. It's nearly three o'clock. Oh dear.'

Robert ran to Rutherford's office; the door was wide open. All he could see was the broad beam of the PROF's posterior as Rutherford rummaged through a pile of papers on the floor in the corner. He looked back over his shoulder, saw Robert and turned purple.

'What do you want bursting in like that? Can't you see I'm giving a lecture in five minutes? It's the first one of the term so it's important for the new students. GET OUT!'

The truth was that Rutherford had lost his lecture notes having tossed them onto the shelf in relief when the course ended during the previous session. Robert sensed immediately what the problem was. This wasn't the first time it had happened. Many times as a student he and his friends had perceived the frequent fluster at the start of a lecture. Word had got around.

'At the end of each lecture Sir, you probably come in and drop the notes in the same place every week.'

Rutherford's eyes narrowed. He picked up a sheaf of letters waiting to be signed, stormed out his office, brushing Robert aside, walked five paces, turned, frowned in concentration, walked back into his office and without thinking, put the letters on the top shelf of the bookcase, on the right, inside the door. He smiled and removed the stack of papers from the same place, blew off the dust and grunted.

'Now get out of my way before I get cross!'

'Yes Sir, I'm sorry. Don't forget the other papers, Sir, on the top shelf. You might need them soon.' Robert thought it best not to call the papers "letters" or else it would look like he had been paying too much attention. Another grunt. Rutherford reached up, took down the papers and blew off more dust. There were more letters than he had just put there, but they would have to wait. Robert thought better of walking to the lecture theatre with Rutherford. His discussion would have to wait. He had arranged to meet Geiger in the basement where the battery of voltage cells were stored. He needed to make arrangements to use some of them for his preliminary experiments. Geiger would not simply hand over the battery of cells.

'Now, Mr. White. When you use the cells, remember this. You must never touch the battery connection when you are standing on a concrete floor.'

'I won't.'

'And you must always keep a dry wooden board to stand on if you are making adjustments.'

'I will.'

'You must always hold one hand behind your back when touching any part of the battery.'

'Of course, Herr Doktor Geiger. But why?'

'So that there is no risk of a circuit being completed through your body.'

'Oh.' Robert started to smile. Dr. Geiger was so concerned for his safety.

'You see, if you get a bad shock, you may kick out before you realise what you are doing, and the PROF would not like it if any of the cells got broken.'

Geiger never used the name "Papa". It was always the PROF. Those in the know, who had visited the local music hall, would use Papa and pronounce it Papaaaa. Others who had heard it once and forgotten, sometimes reverted to Papa, with two short syllables.

'Thank you, Dr. Geiger. When I need them, probably next week, can I just come and get them?'

'No you can't. I am held responsible for the cells by the PROF. If your signature is not in the book and a cell gets broken, then I will receive the blame. Even though I am not to blame. I will not accept the blame for what would be your carelessness, therefore, you must sign my book before I will unlock the door. Then if you break one, I will not have to pay for a new one; you will.'

'I understand. By the way, Dr. Geiger, I need to measure some small electric currents. Have you any suggestions?'

'How small?'

'I don't know.'

'Well, when you do know, ask me again.'

'I think they may be very small. Much smaller than an amp.'

'I shall and must think about that. If I have an idea I will tell you. In the meantime, you must try with the most sensitive meter possible and if you see nothing, you know you have to invent a new instrument. It had better not cost much money. The PROF only has four hundred pounds to spend on equipment each year. That's only about one thousand lunches at the Café de Paris in the Midland Hotel. So think with care.'

~   ~   ~

Dibblee, hands in pockets, peered through the gloom inside the Nelson's Arm. The Kays were not at their usual table. The two visitors to the department from Russian Poland had taken the Kays' usual table and were sitting opposite each other, separated by a bottle of vodka and two small glasses. Except that until that moment, Dibblee had never heard of vodka, let alone seen it. The Russians were attracting attention from the regulars and it wasn't completely friendly.

'What's that stuff they're drinking Reg?' Dibblee needed to know.

Reg Batchelor was the landlord, barman and washer up. He was standing behind the bar drying and polishing some pint glasses with what looked at first sight to be an oily rag but what was, in reality, a tea towel that was kept unwashed for the purpose. Reg was convinced that the accumulation of weeks of dried beer provided a wholesome polish to make the glass shine. Indeed, it made the glass shine so well that he often polished the outside of windows with it as well. Reg turned to Dibblee.

'Vodka, my lad. Russians like it. Poles like it. They are Russian Poles and I'm not sure if they are Russian or Poles. I daren't ask them their names. I'm told they might start throwing the glasses into the fireplace but if they do, they'll have to pay for them.'

'Where's it come from? Who got it?'

'Ah, I had it sent up from Lundun. It cost half a guinea. Half a guinea for just one bottle. It must be some stuff.'

'I think they've nearly drunk it already. 'Have you got another?' Reg turned pale grey. He had thought of having two bottles sent up; it would have been only ten shillings a bottle, one pound instead of a whole guinea, an extra shilling profit for the two. But he wasn't sure that the Russians Poles would like London vodka. He looked over in time to see them pour each other a noggin. They hardly had to tip the bottle. They had barely started. They both swallowed a noggin in one gulp, smiled broadly and slammed the glasses down on the table. Reg matched their smile but then winced. There was clearly no problem with the taste, but if they drank it at that speed he would need another bottle tonight. He'd better have a word with them.

'Be off with you Dibblee. It's time you grew up. You're still a kid.'

'Where's Bill and Ben tonight?' Dibblee was referring to William and Benjamin Kay.

'Over there in the corner where that smoke is. That new chap brought in a box of cigars and they've just about finished them. The cigars seem to have finished off the new chap as well. He went out looking rather green. Any road, I've already pulled you a half of mild. They've paid for it. It's your round next. And it's Mr. Kay and Mr. Kay to you lad. Or else I'll tell them what you call them.'

'Just a half? Are you sure.'

'You're on halves lad. Don't get big ideas.'

'I'm on pints now. And I'm not telling you why. I've grown up.'

Dibblee paused at the foreigners' table.

'Ay, that looks good wodka. Is it strong?' Dibblee knew the men from the department although not their names.

'Yes, excellent. Did you make it?'

'No! I'm Dibblee. I work in physics. I think the wodka has come from London.'

'I am exceedingly pleased to make your acquaintance Mr. Dibblee. I am Stanislaw Loria. I am Polish and you can call me Stan.'

'Ooooh. Poland. That's a long way from here.'

'There are trains Mr. Dibblee. There are trains.'

The other Pole held out his hand. 'And I, Sir, am Bohdan de Szyszkowski. At your service. Would you like a drink of vodka. Patron! May we have another glass?'

Reg realised what was happening and panicked at the thought of Dibblee helping to bring a premature end to the vodka bottle before he could get a replacement. He scuttled over to the table.

'Now then young Dibblee, stop bothering the gentlemen. Your beer is over there.' He turned to the Poles.

'I was just wondering Sirs, since this is a test, as it were, if you'll be wanting any more sent up.'

Loria picked up the bottle, tilted it and frowned. 'We might need another by the weekend. We can only allow ourselves a couple of tots a night because we have important work going on and we need a clear head in the mornings. But it's going to be finished soon and then we'll need a bottle or two for a big celebration. How long does it take to get one?'

'If I write the order tomorrow, Wednesday, I should have it off the train by Thursday night.' The letter was guaranteed to be delivered in London early the next day and the firm would have it on the train the same afternoon.

'Excellent, my Patron. And if the bottle does not arrive, we can always go to the Midland. Monsieur Colbert has plenty. But it's more expensive there of course.' Reg would dearly have loved to know how much more expensive and he did not know quite how much time he had to find out. The Poles liked to pay only after they had drunk up for the evening, not after each drink and he had accommodated their custom, much to their appreciation.

'Right Dibblee lad. Sit yourself down and tell us what's been happening in the big wild world today.'

Dibblee looked chemistry Kay in the eye. 'Not a lot Mr. Kay. That Miss Wilkins is trying to get her hands on that new Mr. White. She's always groping him.'

'Groping lad? That doesn't sound like Miss Wilkins. Secretaries don't grope.'

'Well, she's always got her hands on his lapels, plucking his hairs off them.'

'Hmmm, she's got her work cut out there. Doesn't she know about yon chemistry woman?'

'Oh, and the PROF brought a pile of letters down from his office. They'd been there on the top of the bookcase since before he went away in June. They were supposed to have gone out months ago and it were too late to send them.'

'So what did Miss Wilkins do with them then?'

Dibblee tapped a bulge in his jacket pocket and smiled. Horrified, William Kay erupted. 'What have you done lad? Where did you get them from?'

'It were Miss Wilkins. She put them in a bag and axed me to take them to the bin near the workshop. It's where they throw the waste paper.'

'Give them to me lad. Give them now and don't ever do that again. I'll see they get thrown out properly. I thought you were looking for a future after your apprenticeship? Who do you think is going to take you on if you're not straight?'

William Kay folded the bundle and put it in his inside pocket. 'Ready for another one lad? A pint this time. I'll go and get you one while you gather your thoughts so you can tell us what else Miss Wilkins said.'

Dibblee had a deep thirst. He had been working in the electro-chemistry lab where Dr. Hutton had been trying to make quartz glass. The Kays weren't interested in quartz glass today. It was just loads of electric current into a furnace. That was just amps and more amps. Amps were boring. They just flowed. More amps meant more flow. All right, a wire could get red hot and melt but that was even more boring. It always melted just when you didn't want it to. Whereas volts! Now volts were real man's stuff. Bigger volts meant bigger sparks. Physical Kay had set up a demonstration for the students to show that everything, even air, would conduct electricity if you put on enough volts. Cracking stuff it was when the foot long spark fired across the gap. The students were never expecting it. Usually, Rutherford was giving the lecture in his usual booming style but then dropped his voice to a whisper as he invited Kay to demonstrate the theory. When it happened, a big blue spark crashed out of the blue, it was like clapping hands in a hen house. Everyone jumped in the air and started clucking. It never failed.

'Can I have one of them?' Dibblee nodded at the box of cigars.

'No you can't. They'll kill you. Or at least make you ill. Even Mr. White couldn't manage one without turning all queer and they're his anyway.'

Reg came over. He had tried to put it out of his mind but couldn't. 'Dibblee lad, can you do me an errand? On your bike?'

'Of course, Mr. Batchelor. What would you like.'

'Come to the bar and I'll show you.'

At the bar, Reg continued. 'I want you to go to the Midland and find out how much it costs for a bottle of vodka. I need to know quickly.'

Although Dibblee did not like cycling fast on the cobbles, the prospect of a silver threepence warmed him to the prospect. Twenty minutes later, he was back.

'Yes?' Reg was hopping up and down with impatience. 'How much?'

'Polish or Russian?'

'What!' Reg's chin hit the floor.

'Polish or Russian? Polish costs a tanner more than the other.'

'Polish. No, Russian. No, they're Russian Poles, Probably Polish!'

'Wholesale or retail?' Dibblee was enjoying a rare bout of control.

'What! Retail, of course, they would only want one.'

'Red label or Blue label? Blue label costs a tanner more.'

'Red, no blue, no red. I don't know. They'd want the best, blue. Is that the best? Yes it is, it costs more.'

'You'll get a tanner change from a guinea for the Russian blue.'

'And a shilling change for Polish red? No, no, don't answer that. I've had enough.'

It was, indeed, too much for Reg. He couldn't charge a guinea or else they would be off to the Midland next day. But if he gave them half a crown change off a sovereign pound, they'd both be doing well out of it. In a few days, he'd be covered for all advance purchases and in a couple of weeks, he would have a profit to show in his pocket.

'Er, can I have my thrupenny bit then?'

Dibblee bit into the silver coin, looked at the teeth marks in the soft metal and dropped the coin into his fob pocket. His mother no longer searched his fob ever since he put some frogspawn in it to stop her going through his pockets.

~ ~ ~

Chapter 3

Manchester 1913

T he days and months that followed were some of the most exciting in the history of science. Manchester physicists had charged to the frontiers of knowledge and left the rest of the scientific world behind. Soon, after they had caught up, all the eyes of the world would be on them. Dibblee's eyes, in the meantime, were on the small world of the PROF's office and his ears absorbed everything that Brenda Wilkins was prepared to gossip about. The information thus gleaned found its way into the Nelson's Arm where the Kay twins nodded and murmured, as they thought through the implications. Hans Geiger's work, done with student Ernest Marsden, had caused quite a stir in the department but the paper they had written and published in the respected journal, the *Proceedings of the Royal Society*, had attracted little attention. A few in the world may have been watching, but couldn't take it in. Everyone knew that the PROF had been stunned by the results of the measurements. He had sent the two back to repeat the work to confirm that there had been no slip up. Over tea, Marsden still liked to talk about it, more than a year on. He was confident, almost cocky.

'I've never taken such care in my life. I remember the day when PROF told me that I was going to do these tests with Dr. Geiger. "Marsden, my boy," he said. "it's time you did something useful." Well, I knew from the way he said it that my number was up, so to speak, if I didn't find anything, or if I got it wrong.'

'I still don't get it.' Kay liked to understand the physics so he could talk about it in the Nelson's. 'If I throw an indiarubber ball at a wall it will bounce back at me. So why shouldn't alpha particles bounce back off a piece of gold or brass?'

'Ah well, you wouldn't expect your soft ball to slam its way through a brick wall would you?'

'No course not, I'd need a cannon ball or a shell to slam its way through a brick wall.'

'And you wouldn't expect an artillery shell to bounce back of a brick wall would you?'

'Not with a decent cannon, no! It'd be some wall, reinforced with thick steel, if a shell couldn't slam through it.'

'Exactly. And if you fired a 15 inch shell at a piece of tissue paper, you wouldn't expect the shell to bounce back under any circumstances?'

'Don't be daft. Of course it wouldn't. It would be as if the paper wasn't there.'

'Right, so you've got everything you need to understand what's going on. The alpha particles are swift.'

'Yes, PROF uses that word often enough: swift.'

'Well on an atomic scale, swift means that alpha particles are the 15 inch shells of atomic bombardment. And the gold foil is just tissue paper.'

'How can you be so sure that gold is like tissue paper to these – erm – swift alpha particles?' Kay wanted every last drop of knowledge, up to the limit of his understanding.

'Because, we know what we have to do to slow them down. You could slow them down with a voltage on a plate, just like Thomson speeded up his electrons with a voltage. With alphas, you just swap the connections round depending on when you want to slow down or speed them up. And to stop alphas, you need millions and millions of volts.'

'So, I get it, don't tell me, I've got it.' Marsden had told Kay almost everything, but it was gentle and friendly of him to let Kay himself take the final step. 'It means that the gold must have millions of volts to stop the swift little buggers. And then millions more to speed them up again to send them back the way they came! So gold isn't tissue paper after all.'

'Of course, although it might not be volts doing it.'

Kay's jaw sagged. He had argued and thought his way to the conclusion. He thought he had come to the end of the logical line and suddenly, little Marsden was snatching it away. Marsden noticed the alarm.

'It's all right Mr. Kay, it probably is volts, but you never know, it might be magnetic or something else we don't know about. Like the sun; if the sun is a burning flame like a fire, then it will burn out in only thousands of years. You can work it out. There's only so much hydrogen in the sun to burn. And also, it's not clear where it gets the oxygen from to make it burn; there isn't much oxygen in the sun, if any. Even so, it's been around longer than a few thousand years; so where does all that fire come from? Something unknown?'

'I know that.' Clive cut in with his superior voice. 'It's gravity. The sun is shrinking under its own gravity. When things fall under gravity, they go faster and faster till they hit the ground and all their energy of motion appears as heat. The sun is shrinking about 60 yards a year. It loses energy as it radiates it off as heat.'

'Goodness me, did you hear that Dibblee, lad. The sun is getting smaller every year.' Kay was doing well today. He had two new things to brag about in the pub.

'Well, all I can say, Mr. Kay, it looked the same size as when I saw it last month.' Dibblee smirked.

Kay looked at Clive for help.

'The sun is just shy of a million miles across. It would take 30 years for it to shrink a mile. That means it loses two miles in a human lifetime. You won't notice a two mile shrink off a million, not without extremely fine astronomical measurements. So it's good for a few million years yet, before even Mr. Dibblee could spot it. And with the greatest respect, even our young Mr. Dibblee won't be here in a million years.'

'No, no, no, I don't like that.' Andrade had just puffed in for tea. 'I don't like that at all. It's not so easy. You're right in one sense. Lord Kelvin, remember him? He died about five years ago. He worked out all the gravity stuff that Mr. Clive is talking about and got about thirty million years for the age of the sun. But that just has to be nonsense. Even thirty million years is too short.'

Clive frowned.

'How can you say that?' Kay had the scent of something important between his nostrils and was not prepared to leave without knowing the truth.

'Well, Mr. Kay. Do you remember that Professor Boltwood who came to stay with us from Yale for a year?' Andrade felt the warmth of knowing the whole plot, and how to play Kay like a salmon.

'I'll say. He was a very clever man. One of the cleverest.'

'So if our PROF Rutherford, and Professor Boltwood worked something out and published it in a paper, would you believe it?'

'Would I believe it? What a daft question. It would be gospel, physics bible stuff.'

'Right, then there you are Mr. Kay. Our PROF and Boltwood took all these decaying radioactive substances like uranium and thorium and all the other stuff and as you know, they have worked out the lifetimes and the rate of radioactive decay.'

'Yes, yes. We know all that.'

So if you know all the rates they are decaying at and the lifetimes, you can run it all back to when it started. They have done that.'

There was a long pause while Kay digested. Finally, Kay's flat cap nodded. Dibblee, who was struggling and waiting for things to take a simpler turn, took his cue from Kay's cap and he started nodding too.

'And PROF and Boltwood between them came up with more than one thousand million years.' Andrade finished off.

Everyone except Clive blinked. Clive scowled because he had lost the initiative to Andrade. He had known it all, but had been too slow. He thought Kay didn't need to know.

'What's the problem?' Kay could not see one. 'Thirty million or a thousand million. It's a very long time.'

'Ahah.' Andrade was waiting for this one. But before he could answer, Clive dived in.

'It's quite simple. If you have had this planet with its radioactivity and geology ticking away for a thousand million years, you've got some explaining to do if the sun suddenly switches on only thirty million years ago! There would be quite a few discontinuities, wouldn't there. I mean, life couldn't start before the sun and those dinosaur bones, hundreds of millions of years old, present rather an awkward problem if you think the sun started only thirty million years ago.'

'What about God?' Kay wanted a neat solution. 'He speaks with one voice.'

'Ah. God.' Clive felt extraordinarily at ease. 'God says that it all started six thousand years ago. Or, to be more precise, and this is most important, those people who believe in a creation by God say it started six thousand years ago.'

'What the difference? If God spoke and the prophets wrote it down?'

'Ah. Well.' Clive felt a surge of warmth as he saw his atheism triumphant. 'To start with, I don't recall anyone taking the minutes when God spoke to Abraham and Moses. So those two told us only what they felt and wanted to tell us.'

'So what?'

'Ahah. Do you remember when you were at school? Those especially clever teachers?'

'No!' Dibblee wanted to forget school.

'There was always one teacher who knew it all and wanted to show it. She, and it was usually a she, would lead us up the garden path so she could mark us all wrong when we followed her but misunderstood her clever words, which was what she intended. Then she'd tell us the final truth after she'd marked us with lots of blue crosses. Well, I reckon God's like that and most people fall for it. The earth was flat because God said so. But it isn't and he didn't say it. Then the heavens moved round the earth because God said so. But they don't and he didn't say that. God said women were responsible for the gender of their offspring. But women aren't and when you look at it carefully, God never said that. The prophets did. So if there is a God, he never said the world started six thousand years ago. Only these prophets did. Gentlemen, we don't have a problem.'

After that triumph, Clive decided he had just had enough of tea-talk for the day. It was true that the workings of the sun were not understood at all, but he didn't like to say so. It sounded like a weakness to say it and he almost thought he had gone too far. It was such a common object. It was all right to say an atom wasn't understood, because no one had ever seen an atom in such detail as they had in Manchester. But, not the sun. Everyone had seen the sun.

'Back to Blackmore's Law then, Clive? How's it coming along?' Andrade could sometimes be cruel. But then Clive had invited the jibe by boasting about his law soon after his arrival.

Margaret White breezed in, poured herself a cup of tea and sat down, ostentatiously looking at her rather substantial wrist-watch. She was proud of it. Not many women wore such a new-fangled piece of non-jewellery and most of the men preferred chains attached to the Big-Bens in their pockets. As a meteorologist, working on Glossop Moor in all weather, she needed a quick reliable means of telling and recording the time.

'Ah Robert, I've been looking for you. It's all fixed up for the weekend. Ludwig's new jets are finally ready, he's coming up from Cambridge for one last try. There's no backing out now. Mr. Cook has finished making them and we are going to try them out with the kites on Saturday and Sunday if the weather is fine. I have written to the inn and booked the rooms. It's going to be fun. Just like old times. Eccles is coming as well. There will be four of us. I've asked for two rooms. You don't mind sharing do you?'

On his way out, Clive paused, puzzled. He had been planning to have a quiet word with "Mrs. White" for some time, but the right opportunity had not cropped up. Now he couldn't understand why they were talking about sharing.

Robert had mixed feelings. He enjoyed the enthusiasm of Margaret and her easy-going manner, belying her hard core of prim, proper behaviour with regard to men. She was attractive and well-dressed. Usually, such women made Robert nervous. But he knew exactly where he was with Margaret and he could enjoy the friendship of a pretty female colleague without the baggage of lust gnawing away at his rationality. His relationship with Mary, on the other hand, was developing into something very close, intimate and potentially eternal. He wanted to move it on even faster. He wanted to talk to her parents, especially her father. He had promised Margaret all through the winter that he would see her meteorological work on the moor, but even she had admitted that it was best left to Spring. If it snowed or there was a frost up there above Glossop, getting up in the morning was not a pleasant experience. Margaret remembered how Wittgenstein had become furious one morning up there after a late frost when he had to break the ice on the water jug before inflicting a painful shave on his delicate features.

'In Austria,' he had proclaimed from his high horse, 'the patron would have got up at 5 o'clock to light a fire so we all had hot water from a tap. But this lazy Schweinehund first gets up after we do. I will not light his fires.'

'Two chaperones!' Mary was teasing him. 'It needs two for protection on Glossop Moor!'

Robert misunderstood and failed to see the trap.

'You should not think that way. What have I done to make you think like that?'

'Tut tut, my darling! Is there something I am missing? I actually meant Ludwig. You and Eccles are chaperons for him.'

Another tease, another trap.

'But Ludwig doesn't need anything like that, he's not, he's not ...'

'Not what my darling? What is it that Ludwig isn't? You know him better than I do. I don't work with him.'

'Neither do I.' Robert was biting his errant tongue. 'He just comes up from Cambridge now and then to talk to Margaret and to see if Fokker knows as much as his cousin about aero-dynamics. I find him rather hard work.'

'Methinks thou doth protest too much. Maybe it's you Ludwig likes. Maybe Margaret and Eccles are to be chaperons for you and Ludwig!'

Robert was almost exhausted and felt deflected from his main purpose. Arranging to have a lunch in the refectory with Mary was the first step of a devious plan that he intended to execute that day, Friday, before he left for Glossop Moor the next morning.

Leaving the refectory, he gently steered her towards the Coupland Street junction. Often, Mary liked to take the back route back to the Chemistry building, so she could enter the building alone. Walking through Coupland Street with Robert meant walking past the front of the physics building together and despite the fact that she was proud to be seen with him, it set the tongues wagging. That evening, physics Kay would tell chemistry Kay and it would be even worse for Robert next day if they met the little youth with the big clothes in the street. He always seemed to stare like a sad spaniel.

'Let's just wait for a minute, I want to see one of the new trams they've just put into service. I haven't been on one yet.'

Mary knew by now that he was a techno-phile, loving new gadgets but this seemed to be stretching his love of machines too far.

'But your hawk-eyed Kay will see us and invent a story.'

'Yes.' Robert had counted on this. 'And if he doesn't, yours will. Let's cross over. Neither can see us when we are on the other side.'

'And suppose the next one is a tram-load of professors from Wilmslow Road. They are due about now.'

Robert had not thought of that one. It was true, Lamb, Rutherford, Alexander, and the rest, all swept off the same tram at more or less the same time every day for their first lecture. They probably discuss Faculty and Senate business on the tram.

'Well, they'll be getting off on the other side of the road behind the tram and won't see us either.'

44

He stopped in the middle of the street, after they had skidded over the cobbles and after Robert had watched with close attention as she stepped with exaggerated care over the first tram rail and then the second.

'Do you remember this? Here, last year?'

'Of course I do! And I don't want it to happen again.'

'It won't. I'm keeping an eye on you and the trams.'

He turned to look up to the city centre; he could see almost to St Peter's Square. In the other direction, he could see to Whitworth Park. No trams. This was it.

He took hold of Mary by both of her arms, pinning them to her side, looking her directly in the eye.

'Mary, I love you. I love you dearly. I will always love you. Will you marry me?'

The low weak sun placed a shadow of her nose across her cheek. Her normal pale porcelain yielded to a sudden flush. He couldn't fail to see it. He expected a short reply; but it was not short.

'What happens if a tram comes?'

'Then I will hold you till you say yes!'

'Oh yes! Will you? Then let my arms go, please. Thank you. Am I free to cross the road now?'

'Yes.' Crestfallen.

'Good. Thank you. The answer, by the way, is Yes! But you had better ask papa for permission.'

'Papa? Prof Rutherford?'

'You can ask him if you like but I meant my father. Oh, and another thing.'

'Yes?'

'I love you too.'

Back on the haven of the pavement, neither of them knew what to do. They both had work to do and it would need some explaining and excuses to take the rest of the day off. Moreover, Robert had some arrangements for Glossop Moor to make. He wanted to kiss her. He did. It lingered long enough for William Kay to surprise them as he turned the corner out of Coupland Street, taking one of Ludwig's jets back to the instrument maker to have an extra hole drilled in the mounting. Brenda Wilkins was with him, seeing to the contractual paperwork. Kay coughed. Brenda scowled. Robert jumped. Mary laughed.

45

'I've left that new voltmeter in the basement for you Mr. White. She looks fine and I think she'll do the job.'

Robert did not know if he meant the voltmeter or Mary. He blushed.

'You haven't blushed like that since the cigars, Sir. Very fine cigars they were too, I must say.'

Brenda's scowl intensified.

'I have to go.' whispered Mary. 'I'm helping Chaim with his acetone work and he is at a difficult stage. He'll want to get it finished tonight because he won't, he can't, work tomorrow, Saturday, like we can.'

'Yes. I will meet you here at the usual time, to take you to the station. Will you be finished by then?'

'I must finish by then. I must catch my train. I can't miss it.'

~ ~ ~

Cornelius Ramsbottom had deliberately positioned himself so that his face was in darkness. Robert was standing in the parlour with the sun on his face. He could see the jacket, waistcoat, trousers and shiny boots of the father of his beloved. He could see the sun glinting on the gold chain of a pocket watch. But the voice growled from the darkness above the neck.

'Prospects, me boy. What are yours? Is there money in physic?'

'It all depends on how good you are, Sir. Our PROF, Rutherford, earns a fair amount. It's true I'm not a millionaire but then not many are at my age. I don't think it matters what I am doing, at my age I wouldn't be earning the same as a forty year old, whatever profession I was in. But I will one day, and more.'

Cornelius had already checked with Schuster. Schuster's family were cotton merchants, originally from Frankfurt, and Cornelius would trust the word of another cotton merchant, no matter where he came from. He knew that Schuster and Rutherford both thought that Robert had it within him to make a mark. He had already decided that Robert could marry Mary but he needed to test his mettle.

'And what about children? If there's anything as important as my daughter, Mary, it will be my grandchildren.'

Robert squirmed. He did not know how to deal with this kind of question. He heard the voices of Mary and her mother floating in from the garden. He took comfort from the fact that they were not there to witness his embarrassment.

'Your grandchildren, Sir, will be of paramount importance to me as well. Although I tremble at the thought of the responsibility of your daughter and your eventual grandchildren, if they should be my responsibility, that is, I do not fear the responsibility. I look forward to it with joy.'

'Young man! I thought this conversation would last for ever, spiralling into ever increasing problems, but I can see you are just the sort of man my daughter needs. Now let's have a cigar.'

Robert turned green at the thought of the second cigar in his life.

~   ~   ~

'Mrs. White.'

Before Margaret could correct the title, Clive's voice lubricated itself onwards.

'This is very difficult, but I think there is something you ought to know.'

'Yes?'

'It's about your husband. He goes for lunch with someone in the chemistry department. Often.'

Margaret White looked with unblinking eyes at Clive. Clive was leaning forward with his eyes and mouth open, keen anticipation flowing with the sweat from every pore.

'Husband? What are you talking about?'

'Your husband Robert. He sees another woman. It is not right.'

'You are perfectly correct it is not right, but not for the reasons you think. Are you talking about Robert White?'

Clive's mouth shut. His eyes narrowed and if his expression could be articulated simply, it only needed a paint brush to make a question mark on his face to accurately replace his expression.

Margaret was quicker to his mistake than Clive was. 'You think I am Dr. White's wife? How silly of you. How touching that you should seek to protect me, but protection is neither sought nor needed! I am single and happily so. I like men. I would even admit to being polyamorous because I do believe you can love more than one person at once. But Dr. White is not one of them. I like and admire him a lot. Moreover, he is single and his intentions are

47

entirely his own affair. He is a nice man and a nice colleague but he is not, and never will be, my husband. How did you come across that? We share a name by the happening of pure chance.'

Margaret never received an explanation and Clive could never bring himself to speak to her again.

~ ~ ~

Out in the garden, all the women were wearing hats. They were large hats full of flowers like an array of gardens within a garden.

'I must introduce you to Aunt Mabel. She's dying to meet you.' As Robert approached the bench, he thought Aunt Mabel was sitting under a canopy, in the shade. But then he realised it was a hat, larger than any other in the garden, a good three feet across. She was a large, handsome woman, but succeeded in looking prim by the manner in which she had arranged herself on the bench, sitting on two large cushions.

'Come and sit here, you two!' Her voice was round and fruity and her accent had a curl that placed her childhood within five miles of a straight line between Accrington and Clitheroe.

'That's it. You, Mary, this side on my right; and you on my left Robert. It is Robert, isn't it? Do you know why I have sat you down like that? That Mr. Talbot over there has brought a photographic camera with him and some dry plates. He intends to make some photographic exposures. He has been informed that he should make a photograph of us on this bench and he will come and set up his tripodic apparatus in a moment. And I have chosen the seating positions for posterity. When you are famous Robert, the photograph will be used in all the famous magazines like the Tatler and the London Illustrated. It will say underneath "From left to right, Mrs. Robert White, wife of the illustrious prize winner, Mrs. Oscar de la Rente, aunt of the scientist's wife and Professor Robert White, recent winner of the Nobel Prize." You can afford to come last, Robert, and let the ladies, especially your wife, come first.'

Both Mary and Robert felt a flutter of the heart and a stopping of the breath. Mary had not yet let her new title, Mrs. White, enter her thoughts and to hear it spoken for the first time, before she was even married, induced a shock. Robert had always thought that Nobel prizes only "happened" to people like Rutherford. They happened only to people who were scientifically out of reach. Although Mabel had dropped in the phrase as if it were the most natural thing in the world, it had shocked and embarrassed him.

Mr. Talbot, dapper and fussy, meticulously erected the tripod before them and poured magnesium powder onto the plasterer's hawk that his assistant held. He was overdressed for the day with his winter suit. But he was so thin, having suffered his whole life from the fact that heat poured out of him, even when the sun shone. He was proud of his hawk. Other photographers in the big cities paid five shillings for their magnesium trays. He had noticed that a plasterer's hawk looked identical and cost but a shilling. Except that they were not identical. His wooden hawk had caught fire the first time he used it at a wedding as the magnesium incinerated. He couldn't put it out and had gone and spent another shilling, together with sixpence for a baking tray that he had screwed to the hawk. Now the expenditure was up to two shillings and sixpence and he couldn't afford another fire. The bride at that wedding had screamed hysterically as the assistant had dropped and broken all the photographic plates, leaving the wedding un-photographed except for the first exposure. On this one, the bride's eyes were screwed tight shut, in anticipation of the flash.

'Mr. Talbot will give me a signal when he is ready. We shall be talking so that we look natural and relaxed. Then I shall say a long drawn out "cheeeese" and you shall join me. Then the photograph will show us all smiling. Trust me, I have done this before. Now while we are waiting, tell me one thing, I must know. Robert, where did you propose to Mary. Tell me where and how romantic it was.'

'On a tram line.'

Only Oscar Wilde could have written Mabel's long drawn out reply.

'A tram line?'

Mabel's arms went up in astonishment. Talbot thought Mabel must have misunderstood the arrangements and was giving him the signal rather than the other way round. But Talbot was not a man to argue with Mabel. Flash! Bang! The photograph, when developed and printed and brought round the next day, showed Mabel with both of her arms raised, with her hands level with her face. Her eyes, wide open in surprise, had allowed the light to reflect unhindered off her eyeballs. Her eyes had no structure; they were two white flares. Her mouth was half way through saying "line", which made for a considerably less attractive shape than "cheese".

~   ~   ~

Andrade was looking glum. Apprehensive even. He sat in the tea room with a mug of cold tea, neither drinking it nor putting it down.

'What's up with thee then Mr. Andrade?' Dibblee was in early. He had been working on the electro-furnace, making quartz glass. It was hot work and he needed regular liquid.

'It's that Baumbach chap. Why can't he be more like Geiger? They are both Germans.'

'I know what you mean Mr. Andrade. Thee and me are both English and we're both a bit on the short side. I wouldn't dream of growing taller than thee. I think we're the two smallest in physics and it wouldn't do if one of us were suddenly taller. It wouldn't be right. Please don't grow. I won't.'

Andrade took in not a single word. He didn't even remind Dibblee that he was Dr. and not Mr. He was so pre-occupied with Baumbach.

'He's always going on about what the German Army is going to do to the British. This is England, dammit. He can't say it here: we're in Manchester. He speaks to me in German. He knows I did my doctorate in Heidelberg. But even so, he should be speaking English in England.'

'So what Mr. Andrade? We all know Otto Baumbach. He's got a right sharp tongue on him. Just sit tight and let him eat his words. He'll choke.' Sometimes Dibblee could be wise.

'Too late. I answered him back. In German. I was a bit rude. But only he and I could understand what we were saying. You would have thought that one of these big all-powerful Germans could look after himself in the playground. Oh no. He goes running to the Principal, just like the school bully does when someone finally turns on him. Now I got called in front of the beak myself. I'm finished. The Principal told me off for threatening a

German glassblower. I only told him to shut up or else he would find himself in trouble. He will. They'll put him away if he keeps on saying those things.'

'What did he say, this Principal chap?'

'He told me it was very unworthy behaviour to threaten a poor defenceless German in our midst. He told me not to behave in this way! They'll put me away too now. I'm sure of it. I'm finished.'

'I don't think so, Mr. Andrade. You'll be needed, just like me. They do say the war's is coming and it's only a matter of time. I can't wait for it. It's long overdue. When it comes, I'm going to fight. I'll show them.'

'From what I've heard, young Dibblee, wars are not worth waiting for. But if there is one, I'd rather be me than Herr Baumbach, stuck here in Manchester. I think he might just get his comeuppance if there's a war and he finds himself in the wrong country. I wonder why he doesn't go home now.'

Moseley, who usually worked through the night and was rarely seen in the daytime, chipped in.

'I agree with you Dib, old chap. If there's war then I shall hang up my apparatus and go and fight for King and country. You've got to stand up for things you believe in. Geiger's all right. He's one of us - almost. But I agree that Mr. Baumbach is a bit of a handful. He's got a tongue on him like a duelling sword. Fancy you having to deal with him and then have to go and be told off by the Principal. Told off by that oily old wobbler! How did he ever get put in charge of a University? There's a lot of Baumbachs and they think they own the world and we're just looking after bits of it till they good and ready to take it over. I think those Germans have been planning this for a hundred years.'

'Well, you've noticed that PROF is going to London and Scotland more and more on war work. It means war is coming.'

Both Andrade and Moseley stared at Dibblee.

'How do you know that? Nobody knows things like that. We don't know that about the PROF. Who told you? What's he doing in Scotland.'

Dibblee smiled, tapped his nose and went to swill out his tin mug under the cold tap. The enamel mug was still almost white on the outside but the inside was virtually black.

'Back to the furnace. I wish Mr. Hutton would hurry up and get this quartz business sorted, it's hot work.'

51

Kay had been listening with increasing impatience. He collared both Andrade and Moseley.

'I get on very well with Otto. And PROF values him highly as well. So does the oily old wobbler Principal. If it weren't for Otto there would be a lot of work we couldn't do; think on that. I think PROF would do anything not to lose him. I don't think we would enjoy it if we were in Germany right now and who knows how we would react.'

Chadwick, fiddling with his unlit pipe, overheard and butted in. 'Well, I'll find out soon enough. I'm going to work at the Berlin Institute for a year. Dibblee's coming with me as my assistant. The PROF's approved it. We'll write and tell you what it's like! I don't think there will be a war.'

Dibblee turned his attention to another German visiting scientist, Natasha Bauer, who had brought a gas cylinder into the tea room.

'I wouldn't fiddle with that if I were you, Natasha. Not here, I wouldn't. It might come off and you'd have a dangerous rocket on your hands. Then you'd either have to hold on and go with it or let it go and kill us all.'

Natasha Bauer believed ardently in striving for the true role and position of women. Any woman should be able to turn on the tap of a gas bottle of carbon dioxide. It was just a bit stiff. Robert reached over to give a hand. An icy stare stopped him in his tracks.

'I can manage, thank you.' Natasha never uttered a man's name. It would legitimise his existence.

'Gas bottles and tea don't go together, Natasha. Best take it to the fume cupboard. You never know.' Dibblee persisted.

Natasha huffed and puffed her way into the corridor at the far end of the tea room. She disappeared into the cubicle with her bottle and wedged the tap between the door and the architrave. It was Margaret White, returning from a visit to instrument maker Charles Cook, with yet more turbine nozzles for Ludwig Wittgenstein's kite, who heard the tumbling noise behind the closed door. As she opened the door of the cubicle to investigate, Natasha fell out, onto the floor. Margaret screamed for help. Dibblee ran over. People were always fainting if they got too close to the open electric furnace and he knew what to do. Margaret tried to stop him as she realised she would have some explaining to do if she allowed a man to handle Natasha while she was unconscious. Natasha was not especially friendly with man-handlers. Dibblee brushed her aside and dragged Natasha into the open area of the tea room and started to flap cool air across her face with his cap.

'Stand back. Don't touch 'er. She's all right, it's only carbon dioxide and she were only in there for a few seconds. It's not poisonous.'

Natasha came round and looked up from the floor to see a circle of male faces staring down at her.

'O Mein Gott. I am dead. I am in Hell. How did I get here?'

When Kay heard the words, he knew Natasha had come to no harm. He slipped out of the room and went upstairs to make his report to Rutherford.

~   ~   ~

'What's this I hear, Miss Bauer?' said Rutherford as soon as she had shut the door of his office. 'What's this I hear? You might have killed yourself.'

'Well, if I had, nobody would have cared.'

'No. I daresay not.' Rutherford nodded. 'I daresay not. But I have no time to attend inquests.'

'Oh.' It was no more than a little squeak.

'How is the calcium work coming along. That's why you are using carbon dioxide isn't it? To precipitate out the calcium using lime water and seeing what is left? How much carbon dioxide did you lose? Will we have to buy a new bottle?'

'I'll buy one myself.' sniffed Natasha.

'Oh yes. Do they have carbon dioxide bottles in Affleck and Brown? Where do you think you will get it from? Suppose it had been a bottle of the gas emanations from radium? Radium burns the fingers. What do you think the radon gas would do to your lungs?'

'It wasn't radium emanation gas. It was carbon dioxide. Men drink it in beer.'

'Not all men, Miss Bauer. Only certain men drink beer, and I am not one of them.'

Events were reconstructed in precise detail that evening in the Nelson's Arm.

'When you heard that whooshing noise, Dib, why didn't you realise immediately what was up?' Chemistry Kay liked accidents with gas bottles. They were always having them in the chemistry building. It gave the place its special atmosphere.

'I weren't sure it were real. Me ears had been whooshing all mornin', workin' at t'furnace. Any rate, it were only a minute at t' most till Maggie screamed.'

'Margaret. She's not a Maggie. And she's Miss White to you.'

'Sorry, – till Miss White screamed.'

'What had she done? In the fume cupboard?'

'She'd tucked the gas bottle tap in between the door and the door jamb. Then she pulled the door tight and twisted the bottle. Whoosh.'

'But you saved her! You pulled her to safety and gave her breath!' Physics Kay liked heroes from the Physics department.

Dibblee swelled with pride. His face flushed and he suddenly found the need to look at the floor.

'When she lay there, what did you think? Did you think she was dead?'

'Naw. She were alive all right. My whippet died last week and I know what a dead whippet looks like. She were lying there, a bit pale, true, but compared to my whippet, she were in the pink.'

'So what did you do to bring her round? Give her a kiss of life?'

'No, I didn't. No. Miss White were there. She wouldn't have let me. No, I wafted some fresh air in with my cap.'

'Fresh air? With that greasy thing? It's a wonder you didn't finish her off altogether. Did she say thank you?'

'Not yet. She hasn't said anything. PROF sent her home. Maybe she'll say something tomorrow. I hope . . .'

'Hope? What do you hope Dibblee lad? Are you soft on her? You've not got another crush have you? Not again. Not after that chemistry woman that Mr. White married! And there was Margaret before that! You're always having crushes on women who are out of reach! Oh dear Dib, you do thrive on unrequited love.'

The colour of Dibblee's face betrayed that he did indeed, have another crush.

'Natasha Dibblee! Now that has a ring to it!'

Dibblee cuffed Kay around the ear with his greasy cap.

'So you didn't have a chance to see Miss Wilkins today?'

'Mrs. Blackmore, she is now. She's gone and married froggy dew Mr. Blackmore. Yes, I usually go in cos it's my job to take the letters across to the main post room in time for the mail train collection. She weren't best pleased today. She'd put her old man Clive up to asking PROF for a rise.'

'Goodness me, what happened?'

'He got asked why he needed more than three pounds a week and what could he find to spend it on. He said he would be happy with three pounds a week but he only got a hundred and fifty a year and a wife to feed. He got told to come back when he had done something useful.'

'What's wrong with that? That sounds all right to me.'

'Ah, yon Mrs. Blackmore, she'd only gone and seen a letter from the Principal to the PROF about his salary. He gets thirty pounds a week. Thirty!'

'Get away with you. Humans weren't meant to earn that much; they wouldn't survive, getting so much.'

~   ~   ~

Chapter 4

Manchester, Thiepval and Yorkshire 1916

One by one they left for war. Many would never return. Moseley had gone first, initially to Oxford to write up his work. He couldn't stand Manchester for a day longer and by December 1914, he had negotiated a room in the Oxford laboratories to do his research. They had refused to pay him, so Oxford inherited all his Manchester discoveries for the cost of nothing more than a desk. And then Moseley had been drawn irresistibly into the war effort and volunteered for active service. Not valuing his brain, the British Army shipped it to Gallipoli where it was shot through by a Turkish bullet.

Rutherford's mood had swung from grief to anger. 'This country has better things to do than place its best young brains to be prey to a Turkish bullet. What an extraordinary waste. This young man would have won a Nobel Prize.'

Rutherford had been sad just to see Moseley go. He thought it would not be long before Kay would walk into the tea room, as he had done in 1908, with a telegram from Sweden. Only this time for Moseley. Now the only telegram about Henry Moseley would come from the War Office, for Mr. and Mrs. Moseley and it would not be welcome.

A large cloud of dense smoke entered the Nelson's Arm. Rutherford was at the centre of it. He stood in the doorway, pulling repeatedly on his pipe, scanning the cavernous bar for his prey. He would never completely cross the threshold of the pub, being a teetotaller and Presbyterian.

'Yon professor chap of yours burns more tobacco than he smokes. He must get through tons.' Reg had just pulled two pints of bitter for the Kays and a half of mild for Dibblee who would be round in a few minutes to read the news. He believed in giving a good glass of beer time to breathe.

Rutherford waved and beckoned to his Kay.

'I'm looking for Blackmore and White. They were at the colloquium this afternoon but I spent too long talking to our visitor and they were gone.'

'It's Friday PROF, they have wives.'

'So do I, Mr. Kay, so do I. But I'm still here. You have Ethel and you're still here. If you see either of them, tell them I want them both for a chat. It's important.'

'Mr. Clive never comes in here any road, but I'll tell them. Would you like a pint Sir?'

Rutherford took out his watch from the fob, shook it, flicked open the cover and frowned.

'Sorry, Kay. I'm in a rush.'

Kay smiled and thought to himself "Wives!"

'Ah, there you are Dibblee, come and sit down lad.'

~   ~   ~

Clive and Robert sat side by side, looking at the silhouette of their boss, etched against the window by the late afternoon sun.

'I have just been to a meeting in London.'

Rutherford was often at meetings in London – whenever he wasn't in Scotland, advising the government on scientific matters that might be helpful to the war effort.

'I am afraid that the work you are doing here will have to stop. There are more important things to do. I told London you would do them.'

There was a pause. Rutherford waited and then continued.

'Captain Bragg, you know him of course, is leading a small group near the enemy lines. They are making measurements. We believe you will be a useful addition to the effort. You will leave on Monday on a special troop train to Kent. You will switch off your equipment here, put everything away neatly off your desks and go home to say goodbye to your wives. You may be gone for some time. Marsden is there as well and he has been back here once already, reporting to London when Captain Bragg could not make it. Off you go.'

'What can we do to prepare?' Clive appeared eager.

'Nothing. From what I know it is relatively straightforward and the required skills are the ability to take careful measurements. I don't suppose that much thinking is required. The equipment is there already.'

Although Rutherford had no legal power to send either of his two workers to France, to a war zone, he had the Rutherfordian power, which had the strength of Lord Kitchener. Even Clive dared not refuse the 'order'.

~   ~   ~

In the tent, Bragg and Marsden gave one of the shortest tutorials that Clive and Robert had ever heard.

'Here is a microphone. Here is a large gun, a mile away. Suppose the gun goes off and we notice a flash, or rather the flash-spotters do. When we see the flash, we start a clock. The noise now travels towards us at the speed of sound, about 1,000 feet per second, but variable depending on the weather, especially the wind. When the noise arrives, I stop the clock and I have a time, measured, call it "t". If the gun is a mile away, "t" will be just about five seconds, maybe a scrap longer. But I can measure it accurately enough with a chart recorder. See this map on the table here? We are here.'

Bragg jabbed his finger and covered Thiepval, Ypres and most of the Western front.

'I multiply the time "t" by the speed of sound to get the distance away from us. That's just over 5,000 feet which is a mile, as it should be. We didn't know the guns were a mile away. So with this pair of compasses, I can draw a circle around us, to scale, representing a mile radius. The gun is somewhere on this circle.'

'Yes, I see, but if you see the flash, you have a direction, a bearing, so just draw the bearing and you have the gun. And its range.' Robert was almost there. 'Do you count the flash?'

'Yes, indeed. We do count the flash. We have teams of flash-spotters. More of them later. It's all well and good, but if it's foggy or you blinked when it flashed, or a shell was whistling over your head when the flash occurred, you've missed it. We've got to take out the human element as much as possible. Understand?'

They nodded.

'So we set up a second microphone here. Say half a mile away, parallel to the front, connected to us by another wire. Now we have a second time, "t_2" call it. We can now draw two circles on the paper, they have different diameters because, in general, the gun will not always be the same distance from the two microphones. The circles will intersect. If two circles intersect once, they must intersect twice. They can't help it. Try it. Try drawing it. They must. Two circles must intersect twice if they intersect at all.'

'I know they do; they must.' Robert was up with the argument; Clive was licking his thick lips. He needed an equation.

'If they intersect twice, on opposite sides of the circle, then there are two possible places where the guns might be. Which one is the real one?'

'Well, one possible place will be in front of you, and one behind. I suppose you could assume the enemy guns are in front of you, and your own artillery behind. Your own might let you know when they opened up, I guess.' By now, Clive was gulping, his forehead dripping and his tongue parched, unable to speak and letting Robert run away with the situation.

'Right. But now let us put the diagrams aside and think like mathematicians. We want to find out two things, the range and the bearing. You can think Cartesian if you like.' Bragg liked to pull in familiar scientific words into the unfamiliar surroundings. He felt more comfortable.

'Cartesian coordinates, "x" and "y"; sideways and forwards; or spherical coordinates - range and bearing. That means two unknowns, two quantities that you don't know. Assuming we know the speed of sound already, then how many measurements do we need to make to determine two unknowns?'

'Two.' Clive could answer that without thinking of guns.

'Correct. That is if you start from the flash and measure two independent times. But suppose you missed the flash. What now?'

'You're now back to one measurement.' Clive was getting into his stride. 'The first microphone signal now becomes just a marker, an instant in time. You can call it time equals zero and not change anything. Yes. I see it clearly.' Clive was seizing back control. He was comfortable with equations and concepts. Guns and microphones were now just points on a mathematical curve. 'So you need another measurement. A third microphone.'

Clive preened.

'Well done you two.'

Clive scowled.

'You are quite correct. We have another microphone, another wire, another channel of information. That should have done it. But it still doesn't work. And that's partly why you are here. We need noses to the grindstone, shoulders to the wheel and brains to the battlements. I can tell you something else, if you can't stand the noise of heavy artillery, you are going to learn fast.'

'So mathematically it works. But in practice it doesn't.' Bragg and Marsden turned to look at Robert in pleasantly surprised expectation.

'Go on.'

'That can only mean something is varying. Something you thought was fixed and constant, isn't fixed. The distance between the microphones? Hmmm. If the microphones are under your control, you can't get that wrong. And anyway, it's fixed. You might have measured it slightly wrong but it doesn't change. You can calibrate that out. There may be more than one gun, but that helps. If there are two guns, you should see two clusters for where the guns are. Then you can average them and know it better.'

'Excellent.'

'So what else can change in the problem? Only the speed of sound. That's it. If it varies, then it will mess everything up. How could it vary? Temperature and pressure from day to day! That will change the speed. But that's a slow change and you should be able to track it. Hmmm. Wind. I think the wind must be a problem. Yes. The wind.'

Bragg and Marsden knew it already. But they had been there for months. The new boys, between themselves, had almost worked it out in minutes. Each one helping the other.

'So more microphones. If you have four or even five, you can do away with the flash spotters.'

'Not quite. They still have a critical role to play. They have two roles to play. First, they can sit there and record the bearings. Second, they are nearer the guns so when they see a flash, they can give us advance warning by sending a signal down the wire. Then we can start the charts and not waste precious recorder paper. And the bearings the spotters write down aren't affected by the wind. Put all the information together and it ought to work. But it's not working properly yet.'

'When it all works, Sir, how does it get used?'

Bragg reached into his satchel and pulled out a map. Unfolded, it covered the whole of the table. The quality of paper, linen, and the printing, was high.

'Trench maps. We need to know the positions of all their trenches and guns. It's all on here, the best of our knowledge. Once a trench is dug, it tends to stay there. Same with the guns.'

'Are ours on the map as well?'

'There are maps with our trenches on and maps without. If you are going to go wandering around the fields, you don't want to get caught by the Germans with a map of our trenches in your pocket, do you?'

'But also, you don't want them to know that we know where their trenches are, is that it?'

'In general yes, although I've always thought it wouldn't do much for their morale to know we have accurate maps of their positions. If they knew that, there would be an awful lot of digging and they would be moving their guns – out into the open.'

'It's almost worth dropping a few maps by aeroplane, isn't it?'

'I'm not so sure of that. I wouldn't trust the aeroplanes too much. We might drop more aeroplanes than maps.'

'So what do you want me to do?' With the mathematics and simple physics sorted, and the conversation beginning to drift, Clive stumbled on the sociality.

"Us." thought Robert.

"You two." thought Bragg.

"The two of you." thought Marsden.

'Join the team and get this thing sorted. It will be practical work. That's what you two are supposed to be good at. If there are any new mathematics needed, Darwin will sort it out.'

~   ~   ~

Dinner was boiled turnips. It might have been France, but this was 1916 and that's all there was. Charlie, the cook and forager, had been out foraging all day on the neighbouring farms because the ration run was late. The ration run was always late, bogged down in the autumn mud. Most of the farms were empty, burnt. Many cooks had foraged before him. Some had been used for billeting but they immediately became a target and it could not have been clearer to enemy guns if they had hoisted a large flag with the words "The English are here" blazed in big letters. Charlie finally found one with life. The farmer had gone to war, probably never to return. His wife had been plump before the war but was

61

now ravaged with the consequences of having to supply endless passages of troops with beef, then mutton, then eggs, then most of the chickens, till all that remained was turnips and milk from the two old cows. Her restricted diet showed. Her unsatisfied appetite for food was matched only by her appetite for sex, also long unsatisfied. For Charlie, the choice was stark. Either I fuck her and get the turnips, or we starve. Dinner was boiled turnips.

Bragg picked out three bay leaves from the now empty billy-can. Charlie was an artist and had seized the opportunity to pluck a branch of bay leaves from the tree in the farm yard. He knew the edible variety *Laurus nobilis* from long experience. The leaves would add much needed flavour. Boiled turnip with bay leaf marinade.

'Charlie.' Bragg wiped his bowl with the leaves and licked first the leaves, individually, and then his fingers, spotlessly clean. 'Charlie. Do you think you could persuade her to tell you where she has hidden the remaining chickens?'

Charlie knew exactly what he would have to do to release the intelligence on the hidden chickens.

'She's a rare bird Sir. I've never met a woman like her. She's tough as our old boots, Sir. I think if you brought her in and worked on her all night, you might find out where she's stuffed her chickens. But I have to say Sir, I think she's stringing us along. I don't think she has any chickens anymore.'

The whole squad, all but Charlie, stared into their empty turnip bowls and thought of chickens. Charlie thought of the afternoon and wondered how he had done it. Then he realised. He had lain on his stomach and thought of England.

'Why would she want to do that? If she doesn't have any chickens, then she'd best convince us of it sharpish, to get us off her back, like. Unless she likes you on her back, Charlie.'

Ernie, a regular sapper, deployed to the squad to handle the sparks, had a nose for human relations. Charlie was betrayed by his involuntary, uncontrollable, stare of anguish.

'I was also thinking.' Bragg again. 'Perhaps we should think of setting up billet there, in the farm. Quietly, at night, then we don't attract fire. Then decamp out here during the day. We would be nearer the action. Charlie, you could cook in her kitchen. We could dine in the barn.'

Charlie's look of anguish intensified.

Perkins, the NCO, deployed to maintain discipline among the juniors whenever bombardment became intense, disapproved of comforts like farm kitchens and barns. 'We should be looking forward, Sir, if I may be so bold as to suggest.'

'Forward?' Bragg was not so sure.

'I mean we have not yet swept the MacFadzean trench.'

There had been an accident a few weeks earlier before the sound ranging team had moved forward into the area. Private MacFadzean, of the Irish Fusiliers, had been cutting the straps on a box of grenades when the box slipped, tipping the contents into the trench among the troops. MacFadzean had spotted that the pins had fallen out of two grenades and had thrown himself on top of the pile, sacrificing himself to save his colleagues. His few remains had been taken back to Belfast to a muted hero's welcome. He was posthumously awarded the Victoria Cross. The trench had been evacuated and was still deemed unsafe. Three grenades were still missing. It was suspected that some of the foot soldiers might have seized the opportunity to acquire extra weaponry to supplement their inadequate ordnance. But by then they had gone off into battle. Most likely the grenades had already been used in anger, but no one could be sure.

'Yes, it is down to us.' Bragg agreed. 'And it needs to be done. If we move on without doing that, who comes next has every right to believe that we have done our job. They may not even know of it and then how would you feel if someone got blown up in that trench?'

'What if we have to retreat and it's the Germans?'

Bragg pursed his lips for 10 seconds. Everyone thought they had stuck. He finally spoke. 'We shall not be retreating. Our boys will see to that. Yes, Sergeant Perkins, create a team of volunteers for tomorrow. One team for the morning and if they don't find anything, a second one in the afternoon.'

'Do you think two sweeps will be enough, Sir?' There was nothing Perkins liked more than creating teams of volunteers and giving them orders.

'Probably not, Sergeant, but let's see where we are this time tomorrow and take it from there. Oh, and another thing, Sergeant, can you make absolutely sure we don't lose anyone this time?'

'Of course, Captain Bragg, Sir. It's more than my reputation's worth to lose anybody. Some people might think that to lose one might be an accident and to lose two carelessness. But I never did like Oscar Wilde, Sir, and even losing a leg or half a leg, I'd consider carelessness, punishable by court-martial. And there's none of us would want that.'

The new recruits were not sure what was meant or what was worse: losing a leg or being court-martialled.

'What's for dinner tomorrow Charlie? Have you got anything nice saved up? Not turnip again, I hope?'

Charlie's anguish returned.

'It's not that I don't like turnip. I do. But there's something about your turnip that I can't quite put my finger on. It almost tastes like foot grease sometimes. You wouldn't be using that stuff to cook in would you, Charlie?'

'Goodness me, Sir. Even if it wasn't poisonous, I'd be in serious trouble if you all got trench foot because I'd been cooking in the foot grease.'

~   ~   ~

Perkins, Clive and Robert had moved to the MacFadzean trench before sun up and by seven o'clock were in the trench ready to start work.

'Right. We are going to split this into three sections. You, Corporal Blackmore, will start on the left and work towards the middle. You, Corporal White, will start in the middle and work to the right. That way you are always half a trench apart. So if we do have an unfortunate accident, then we will lose only one of you. That's why you will not work together. As soon as you, Corporal White have moved out of range in the main trench, I shall start on the sap, working outwards and away from you. You are going to be on your knees for most of the day so you will need to wrap two extra puttees round your knees for padding. I'm not going soft, so don't get any ideas. You're just no good to us with housemaid's knee. And housemaid's is not a Blighty wound, so don't come running to me tomorrow if your knees are aching. That's if you survive today!'

Perkins believed in keeping his charges, especially new ones, alert with regular reminders.

A quarter of the way along the left hand trench, Clive found two grenades. One was lying on the surface and the other a foot away was half buried in mud. His mouth went dry. He reached to touch one and then pulled away. Laying flat on his belly on the duck-boards, he looked at the one on the surface from all sides. It seemed intact with the pin in place. He lifted it, took a small towel out of his bag, wrapped it up and put it back inside the bag. He then got up and walked, stooping, to the junction of the trench with the sap and called gently to Perkins.

'Sergeant Perkins! I think I've found one.'

'You have indeed found one,' Perkins' eyes gleamed as he looked at the stump of the grenade sticking out of the mud.

'You go and get your mate and go and wait at the end of the sap, as far away as you can till I've lifted this. It looks all right but you never know. Tell him to mark where he's got up to so he can carry on when I've sorted this out.'

Perkins used the tip of a screwdriver to slowly lift the mud and reveal the whole body of the grenade. He worked especially carefully around the pin, in case it was half out and held in by the mud. Fifteen minutes later, he sent the two back to look for more. None was found.

~   ~   ~

Bragg pulled his greatcoat tight to feel its warmth. He used one of the flash-spotter's stools to sit on while he opened his letters from Blighty. There was one he recognised from the jumped up clerk sitting at his comfortable desk in London who was doing his best to recover fifteen shillings of excess pay he had received in error. Acting majors should not be paid at the rate of real majors and someone had made a mistake for four weeks. Now the clerk wanted it back. Bragg put it to one side and turned the other one that looked more like a package than a letter. It was in a large envelope, foolscap size and inside was another letter. This one was covered with embossed printing with the sender's address printed in the top left hand corner. Nobel Committee, Stockholm. Bragg read the letter numbly, then read it again but couldn't absorb it so he read it again. He then sat gazing with unfocussed eyes on the pages that drooped from his hand.

'Not bad news, Sir?' Charlie could be gentle.

'No, no, not at all.' Bragg gazed across to the German artillery. 'No, I've just got a Nobel Prize.'

'A prize, Sir? Is it a lottery?'

'A kind of lottery, yes, Charlie. A kind of lottery. I share it with my father.'

'Oh, does that leave enough for both of you?'

'Hmmm, what? Oh yes, it's the sort of prize that you can cut into several pieces and each piece is worth almost the same as the whole. Charlie, does your farmer's wife have any decent wine? And Charlie, why do you always look like that whenever I mention that woman. Don't you like her or something? When we went there to plead for the chickens, she acted most familiar with you. One could have almost imagined you were the farmer and not our cook. Now there you go again. What is the matter with you?'

Later that afternoon, sitting on a tea chest along the trench, Clive ran through the list of Nobel physics prize-winners in his head as if reciting the times table. Roentgen, Lorentz, Zeeman, the Curies, Becquerel. He knew them all. Rayleigh, Lenard, Thomson, Michelson, Lippman, Marconi, Braun. He knew them all in order from 1901 to 1914. Van der Waals, Wien, Dalen, Kamerlingh-Onnes and von Laue. Throw in Rutherford for chemistry and it was a roll call of the high and mighty. The hall of fame. And now Bragg. Clive had calculated backwards and forwards and inserted every parameter he could think of but the fact remained, Bragg had won the Nobel Prize at the age of 25. The fact that he had shared it with his father made it worse. Clive was 24. He had done nothing remotely capable of winning a Nobel Prize. Indeed, if he were honest with himself, he had done nothing at all.

'Cheer up Clive.' Robert was feeling the surge of excitement at being present at the unveiling of a new Nobel prize-winner. Clive's sulking was out of place. 'It's a great day for Blighty's physics. We've beaten the Boche. People thought Planck would get it this year but the Braggs have beaten him on their own.'

Clive frowned as he tossed aside the logic of two people beating a German on their own.

'You haven't got trench foot have you? Charlie told me it was nasty. He said he had seen exhumed limbs that looked healthier than a dose of trench foot.'

Robert had seen Clive earlier removing his boots and socks and scratching between his toes. A bit of teasing would not come amiss. The effect was far beyond Robert's expectations.

'I have not got trench foot. I will never get trench foot.' Remnants of un-swallowed turnip were forced from between Clive's teeth by the explosion of his response.

'But I saw your feet earlier. I couldn't see any grease. I know it's nasty stuff but you don't want to find yourself on a charge do you?'

'I do not need you to tell me about the grease. Now leave me alone, White, now.' Clive was venomous.

Charlie chirped at Robert when he returned to the group. 'What's up with him then? He's worse than me missus on her dark seven today he is. What's bitten him? The chats?'

'No Charlie, I saw his legs today and they were as white as a slug's belly. And he swears he's greasing himself properly.'

'I'll get Sergeant Jenkins to check his grease tub every day to make sure it's going down. It reflects on all of us if anyone gets the foot. It's like we don't look out.'

The influence of the wind on the sound ranging accuracy was a problem that had to be overcome. It was discussed at every meeting convened by the technical co-ordinator Marsden. Bragg thought it was a good idea to participate in these meetings as one of the team and not as leader. He thought he could contribute more than he would if he were organising the structure of the meeting. Marsden was a good organiser, so he ran the meetings.

'All the calculations show that we should be able to achieve an accuracy of 50 yards over a distance of fifty thousand feet, almost ten miles. Yet we don't. So we need to find out why, and then fix it.' Bragg got the meeting started and others chipped.

'One of the problems, I think the main problem, is that our bank of microphones is in a straight line behind us, more or less parallel to the trenches. So if one microphone has a wind error then all of them will have the same error, more or less.'

'Yes, we know that, we've tried zig-zagging them. It doesn't help.'

'What about the forward position, Sir?'

The forward position was an exposed location half way between the two lines of trenches. When the observer at the forward position heard a gun blast, he pressed a key, that which sent a signal back to the recording station. This signal travelled almost instantaneously down the wires and started a pen chart recorder. The sound would then take about five seconds to travel each mile to the microphones whose signals were then recorded on the chart. This saved a lot of paper on the chart recorder.

Clive became visibly more nervous, although he did not realise it himself. He never noticed if he sweated more or less. He just knew he sweated. Never having done it before, the experience of carrying around a live grenade in his bag preyed on him every minute of the waking day and made his sleep more fitful. He knew he had to move on, even drive the situation on. He and Robert were deployed to the forward station. One of them was deployed to spot the flashes through a pair of binoculars and mark the direction on a chart. The other would look over the whole horizon for flashes and press the key to start the chart recorder a mile away.

'I think I know how to solve the wind problem.' Clive had chosen his moment with just the two of together.

Robert pricked up his ears.

'Just think.' Clive was slowly moving his moment on. 'If the forward position were a mile nearer their trenches, the problem would be solved.'

'I don't think the Boche will take kindly to us sitting just outside their trenches pressing keys.'

'You're not thinking, White. If you are pressing a button, you don't need to be right on their trench or gun battery, especially if you have a microphone there. I'm saying, put a microphone near the trench, sit back a mile and just correct all your readings by five seconds. You know exactly where the microphone is because you put it there.'

'It's not just a straight five second correction. The gun may go off some distance to the side of the microphone. All the angles come in to play.'

'Yes, that's obvious, but it will solve all your wind problems if you have a microphone right on top of the artillery.'

'So how are you going to get one there?'

'We can run a cable under cover of dark. It's a waning moon and it will be totally dark at night in about a week.'

'Bragg won't agree to it. Too risky.'

'He's going away for ten days tomorrow. He's back to Blighty for meetings. Marsden's in charge.'

'Marsden won't agree to it.'

'We're supposed to show initiative and solve problems. That's why we are here. That's what we were told.'

'So.' Clive licked his lips, a stroke to the left, a stroke to the right. 'So why don't we just do it one night. It would be so easy.'

There was a silence of minutes. Clive broke it himself.

'We get a drum of wire. Run it forward a mile towards the trenches. Fix the microphone there and it's done. Nothing ever happens after eleven so we have oodles of time. It will take half an hour, maybe an hour, depending on the terrain to get it there and barely a half hour to scamper back. I've got it all worked out. I have this clasp, it snaps onto loops on your webbing. We fix it to our back and crawl, pulling the wire. One of us stays just behind checking it doesn't get tangled. I think it's best you pull the wire, just from sheer physical size. I'd do it. I'd prefer to do it but I am a bit flimsy. We'll be heroes!'

Robert could not argue with Clive's logic although he was concerned with his initiative.

'I'll sort out the wire and the microphone. I just need your support and discretion.'

Robert slept badly. He knew there was a flaw. If there was one person whom he respected to carry common sense through a situation like this, it was Perkins. Yet Perkins was out of the loop.

Clive was ready in two days. The drum of wire appeared at the forward post as if by magic.

'It's lighter than you think. I was worried that we might not be able to unwind it any further if we got a few hundred yards off the roll, but now I'm sure we can. What I suggest is, and I've been thinking about it, is that I fasten the clip to my webbing and drag it for as long as I can before I get fatigued. Then you take over if you're needed.'

Robert was duped by Clive's solicitation.

'I can manage it all. It can't possibly be a strain.'

'No, no. I have to do my part of the physical stuff.' Robert fell for it. To insist on doing all the physical stuff meant that he conceded all the intellectual stuff to Clive. He could not know that even conceding the intellectual stuff would have been easy, but not to his advantage.

Two hours after the last noise, Clive and Robert moved off. The clip on the end of the drum of wire was snapped over a metal loop on Clive's webbing in the middle of his back. Clive moved off, twenty yards ahead of Robert who fed the wire. After thirty five minutes, Robert noticed that the wire ahead was no longer moving and he no longer had to feed it off the drum. He crawled forward till Clive's pale face appeared out of the darkness.

'I'm finished.' He whispered. I've been finished for ten minutes but I have tried.'

Robert unclipped the clasp from Clive's back.

'Have you got the microphone ready?'

'Yes. It's in my bag, all ready to connect. Very soon, the wire won't unwind any more and that means we've done our mile.'

Clive counted as best he could up to three hundred. Five minutes. He paused and waited, feeding out the line. Two miles an hour, three feet per second. Count to thirty. A safe distance. Robert felt the sharp tug and thought that Clive was signalling him to stop. There was a curious, unfamiliar metallic click and the tugging stopped. Robert half turned. He couldn't see anything in the darkness anyway.

~   ~   ~

Mary stood in the bay window, waiting for the postman, waiting for one of those precious letters, written in pencil on scraps of paper, sent from afar. Sometimes, words were obliterated by a thick heavy indelible stroke.

Today the rain slanted down off the moor; the village was grey and shining under the unrelenting drizzle. Then, there he was, the telegram boy, struggling up the hill on his bicycle. He was back at work after that mysterious altercation when he had delivered a telegram to the detestable Smiths at the other end of the village. A sudden lurch of fear swept through Mary as she realised that someone, either in this village or in the small hamlet a mile further on up the hill was about to get some bad news. Bad news? Dreadful news. The worst possible news that any wife or mother could ever receive. The fear intensified as she realised that the boy had already cycled past more than three quarters of the village. That was the trouble with a scientific mind. It could never stop calculating.

'He's stopped. He's got off his bike. He's not coming here. He's wiping his face on a little towel he keeps in his bag. Who lives there? No one with a husband at war. He's puffing and panting.

70

He's just tired. Oh my God, now he's moving again, he's not even riding, he's pushing his bike. He's too tired to pedal. He just wants a rest. He'll get on and start pedalling again.'

This was the third time in a month that Mary had watched him pass through the village and each time she had suffered this routine. It was now becoming a charm to keep away the evil spirit. Imagine and anticipate the worst fear that the telegram is coming your way. Bad news comes without warning so every time she saw the boy early enough and went through the routine of frightened anticipation, it could not happen to her. If she anticipated it happening, it would not happen. She knew it was totally unscientific, but science could not help her.

'He's stopped again. Oh my God. He's leaning his bike against the wall. He's got his bag. He's coming up the steps to the path in front of the terrace, Moor View Terrace, a row of stone cottages built about 30 years ago to house the tannery workers. Oh my God, it's only Billy. He's calling in home to see his mother, maybe have a hot drink. Oh my God, I can't stand this any longer.'

Billy Frith lived with his mother at the end of his terrace. They kept themselves to themselves. Mary hadn't even known that Billy was the telegram boy. Suddenly two people became one. Mary had only seen the boy on his bike twice before and his flat cap covered most of his face.

Billy had delivered a fateful telegram to the Smiths a month ago. He had swung into the drive on his bike. Crunched to a halt on the gravel and following instructions from his senior colleague in the town, had walked to the side door, the tradesman's entrance. Tradesman! This was an ordinary detached house. All right, a bit bigger than most, but there were no servants here, no upstairs and downstairs. The Smiths were not liked in the village. Arthur was a big cog in a small wheel at the Building Society in town. On Sundays, he walked briskly up the hill to the Methodist chapel, side by side with Hortense, his wife. There, once a month, he practised his public morals and vocabulary as a lay preacher, before returning to home and work to practice his private ones. Hortense, the wife, complained about everything. She had married beneath herself and aspired to servants and power and one day being Lady Smith. She had already discreetly checked through a relative, who had connections in London, if a peer by the name of Smith, could call themselves Lord Smith of Ladysmith. She would have to contrive a connection with the South African battle site but if a dear relative had fought there, it might be possible.

The thought that she could be Lady Smith of Ladysmith consumed her and once the thought had entered her head, it would not leave. Lord Smith of Lady Smith. He would belong to her. It would not be Lady Smith of Lordsmith!

She had taken the telegram with a supercilious sneer. 'Wait a moment, boy. There may be a reply.' Obviously, she received routine telegrams almost every day of the week, for nothing had prepared him for what leapt off the page.

```
POST OFFICE TELEGRAM
OHMS
War Office London Handed in Received
To Mr. and Mrs. Arthur Smith
We deeply regret to inform you that
Private Aubrey Smith, 14 Bat Royal Inf Rifles
was killed in action 2nd June.
Lord Kitchener expresses his sympathy.
```

'Kitchener!'

Billy stared, open-mouthed, bewildered by the response.

'Lord Kitchener is dead. He died a hero last month. Everyone knows that. Who wrote this? Did you write this, you wretch? Is that it? You can't even keep up with dates and events and you sit there and scribble this monstrosity. Take it back and write it properly. I want it signed by the King.'

She had screwed up the telegram and thrown it at Billy. The thought that she would have to explain to her husband where the telegram, informing them of the death of their son, had gone, did not occur to her.

The sudden attack on Billy had caught him completely unawares. Mrs. Lady Smith had reached behind the door and seized a heavy walking stick, a weapon. She flew at Billy in a frenzied rage. Not for her the caricature of an exasperated school teacher with swirling gown and a thin cane swishing the air. The face was contorted with fury, lips withdrawn in a snarl. The stick, thicker than Billy's arm, fashioned from the trunk of a hazelnut tree, knurled and with a brass collar at the end came swinging down in a vicious back-handed arc.

'You wretch. Why are you living? Why not you? Why are you not there, fighting, dying?'

The first blow struck Billy across the eyes and hit the bridge of his nose, causing an instant fracture. The second broke two fingers in his left hand as he raised his arm in defence. The third, fourth, fifth and sixth bruised his spine, kidneys, spleen and liver as he lay on the floor. The seventh was intercepted by Frederick Townsend, retired banker, who lived next door and who had been laboriously pruning a hawthorn bush with a pair of small clippers. He burst through a gap in the hedge and ran over.

'Steady on, Hortense, steady on. What on earth is going on.'

Billy had been transported to the town hospital in Jack Read's horse and cart. When the police visited the Smiths to enquire into the injuries, Arthur Smith, market town building society magnate, had refused the officer entry to the house. He also made it clear that Mrs. Smith, bereaved, would give no interviews. He also handed over, typewritten on the Smith's 32 year old Remington, one of the first machines of its kind ever manufactured, a formal complaint about the provocative and insulting behaviour of the telegraph boy who, it was claimed, had smirked and sneered as his dear wife had read the dreadful news. Arthur Smith made it known that he was a personal friend of the Chief Constable and he expected results.

P.C. Hawksworth, dour but honest had indeed been hauled before the Chief Constable Brooksbank of the West Riding Police and been told what would happen, nothing less than six months in Borstel would suffice.

'We can't have the wives of our Chapel lay preachers being treated in this way. Pillars of society. This ruffian had better learn that.'

Hawksworth knew his Chief better than the Chief himself did and when Brooksbank had left the next day for a three day war meeting of Chief Constables in London, Hawksworth had visited Billy in the almshouse in the town and issued a formal caution warning him about his future behaviour. Billy had been unable to speak, but had heard and had been unable to comprehend what he had done wrong. Hawksworth had returned to the station, placed the three relevant documents in three separate unrelated files and put them to the bottom of the hundred files that Mrs. Wheeler came in to sort once a week. She was about six months behind, even with crime at its lowest level since the Boer War.

"Nothing like a war to slow down the chummies." thought Hawksworth.

The charm was invoked again. And again. The telegraph boy Billy, always had to dismount half way up the hill, unable to pedal further. Once again he leant the bike against the wall.

'Oh my God, You are calling in home Billy, aren't you?. Call in to see your mother. That's why you're here. Oh my God he's walking past his own home. Oh my God, there's just three of us left. It's either Mavis, me or Elsie. Oh my God, let it be Mavis. Oh God no, I can't think that. Why Mavis? God will decide. He already has. Oh God, he's walking past Mavis, it's just me or Elsie. Oh God, Oh God, no.'

The last 'no' was a long drawn out groan of despair.

Billy now watched Mary intensely as she opened the telegram with trembling hands. She was fumbling as she tried to reach the envelope with one arm round the baby, Harry. Billy had been advised and trained on how to retire from the scene after the telegram had been handed over. Don't rush away with unseemly haste. Don't hang around as if waiting for a tip. It was a delicate balance, as Hortense Smith had demonstrated.

```
POST OFFICE TELEGRAM
OHMS
War Office London Handed in Received
To Mrs.Robert White,
We deeply regret to inform you that
Corporal Robert White, 4th Field Survey Bat
Royal Engineers was killed in action 1st July.
Lord Kitchener expresses his sympathy.
```

So ended a life, with six mean lines of text. Thirty mean words; seventeen of which had already been deposited in all the Post Offices in the Kingdom to save the cost of repeatedly sending them. All the local clerk had to do was to insert the personal details. The War Office did not believe in wasting money in sending the words: 'To Mrs. "blank", We deeply regret to inform you that "blank" was killed in action. Lord Kitchener expresses his sympathy.' thousands of times, when once would suffice. Four hundred thousand had died in the Somme campaign during that summer. Four hundred thousand telegrams. Eighteen repeated words. That would have been almost eight million unnecessary words to be paid for and transmitted. Such a waste of words. Such a waste of life.

The fact that Kitchener himself had died six weeks earlier would have been lost on Mary. She did not know, that as well as having simple orders on how to fill in the names into the template, the Post Office clerks were also under strict orders not to deviate from the official War Office wording. So until a clerk in the War Office got round to sending a new template of standard words to the thousands of Post Offices in the realm, Kitchener would continue to express his sympathy from his watery grave.

In any case, Mary's eyes had filled with tears and she never read the last sentence, although she would read it a hundred, if not thousands of times in the years ahead. Billy knew it was time to go. He tipped his hat, uttered a quiet 'Ma'am' and turned to go.

'Wait.'

Mary turned and reached inside the door and fumbled with her purse on the hall table. Billy froze in panic.

'Oh no, not again. I don't like this job.'

Mary held out a sixpence, a small flat disk of almost pure silver. 'Take this.'

'On no ma'am, I can't. I'm just doing my job.

'I want you to. Please. Robert would want you to.'

Billy was in no mood to argue further with a fresh widow and took the coin, leaving it flat in the palm of his hand.

'I won't spend it. I know I am nothing but I won't forget this day. I will keep this. I promise.'

~   ~   ~

Chapter 5

Manchester 1919 and 1921

K ay sat in the corner of the otherwise empty Nelson's Arm. He looked across the empty pub to the bar, where Reg was polishing glasses with his brown rag. There was a clear view across the cavernous Men's bar with not a trace of tobacco smoke, because there was no one left to smoke. Dibblee was gone. Kay's brother was gone. The Poles were gone. And on top of that, Rutherford was going. He had been offered the top job at Cambridge, the Cavendish Chair and no one said no to that. Kay had just come into the Nelson's after the final argument with the PROF. Except it wasn't an argument. Kay had wanted the PROF to shout at him, complain and bellow. But he hadn't.

'Well Kay, my boy.' Rutherford was pragmatic. 'If your wife doesn't want to leave Manchester and move to Cambridge, you'll be no use to me. I'm going to miss you.'

Rutherford had then picked up some papers and pretended to read. Neither of them had known what to say and Kay had left, bowing and walking backwards like a serf leaving the presence of royalty. Rutherford never showed sadness or disappointment. The drowning of his elder brother before his eyes in a boating accident when they were both lads had seen to that. When he was upset or sad, he either became angry or quiet, depending on whether equipment or humans were involved.

Reg waved. He took the straps of his special tray and slipped them over his head onto his shoulders. He had got the idea from seeing the women who took round the orange juice and lemonade during the intermission at the theatre. Now he reached under the counter, took out a dusty bottle, wiped it with his rag and put it on his tray. He added two glasses and then, fitting his crutch under his left armpit, hobbled over to Kay.

'I've still got this Bill. Remember those days? I don't think those Poles will be coming back for it, do you? Do you fancy one? It must be nice and mature by now.'

Kay forced a smile that wasn't a smile. As an athlete capable of near Olympic times for the half mile in his younger days, and still able to outrun anyone in the University, he always found physical disability and loss of limbs hard to accommodate. He didn't realise he was staring.

'It's all right Bill. It doesn't hurt and it could be worse. You should have seen some of the others. There was one chap, Shillitoe, he took a round, maybe two, right to the stomach. He took an hour to die, screaming. I took a peep at the orderly's notes to see how they describe such things. "Total evisceration", I'd never heard of the word till then. Mine was much simpler. It was a piece of red-hot shrapnel the size of a broken-off pencil point. It went right in above the knee and stuck against the bone. It just felt like someone had jabbed me with a needle. It hardly hurt at all. Then it turned red and started to swell. Then it turned green and I got a fever. I woke up with my leg off and they told me I was lucky to be alive. I suppose if I was going to pick up a Blighty, it didn't need to be a whole leg. I'd have settled for a toe to get out of that hell. But any road, cheers! Let's be cheerful. I asked if I could have my leg and have it stuffed and then I could hang it over the bar. But they said the green would never go with the tobacco decor and unless I hung it properly first in a cool cellar, it would go off before I got home. Cheers leg, wherever you are. Probably eaten by a French fox by now.'

Clive looked around his old office with a sense of growing excitement. It was the same feeling that had grown to engulf him in the days after Robert's death. He only ever said "death", even in his own thoughts and he banished the seeds of the unspoken and un-thought "murder". He must not, dare not even think the word. If he ever thought it, he might one day inadvertently say it.

He took the towel he had brought and wiped his chair, covered with almost three years of Manchester grime. He picked up his notebook, exactly where he had left it and noticed the shadow of the book, picked out by the rectangle of clean desk in the midst of the sooty dust. Round the corner of the partition between the desks, he started on Robert's desk. Neatly placed in the corner was a notebook, the same dark blue regulation University issue with the University crest embossed in gold on the front. It too was covered in grime. The towel did its job. Clive took the book to his side of the room and opened it at the first page. "Book 3 Oct 1914 – Sept 1915." The second date was in a slightly different colour ink, in a slightly broader nib. He reached into his drawer, and took out an identical looking book. It was the one he had brought back from the Somme, the one he had promised to return to Mary White along with the few other personal effects. "Book 4 Oct 1915 — " The end date had never been entered because the dead cannot write up the date of their own death.

Up on the shelf was a small pile of new, unused notebooks, four of them. They had been new once, but now shared the grime with the others, especially the top one. Clive took down all four, thought for a moment and then put the bottom two back. The other two were about to get the towel treatment when Clive paused, looked out the window, thinking, thinking. He sat down and realised his plan was not yet refined. The details were important and they were not yet right. Then he took down the other two books as well. He would need them after all. He wrapped the dirtiest unused book in brown paper and put it, un-wiped, in the bottom drawer of his desk. He would make a cover for it, to protect the grime. The other cleaner notebooks were placed on top. Robert's book 3 and book 4 went home with Clive that evening, forever.

For the next four weeks, he worked like he had never worked before. Indeed, he had never worked so hard on his own research. His plan unfolded as he carefully developed it. He had a plan, a general plan, but he was no Bragg with disciplined vision. He had to work it out as he went along. He began with a set of red soft cover exercise books, bought from the University stationers. Into these books he wrote, slowly, carefully and verbatim, every word, number and equation from Robert's notebooks, book 2 and book 3, exactly as they were written. Then he tore three pages out of Robert's books and burnt the rest. Brenda watched with concealed curiosity as he broke the hard covers into shreds, tore the pages into strips and burnt everything in the hearth.

'It's pre-war stuff. I got it all wrong. I don't want it messing up my thoughts and now I can start afresh on a clean sheet. I have some good ideas. Some very good ideas indeed. Trust me.'

The red exercise books never left the desk in his study at home. Brenda would go through them when he wasn't there, wondering about the dates, trying to reconcile the fact that Clive had burnt his past and yet had kept this copy, a tangible record of the past. Even when Clive started locking the drawer, it didn't stop her keeping a check on him. She called in a locksmith and told him she had lost the key. He scrutinised the lock, went away and returned in half an hour with a bunch of 20 keys, one of which fitted. Thereafter, even when they eventually subscribed to the telephone company, and Clive spoke down a wire instead of writing it on paper, he held no secrets from Brenda, although he thought he did.

The seeds of a conspiracy were sown. If you know of a plot, if you watch it unfold, if you understand every step, if you match his steps with steps of your own, accepting every advantage and pleasure that the plot should yield; then you conspire, in silence. On the day she took the key, Brenda became a silent conspirator. She did not stop to think, nor flinch. Her only saving grace was that she did not know that her husband was a murderer, until later.

Over the next weeks, Clive dismantled Robert's apparatus in the laboratory basement, cleaning off the dirt with more towels. Brenda had to wash the towels and she complained. There was no Geiger to admonish him about the batteries. Geiger was at Kiel University. Rutherford was leaving and everyone was moving on as well. Moseley was gone, for ever. Chadwick returned from internment in Germany and went to work in Cambridge. Dibblee, who had gone to work as Chadwick's assistant in Germany before the war had disappeared, believed dead. Marsden, Andrade, Robinson had all gone. The only two left were Jimmy Nuttall and Kay. Nuttall had never been interested in Robert's or Clive's work and Kay popped downstairs rarely. He was helping Rutherford to finish off some "epoch making work" before he left for Cambridge.

Clive wanted to turn the clock back seven years, but managed only five, since the first two books were missing. Each day he traced the research steps taken by Robert from October 1914 until the time they had both left for Thiepval in 1916. Each day he would write rough notes on a pad in the laboratory and then go home and spend an hour combining his notes with the red exercise books and writing the product into one of the grimy books he had found on the shelf. Although the written log described what he had done for that day, the date was transcribed backwards to 1914. He had thought long and hard about going further back in time but dare not. Before 1914, Rutherford knew too much about what he and White had been doing in the basement and who was doing what. After the start of war, London had beckoned and Clive took a chance that he could defend his own books.

The next stage was the most difficult. He bought six, scratchy pens and two bottles of ink, both blue but differently blue. He then began to create the myth, producing the "real" Robert notebooks. He created the books containing the mistakes, the poor readings, the blind alleys and the fruitless research that never happened, except in these books. Clive wasted a red exercise book practicing the handwriting using the three torn out sheets as a guide. He practiced until he reproduced the special form of Robert's r, the l and the q and the e with a special serif emerging from under the "chin" of the e. With the wooden steel-tipped pens in his hand, a grimy book in front of him, he became Robert. Except it was Robert the failure that he became, writing a new history of Robert's "wasted years".

Brenda became driven by a compulsion to work out what was going on. She had a compulsion to become part of a conspiracy before she even knew what it was. She laid out the books side by side while Robert was in the university. On the left, she placed the red book with soft covers, all in Clive's pencilled handwriting covering the pre-war years. Next, the three torn out sheets were in someone else's handwriting but the dates and contents matched the pages in the red book written by Clive. The two other outwardly identical books had similar contents. She could not of course understand the differences in content because the physics was beyond her comprehension. They both were running about five years behind the current date. Each day that passed, the books moved on a day, sometimes two or even three. One of them was in Clive's handwriting. The second book had been written by the same person who had written the torn out sheets. And yet Clive was writing them both. It took Brenda a week to work out what was going on.

~   ~   ~

Bragg was standing, somewhat apart from the tea-drinking group and addressing them, his thumbs tucked into his waistcoat pockets. He was in army major mode.

'He's coming. The arrangements are all made.'

Ten faces looked puzzled. They had not spent the morning, like Bragg, with the new incisive Vice Chancellor, Sir Henry Miers, and so they didn't know who "he" was. Clive frowned. Whoever "he" was, it sounded like "he" was coming to work in Manchester, enlarging the pond of physicists even further. His fears were soon assuaged as Bragg continued.

'His lecture will be in the Whitworth Hall and we expect it to be full. You will all get invitations, so don't lose them. You might not get a chance to hear Einstein again in a hurry.'

'He's going to be speaking in German!' Jimmy James was reading the Manchester Evening News and had spotted an article announcing Einstein's arrival that day. 'He's coming over by car from Liverpool; must have arrived by boat. That's why Cook has been working on Schuster's roller. They must be using it to collect Einstein and don't want it to break down.'

'I thought he was in Berlin. What's he doing arriving at Liverpool? It's a long way round.' Clive wanted to disprove the hypothesis of Einstein's imminent arrival.

'He's been on a lecture tour in America. He's on his way back.' Jimmy James was quoting from the newspaper.

Bragg had been flitting in and out for days in a state of high agitation. He had to make a short response at the end of Einstein's lecture and since he would be speaking in English, everybody in the hall would be listening more closely to him. Einstein had no fewer than five laws to his name compared to Bragg's one law. In the end Bragg calmed himself with the thought that there is no greater achievement one could hope for than to have a law of physics named after you and to be rewarded with a Nobel prize. None of Einstein's five laws had got him a prize yet.

The Whitworth Hall was filled to capacity for the degree ceremony that was to precede the lecture. Einstein was to be awarded an honorary doctorate. Clive, well back in the hall, craned his neck to see who was sitting in the front row. He usually sat in the front row at lectures where everyone could see him nodding sagely. But every seat had been occupied or covered by a reserved label and by the time he had realised it, the next rows were full as well. He could see the Vice Chancellor with Bragg next to him. Rutherford was over from Cambridge for the day and had brought J J Thomson and C T R Wilson with him. That made three Nobel prize winners next to each other, plus Wilson. Clive had been seething ever since Bragg had predicted that Wilson himself would soon get a prize for his invention of the cloud chamber. He had seethed, year on year as people he knew were recognised with the highest accolade. Even that impenetrable Danish guy, Bohr, had got one. No one had ever been able to understand what he was saying so how could they give him a prize? Rutherford got on well with him so he must have put in a word.

Since hearing yesterday that Einstein's English was not up to a full lecture, Clive had spent half the night cramming from a German phrase book. He felt able to greet the famous professor and introduce himself. He had suddenly panicked when he realised that if Einstein responded with a long deep question about Clive's interest in relativity, he would be sunk. He had then constructed an escape sentence which said "Ah, if only we had time to discuss that." It had taken him two hours with a grammar primer. He had realised after an hour, with a shock, that it would need the subjunctive and had started again. His school text book had warned that Germans were much less forgiving of mistakes with the subjunctive, than were the English.

The lecture, in German as it was, was lost on the bulk of the audience. Clive had again been driven to scowling as he heard another Manchester man mentioned in the middle of an explanation of how the new relativity theory had been confirmed by the measurements two years previously at the 1919 eclipse. Einstein was glowing in praise of the former Manchester lecturer, Eddington, who had led the eclipse expedition to the South Atlantic. Clive could see the big men on the front row, nodding their heads in agreement with the flow of scientific German, with extra large nods when Eddington was mentioned. At the end, Clive had struggled through the crowd to get as close to the great man as he could, hoping to exchange a word. He had no chance. All he got for his trouble was to hear Einstein, speaking in broken English to the Vice Chancellor, Miers, saying what an honour it had been to be invited to speak to such eminent physicists as Bragg, Rutherford and Thomson. Then Einstein was whisked away and Clive was left, isolated and ignored. He felt the pain of being treated as ordinary but stirred with the knowledge and determination that it was all about to change.

~   ~   ~

Chapter 6

Manchester 1926

C live was unhappy, whereas Bragg, sitting across the professorial desk, was as usual, cool calm and collected.

'But your name is going to be on the paper, and with respect Sir, Professor, I have done all the work'. Clive was whining.

'My name will not be on the paper. The format will be the same as for any paper submitted to the Proceedings of the Royal Society by a member of this department – except me of course. The title of your paper will be printed in italics at the top. Immediately below, on a line to itself, will be your name printed in that font where even the lower case letters are capitals. Then beneath that, in brackets, in a smaller typeface, it will say "(Communicated by W L Bragg, FRS – Received whatever date it was received.)" What can you possibly have against that? I haven't checked but it was almost certain how Newton's paper was first published before he became a Fellow of the Royal Society. He probably had to get Robert Hooke to communicate his paper and the two of them didn't get on well at all. Are you going to have all my portraits destroyed like Newton had Hooke's? When I am dead and gone!'

Even Blackmore could not argue with that. But that rarely stopped him from arguing. 'So if I were an FRS, I wouldn't need someone like you to communicate my papers.'

'That is a treat you have in store. But for the moment, it is denied you.'

'But can't I just join? How much does it cost.'

'Alas Dr. Blackmore, you can't just join. You have to be nominated by at least six people and preferably those from a different university. Then the fellowship meets and votes and if you get that far, you have to pray that you have not upset anyone because out of the hundreds of Fellows who can vote, it only needs one of them to slip a black ball into the bag and you would be sunk.'

For the first time since 1916, Blackmore felt that he was facing a situation that he could not handle. He would normally have expected to have some input, to exert some control.

'So I have no say in the matter at all. What kind of a club is that?'

'It is not a club. It is our National Scientific Academy and you do have a say. If your scientific research and your papers speak for themselves, you have all the say. The sooner you get your papers published, the sooner you are in with a chance. And I suggest you present your results in a colloquium in the department before the paper goes off. That way you will get some intelligent feedback.'

'I was hoping to send it off without others reading it, Sir. Do you have to read it as well?'

Bragg felt the hairs bristling on the back of his neck.

'You expect me to communicate a paper written by you to the Royal Society without having read it? It's a two edged thing Blackmore. You get my support by virtue of my name printed as communicator and I take the chance that my reputation might suffer if someone comes along and proves you not only wrong, but stupidly wrong. The colloquium will be on Friday and you can let me have the paper when you are happy with it.'

If Blackmore had not been clammily humid as usual, he would have discharged his high voltage of anger on the door knob as he left the room.

$$\sim \quad \sim \quad \sim$$

Once again Bragg faced Blackmore across his desk. This time, Blackmore looked unusually smug.

'I've been offered a job at King's, subject to references and Brenda says she wants to live in London.'

With an ease born of hearing premature good news in the trenches of the Great War, Bragg suppressed his desire to burst into a bout of uncontrolled manic laughter. He paused and thought.

'Oh dear, Blackmore. We shall be so sorry to lose you. I hope you don't mind me asking but when do you have in mind? I have a chap who is well spoken of and I can only hire him if I know your salary is available.'

Bragg suddenly hoped he hadn't pushed things too far. Blackmore was funnily cunning. If he knew too much he might try to scotch the new appointment, just for the sheer hell of it, or so it seemed. Bragg had a way of writing references that appeared at first sight to overflow with praise, but if read carefully, suggested ordinariness.

'Next month if the references are received. I hope that can be managed, without leaving you in the lurch.'

Bragg contemplated a serious bout of delirious lurching. He bent as if to study papers on his desk, gave a friendly wave of dismissal and bid Clive farewell out of the department.

'Leave it with me. You can safely leave it with me.'

As the door closed behind Clive, Bragg allowed himself the briefest of smiles in case Clive should come back having forgotten something. Then he reached for his pen and immediately wrote the first draft of his letter of recommendation. Bragg knew that he was an expert in writing references and it was his golden rule, never to tell a lie. He had just written a superb one for a former student, whom he could barely remember, even though there were only half a dozen of them in the class each year. He had confirmed that the applicant, without mentioning that he would have been doing research if he were any good at physics, would make an excellent deputy director of the department of education in the City Council, because after all, he had got a third class honours physics degree at Manchester. As he wrote the carefully crafted words, Bragg had no inkling that Blackmore would be awarded a Nobel Prize within ten years and even if he had known, he would not have changed a word.

$\sim$ $\sim$ $\sim$

Chapter 7

Manchester 1934

In the Nelson's Arm, Kay was restless. He had work to do and the conversation, as usual, was uninspired. Albert Hunter and Freddy Fisher were good company, but neither of them matched Kay's brother for repartee, nor even the long gone Dibblee, who had provoked more conversational topics with his gossip stream than even Kay could manage. Bragg had been to the pub once during his 13 years as head of the Department and even though the number of physicists had grown relentlessly, year on year, as Bragg sought to expand, few of them brought in the family spirit of 20 years ago. Only Jimmy James, having survived Shackleton's expedition to the Antarctic and then the Somme, found the Nelson's a haven of luxury. The few that did come, during the period of economic depression and its aftermath all agreed. The last war had not finished off the business with Germany. This Hitler bloke, who had just come to power seemed an awkward customer and the Germans were becoming ominously restless.

As Kay got up to go, the main door opened and let in an icy blast, followed by a smart foreign looking couple. He, of medium build, had close cropped hair and a neat moustache. She, slender, and attractive in a schoolmistress kind of way, looked around the cavernous bar with keen anticipation. She wore a winter coat of black, with a large black Astrakhan collar, lambswool, so tightly curled that it could only have come from an unborn lamb, as it should. Such nuances were lost on the Nelson's Arm, except for the general aura of class thus created.

'Natasha, Schätzchen, sitzt Du hier und ich hole Dir was zu trinken. Was möchtest Du? Ein Wein?'

'Thomas, speak English. We're in England again and I haven't forgotten how to speak the language. You'd better get used to it again.'

Kay had watched the couple's arrival and hairs had started to tingle on the back of his neck. There was something about the man, something irresistibly familiar. At first he was reminded of Geiger, with his precise German ways. Kay, who had been preparing to leave, paused, walked a few paces towards the bar where the foreigner was standing, waiting for Reg to serve one of the porters from the Infirmary. Kay stopped, walked forward a step, paused, stooped, blinked, walked another step, blinked again, stooped, staring in-between each blink and stoop. The foreigner turned to face him with a smile.

'It isn't. Is it? It is! It's you! It's Dibblee! It is! Good grief. What are you doing? Where have you come from? Where have you been?'

'Good Evening, Mr. Kay. Yes, it is me. I'm back. May I buy you a drink. A pint of bitter still? Thwaites? I must introduce you to my wife.'

Behind the bar, Reg turned from serving the porter and addressed Dibblee. 'Yes Sir, what'll it be.'

'What's up Reg?' Kay was beaming. 'Don't you recognise one of your old customers.'

Recognition dawned more slowly on Reg until eventually, the images of the boy with the ever smiling face, the boy dressed in men's clothes and a flat cap, came flooding back.

'Well I'll be damned. Dibblee, you old rascal. What have you been up to? Marrying a foreign wife by the looks of things! Well, well Mr. Dibblee, what will it be? Half of mild? It's on the house!'

'I'd like a glass of wine for Natasha and a schnapps and ice cold beer for me.' Dibblee almost clicked his heels.

Reg rocked back on his single heel but as a landlord of thirty years experience, recovered in a flash.

'I think I have a bottle of red wine in the cellar. You know how it is? Not much call for it here in Chorlton-on-Medlock.'

On the way to the cellar, Reg looked into his reference book, kept for when the scientists brought in their visitors who always wanted something obscure.

'Hmmmm, schnapps. Ha, good. That's easy!'

In the cellar, Reg moved some boxes and found a heavily grime-caked bottle lying in the corner on an old sack. A French scientist, von Laue, had visited the department and given it to Kay as a present. Kay had no use for it and has swapped it for two pints of bitter. He put the bottle in the satchel hanging from his shoulder, leaving his two arms free to manhandle himself back out of the cellar. He had found a way to hop down the stairs leaving his crutch at the top with a second one at the bottom for getting around.

'Now, where's that corkscrew, I had it last Christmas, or was it the Christmas before?'

On his way back to the bar, Reg went out into the yard and snapped off two large icicles, hanging from the gutter. He wiped off some moss with his towel rag.

Back in his bar, Reg took down a brass bucket and half filled it with water. He broke one of the icicles into the water and then drew a quart of best Thwaites bitter into a jug. With the jug placed in the bucket, he gave Dibblee an empty pint glass and the bucket.

'Give it a minute to chill, Dibblee lad. You've picked up some queer habits along the way. Thank God you didn't come back in the summer. I'll bring the wine and schnapps over.'

Reg broke the second icicle into another bucket, poured in some water and then opened the cupboard under the counter and fished out one of his five remaining bottles of blue label Polish vodka. "Served cold", his waiter's guide book had said. "It is advisable to chill the glass with ice." He dropped a small glass into the bucket of water to cool.

Kay took his warm beer back to the Dibblee's table. As he stood and held out his arm in greeting, recognition swept over him for the second time in five minutes.

'Goodness me. It's Miss Bauer!'

'No it's not! It is Mrs. Dibblee if you please!'

'Pleased to meet you, Mrs. Dibblee. Well, well, well. No lasting harm from the carbon dioxide bottle I see. This is going to take a week or more, isn't it, to get up to date with all the news.'

Reg prepared the glass for the schnapps, wiping it off on his rag and then fished out a few strands of stray moss with his thumb. He hobbled over with the vodka and glass of wine on his neck tray and stood awkwardly on his one leg, which Dibblee saw for the first time.

'Oh dear, Reg. I'm so sorry. Was it the big, bad war that did that? Hmmm. You'll have to tell me all about it, that's if you want to.'

Dibblee downed the schnapps in one gulp and looked admiringly at the empty glass.

'That's a Polish blue if I'm not mistaken! Well done Reg! Excellent taste.' He then took a glass of cold beer, pouring the jug from a height to increase what little froth a pint of Thwaites could offer. He pushed the wine glass over to Natasha, bid Kay to raise his and then proposed a toast:

'Je ein Glas auf was uns freut! To each, a glass, a toast to what makes us happy.'

'Hark at you, Dibblee lad! I always knew there must be a language you spoke better than English. And your English's pretty good as well. What on earth happened?'

Dibblee winked.

'How was the wine, Mrs. Dibblee?' Reg was worried.

'You may call me Natasha.' She picked up the glass, swirled the liquid and had a sniff. She took another sip, letting the dry, exceedingly mature wine bathe her taste buds. Her face screwed imperceptibly at the light taste of tannin and the faint memories of summers long gone, all overlaid with antiquity. She swished the wine round her palate and swallowed. 'This wine ... this wine ... is quite extraordinary. It is quite the most extraordinary wine I have ever tasted. May I see the bottle?'

'The lady is so generous.' In truth, Natasha was not lying. Reg brought the bottle over and stumbled through the label, pronouncing, where he could, every letter of the French words as if they were in English.

'Margo, Chatto La, la la something. Premier cru whatever that is. Nineteen hundred and eight. Now that was a good year wasn't it Bill. That was the year your Prof won that Nobel prize thing. I remember bringing all that beer over for the party. Cor, it's nearly thirty years ago! I hope that wine's all right Mrs. Natasha.'

'Oh, it's all right Mr. Patron. It is very much all right. We don't produce much red wine in Germany. But this will do. Can I have another glass, please?'

When Reg had gone back to the bar, she asked Dibblee how much he has been charged for it.

'It's on the house, but I saw him write sixpence on a slate with a chalk. I suppose that is his own house slate to pay.'

'Hmmm, then how much is five glasses? That would be a whole bottle. I can't remember your silly money.'

'Half a crown; there are eight of them in a pound. And if you're going to have a go at English money then don't forget this!' Dibblee slapped a ten million Reich Mark note onto the table and used it to wipe away a few drops of Margaux.

'Goodness, you would have paid twenty Marks even before the ruin over ten years ago. That's two pounds of your money. I hope the Patron's cellar if full.'

'Thank God for your father, Natasha. He saved us from the ruin. If it wasn't for him, we wouldn't be here with a future.'

Natasha's father had been a bank manager till his premature death two years ago. Now both the Dibblees were orphans. He had advised them, before the German hyperinflation more than ten years ago, and then again as it started to take a grip, to buy gold, gold and more gold. Every pfennig they had, and every pfennig, many of them, from Natasha's inheritance, had gone into gold. They had a bedroom full of gold and a kitchen full of millions, billions of worthless paper Weimar Republic Marks. It had been an exciting ride as the German economy had spiralled into virtual extinction until rescued on it death-bed by the director of the German Central bank, Hjalmar Schacht.

Natasha's father had chosen his moment well. The family owned two houses, one outright and one that had been bought using a large mortgage. He had waited until the value of the mortgage had fallen to the equivalent of ten Marks. Then he had gone into his own bank as a customer to redeem the debt. If he had waited until the value of his debt had fallen to less than one pfennig, there would have been no banknotes, no coins with which to redeem the debt. He had been worried that the bank might claim it if he physically could not find a coin to repay them with. Not long after the time when Schacht had stabilised the Mark, Natasha's father had died and she had sold the house overlooking the Grunewaldsee. They were rich, even richer if they could take their wealth out of the new Nazi Germany.

Getting the gold out of the country had been an adventure of science and steel nerve, except that Dibblee had used lead and not steel. He had done the calculations himself and used the Berlin Institute's workshops to do the smelting at night. Siegler, the workshop assistant, one quarter Jewish, who had already arranged an exit for himself, sorted out the night-time access to the workshop in return for two gold ten Reich Mark coins. It was a perfect place to carry out their nefarious work without observation. All of the Germans in the Institute went home for Abendbrot and by six o'clock, they were long gone. There is no German word for "midnight oil"; they do all their hard work in the daytime. No one came round snooping at night on the Institute campus.

Dibblee had used a set of callipers to carefully measure the dimensions of the lead bricks that were used for shielding away the nuclear radiation in their experiments. He had a ton of it, more than two hundred brick-sized lead bricks, more than enough for his purpose. Those radiation workers who had been careless, not using lead screens, were dying like flies, or if they were unlucky, living with debilitating radiation sickness, as it was called. When their neighbours got colds, they got pneumonia. When their neighbours got pneumonia, they died.

He measured the volume of twenty different bricks in a displacement vessel and took the average of the readings. He used this average result to work from. Dibblee then made several sand moulds of the lead bricks. The next step was to make some smaller bricks from aluminium, now a cheap metal since the advent of hydro-electric power. Aluminium was a light metal - barely three times heavier than water. Lead was almost twelve times heavier than water and gold a massive twenty times heavier. Dibblee imagined a bucket of water twenty times heavier than it should be; un-liftable. Dibblee had laughed in the German Kino, the cinema, when the robbers had run up the stairs with a pile of gold bricks under their arms. In reality, you would crawl, stagger, and finally give in, defeated by gravity. Therefore, gold bricks plated with a thin layer of lead would be far too heavy; they would be nearly twice as heavy as they should be – if they were supposed to pass off as lead.

Into each aluminium brick, Dibblee had machined a series of slots, each one a fraction, a measured tiny fraction, wider and deeper than a twenty Mark gold coin or sovereign. With the coins in place, an aluminium lid fitted snugly on top. Now came the test, the acid test without acid. He measured the volume of five such assemblies using a displacement vessel. Then he weighed them to an accuracy of a tenth of a milligram with the coins in place. Dividing the weight in grammes by the volume in cubic centimetres gave him the overall density of the aluminium and coin assembly. If his calculations and machining were good enough, each assembly would have a density that was a small amount greater than pure lead.

For safety and peace of mind, he had weighed the coins individually on a micro-balance and found them to be remarkably consistent. He had always bought the coins in mint condition and refused any with scratches. He had travelled the length and breadth of the republic to buy thousands of twenty Mark gold coins and sovereigns. The German coins looked and felt the same size as sovereigns, but they weighed just over two percent less, 0.2304 troy ounces, than their British counterparts, which weighed 0.2354 ounces. This was easily dealt with. Each aluminium brick was loaded with twenty German and twenty British coins. So a pair of such coins weighed 0.4658 troy ounces. Easy, thought Dibblee, double them up and treat them as unit. There were a few unpaired German coins left at the end. Good for ready cash.

It was important for the next stage that each assembly was slightly heavier than the equivalent size of lead, and not lighter. He then calculated how much aluminium he needed to shave off the inside of each lid to bring the density down to be exactly the same as lead and he shaved that much off, using the micro-balance to weigh the shavings. It was easier to shave off bits than to add shavings. By shaving off the inside, the overall volume did not change, but the mass went down. It was crucial that each assembly was the same as lead, not nearly the same. He took the best known value for the density of Czechoslovakian lead, from the mines of Silesia, that he found in the published tables of Landoldt, held in the Institute library.

Then, he went to the smelting furnace. He felt at home with the high temperatures, having worked in front of furnaces for many years. Each aluminium gold assembly was placed on top of a small lead base in the mould and molten lead was poured in slowly, so as not to melt the base, nor to disturb the assembly. It must not float. The end product was a pile of what looked like lead bricks. They were shiny as new but rapidly oxidised to dull grey in days. They had exactly the same density as lead. If a piece of lead were to be cut off, what remained would have exactly the same density as lead. Provided the aluminium core was not disturbed, and it lay a centimetre beneath the surface, each brick would behave like lead. From the outside, it would look, feel and weigh like lead. Brilliant, thought Dibblee. Prof would have been proud of me.

Siegler had stamped each brick with a steel die, to impress a batch and brick number and an ownership tag. "University of Cambridge. Batch 057. Brick 097." It was Siegler who remembered to file the cross stroke off the die for number seven, to convert the German into an English seven.

'Let's be quick, but careful. I have another job after this one. You haven't patented the process yet have you?'

'What? Patented a method to smuggle gold out of the Reich? That's a nice one, Mr. Siegler!'

Siegler had his next job lined up – to export Silberman's gold. He had squeezed twenty gold coins commission out of Silberman for a consignment only twice the size of Dibblee's. Silberman had left it late. He should have left six months ago and was paying Siegler five times over the odds for his belief that Berlin would be a safe haven for people with only one Jewish grandparent. Now Siegler had to think of a new ploy to bury it in lead or some other material. Dibblee had promised to think of something that would work. He couldn't use the lead brick ruse a second time and in any case, Dibblee, the careful measurer would be gone. Very few people exported scientific lead bricks and two lots in one year would arouse suspicion. Siegler would keep the best method for himself at the end. At this rate, he would be rich beyond dreams in six months. "New York, New York!" he hummed to himself.

Dibblee had written to his former boss, Chadwick in Cambridge with an outline of his request: he needed a letter from Chadwick demanding Cambridge's lead back for essential research. It wasn't Cambridge's lead but no matter. The neutron had been discovered in Cambridge and now lead was needed to contain them. The fact that it was never Cambridge's lead in the first place was lost in the turmoil of the Great War and the Weimar Republic. Rutherford had received a gift of a large amount of lead from the Austro-Hungarian Empire, the rump of the First Reich, and Dibblee knew where to find reference to it in the Institute library.

At the border, the crated consignment had been opened as expected. The German customs officer was genial and had engaged in scientific conversation with Dibblee about the purpose of the shipment. He was a specialist metallurgist whose brief was to assay shipments of metals, whether precious or otherwise. He had a bald head, rimless spectacles and blue lips.

'I am Herr Emil Schaeffler, your obedient servant.'

It was most unusual for a civil servant to give his name. Officials of the Third Reich expected obedience; they did not dispense it. But then, Emil was no ordinary civil servant.

'Let us look at your lead. I must prove to my masters that it is lead and not gold in disguise! You would be surprised at the people who think they can paint gold to look like lead. But they do not know the atomic weights and the densities, ha ha! Oh no, they are not chemists.'

"Neither am I," thought Dibblee. "Two hundred and eight for lead, one hundred and ninety two for gold were the atomic weights. Lead ought to be heavier than gold in a fair world. But for some reason, maybe chemistry, lead atoms, although individually heavier than gold, spread themselves out when they joined together to make a metal. Gold atoms stuck close together. So gold was denser."

'The chemistry of lead is extremely interesting, no? Ah yes, very interesting. Now I shall determine the density of these blocks using my apparatus. I have developed this myself because the Reich's method is too inaccurate. It only scratches the surface. I go much deeper. You are a scientist; you will appreciate this! I hope.'

Dibblee had turned pale and would have given himself away had not Emil been transfixed by the lead. Emil had gone on to measure the volume of one brick using his own displacement vessel. Dibblee had looked on, understanding every step. He was convinced that Emil could hear his heart beating. Yet he had been able to ask illuminating questions, based on pretended ignorance, every step of the way.

'Now, we weigh this thing, so, to an accuracy of a milligramme, I think. Gut! Better than a milligramme is not necessary. I think not! Are you a milligramme man? Some people think a gramme is small enough. But I like to work a thousand times smaller than that!'

Dibblee felt a lot better as Emil showed that he was good, but not that good. Any discussions were likely to be sensible, but kept his thoughts to himself. "I work to accuracy ten times finer than you. Thank you Emil. I feel a lot better already." But he still felt moved to say something.

'Ich meine, Sie seien der groesste!' Dibblee felt confident enough to give Emil scientific praise. 'I think you are the greatest!' Whether the greatest metallurgist, or government scientist, Dibblee left unsaid. But his correct use of the German subjunctive was not lost on Emil.

'Where did you learn to speak German? And the accent is certainly there.'

Dibblee turned to smile at Natasha, unmistakably German, reading from a small pocket book, through a pair of pince-nez.

'Ahah, a bed dictionary. The best way. I wish I could speak French.'

Dibblee guffawed. It was rare to find a German civil servant with a sense of humour.

Emil was measuring accurately. But Dibblee had measured with super precision. It could be the telling factor.

'Ahah, I now calculate the density and yes, I have it. Now specially, by courtesy of Emil, in the name of the German Reich, I look in my book and I will tell you where this lead came from!'

Dibblee nearly died.

'Not many people know that the density of lead depends on where it comes from. Some lead is heavier than others! Is that funny or is that serious? It is all a matter of isotopes and what was happening in the ground before the miners came. But you know all about that don't you, you lucky scientist? I wish I could work as a scientist in a University. The isotopes are all the same if you disregard one tenth of one percent. But I am Emil Schaeffler, a customs officer of the German Third Reich; I deal in tenths of one percent.'

Emil winked.

'Ach sooooo, allowing for experimental error, which will be very small, I see here that your lead has come from our mines in Silesia!'

"Your mines!" Dibblee had thought. "The last I heard, Silesia was in Czechoslovakia and Poland. Czechoslovakia might not have been independent for long, true, formed in 1918, but then this third German empire had only been formed in 1933, eighteen months ago."

Dibblee had experienced a flash of inspiration that scientists know, when they realise some aspect of the world, previously hidden from human gaze, for the first time.

'Brilliant, Herr Schaeffler!' he had replied. 'Our professor in Manchester, Rutherford, now Lord Rutherford, received it as gift from Austria who temporarily held Silesia before you did. They gave him some radium and a lot of lead. He sent me to Berlin and

Heidelberg with the lead to do some experiments with Professor Lenard. Now Professor Rutherford wants his lead back.'

Emil had beamed, wagging the tail he had never been born with.

'Rutherford? The Lord Rutherford? The Chemistry Nobel prize-winner of 1908? You worked for him? My God! No, no, not you! You are not God, excuse me. I knew it! My method really works. This is the first real test! You have helped me to prove it! You and Rutherford, Lord Rutherford. Mein Gott, Danke, Danke!' Emil had grabbed Dibblee's hand and pumped it vigorously.

'That explains the weight of the bricks as well! They each weigh 6.3602 kilograms, which is most unusual to us, I mean the Germans in general, but not me. That is your English measure of a stone isn't it! I know about stones even! So this German lead was made into bricks in England. You see, I can work it all out! You can't fool me.'

Dibblee nodded in approval.

'I wouldn't even try, Herr Schaeffler.'

Then Emil cooled.

'But now we must satisfy the Reich.'

Dibblee again blanched, but Emil, opening his instruction manual, page 82, lead, did not notice.

'First, I read the instructions that I must follow and I take this instrument here. It is like those that carpenters use to mark straight lines on wood; a scribe, except it has a tungsten tip. Tungsten, you English call it; Wolfram, we Germans named it. Nothing is harder! It will make an easy groove to the depth of one millimetre. Superfluous, redundant, I have already looked deeper with my Emil-eyes. But I must do it, for the record, for the Reich.'

Emil scratched, got out his magnifying eyepiece and inspected the groove.

'I see only lead. Jawohl, sieht aus wie Blei; it looks like lead. Fuehlt wie Blei; it feels like lead. Wiegt wie Blei; it weighs like lead, and,' Emil bit into the corner of the block, revealing teeth impressions in the soft metal. 'Schmeckt wie Blei; it tastes like lead! So I say, on behalf of the German Reich, it must be lead!'

Dibblee allowed himself a bleak smile.

'Unless of course, Herr Englishman, you have used very thick lead paint!

Emil waited until the smile had completely vanished.

'A joke, Mr. England! You have made me happy today. Normally I would have the final right to saw one of your blocks in half, just to be sure, but only an intellectual weakling would need to resort to such crudity. I can see right through lead with my special eyes.'

Dibblee wanted to return the compliment, but eschewed the opportunity. Emil had torn seven pages off a thick pad and started on the first one, the official form. He had laboriously written in the entries, line after line, sucking the indelible ink-pencil between lines. That explained the blue lips. He had finished with the finale: "lead", signed the form and taken out an impressive rubber stamp which he had tamped onto an ink pad and then placed in the corner of the form, pressing and counting, eins, zwei, drei, vier, fuenf. He had removed the stamp to reveal a perfect eagle impression and the paraphernalia of the German Reich, correctly placed to a fraction of a millimetre. He repeated the stamp on all of the six copy pages beneath.

'Gut. That is the first block finished with! You have ninety-nine more?'

Dibblee could not help his face.

'Another joke, Englishman! German humour! I only need to test nine more blocks, at random, not all hundred!'

"Now that is funny." thought Dibblee.

'Mr. Emil. May I call you Mr. Emil?'

'You may call me Emil, English scientist!'

'Emil, although I have lived in Germany for, oh, twenty years, and I am not leaving for ever; I will be back, soon, there is one thing that I have never understood about Germany.'

'Yes, Mr. Englishman, I am your obedient servant. What are you missing?'

'It is now the third Reich.'

'Yes, indeed it is!'

'What was the second Reich? And indeed the first one?'

'Ah! All the foreigners ask that. Let us dispose of the second one quickly. Our great Count von Bismarck, he created the second Reich in 1871.' Emil did not go on to say when it ended.

'And the first Reich, the Roman Reich and the Holy Roman Reich together. It lasted for one thousand and six years. The famous first emperor, Carl the Great, sat here in Aachen. But poor Bismarck, he will eventually not go down in history, German history, for his second Reich. Because the third Reich will also last for one thousand years. At least!'

One hour later, Dibblee left the shed with his gold and a valid certificate of exportation for the lead. Two hours after that, he was in Belgium with his German doctor's degree, his German wife and nearly £10,000 of the German Reich's gold, most of it Natasha's inheritance. The "lead" consignment weighed just over half of a ton. Sixty pounds of it was gold, in the form of one thousand coins.

Natasha had stayed in the background in the customs shed, reading, watching and listening. On the train, she waited patiently during the German passport control and then the Belgian. Not until the Belgian uniform had been to check their tickets and departed with the words "Next stop Lüttich, Liege, Welcome to Belgium," did she release a huge sigh, turning to Dibblee with the words,

'Du bist meiner Held. Der Held des Tages und meines Lebens! You are my hero. The hero of the moment and my life! I want to make love to you now.'

'We'd better wait till Manchester, Natasha. We don't want to get thrown off the train without our lead.'

'Wake up Dibblee! Where are you? Your lady wants another glass of wine. You've been sitting there with your eyes closed and your mouth twitching. What are you thinking about?'

'Lead, Mr. Kay. Lead. Do we still have an electro-furnace?'

~   ~   ~

Chapter 8

Manchester 1934

'Now Dib, we want the whole story, everything.' Kay had hardly slept the previous night. It was just like old times.

'Dr. Dibblee to you, Sir!'

'You know that I called them all Mr. even when they were Dr., except the Prof. He was always the PROF. Still is. But I'll make an exception for you Dib. Dr. Dib.'

Reg brought over a warm pint and a bucket of chilled bitter. He had poured water into the gutter to make more icicles and had no idea what he would do for ice if Dibblee stayed till Spring. He had kept the bottle of left-over Margaux for Natasha, with the cork stuck back in and had left it in the back yard to keep cool. He had no idea what he would do if she developed a thirst or came back tomorrow. He needed a Dibblee to cycle to the Midland to find out the price. In the meantime, he prepared a cold schnapps and poured a glass of wine, holding back a finger to stretch it to four more glasses, enough for tomorrow if she kept to two a night. Tonight, it was sixpence a glass. He had a living to make.

'So? So? You left with Mr. Chadwick before the war to go and work in Berlin for a year. It's been a long year!' Kay was leading the questioning.

'Yes. I worked for Mr. Chadwick as his research assistant in the Institute in Berlin and then when war broke out, we hadn't been paying attention and they put us both inside the nick. Not the same one; Mr. Chadwick, Chadders, was put in with all the toffs in a shed. I was sent downstairs, as it were. We had tents.'

'Goodness me, our Dibblee, a prisoner of war. Without fighting!'

'You remember Natasha from the Manchester days? She had been in the institute in Berlin with us working on something and then one day, they pulled me out of the nick and asked if I would work for her, making quartz glass in the furnace. I wasn't too happy about that at all, it might have been for submarine windows, but Natasha promised it was pure physics research. She wanted some windows for a new cloud chamber she wanted to put on a high mountain to look at Hess's rays – you've heard of them?'

'We've heard of them all right. Cosmic rays we call them.'

'Well, believe it or not, I felt that Natasha was telling the truth and it was true, we only ever made windows for her cloud chamber. Even that's not true, only one ever turned out right. But we only needed one.'

'Yes, yes, but you don't get married over a cloud chamber. What next?' Kay wanted to know every detail.

'Ever since that day with the gas bottle, I'd felt funny whenever I looked at her. It wasn't like that chemistry woman or Miss Margaret. It was different. And I just knew she was warming to me. She didn't have to get me out of nick, it was a risk for her, so why did she do it? But I did notice that she didn't have much time for men and so I couldn't move in on her fast. I had to woo her.'

'Woo her! Dib, you swain!'

'I was taking German lessons in the afternoon. I could just squeeze it in before returning to the prison camp. There were a few of us working in the institute; I wasn't alone. But I never saw Chadders again. For all I knew he didn't make it. Though I hear he's in Cambridge now, and the Prof, and Mr. Blackmore. Funny enough, as I learnt German, and it came quick, living among them, I learnt to read and write English as well. I read all the Prof's papers about the nucleus. Gosh, I could tell you a thing or two about the things we didn't understand back then. When the war ended, Natasha got me to enrol as a physics student to get a diploma. And I got my Ph.D. working on her cloud chamber. We saw the positron a year after Anderson and Blackett. If we'd made that cloud chamber window a year sooner, she'd have a Nobel prize.'

'My, my, who would have thought it. Another schnapps? Can I try one?' Kay felt boundaries falling away.

'I proposed to her on top of the mountain, the Jungfraujoch, where we were doing the experimental measurements with the cloud chamber.'

'Jungfraujoch?'

'The name of the mountain, it means "virgin's harness" in English, chastity belt almost.'

'I see. How romantic! What did she say? Yes please?'

'No. She said that at high altitude, oxygen starvation makes the brain work in unusual ways. Therefore my judgement might be affected and I might not really have meant to ask her to marry me. Similarly, her judgement might also be affected and she might give the wrong answer. Therefore we should go down the mountain, rest, think and then see what happens next.'

'How Germanic! So what happened next?'

'We went down the mountain to the little guesthouse where we were staying. Separate rooms of course! Neither Natasha nor the woman who ran the place would have allowed anything else. I was in the annexe across the courtyard, past a large dog, tied up it was. I had to squeeze against the wall each time I slid past, to stop it biting my balls off. That day, I went to have a long bath. So did Natasha. We met in the dining room and I asked her again and she answered, "Yes please." She made the landlady bring a candle for the table and told her what had happened. Then we had some Sekt.'

'What?'

'Sekt. It's the German name for their sparkling wine. They didn't have any champagne.'

'Oh.' Kay sounded disappointed.

'I had to ask her father for permission when we went back to Berlin and he wondered why it had taken so long; he had been waiting on me to ask her for a year. He liked me and said in some ways I was more German than the Germans because I had thought about it and had become a German. I did not like that. It is one reason why I decided to come back, even though it took a long time to achieve it. I am not German.'

'But didn't the inflation ruin you? We read all about it. But you have money, I can see that. Where did it come from?'

'Ah everyone thinks that the whole of Germany was ruined by that business but it only really hit the middle classes, not the rich, nor the poor. If you had nothing, like I had, then you had nothing to lose. You might even make, if you were smart. If you were rich, you switched to gold or gold shares. That's what Natasha's father did. The middle classes were paying rent and they couldn't afford it. They all had to sell furniture to pay the rent so furniture prices fell like a stone. With some of father's gold, we bought antiques and paintings. Then after the finance minister Schacht sorted it out, it was all over. We were rich and sold off the antiques and paintings when prices recovered.'

'Goodness. And what about the physics work, lad?'

'Oh we kept that going. The other stuff was just weekends. Then father died and Hitler took over last year. It's frightening what's happening and even Natasha wanted to leave. And here we are!'

'So you've been married a few years then. Where's the kids?'

'Nothing I'm afraid. No little Dibblees. It just doesn't seem to happen.'

'Just like that Mr. Blackmore! He and Brenda didn't have kiddies either. But he's just got a Nobel Prize now for the work he did here. Bit of a shock that was. We'd all forgotten what he'd done.'

$$\sim \quad \sim \quad \sim$$

'Good morning Mr. Kay. My mother sends her greetings. She hopes you still remember her – and my father.'

Kay looked and frowned. There was something vaguely familiar about the fresh faced young man with dark wavy hair. It was unusual for new students to address him by name, even if they spoke to him at all.

'You'll have to give me a clue lad.'

'White. Harry White. My father was Robert White who worked here before the war. My mother was in chemistry.'

'Mr. White! You're his son? Well, well well. We do remember your father. You don't look a bit like him. So sad. Mr. Moseley too. It was all so sad and unnecessary. So you are our new research fellow, come to work for the PRof!'

PRof was now the pet name for Rutherford's successor Bragg; the "r" was rolled for semi-emphasis. Appointed in 1919, he had been the main reason why Clive had moved to London. With Bragg a Nobel prize-winner at 25, a professor in Manchester at 29, Clive did not want that success stuffed down his throat every day. Clive was now talking openly about "his" work and his reputation was growing.

'Oh Mr. White. I do hope you do well and stay on to do research. It would be quite like old times! I suppose your mother has warned you about women in the chemistry department! Watch

102

out for them, especially when they are crossing the tramlines on Oxford Road.' Kay loved "old times".

Harry had come to Manchester to get a degree and then work under Douglas Hartree on mechanical computing machines. Hartree and his research student Arthur Porter had built a model computing machine out of Meccano that could do physics calculations. Harry was an avid young Meccano mechanic and had read all about the mechanical computer, the differential analyser, made out of Meccano and he had set himself the task of building one himself before he got his degree.

'You'll have to hurry up lad! We're having a big one made by Metropolitan Vickers in Trafford Park.'

The times were becoming exciting again.

~   ~   ~

Chapter 9

Cambridge 1937

T he shock of Rutherford's death in October 1937, coming as it did when he appeared to be in robust health, echoed throughout the scientific world. One moment he strode the world like a Colossus, booming his way through the corridors of physics in Cambridge and through the corridors of power in London. One of the most famous chairs in a British university, the Cavendish Professor of Physics, was vacant.

Clive, 46, now a Nobel prize-winner himself, and finally a professor at Cambridge within months of him getting it, started designing his new visiting card. Wrapped, as he had been for two years, in the dazzling cloak of fame brought by his prize, he continued the cycle of accepting invitations to dinner and honorary degrees. A lifelong frog, he was starting to look like a bloated toad. Complacency brings its own rewards. He had been looking forward to Rutherford's retirement for some time. His move to Cambridge from London, following his Nobel Prize and knighthood had been almost a formality. They even came looking for him. Rutherford, who had thought he had made a mistake when he had hired Clive to Manchester now thought he must have made a mistake thinking he had made a mistake. Nobel Prizes are not lightly given. He did not know who had nominated Clive for it because he himself did not think much of the subject of semiconductors and solid state physics.

Rutherford's death brought everything forward a few years. Clive had already perceived his main competitor to be his former leader Bragg, all powerful in Manchester after a reign of eighteen years, but had been elated earlier that year when Bragg resigned from Manchester to become Director of the National Physical Laboratory. The finishing line was in sight and he could hear no footsteps behind him. Within days his dreams were shattered. Twice he had picked up the Times and twice the words leaped off the page. "Professor William Lawrence Bragg appointed Cavendish Professor in Cambridge." "Professor Charles Galton Darwin appointed Director of the National Physical Laboratory."

He had not thought of, nor heard of such plans. They had done it behind his back without asking him. He told Brenda he needed a second honeymoon in the Lake District to clear his mind. It had been a repeat of the first. It was November, cold and wet and they had barely spoken. Left alone one afternoon, she walked through the town of Windermere and was astonished to see Clive having lunch with three people, two of whom she recognised from Cambridge. They weren't even physicists, there was that arts man, Blunt and what's his name, oh yes, Cairncross. The woman looked as prim as a schoolmistress, with hair swept back in a bun. The three men wore suits, the woman had on a grey, shiny, glistening raincoat, even inside the restaurant. She looked very foreign.

Back home, sitting down to lunch, Clive had thought: "University politics: a funny business. Fancy appointing Bragg." Clive could not change that now. It was time to turn to other things. He had achieved everything he could in physics and the goal of being the Cavendish professor in Cambridge had been torn from his grasp. The Establishment had betrayed him. The Establishment must pay and he had set the payment process in motion.

'Who was she?' Brenda was not in the least bit interested in why Clive had met Blunt and Cairncross, but she was interested in the woman.

'Ilse. That's all I know.'

'What! On first name terms already? It was six months before you ever spoke my first name. What was it all about?'

'Urgent University business. It couldn't wait. If I had not dealt with it, I might not have a job when I get back. I do now.'

The Establishment, unwittingly, was now starting to pay. As a Nobel laureate, he did not have long to wait before he received a discreet phone call, followed by a letter informing him that King George VI would be delighted to confer a knighthood on him. He had already been discreetly told, more than a year previously, that King George V was going to do the same but the King had inconsiderately died and then that Edward chap had made a mess of everything and Clive was not the only aspiring knight who had been made to wait. But the new George was wasting no time in rectifying omissions.

Chapter 10

Manchester and London 1944

Kay slipped quietly into the cosmic ray laboratory and glided unnoticed into the corner where the physicists were having tea and discussing all the things they did in the afternoon: physics, sport, politics, the war and occasionally women.

'That is an unbelievable amount of energy.' Douggie Broadbent always had something to say and it was usually worth listening to.

Kay gently tapped Harry on the shoulder and growled 'Prof wants to see you, now.' Kay couldn't whisper. He was a robust Northern athlete.

'Prof!' It was out too loud, too strong, before Harry could control his voice. Harry also did not know how to whisper. 'I thought he was in London.'

'He got back just after dinner.' Said Kay. 'Though God only knows how the train found its way here.'

Manchester was enveloped in sooty fog, as it had been for over a hundred years. Kay, of course, did not realise that the sooty fog only extended as far as Stockport and held only its beloved Manchester in a dark bronchitic embrace. Wilmslow, Crewe, Tamworth and Bletchley were all enjoying autumn sunshine.

'Dinner?' queried Harry, thinking that Blackett must have returned the previous day, before remembering for the thousandth time, but still not storing the unusual fact that in the North, dinner meant midday.

'He wants you now.' The growl became almost a purr as Kay recovered his breath. "Dammit." Thought Kay. In the good old days he used to be able to run up and down these stairs and still be able to shift half a ton of lead bricks before dinner. And not only that, in the old days, in the days of the 'PROF', the PROF would have come to Kay's room when he wanted to see him. The PROF was Rutherford, dead now for six years, before his time and sorely missed by Kay. PRof was Bragg, who had let Kay stay in his room when he took over from PROF in 1919. But Blackett, the Prof, who had arrived in 1937, had ejected Kay from his allegedly "cosy" room within days of his arrival and put him in a glass cubicle by the front door, like a receptionist. Not only that, he didn't come himself when he wanted Kay to do something; he used the internal telephone to ask him, nay tell him, to come up to the Prof's office. Kay did not like the telephone. It had not been invented by a clever, friendly, Manchester physicist. Even a Geiger counter was better than a telephone. A Geiger counter could make a man happy, nay, well nigh ecstatic, for life.

'Better not keep him waiting.' urged Kay in a slightly elevated tone. 'He's not best pleased today.'

Harry's heart and spirits sank. 'He knows.' The thought could not be contained. 'How on earth did he find out? He couldn't have known when he left on Monday because I hadn't done it then. Nobody knew but me. And if he was on a train till midday, how did anyone tell him? It's got to be something else!' Logic was Harry's speciality and he applied it everywhere. He could take ten facts, all intertwined, and come up with the logical consequence while everyone else was asking for the details to be repeated. Faced with two habitual liars who held the information he needed, he would know to ask one of them what the other would answer if asked. Two logical lies make a logical truth. Easy. For Harry. But Harry was not good with fear. He now felt, as he often had done at boarding school, after the laxatives had been administered.

'You'd better go home now and get your things ready.' Blackett barked out the order like a ship's lieutenant. Naval college had served him well, while others of his age were wasting their time as undergraduates. He had gone straight from naval college at Dartmouth into physics research at Cambridge, working in Rutherford's group. His Nobel prize would arrive with no more surprise than a Christmas card from his mother.

'You're expected in London tomorrow. There's a train just after nine. Sally in the office has a rail warrant and your expenses. If you spend more than you're given, you'll have to find it out of your own pocket. You need to be at the Cabinet Office for two o'clock. Don't get carried away, it's not the War Office. The Cabinet Office deals with scientists – among other things. It's just around the corner from Downing Street. I'm sure you can find that. If His Majesty's constabulary should impede your progress, then show the letter that Sally will give you. Don't lose it.'

Harry hated the patronising additions that Blackett frequently added to his commands. Blackett wouldn't lose his passport, but others might. Blackett wouldn't forget to charge the batteries overnight, Harry might.

'What's it all about?' juddered Harry.

'You simply don't ask those sort of questions in a war, White. That's the first thing to learn if you are to progress.' It was meant to be helpful but Harry's stomach seized up. Laxatives couldn't help him now. Matron would have recognised the bilious look on his face and administered something stronger. Probably she would have delivered the dreaded castor oil. Whereas Blackett's whole life and being did not admit or acknowledge even the existence of laxatives.

'Go home now, before the trams stop. The fog's bad today. Even worse than London.'

'I don't live on a tram route.' Useless information. 'But it is not a problem. Shall I go now?'

Blackett had already opened a file and was pursing his lips in concentration, Harry was already forgotten and filed away. Sally, in the department office, handed over an envelope.

'What's this all about then, Mr. White?'

Sally called everyone Mr. It was too difficult to remember who was Mr. and who was Dr. and the Misters became Doctors very quickly anyway. Sally also needed to know everything that was happening so that she could tell everyone what was happening. It was simple obvious logic to her, but a source of endless problems in the department. She knew who was going to be courting whom, even before the couple knew it themselves. There was one little secret she kept to herself because she quaked just to think of it. She had seen Blackett with a woman in a cafe in Didsbury. There weren't many cafes any more, so if you went to one, there was a high chance of meeting someone else who also did. The woman was not Mrs. Blackett. She had assigned the assignment to business.

'Haven't got a clue.' replied Harry. 'The Prof told me to pick up the envelope and go to London. Very mysterious.'

'How exciting!' chipped in Daphne, the junior secretary. Daphne had a huge crush on Harry and it showed all over her chubby freckled face every time she saw him. 'I've never been to London. Can I come?'

Harry smiled back and nodded. He was rather frightened of Daphne with her ruddy face and five feet nothing of unrefined sexuality. Daphne had exceedingly large breasts, out of all proportion to her height. At normal conversation distance, she was usually in physical contact with whomever she was speaking to. Some men backed off. Some didn't. Harry was one of those who did.

'I'll have to ask my wife, Daphne. She vets all my girlfriends.'

Daphne frowned with incomprehension.

Harry went back to the laboratory to find that Michael Polyani had joined the tea group. Polyani was a Hungarian émigré, now a professor of physical chemistry. He spent a lot of time in the physics department on account of the more stimulating conversation over tea. His skills and interests covered logic and philosophy and Harry valued his visits for tea. Today he was steaming with rage and not in the mood for two-way conversations. He was half-way through an explanation of what happened in Cambridge where he had just given a seminar.

'... and that Wittgenstein, he thinks he owns philosophy and can't accept any idea that isn't his own. When anyone says anything remotely radical, he gets up in a pique and leaves. he leaves! he says he has to go to his room and have a think about it. People with brains stand there and discuss it. Ow can you have a debate with a missing brain?'

'Should have stayed here and stuck to kites.' Kay was still there.

'Kites!?' Polyani again.

'Ooooh yes.' Explained Kay. 'He was here as a student before the war.' Kay meant the first one. He used to go up on Glossop Moor with Margaret, Margaret White that is. We all thought there was something going on, Margaret would come back so flustered. But then him being what he is and Margaret being what she was, they'd probably have been arguing about certain things in the Bible.'

'I wish I'd known that yesterday.' Polyani.

'What are you talking about?' Douggie was sometimes slow to catch on when it wasn't physics. Kay replied by tapping the side of his nose.

'I'm off to London for a few days.' Harry felt he had to hurry things along. 'I don't know what for, but I'll be back in on Friday to set up the chamber for the weekend run.'

'War work.' Polyani grunted. 'It's always war work when they say that, or rather, when they don't say that.' It had to be logical with Polyani. 'At least they don't send our young Turks up the beaches of Gallipoli to be shot by their Turks any more, like they did with Moseley.'

Thirty years later, together with the loss of Harry's father, who had not had time to make his name, the deaths of Moseley and White still hung over the department like the densest coal-loaded Manchester fog. Moseley had been destined for a Nobel prize for his X-ray work, offering as it did, a key understanding of Mendeleyev periodic table in terms of atomic number – the number of electrons in orbit round the nucleus of an atom.

'Moseley wasn't sent.' Kay had stayed to find out what Blackett had wanted with Harry. Although he knew he would not now find out, he did know that the department was losing another of its youngsters to the war, hopefully not for ever. He'd counted them out and he had failed to count them all back. The PROF had always told him what was going on. The PRof told him half of it. This Prof told him nothing.

'He couldn't wait to get into action so he volunteered, damn fool. Say mannifeek, mare sir nay pa la gar.'

It was some time before the assembled group, which had remained silent, realised that Kay had been trying to speak French, overlaid as it was with a heavy Manchester accent.

'Ah yes! Charge of the Light Brigade.' It was George Rochester who had sorted it out first. 'I've been to Gallipoli. I went to a conference in Taranto a few years ago and hired a bike one afternoon and cycled down the coast to Gallipoli. Damned hot it was.'

'Gallipoli's in Turkey, in the Dardanelles and Taranto's in the south of Italy. How did you manage that on a bike?' Polyani leaned back smugly and pulled on his pipe. 'Check.'

George gave a short laugh, more of a cough. 'You're not the first to fall into that trap. There are two of them – Gallipolis that is. There was also a ferry from Bari just up the coast from Taranto sailing across the Adriatic to Bari in Albania. Most confusing. I'd get the return ticket portions mixed up.'

'Ah; that Gallipoli.' Polyani shared with Wittgenstein a need not to make mistakes.

Harry picked up his cup of tea, left un-drunk before he went to see Blackett. He pulled a face as the cloying skin of tea and milk wrapped itself round his tongue.

'Best be off.' he chirped, getting to his feet. I need to persuade my landlady to starch a few collars. 'I'm told London is just as grubby as here.'

A shirt collar became dirty in about two hours in Manchester and Harry didn't like grubby collars. So he used replaceable collars on his shirt, not being able to afford changing shirts twice or thrice a day. He couldn't afford a decent collar stud either and usually had a small green smudge in the region of his Adam's apple caused by the action of sweat on the brass.

'Doesn't Debbie do your collars?'

'She's got her hands full with Bobbie, our little one. I tried it but I left the iron on the gas too long once and the starch went all black. How is one supposed to know when the thing is the right temperature?'

'You should comprehend that better than anyone.' Friz Quarmby chipped in. He was a young, verbose physicist who specialised in the meticulous and fastidious application of other people's ideas, without having any original ones of his own. He had been hired by Bragg in the months before Blackett's arrival. Bragg, having been distracted by his own imminent departure, had paid less than normal attention to Brown's details and originality. It had been most unlike Bragg. Blackett would have got rid of him by now if it were not for the fact that he was losing staff faster than he could hire good replacements. 'You're a physicist. Why don't you time how long it takes a kettle of water to boil on your gas ring? Weigh your flat iron, look up the specific heat of iron and there you have your panacea.'

'And what's the right temperature for not scorching the starch?' Douggie had joined the debate and usually found it easy to shoot holes through Quarmby's flimsy arguments. Douggie liked soft open necked shirts with wide collars, unconventional for wartime and pre-war England. Douggie had spent time in Italy.

'Oh, why do you always spread such a cornucopia of irrelevance? Where is your mantra? I would make some test strips using old cotton. Shouldn't take long. You could even do it with panache.' Friz Quarmby needed the last word even when he didn't have one.

'There must be an easier way.' Douggie again.

'There is.' Harry wanted to terminate the discussion. 'I ask my landlady to do it. She's figured it out after years of experience.

She spits on her finger and touches the iron. When it squeaks, it's ready.'

Harry left the building and stepped into a blanket of pitch darkness. He stepped back inside the porch to check the time. Two minutes after four and it was darker than midnight on a moonless night. All this from just soot and fog thought Harry. Why do people put up with it? The University buildings were only sixty years old, the physics building not much more than forty and yet they might have been hewn out of coal themselves instead of the near white stone that lay under the microscopic layer of sooty grime. When the physics laboratory had been built in 1900, a contraption had been installed to draw air in from outside over a large vat of oil so that most of the soot would stick onto the surface of the oil, like it was fly-paper. The oil was replenished annually. But this was for the benefit of the apparatus, not the occupants. Harry could barely see the tips of his fingers when he stretched out his arm. This was his test to check whether the buses would be running. If he couldn't see them, the bus drivers would have all gone back to the depot on Princess Road and walked home. He decided to walk. He would be home in an hour whereas he would need about half that time to find out they were not running and then he would still have the hour's walk. Logic again. He tugged his trilby an inch lower than usual and tightened the belt on his gaberdine coat a further notch. If the war went on for as long as it had done already, he would need extra notches making in the belt.

Out on Oxford Road, the fog blanket smothered all sound. Harry could hear faint footsteps but nothing else. Then there was a distant sound of a motor engine, not heavy, definitely not a bus but getting louder. A small car, perhaps a Morris 8, loomed out of the fog, travelling not more than ten miles per hour on the pavement. How it had mounted the kerb without the driver realising, Harry could only guess. The Morris squawked as the driver used his horn in preference to his brakes. Harry jumped back, his reflexes being more than a match for the myopic Morris driver. The car continued a few yards before smacking into a lamp-post. At ten miles per hour, the car was no match for the Victorian cast iron and the vehicle stopped within its own length, hissing, with its front bumper bent into a gentle curve.

'Why can't you look where you are going? Look what you made me do.'

'Are you talking to me, or the lamp-post? You're on the pavement don't you know?'

'I've got a meeting in the Town Hall with the Mayor at half past.' The plummy voice was resplendent of Fallowfield or even worse Didsbury.

'Town Hall is ten minutes walk. You'll make it.' Harry slipped away into the gloom, quickly forgetting the idiot. He now needed all his stored knowledge of the details of the route home if he was going to make it in an hour. He had devised a special route for days like this. He tightened the belt on his gabardine yet another notch, turned up his collar and pressed his trilby firmly down on his head. With a large handkerchief pressed over his nose and mouth, a stick in his other hand, he could tap the walls as he progressed, never straying more than a couple of feet from the wall. Care was needed at junctions, which he would cross as quickly as possible, listening for engines. In the blackout, even when there was no fog, cars were not allowed to use headlights and drove with their lamps covered by opaque material except for a small torch sized hole. No wonder death rates had risen. Bats with earplugs would have had a better sense of direction. They were probably killing and maiming more of their own countrymen than the whole of the German Luftwaffe in their air raids on German cities. What a war. Manchester had its share of the bombing and the targets were usually the industries in Trafford Park. But some of the bombers didn't seem to care where they dropped their fire-bombs.

With these thoughts and those of tomorrow, streaming through his head, Harry soon found himself past London Road and Piccadilly and almost back to his rented home in Ancoats. It was a grim part of a grim city, but it was cheap, less than a pound a week. Harry and Debbie were looking forward to a home of their own. He would settle for Victoria Park so he could walk to work in ten minutes. Debbie preferred the leafier avenues of Didsbury or Fallowfield. But Harry flinched at the thought of driving a Morris 8 and talking like an idiot who drove on pavements.

Suddenly, Harry remembered the electronic logic circuits he had modified on the cloud chamber. "Oh my God." He thought in a panic. "What will Blackett say?" More to the point, "What will Blackett do?" He would surely notice; Blackett never missed anything. He thought briefly of walking back – an hour, changing and testing the circuits – at least another hour, walking back home again – another hour. He'd just have to take a chance.

Debbie's face lit up as he entered the room. 'You're back early. That's nice. The fog is so bad and I thought you would be very late.' Debbie was sitting with young Bobbie in front of the fire. They had been engrossed in a book. Little Bobby was only four, but had been at school for six months and could already read and do arithmetic. He had a natural appetite to learn and Debbie and Harry fed it.

'Daddy!' Bobbie ran to his father and grabbed his leg, holding tight as Harry swung his leg back and forth.

'I need to clean up. This muck gets into all my orifices. I won't be a minute.'

'Daddy doesn't have a hairy face.' asserted Bobbie.

'Orifice, young man, not hairy face. It means a hole and I've got a few of them on my head; my mouth, my nose and my ears. They're all orifices.'

Bobbie would now use the newly acquired word mercilessly for at least a day or until he learnt a more interesting one.

'Daddy's hairy face has got an orifice.' he chanted and laughed.

Harry thought of the kids he sometimes passed on the way to work. Scowling and wordless, with a total, life's complete vocabulary of a dozen words. They were at least twice Bobbie's age, knew nothing and didn't want to learn anything.

Harry used the kitchen sink, a large white Belfast monolith. Closing the kitchen door behind him, he proceeded to clean up his face. He blew out the contents of his nose into the sink and noticed with disgust the dirty slime, streaked with filaments of soot, as it was sluiced down the plug-hole. He cleared his throat of an equally obnoxious mixture of bodily fluids and the product of the industrial revolution. He then scrubbed his hands and arms with the red carbolic soap and finally washed his face, ears and neck. Debbie did not like him using the astringent carbolic tablet on his face but Harry insisted on washing the Manchester grime off as soon as he got home. He said that the carbolic only removed the top half and second wash with the green Fairey soap block took off the rest down to the skin. At least Manchester had soft water. Incredibly soft. Kettles never furred up in Manchester, even after decades of use. Virtually all of a bar of soap was used for washing and not removing the chalk from the water. Harry put on a thick pullover and went back to the living room. Now he felt able to give Debbie a hug and a kiss without feeling that the dirt would rub off onto her. Bobbie now tugged at both their legs, impatiently waiting for his turn to be admitted into the close physical bonding.

'Blackett is sending me to London. I've got to catch the train at nine o'clock tomorrow morning.'

'What!' Debbie panicked as she misunderstood the information, thinking that Harry was being transferred.

'It's some meeting in the afternoon. I'll be travelling back on Thursday morning.'

'Oh, I see. I thought for a moment, . . . What's it all about?'

'I don't know for sure. Blackett is being cagey as usual. The meeting is in Downing Street, or rather just round the corner.'

'Wow, are you going to see Churchill?'

'No! I'm pretty sure he won't be there, too busy to see scientists. It's something scientific. They wouldn't want me for anything else.'

'Do you think you will be going off to America, like Chadwick and the others?' Debbie had a secret longing to go to the USA, to get away from all the bad things England had to offer; war, bombing, near starvation, low wages and an uncertain future for the family, especially young Bobbie.

'I don't know. I'm not a nuclear expert like Chadwick or even Flowers, but you never know.'

'What are they all doing over there? What is this nuclear stuff?'

The answer to that question was a highly classified secret but physicists could guess. You didn't just ship away all the nuclear physicists to the United States, leaving the rest behind, unless there was something to do with nuclear physics going on in America. It didn't take much logic to figure that out. Most physicists knew of the huge energies locked in the nucleus and capable of being released. A few of the physicists had converged their thoughts onto using it as a weapon, but many scientists, like Harry, thought of it as a likely power source, an alternative to oil and coal as the war went on.

'Hmmm, you see that coal. It burns and gives off heat. Well the nuclear guys have found a material that will give off thousands and thousands times more heat than a piece of coal. One shovelful will last a whole family a lifetime.'

'Goodness! When can we get some?'

'Well, the problem is that the material doesn't come pure when you dig it up out of the ground. Not like good coal. And it's not easy to refine. And no one is sure how easy it is to set on fire. And once it is on fire, it burns so fiercely, no one is sure how to put it out. Even the air might be set on fire. Think of that.'

'I'm not sure if I like the sound of this at all. If it's so nasty, why work on it?'

'Because if we don't, the Germans will, probably are, right now. And I wouldn't like a shovelful of that stuff dropped on Manchester. On second thoughts, . . . I'm not so sure.'

'So we are going to drop a shovelful on Berlin first, is that it? Is this civilisation? Is that what you are going to London for?'

'No Debbie, no. I told you, I am not an expert in that. But let me tell you, if it comes to a choice, a shovelful on Berlin or a shovelful on you, I'm in there, working on it. I can tell you.'

Debbie was a dedicated pacifist and Harry had long since abandoned the notion of convincing her that civilisation sometimes needed protecting from aggression using controlled aggression.

'I'll make tea, you look after Bobbie, he's had a tiring day at school.' Debbie smiled and the warmth and softness of her eyes mollified the sharpness of her tongue. 'I need to ask Mrs. Fletcher to do some collars. I'll need them in London.'

Debbie turned and picked up a neat pile of starched and ironed collars. 'I had a starching and ironing tutorial this morning. I'm now an expert.'

~   ~   ~

The ticket inspector at the barrier looked at the warrant, holding it arm's length and turning it over.

'This is no good.'

'What?' Harry's heart sank and his voice quivered. Blackett's face swept into full view, replacing the bald head of the inspector.

'You'll have to go to the ticket office and change it into a ticket. This is just a warrant to issue a ticket. Over there.'

Five minutes later he passed the ticket inspector again. 'That's more like it. Off you go.'

Through the barrier and through the steam. Harry coughed as he caught a lungful.

'There you are White. I thought you'd got lost.' The unmistakable bark of Blackett sliced through the complex mixture of sounds on the platform. 'What kept you? You'd better hurry and find a seat or you'll be standing all the way. Look there.'

Blackett pointed back up the platform towards the barrier, a group of about twenty lads in khaki, swinging kit bags over their shoulders, were now jostling their way towards the train.

'I'll see you on the platform at Euston.' Blackett was standing by the coach doorway which was marked with an appropriate "1st Class". 'You'll be in 3rd. I'm afraid I have a special badge that gets me into 1st. I need to be able to work.'

Although Harry accepted that Blackett had first class written all over him, he could not totally suppress the stab of indignation, more at the implication that he didn't need to work on a train or that his work might somehow be unimportant. First class fitted the imminent Nobel laureate like a glove and Harry found himself, not for the first time, drawn to stare at the imposing figure, now with one foot on the steps to his coach. The black wavy hair, the handsome chiselled features, all set off by the pipe. Blackett could have been a film star. He was far more imposing than Leslie Howard and now with Howard dead, there was a vacancy for the dashing handsome English hero. Harry picked up his suitcase, nodded his departure to Blackett and set off further down the platform without waiting for his boss to board the train. He's not King, thought Harry. I don't have to walk backwards out of his audience.

The 3rd class compartments were filling up rapidly and Harry eventually found a seat in one already occupied by five smoking privates, all returning to base camp after a week of special training at Padgate near Warrington. It was already almost impossible to see across the narrow compartment out of the window.

"Why do they do it?" thought Harry. "They live and breathe the muck and then when there's a chance to get out of it, they create the filthy atmosphere to take with them."

One of the soldiers, with a leer, slowly scanned Harry from head to toe and back to his head again. Two things in life caught his attention and both attracted the same dedicated scrutiny. Woman, and eligible males in civvies. Eligible in this case meant eligible to fight. For Harry the special ingredient reserved for women was left out. There were no breasts to pause at on the way down, and this saved a quarter of a second. The half a second pause on the way up was also omitted and so the manoeuvre was completed significantly earlier for men, allowing the cutting phrase to slice through the already nervous victim. An inch of cigarette was stuck to the soldier's bottom lip in a futile attempt to look like Humphrey Bogart. It was futile because Bogart never dressed as a private.

'And where's Mummy's boy off to then. Back home to Mummy?'

'Give it a rest Sid.' The soldier next to Sid had put down his copy of the Daily Mail with a bored expression. 'We had enough of that on the way up.'

Sid tried to sweep the cigarette off his bottom lip in the way he had seen endless times at the pictures. He immediately wished he hadn't as the thin skin, hardly healed from the last attempt, was ripped off by the cigarette paper. Part of the paper remained stuck to the lip, providing a white contrast to the red now trickling down Sid's lips.

Harry has met this attitude before and he had not yet learnt how to deal with it. Polyani had made a promising suggestion and he decided to try it out.

'My father died in France in 1917, blown to bits fighting the Germans the last time. I'd gladly take his place and risk the same fate but I've been given other work to do.'

He wanted to add that he could easily do Sid's job but Sid could not do his, but the last time he said that to a wiry Scottish dwarf of a soldier in a pub near the University it had back-fired and turned nasty. 'I'm a professional boxer you Sassenach shyster.' Harry hadn't even seen the punch coming. The day turned black and red and Harry consigned the provocative phrase to history.

'Oh yeah?' Sid had picked up the "yeah" early in his infatuation with the American moving picture industry. He licked his lips and tasted blood. 'And what does Mummy's boy do then? Polish Winston's shoes?'

Harry nodded at the poster above Sid's head. "Careless talk costs lives." From Polyani, Harry now had a fictitious job lined up for circumstances like these. 'I design and test new ordnance so that you have better weapons to fight with. If it weren't for us, you'd still have long bows. And we take the risks so that you don't have to.'

Harry showed his left hand with the missing two fingers, the scars still red after a year. The lack of the digits was usually enough to shut most people up, especially those who had seen death and a person who had escaped scarred was someone to be respected.

'My friend and colleague took the full blast and it took out everything from his navel to his knees. I got a scrap of shrapnel.'

Sid had never seen action; he had never even seen blood, except on his own lip. 'And how's he doing then?' The words came out as a nervous croak.

'How's he doing? He's not doing anything. You don't do anything when your stomach and balls are smeared all over your mates. You are glad when you die quickly. But you must have seen that yourself at the front?' Sid had never left the shores of England in his whole life. He'd never even been as far as the Isle of Dogs.

'Are you always so careless when you are testing?' Sid's neighbour spoke up. Almost a cultured voice. You could imagine it reading the lesson at church. 'My name's Rufus by the way.' Sid smirked. Names like Rufus amused him.

'We thought we would be all right. We were testing new armour plating and a new type of shell. We should never have done both together but there are not enough minutes in a day sometimes. The new plating won and the shell ricocheted off. We were behind conventional shielding plate and now the new shell won. We learnt a lot that day. I think I've said enough.'

Harry looked up at the poster again, nodding at it to close the topic. The train was just pulling into Stockport. Twenty minutes down, four hours to go at least, thought Harry. Meanwhile, Sid dabbed his lip with a filthy handkerchief.

Harry peered out of the window and noticed that the fog was getting thinner. He was able to see small stations flashing by. Goostrey, Holmes Chapel. Harry had visited the University's botanical field station at Jodrell Bank with lecturer Bernard Lovell. Bernard was an extremely clever physicist who had been in the department for about five years, working with George Rochester and Blackett on cosmic rays. They had plans to see if they could detect the cosmic ray particles by bouncing radio waves off them, much in the same way as enemy planes were detected by the new radar system. If anyone could detect the elusive cosmic rays by radar, it would be Bernard Lovell. Bernard himself was now permanently absent from the department leading a project team at Malvern. Harry noticed the cleaner air around Jodrell, here not much more than a standard Cheshire mist. He resolved to look into the possibility of working at Jodrell when things settled down. A village in Cheshire looked a nicer bet than Didsbury or Fallowfield. He would take Debbie and Bobbie out for a day trip on the train on Sunday if the weather was better. Actually, he would do it even if the weather was bad, because it would be better in Cheshire. Logic again.

At Euston, Harry found Blackett standing near the ticket barrier. The statuesque figure looked as if it had been transported from the platform at London Road station in Manchester without a hair being displaced.

'Good, let's go.' Blackett held out his arm and ushered Harry through first. Harry fumbled for his ticket, having forgotten which pocket he had put it in. He looked back instinctively and noticed Blackett pulling back his coat lapels to one side to reveal a metallic enamelled badge pinned to his jacket. Blackett did not normally wear a badge there. The only thing that often drew attention from his otherwise immaculate appearance was the edge of a card sticking out of his top pocket. The card was legendary and struck fear into the staff at Manchester. Blackett would pull out the card with a flourish and pronounce: 'Now White.' Or 'Now Rochester.' Even the flourish accompanied by 'Now Braddick.' would reduce the normally pugnacious and garrulous Jimmy Braddick to a state of anxiety. Braddick himself could terrorise students with a cutting remark 'Are you incapable of coherent speech?' so he must have known the effect he was having on young inexperienced undergraduates when he turned on them. The card would contain a prepared list of topics that needed immediate attention; usually things that had gone wrong. Today there was no card.

Blackett led the way out of Euston to a side street where a black Wolseley was parked. The driver put out his cigarette and folded his newspaper as soon as he realised that the sudden darkness was caused by Blackett at the window and not a heavy cloud.

'Afternoon Sir. Straight to the office?'

'No, I think we shall stop at Lyons for something to eat. We'll find our own way from there.'

'I didn't think you would be travelling with me Prof. You told me how to get there.' Harry was confused.

'No need to say everything is there? You'd better learn that. And I might have missed the train.'

Harry could not imagine Blackett missing a train, especially when he was already on the platform.

After a brief and frugal lunch at Lyons, a luncheon meat salad each, Blackett and Harry walked down Horse Guard's Parade and took the back route towards Downing Street. The entrance was indeed just round the corner and the dingy doorway was not at all what Harry had been expecting, nothing like the picture he had seen of Number 10 with a smiling or stern Chamberlain and then Churchill, with an automaton of a policeman standing guard.

Inside the building, Blackett quickly went his own way, leaving Harry with the receptionist, a middle aged dumpy woman in a smart grey cardigan and plain glasses.

'Doris will take care of you now.'

'You'll be all right Sir. They are all quite friendly really. Nothing like as fierce as they look.'

The accent was Northern with the peculiar twirl of vowels that Harry recognised from the Accrington, Clitheroe and Blackburn triangle. The problem was that Blackett was fiercer than he looked. And why should Harry need reassuring that it would be 'All right'. It was the first indication of what was in store. He almost responded with a query but realised that he ought not to demonstrate that he was in the dark.

'Yes, we have some pretty ferocious looking people in Manchester as well.'

He wanted to add that they all shat and fucked like anyone else but Harry couldn't even imagine the full spelling of the words, let alone use them in front of a woman.

'Cup of tea? They're not all here yet so it will be a while.'

'Yes please.' Harry had settled for a coffee in Lyons and he could still taste it. It was clear that tea was still being made from tea-leaves but he had long since stopped wondering what went into coffee these days. It wasn't just the over-boiling or scorching of the milk that wrecked the taste, the English always did that. It was whatever was in the brown grindings that had not come from a coffee bean. The tea was good. Hot and with the right amount of milk added, and not put in first.

'Nice cuppa tea Doris.' He complimented her.

'Thank you. You're welcome. They let me make my own since they got fed up of me complaining about Sandra's stuff. She stews it for an hour on the stove so she can get fifty cups out of four teaspoons before setting out with her trolley. She always got to me last, uugghh. Now they're all sneaking down here to get one of mine. It's alright if they bring their own milk and sugar and a bit of tea now and then. But I can't feed the five thousand on my ration book.'

Harry sat in the reception area, slipping and sliding against the polished hard leather of the couch. What was this all about? It looked like an interview, that much he was sure of. Why didn't they let him prepare. Probably part of the plan. Harry had figured out interviews very early on in his career and took them in his stride. It was no good pretending to be something you were not. Too many people polished themselves up to present an image of something they had imagined and too many of them pulled the wool over the interviewers who had probably got themselves into the position they were in by similar sleight of mouth and a jar of Brylcreem. They couldn't do the job they had talked themselves into and spent the rest of their careers obstructing the progress of others who were more talented. Friz Quarmby was one of them. He had seized an opportunity between Bragg and Blackett when he was interviewed by mild Harry Nuttall. Neither Bragg nor Blackett would have hired such an ordinary physicist. He'd do well in Gallipoli thought Harry, before dismissing the negative thought. Harry got incensed by the English recruiting system because he thought that the war would have been over by now if the right people, in the right jobs, had been given the right tools for the job. At that moment, it did not occur to him that if what he thought was totally true, then he might not be in London at that moment, about to be interviewed by the power and might of the British scientific hierarchy.

Doris had poured out three cups of tea for a thin young man with a thin balding head who had appeared silently. The young man wore a pin striped double-breasted navy blue suit that was a size too large for him. Probably his mother had bought it for him in his late teens with the expectation that he would grow into it, but he had stopped growing. Almost everyone had stopped growing in the war. Pin stripe had stacked the three cups and saucers like a Balinese temple and had opened the door through which he had come using his elbow. Holding the door open with his foot, he manoeuvred his way through the opening with practised skill. Harry was watching the dexterity in amazement until he noticed two figures at the end of the corridor. One of them was Blackett, pipe in mouth, gently nodding to a bull walrus. The walrus also had a pipe which he was repeatedly jabbing in Blackett's direction, emphasising whatever he felt needed emphasising. Blackett was tall and imposing enough but the walrus was awesome. Harry felt the stirrings of recognition but it wasn't until the head went back and the mouth opened that he realised it was Darwin. He hadn't seen Darwin for over five years, since he was a research student when Darwin had come to Manchester for a seminar, to talk about the golden years. Stuff the golden years thought Harry. They've gone. Rutherford's gone, Marsden's gone, Geiger, Chadwick and Moseley, they've all gone. Darwin's gone, but it was clear that now being Director of the National Physical Laboratory had not slowed his growth. His mother would not have saved much money buying clothes to grow into. This Darwin was the 5th generation counting Erasmus as the first. Harry could not help wondering to what extent genetics or the possession of the surname had brought Sir Charles Galton Darwin to this position. A bit of both he thought. Plus his education at Marlborough College and Trinity, Cambridge of course. Darwin was good, no doubt of that; Rutherford would have ensured that he would have disappeared without trace, family name notwithstanding, if he had not been good. And when the chips are down and all things are equal, having a Darwin on the team wouldn't hurt, particularly if he towers over the opposition, bristling his walrus whiskers. Pinstripe had slid through the door, tea intact and the snapshot of Blackett and Darwin clicked from view.

'Another cup?'

'Thank you Doris, but no. I'll save the pleasure for later.'

Tea was a strong diuretic for Harry and he did not want to find himself uncomfortable half way through whatever was coming up. Doris poured herself another cup from the large aluminium teapot but managed only three quarters before the dense brown liquid ran out. Harry noticed the slight grimace as Doris met the bitterness of the tannin and he was glad he had said no. The last cup from the pot with a swollen fat tea leaf to wrap round the tongue was never the same pleasure as the first.

Harry picked up the Daily Mail off the coffee table and read it in about five minutes, all four pages, a single sheet of paper. Pinstripe came back through the door and bent over to whisper something in Doris's ear, looking at Harry as he did so. How subtle, thought Harry. Doris put down her knitting and smiled.

'They're ready for you now, Sir. Would you like to use the room over there Sir, straighten your tie, do you have a comb?'

Men usually didn't. Harry was in the toilet and out again within a minute, relieved, tie straightened and hair combed. Doris led the way down the long corridor, round the corner and down an even longer corridor and opened the door at the far end. There was a sign "Silence – Council in Session" on the door, which seemed rather redundant to Harry since all the people in the building except Doris were now in the room. Even in the room, one could have heard a flea cough.

'Mr. White, Sir,' Doris from the doorway, addressed the old distinguished bishop-like man at the centre of the group, seated at a table at the far end of the room. The room itself looked like a large corridor and it seemed to Harry as if it took five minutes to reach the chair which the bishop was gesturing at.

'Dr. Harry White?' The bishop looked up from his papers with a benevolent smile. His hands were almost pure white, yellowish at the knuckles and blotched with brown liver spots on the back.

'Oh I'm sorry,' Doris again. 'It didn't say Doctor on my sheet.'

'Thank you Doris. That's perfectly all right.' The bishop dismissed her gently. 'Scientists tend not to brandish their qualifications. At least most of them don't.' Blackett pulled back the start of a frown as he pondered whether the bishop was having a dig at him.

Harry turned slightly to the right so he could take in those seated to the bishop's left without scanning his eyes. Blackett was seated immediately on the bishop's left. Next to him was Darwin tamping his pipe with the flat end of a pencil. Next to Darwin was a younger man, younger looking anyway, with dark, lanky hair, sallow face and a classic seven o'clock shadow at two o'clock in the afternoon. Harry recognised him but in the stress of the moment, the name would not come to mind. To the bishop's right was a person in uniform, white haired, white clipped moustache and a pair of incongruous black shaggy eyebrows topping a pair of rimless glasses. Harry was weak on uniforms and ranks and hoped the introductions would make everything clear. The uniform was obviously not navy or air force so had to be army. Simple logic. Next to the army sat a diminutive woman with darkly lip-sticked thin lips. If anything, her lipstick had been applied to make her lips seem even thinner, Harry noticed. There was a sixteenth of an inch of un-lipsticked lip at the margins, perhaps nearer a thirty-secondth he estimated. Harry's mother would never have gone out like that. She would rather have stayed in till she could afford more lipstick than go out looking like that. His mother had performed a ritual before leaving home on a shopping mission or to see a friend. Dressed immaculately, often in clothes she had made herself, she would lean over the fireguard to inspect her face in the mirror before leaving to face the outside world. A small unnecessary dab of extra lipstick would be added to the perfectly executed bow and she would compress and smack her lips silently. She would often catch sight of Harry in the mirror watching her from behind.

'I look like the wreck of the Hesperus.' Harry had found out that the Hesperus was a ship and always held the image that his mother must look like one of the wooden female heroines at the bow of the ship.

The woman wore a faded purple cardigan. At least it had once been purple. She must have saved some wool to darn the worn-out elbows after a thousand washings because the patches, still bright, stood out stridently. I wonder why she didn't wash the spare wool in with the cardigan every time,' thought Harry. It's so obvious. Logic again. Her greying hair was scraped back and tied in a bun. Thick glasses, with even thicker rims, perched on the end of her disproportionately long nose, the glasses attached to a looped chain.

Next to Cardigan sat Pinstripe, looking at his fountain pen with a pained expression. He had just had an argument with the Bishop who had told him to write the minutes in ink and not pencil. Moreover, the Bishop had told him that he would have to hand them over at the end of the meeting. Pinstripe was acquiring a dislike for government scientific advisors. Minutes sometimes needed "minor" adjustments in the cool light of day and pencil was much easier to change. Unfortunately, the Bishop knew that.

Harry had taken all this in as he sat down, tugging up his trousers to save the crease. He then caught sight of the card sticking out of Blackett's top pocket. A wave of panic swept through him. The last time he had encountered the card was when he had fiddled with the logic switches on the cloud chamber, trying to test out an idea to improve the triggering efficiency. Blackett was already being touted for a Nobel prize for this technical invention, triggering the hitherto random cloud chamber and ensuring that every frame of film on the reel of expensive photographic emulsion recorded a piece of new and interesting physics. Fiddling with Blackett's logic circuits was an act of folly, unless you were a brilliant logician, which Harry was. After the row, which Blackett won, they then went to the Prof's office where Harry was asked to explain slowly what his improvement was. He was stunned, he thought he was about to be sacked but had accepted Blackett's explanation.

'What would have happened,' barked Blackett, 'if your damned "improvement" had fogged the physics and produced artefacts instead of true phenomena? And then imagine you had got run over crossing Oxford Road and nobody knew what you had done because you hadn't told anyone. So we publish silly physics not knowing that it is wrong, let alone why it is wrong. And then someone in America, or even worse France, proves that we had messed it up and got it wrong. End of Manchester's reputation, bang.'

Harry had been forced to accept this logic and it took some of the gloss off being able to explain his idea to the boss. Blackett had said it sounded good, but that some test runs would need to be made before it was taken as standard practice. Now Harry quaked as he contemplated the possibility that Blackett would get to the cloud chamber on Thursday before him. It would be a lame excuse to say he hadn't had time to tell anyone because Blackett could have replied that they had been almost an hour in Lyons and discussing the trigger logic would have been more interesting than eating spam.

"Snap out of it." Harry thought. "Grow up. He's not got a reminder to have a row about the trigger written on the card. He wouldn't do it here. He would have said something over lunch."

'Good afternoon Dr. White.' The Bishop continued. 'I am Toby Mauritzen and I am your chairman for today.' Sir Toby had never completely got used to his knighthood and rarely flashed it around.

'You know Professor Blackett of course and you probably know Professor Darwin and Dr. Turing.'

Harry nodded; the time and place of the lecture he had attended when Turing had blazed through his mind and changed all his preconceptions was as clear as if it had been yesterday. Curiously he had been so wrapped up in what Turing had been saying that he had almost forgotten what he looked like.

'Let me introduce you to General Thorndyke whose present wartime task is closely connected with science. And also Dr. Marion Masterson from the Cabinet Office.'

Cardigan's lips disappeared altogether inside her mouth as she gave either a grim smile or an acknowledgement that she indeed had the misfortune to be the person just introduced.

'Mr. Mather will take the notes.'

'Dr. White, we want to talk about codes and encryption. We understand you are something of an expert and we would all like to learn a little bit more about it ourselves.'

The word "more" was not lost on Harry. They weren't about to hear about codes and encryption for the first time. Harry had nodded a greeting to each person as they were introduced and so he felt able to dive straight in with a response.

'Well Sir, codes and encryption are a kind of by-product, a hobby, arising out of my main subject area which is the development of binary logic. That is my area of expertise.'

'We'll see,' answered the Bishop. 'Professor Darwin will start by asking you some questions and we'll take it from there.'

It sounded rather unstructured but Harry realised that this was because he did not know the structure.

'Dr. White.' Darwin's voice was plummy, phlegmy and resonant. 'Suppose I wanted to send a message by radio to someone in France, an important message critical to the Nation's security and war effort. Can this be done in such a way that even if the message is intercepted, it cannot be understood by the enemy, now or at any time in the future?'

'I would start by saying that you should work on the basis that the message will be intercepted and that the enemy will make every effort to understand it. Part of the strategy would be to eliminate any trace of complacency.'

'Complacency?'

'Any complacency that the code is secure. All codes can be cracked one way or another given enough time.'

'So if you were given the job of cracking the enemy codes, you could promise to deliver?'

'No, I didn't say that at all. A team big enough and clever enough could do it sooner or later. The problem is that it might be later rather than sooner and by then it might be too late. But some of the time it will be sooner rather than later and you will have to work on the basis that on average, it might take slightly longer than you like.'

The general nodded. Blackett, Turing and Cardigan did not even blink and Pin-stripe wrote down every word. The general decided that Harry had pushed on too fast and for the benefit of Cardigan, brought the discussion back to a simple level.

'But if you jumbled up the alphabet and then substituted – say – a letter "f" every time there is an "a" and put in a "q" every time there is a "b", and if only I and the person at the other end knows the substitution list, that must be pretty safe.'

Harry couldn't believe that Darwin could be so naïve on codes so he followed his usual interview strategy of assuming that the interviewer wasn't naïve and that he could use apparently naïve questions to elaborate coherently and flatter, rather than patronise the questioner.

'If you were sending a single word whose context was unknown, i.e. the main course or dessert on the menu at the regimental dinner, or the main landing site for the invasion, then you might just get away with it. But if it's more than one word, or a sentence, or a paragraph, then you give any decent code breaker a good chance to decode it. And then there is the ultimate weakness of any code, the weakness that has undone most attempts to encode language throughout the centuries: the key to lock and unlock the code itself, in your case, the list of substitutions, has a nasty habit of falling into the wrong hands. Much more easily than you might anticipate. You need to have the key to lock the message into code. The person who receives the message needs to have the same key to unlock the message and as soon as two people know the same thing, you may as well say that the whole world knows it.'

'But surely,' Darwin wanted to guide the discussion his way. 'You can rely to a certain extent that a patriotic Englishman will not betray King and Country.'

A snort from Harry. 'Not knowingly, I am sure. And not willingly. But if I knew the key and a team of Germans was about to take my testicles off with a circular saw if I didn't tell them, I think I might temporarily forget about the existence of King and Country.'

Cardigan's mouth, up till now a small horizontal crease in a puce expanse of skin, momentarily opened to a black gash as if someone had slapped her across her face with a tar brush. It then snapped shut and tightened into a fair impression of a cat's anus. The Bishop's mouth broadened perceptively into a hint of a smirk. Darwin leant forward and his voice boomed with resonant sarcasm.

'I suppose it would be a bit a problem if you actually didn't know the key and the Germans thought you did, and they got out their circular saws.'

'Too true.' Harry was buoyant. 'It's one of the classic cul-de-sacs of logic and even cryptology. How to prove you don't know something. It's the sort of thing Wittgenstein would have a name for, whilst still regarding it as frivolous.'

Darwin didn't like Wittgenstein and allowed himself another snort, moustache bristling. 'I don't think Wittgenstein will help us.'

The general's eyes were beginning to glaze over but he pulled himself back into the arena. 'Why Wittgenstein?'

'Well sir, Wittgenstein is not totally irrelevant because he does have the skills of logic and mathematics as well as philosophy, whatever that is. In this case, Wittgenstein would probably cut through the debate. He didn't like discussions on statements like "I am a liar", which is the parallel, actually the diametric opposite of the hapless ignorant captive in the hands of the Germans. The "I am a liar" statement leads to contradictions whether he is a liar or not. If he is a liar, then the statement he has just made is false, by definition. If he is not a liar, then it is also false. Although Wittgenstein considers arguments like this to be shallow, the principle becomes a general tool of logic analysis and has wider applications. Unfortunately, rather desperate things arise if you say "I am not a liar." It is not possible by logic alone to establish whether a person who says this is a liar or not. There are no contradictions.'

'Bring on the circular saws!' The general had a sense of humour.

'Of course, the problem is that liars sometimes tell the truth and sometimes don't.'

'Exactly.'

All the while, Cardigan had been pursing her lips, Turing had barely been concealing his boredom and Blackett had been continuously tamping his pipe. It was time the interview moved on and Cardigan provided the impetus.

'How would you feel about working away from home for a while?'

'I'm married with a small child. But then there are a lot of our soldiers in the front line who could say the same thing.'

The face of Sid flashed through his mind and he fought the moment to feel more shame.

'I would expect that I can be sent anywhere. It's a war and we have to win it, at least our part of it. If we disappear into the German Union of Europe, then I suspect the USA will stop fighting our war in Europe and concentrate on making Asia safe for themselves and then selling as much as they can to the new Germany.'

'What do you think ...' The general now burst into life. '... what do you think about academics and intellectuals like yourself fighting in the front line?'

'Hmmm, there's no single answer, Sir. First of all, who decides whether the academics are more useful at home or the front? And who decides the importance of the scientists work to the war effort or even civilisation? My father worked in Manchester with a colleague called Moseley. Moseley was simply brilliant. He sorted out the Periodic Table and why everything is ordered the way it is. Elements that were unknown at the time were predicted to fill gaps and they had to be found. The impact on scientific knowledge and the impetus for further development was enormous. Nobel Prize material. The stuff that history and culture are made of. The stuff that makes you proud that it was done by a citizen of this country. But Moseley volunteered for active service and instead of using his brain to help our country win the great war by applying it to the scientific effort, the army sent it to Gallipoli where it was shot

130

through by a Turkish bullet. Bit of a waste. But then, we are not all Moseleys, so who is going to decide?'

'But what do you think of the front line yourself?' insisted the general.

'It's not a problem at all. I don't pretend that I would enjoy it and I honestly never had the urge to take the army as a career. But I would join the front line team if required without a moment's hesitation, like my father did 30 years ago.'

'Ahah, where did he see service?' The general leaned forward with interest.

'In France, at Thiepval Wood.'

'Good God. Was he there on the 1st of July?' He did not even have to state the year. Everyone knew it was 1916.

'No. He went a few weeks later. He was a member of the team assigned to locating enemy guns with microphones.'

'I remember that, it was Major Bragg's lot wasn't it? If I remember right, if their results were to be believed, they had the German guns whizzing up and down the trenches at 50 mph.'

'Hmmm yes, the wind could be a problem. But all the same, I think they did better than that. The number 50 that I have heard of, is that they could locate the guns to an accuracy of 50 yards at a distance of ten miles. That's not bad at all for scientists in a war zone.'

'You boffins never call yourself boffins do you?' The general beamed a triumphant smile.

'Well,' dared Harry. 'I guess only generals call themselves generals.'

'And not what the ranks call us!' boomed the general with a huge laugh. 'But seriously, there was some funny business with that sound ranging team, wasn't there? One of the section died in curious circumstances. I hope your father wasn't involved in that.'

Harry wished he hadn't introduced his father into the conversation. Now he would have to pick his way carefully.

'I'm afraid he did die in action Sir, and his body was never recovered. But it's all in the past now.'

The general frowned and the topic came to an end.

'I think Dr. Turing has some questions for you and I think it would be useful at this stage if we left you to be alone for a chat.' The voice emerged suddenly from the Bishop who had said nothing since the start of the proceedings.

All except Turing and Harry left the interview room and gathered in a small airless chamber down the corridor which still stank of a mixture of Darwin's pipe from the pre-interview discussion and the dank smell of burning coal and damp wool given off by the row of overcoats hanging on the hat-stand.

'Well Marion, I guess you will just arrange the papers ordering Dr. White to report for duty at the Park asap. Usual arrangements regarding the family.' The general beamed.

'They're all the same, Sir. Such indiscipline. Why are scientists like that?' Cardigan hadn't finished.

'Marion. Imagine we put White, or even Turing here in charge of a crack commando whose task was to get themselves and some heavy encryption machine back across a 20 foot wide and 500 foot deep ravine in the face of enemy fire. The safety of Atlantic convoys depends on that encryption machine. How do you feel about that?'

'A disaster. Such indiscipline would effectively guarantee failure.' Marion was, if nothing, pragmatic.

'Exactly, for that specific task you need discipline, training, courage, experience and a strict code of operation. It would be hard to imagine anyone less suitable than White and Turing. And if we put them in the ranks, their brains and special skills are wasted. But in the right environment, their indiscipline can spiral upwards and outwards, encompassing complex problems and solving them. Yes, it is the equivalent of a military ivory tower, but solving the German and Japanese and of course Russian codes, and at the same time improving ours, saves lives, hundreds and thousands of lives. It saves tonnage. Hundreds and thousands of tons which would otherwise plunge to the bottom of the Atlantic instead of arriving on our shores. White is another R V Jones, better perhaps because his character is stronger and he won't claim he is winning the war on his own and demoralise all his colleagues. He's a good complement to Turing.

Turing entered the room in time to hear his name mentioned and raised his eyebrows. He was already dressed in outdoor clothes, having taken his heavy, still damp raincoat into the interview room. Cardigan frowned. She felt uncomfortable in the presence of Turing, outside of the interview environment, and didn't know why. It wasn't intellectual superiority; she felt his equal. It was something about the man that made her uncomfortable. Blackett also made her feel uncomfortable but that was a combination of extremely handsome looks, piercing intellect and his overall stature. She couldn't bear even to look at Blackett; he made her old knees tremble. But Turing was a different case altogether. Blackett's hand on her shoulder would make her swoon. Turing's hand anywhere would make her sick.

'There's no question,' continued the general. 'I want this man on board; now. Professor Blackett?'

'Nothing he said today changed my mind about him. He was in a room of top brass and he didn't flinch mentally. He wasn't flippant or disrespectful.'

'Not disrespectful!' Cardigan was throwing her last dice. 'What about talking about circular saws and male, er, male, private parts in front of a woman?'

The general was about to say that Harry probably hadn't regarded her as a woman and she should be proud of that during a war, but quickly shifted his response.

'This is a war to the death, possibly the death of our culture and ideals, and circular saws are childrens' toys. If you think we English have got worse over the years then you only have to remember what we did to put Edward II to death in Berkeley Castle. The history books are bad enough but they only dare tell part of the story to sensitive readers. We all know about the red hot poker and the screams heard 20 miles away but the bit of equipment left out of most narratives, the greased lead pipe, big enough to take the poker but small and tapered enough to ...'

The general was unable to finish his sentence as Turing crashed to the ground in a faint.

'What on earth's the matter with him?' boomed Darwin.

'Probably not feeding himself enough.' mused the general. 'He doesn't like Camp food at the Park and takes two hours to eat an apple. It'll be the death of him if he doesn't watch out.'

While the men talked and gazed down at the fallen Turing, Cardigan had clicked into action as soon as he hit the deck. She took off her cardigan, folded it and placed it under Turing's head, checking that he had not swallowed his tongue. She felt his pulse and then picked up the telephone in the corner of the room and called Doris. She fought to suppress the thoughts of carbolic soap. She then turned to Darwin and snapped 'Put that pipe out

133

and open the window and the door. Get some air in, we are all suffocating.'

In this moment of mini-crisis, the men stood around helpless as cardigan-less Cardigan showed her mettle. Doris bustled into the room. Five minutes and a waft of smelling salts later, Turing was on his feet again, pale and sweating, but sipping a cup of Doris's hot sweet tea. Cardigan was about to put her cardigan back on, thought twice and tossed it onto a chair in the corner. She turned on Turing and removed his heavy trench mac.

'Why on earth do you wear this thick hot thing indoors? No wonder you feel dizzy.'

'So I don't forget it. Watch out, my keys are in the pocket.'

'I'll see you don't leave without it. Now here, sit down and finish your tea.'

The discussions were concluded briskly. Cardigan took no further part as she concentrated on mothering Turing. She had become overwhelmed by an uncontrollable urge to strip Turing and get him into a bathtub, to scrub him with carbolic, especially his lank hair, to cut his hair to a sensible short length, back and sides, shave him twice and then get him dressed in crisp clean cotton. She would burn the mac. Then she would introduce him to her unmarried niece, Emily, who always dressed as if she were about to step out onto a hockey pitch. It was about time that Emily, now 35, got interested in men. There was already a shortage in that age group as more and more left for war and didn't come back. Now if Emily would only let her hair grow as long as Alan Turing had his now. But, one thing at a time. Cardigan's mind was racing; she had never been a mother and she simply hadn't a clue. She turned to find the men shaking hands and taking their coats from the pegs. Business concluded.

After the brief discussion with Turing, Harry had been led to the main entrance by Doris and told to return to Manchester and wait for them to get in touch. He would be travelling alone because Blackett had further business in London. He wanted to say he had travelled down alone anyway, but thought better of it.

The one o'clock train back to Manchester was totally full and Harry stood for most of the journey. He briefly sat on his small suitcase but found it less comfortable than standing. Five hours later, the train crawled into London Road Station into the customary blanket of dark smelly fog. Except that it wasn't the usual fog. The usual fog smelt of burning coal. This was more pungent and complex. It had traces of burning wood and even traces of the smell Harry had made when he scorched his woollen trousers with an overheated iron. There was also a smell he remembered from pre-war, from his childhood; bonfire night and the smell of fireworks. It was all accompanied by a distant hum of noise. The smell intensified as he approached Ancoats and so did the noise. There was a hubbub of voices and motor engines, the crackling of fire and the sound of water. The small rivulets of water in the gutter were getting wider and debris, most of it charred, floated with the stream.

Harry paused, concerned, and tried to make out the context of the shouting and the unfamiliar noises, the creaking and the occasional crash. The crashes reminded him of the time he had helped his uncle and cousins on their farm to take the roof off their barn. Visibility was about 40 yards; better than yesterday. He approached the corner of Waterhouse Street where he lived, except it wasn't the corner of Waterhouse Street anymore. Heavy vehicles filled Cobden Street at the entrance of what should have been Waterhouse Street. The grocery store on the corner, Kenyons, the corner shop, was no longer there. Nothing was there as far as he could see in the fog. Twenty yards, there was nothing, thirty was getting murky and forty yards was the limit, shadowy walls and roofs in the murk. Ten yards a house he thought, optimistic, make it seven. Number 1, number 3 and 5 and 7 and 9 and then his 11. What number was the first one in the murk? Let it be number 7 he prayed. Number 7 there, number 9 and then his number 11.

Wardens in tin hats, police in helmets barred the way.

'What do you want Sir? You shouldn't be here. It's a barred zone.'

'Yes I should. I live here. I've just got back from London. I've been away since yesterday.' Harry was choking on his words. 'What's happened?'

'Over there Sir, in the tent. The WVS will help you. You'll be all right.'

'I'll be all right ...!' Harry started to contradict, but broke off and ran to the tent. Inside, members of the Women's Voluntary Service, uniformed and quietly spoken were in close conversation, each one paired with a civilian, all anxious, distraught or weeping civilians. At a desk, illuminated by a dim oil lamp, a woman got up and escorted a smartly dressed man in his 60s to a row of chairs. She turned back and faced Harry with an expression that brought warmth without a smile.

'Yes Sir, what can I do for you?'

'I live at number 11. I've been away. I've just got back. What happened?'

'Just a moment, Sir. We have a lot of information and we are trying to put it all together.'

'I want to go there now. I need to get to my family.'

It's all right Sir. Don't rush. It happened last night. They missed Trafford Park in the fog and hit us instead. There is absolutely nothing you can do. Everything is being sorted. Now tell me your name. Number 11 you said. That's Waterhouse Street isn't it?'

'Yes, Number 11, Waterhouse. There's my wife Debbie and young Bobbie.' He wanted to say "Are they all right?" but he didn't want the woman to look down at her papers, shuffle them and turn grim.

'Right, number 11. We have Mr. and Mrs. White and son Robert. Yes? So you are Mr. White? So you were not with them?'

'Were?' shouted Harry as he thought "Why not – are not with with them?"

'Just a minute, there's another note here. Mrs. Fletcher, Edith, from number 12.'

'Yes, Mrs. Fletcher is our landlady. Our house belonged to her grandfather. She lives across the road at number 12. What about her?'

'She's marked EH, evacuation hall and linked to you. They will know all about it at the hall. It looks like Mrs. Fletcher has been taken there.'

'Why is she in the evacuation hall?'

'Everyone from the Street has been taken there. It's not safe with the broken gas pipes.'

'Are Debbie and Bobbie there? Are they marked EH?'

'There's no marking against your family names but then you were away and we haven't marked that either. We don't know everything. We are doing our best.'

Harry wanted to shout. He wanted to shout at this woman who seemed in control although he knew it wouldn't help. He was a man, an Englishman and Englishmen did not become hysterical when things went wrong.

'Mr. White.' The woman's voice had softened markedly. 'It's awful not knowing, but you will. I didn't know about my George for a month and I know what it is like. That's one of the reasons I am here. I do understand. Now Joyce will take you over to the evacuation hall. We're having to use the Temperance, over towards Shude Hill.'

'Come on Mr. White, let's get this done.' Joyce led the way briskly. She had a lot of experience of wartime tragedies and she firmly believed that there was no point in behaving as if you were going to a funeral unless you knew there was actually going to be one. Hustle and bustle, swing those arms. Onward Christian soldiers. In less than five minutes they were at the Temperance Hall and Joyce was letting them in through the side entrance. They came into the hall, with its balconies and galleries. The upper floors were empty and small groups of people were huddled around the floor, some wrapped in blankets. As the noise of Joyce and Harry's entrance caught their attention, fifty pale anxious faces turned to the pair in a communal act of desperation, hoping to see a familiar face. After the briefest interval of dashed hope, forty nine faces turned back to the floor leaving one, Edith, to catch Harry's eye. Edith was crying.

~   ~   ~

Chapter 11

Yorkshire 1944

H arry sat on his rock, on the crag. He looked over the valley and waited. He cursed the world. And the war. He shouted down to the river in the valley and demanded answers to his questions. They were illogical questions from a master of logic.

'Why?'

'Why me?'

'Why her? Why him?'

Tears and snot. The visible, physical manifestation of grief. He hunched his shoulders, shaking, with the cold October wind tugging at his collar. Not a trace of fog in the Yorkshire Dales. Not a trace of smoke. Pure clean air, blown across the Atlantic, across the north of the Irish island, across the Irish sea, over the plains of Lancashire and pushed upwards by Pendle Hill to chill the home of witches. As the air was pushed up by the slopes, it expanded into the lower pressure at higher altitudes. The air molecules are attracted to each other at all times and when they are forced to move further apart, they need energy to overcome the force of attraction. This energy comes from their motion and so they slow down. Slower molecules are cooler so the air gets colder as it rises. The temperature can fall below the dew point so the water vapour, swept up from the oceans, condenses and falls in drops on the slopes of Pendle. The chilled air is pushed on into Yorkshire. When the wind is from the West, Lancashire rain and Lancashire air is warmer than Yorkshire rain and Yorkshire air. This cold wind of air tore on, into the Dales of Yorkshire and onto the crags, there to pull a chilling draught on the speck that was Harry's tragedy. These were the thoughts of science that Harry would normally think, understanding the winds and the rain in terms of the gas law and Van de Waals equation. Pulling the chill out of the physics of the atmosphere. But not today. He pulled up his collar to exclude the wind and the physics. And he sobbed.

The bracken behind and below Harry and down to the left crunched, swished and parted to reveal a gamekeeper, fit, his breathing barely elevated by the climb, smart in heavy tweed with plus fours. Harry Frith was the youngest in a long line of Friths who had kept the game over the years for the Duke. He was about to bark firmly at Harry, using his stick for emphasis. But the sight of the sunken figure, the sunken face and the mess of mucus restrained him from his intended brusqueness. Gamekeepers understand and recognise an animal in distress and here in its simplicity, was a human animal in stress.

'There's a beat coming through soon, Sir. Last one of the day. You'd best make a move or else you'll be caught up in it. And it's coming on dark so they'll arrive at a gallop.'

'Yes, yes. I'm sorry. I should have known it's October. I haven't been here for a while and I've forgotten. I used to be a beater. That's why I come back here.'

'If you go down the West slope, off towards Crookrise Wood and then down the gully before Deer Gallows, you'll get to the gate into Moor Lane.'

Gamekeeper Frith was ordering Harry off the Duke of Devonshire's estate but he was doing it with skill and sensitivity; pointing the way home for Harry. Off the top, the wind cut less deeply into the folds of Harry's face and the thin sun almost cast a warmth. But in mid-afternoon in October, a thousand feet above sea level, warmth was a scarce commodity. Harry was inadequately dressed for a night on the moor. One shoot to go and that was cutting it fine before the darkness closed in. If you were not off the moor and crags by dusk, you would stay there till dawn or else fall and break your neck in a gully if you tried to walk off. Harry Frith and his predecessors could walk off the moor in the dark but not everyone was a Frith. If you stayed all night and stuck it out, the best you could hope for would be pneumonia. It took too much of the estate's resources to deal with the dead, hyper-chilled bodies when they were found the next day. Tracts of shooting moorland would be closed down while the police checked if it was murder; it never was. They had always died of cold. Two deaths in 30 years were not a bad record for an estate of this size, with leaky boundaries. Harry Tweed would keep an eye towards the West to make sure that Harry Blazer was getting off the moor. It would keep him on the ridge for longer than he cared, taking the wind on his face.

Harry was off the ridge in a few minutes and down the gully onto the firm moorland grass, grazed to perfection by the moorland sheep. Frith frowned as he saw Harry silhouetted against the bright green as he recalled the day-trippers from Ilkley whom he had caught two weeks ago digging up the perfect turf for their lawn. Where did they get the petrol to come to the moor in their posh Lanchester? The woman had been arrogant, reminding him of one of his schoolteachers. This one had slapped her fancy thin leather gloves against her wrist, trying to emphasise her futile attempt to justify their theft, claiming the turf for God and herself as trustee. He had sent his son, Billy, who was out learning the skills of the moors, to block the moor road with farmer Beck's tractor. They had been told to replace the turf or else the tractor would stay all night and all week if necessary. The woman had pouted, claimed personal kinship with the Chief Constable and then sat in the Lanchester and sulked while her husband, showing every sign of an oncoming heart attack, had carried the stolen sods back to the scars they had just created.

'You have not heard the last of this.' The woman had snarled. She had slapped her husband across the face with her gloves as he tried to restrain her.

'That's quite all right ma'am.' Harry Frith could have been a diplomat, apart for his accent. 'The Duke'll be seeing the Chief Constable tonight; he and his missus are coming round for a grouse.' The subtle ambiguity would be lost on Mrs Leather Gloves. 'I'll get the Duke to mention it all to the Chief shall I? What did you say your name was?' Young Billy had wanted to do something naughty to the Lanchester, like making a small hole in the petrol tank with his penknife, but father Frith had admonished him.

'That'd make you as bad as them lad. I'm ashamed of you. They won't come here again and if anything like that happened to their precious car, it would give them a moral advantage. As it is, they're going away after a wasted journey. They might have saved their juice for weeks. Now they have no petrol and no grass. And her husband is non too well pleased. I'm sure he's running a risk. You're not allowed to use petrol for leisure these last two years and they'd have a job explaining to old Hawkesworth what business they had up here. I'll bet he didn't want to do it anyhow. I wouldn't like to be him when she gets him home tonight. It'll be bread and water for a week if he isn't on it already for some other misdemeanour.'

Young Billy had run down into the village to alert PC Hawkesworth to the crime of petrol wastage. Country had triumphed over town.

The impetus of the downward walk off the crag had turned into a run and Harry was soon at the moor gate. He stopped, looked back up to the big rock of the crag, his rock; his rock although it belonged in law to the Duke of Devonshire.

'Bye rock.' Harry stared unblinking at the silhouette of the crag, now barely outlined against the grey sky. The pinprick of the gamekeeper was just visible as he moved off the eastern ridge. 'Goodbye. I won't be coming again. Ever.'

It was milder in the village and he stopped hurrying as he passed the school where he had spent the first eight years of his schooling. He could still remember his first day there when he had asked not to play with bricks but do some sums instead. They had brought him a slate and chalk; infants were not trusted with pencils and pen nibs.

The infant class teacher had written a few examples of simple addition which he had polished off in seconds. Then some subtraction and finally, simple multiplication. He had learned his tables up to 4-times which placed him ahead of even some of the eleven year olds from the village. And he was only three. He had been sent with the slates to see the head teacher and felt the first anxiety of meeting authority. He thought he must have got the sums wrong and was being sent for punishment. Thereafter, the village teachers had nurtured and fed his thirst for knowledge. He would always be a target for bullies but at this school, the teachers were wise to bullying and had snuffed it out at the first signs. Bullies and victims had been encouraged and manipulated into being friends. Harry felt as if his life was flashing before him and jerked himself out of the reverie. Instantly he was confronted with the grim reality of the present, but was unable to recapture the totality of the memories he had just caressed. Debbie was back at the front of his thoughts. She was surely going to stay there for ever.

Back at his mother's cottage, he could see two familiar figures in the parlour, drinking tea. Blackett towered over his mother. His mother, Mary, once a tall stately figure had shrunk and shrivelled. She was sitting on a couch, crying, holding a shoe; the shoe.

'It's only a shoe, but it has changed so many lives for the worse. I remember being taken to Affleck and Brown's and seeing them. I just had to have them. Then this one stuck in the tram line and I was rescued by Robert. We married, had Harry, but two years later, I was a war widow. And now Harry is a war widower. If I had never bought the shoes, I would never have met his father. His father would still be alive and Harry's wife Debbie would still be alive. Two people dead all because of a shoe.'

'But Harry would never have been born.' Blackett was gentle but logical. 'Would you want that?'

Mary looked up at Harry, now in the room. Her bewilderment, grief and hopelessness were beyond the capabilities of Blackett and Harry to repair. She let the shoe fall to the floor. Harry wanted to throw it on to the fire, but dare not. If he did, he would never hear the end of it. But if he did not, he would never see the last of it.

~   ~   ~

Chapter 12

Manchester 1957

'I shall be leaving Manchester, Robert. I have chances at Cambridge and Oxford and it is far better that you have the freedom to be yourself in the Department without my shadow taking away your brightness. It is just a matter of time, but I shall be off very soon.'

Robert had two minds. He did not wish to lose the closeness of his father and yet it was true, he did not really want him around in the building as he launched his own career. He was determined to come through the undergraduate school with a top first class degree and he wanted it to be seen that he had done it on his own. He wished his father had married again instead of devoting his whole life to physics, or rather computing logic, and to him, Robert. Harry and his mother together had raised Robert and here he was, tall, dark and Robert-like. Kay now retired, had almost swooned the first day he had walked into the building and seen Robert, almost forty years after he had seen his grandfather.

'Mr. White, oh Mr. White. I don't know what to say. Here you are again.'

Robert and Kay became good friends, meeting regularly in the Nelson's Arm for a pint of Thwaites and chatting with others from the department and with the now elderly but still nimble Reg.

'I have to say, Mr. White, I didn't know your grandfather very well. He only came in here once or twice before the war. Fair stank the place out he did, with cigars.'

'Cigars? My grandfather? It doesn't sound right!'

'Everything was possible in them days. Dibblee went and married Fräulein Bauer and everyone would have said that were impossible. Also against some physics law you would say. But look at 'em now. Goldsmiths and jewellers in town. Still, they do come in here still once in a while. I have to get this special wine in for the Missus. French stuff, Margaux it is. She won't drink nothing else. I'll introduce them to you. They worked with your grandfather.'

Bragg, Cavendish Professor, was in charge of Harry's interview in Cambridge. The pale sunlight seemed amplified as it reflected off his now bald plate and caused his moustache to grow extra bristles. Harry outlined his research and fielded the questions easily. It was less intimidating than the fateful one in London fifteen years ago. He relaxed and thought it was all over until a globular bald head leaned forward out of the shadows, where it had been hiding. Despite the coolness of the room in the Cavendish laboratory, barely heated even in the depths of winter, Harry was sure he could see sweat glistening on the dome of a head.

'Dr. White. How do you think that computers and logic fit into a physics department? Especially this one.'

'I say.' Hartree responded on behalf of Harry. 'Have you never needed the wave function for electrons in materials like carbon and silicon? They don't grow on trees you know. Someone has to calculate them.'

'That's exactly what I mean.' Clive pulled back his wet lips into the kind of sneer that had petrified Brenda in the days when they had slept in the same bed. 'There is no physics innovation in doing those computations. You did all that many years ago, Professor Hartree, and you are recognised for it. You were innovative.'

Clive, the Nobel prize-winner, could afford to be economical with his criticism. He could pin Harry to the table with a few words and a single bony finger. He could give faint praise to Hartree and leave the rest of the committee to behave like any other University committee he had ever seen, namely like a bunch of starving hyenas sizing up a rabbit. Hyenas eat anything, especially carrion. With Harry out of the room, the hyenas lost no time in tearing Harry to shreds. They started without warning and Bragg was unable to stop them, all chattering and snarling away. It was vindictive committee pack behaviour at its worst, frequently using words they had once heard but never understood the meaning of. One said that Harry was hardly likely to enervate the department, blissfully and dyslexicly unaware that the word meant weaken. It was easy. If Max Perutz, tipped for the highest Nobel recognition, could be bounced out of the physics building and into a porta-cabin in the car park, Harry stood no chance. Clive's research assistant got the job and Harry was sent back to Manchester. It was a rare aberration of Cambridge. They had accepted Thomson, Rutherford, Chadwick, Blackmore and Hartree from Manchester with open arms. But Blackmore could not stomach any more Mancunians.

Two weeks later Harry was in Oxford, thrusting and parrying with an appointments committee of dedicated dons. He was only two minutes out of the committee room, elated, looking for a cup of tea when they called him back in.

'When can you start?'

~ ~ ~

'Oxford it is then!'

Kay was in an expansive mood. He even put his arm round Robert, beamed at Harry and turned to Reg behind the bar.

'Reg, do you remember that stuff you served when Dibblee came back with his wife and that pile of lead? What was it? Schnapps and lager? Can we have some?'

Reg beamed from ear to ear.

'I've had this bottle waiting for over twenty years. My last Polish blue!'

'What about the lager then, Reg? Surely it's still Thwaites.'

'Haven't you heard of this new way of drinking beer? Lager and lime? Eh lads, we're going to have a right good night here!'

Robert cruised through his undergraduate years and got his expected first class degree. Harry thrived in Oxford, his computer logic path rarely crossing or overlapping with Robert's chosen career into sub-atomic physics. After his PhD, Robert was in demand as a rising young star and could choose where to hold his first fellowship. For reasons his father and colleagues could not understand, he accepted a post at the relatively unknown electron accelerator laboratory in Hamburg, Germany. He became a big fish in a relatively small pool. With no family ties, he buried himself into his research and soon became the undisputed leader of all that he did. It was a long time before he came back to England from Germany. Indeed he overstayed his welcome and remained longer than he himself would have wished and certainly longer than many powerful Germans wanted. And even more than that, he would never escape the multiple embraces that engulfed him in that country.

~ ~ ~

145

Chapter 13

Dresden 1962

Robert entered the café, empty apart from Ursula who was sitting alone at a table in the window huddled over a pot of black tea. A thin old man in a thin threadbare jacket shivered in the far corner. The premises were typical East German, drab, and with a pervading smell of boiled cabbage. If there was any heating, it was set low and Ursula had wrapped her fawn coat tightly round her. Her shoulders were soaked from the drizzle. A Wagnerian looking waitress sat behind the bar with a cigarette hanging from the side of her mouth. Her eyes narrowed as Robert entered and she scanned his foreign clothes from head to toe and then back to his head again. Robert took his place across the table from Ursula without speaking.

'One coffee please.'

It was Ursula who placed the order, confident in her belief that Robert would drink nothing else. He was about to say he preferred a beer but decided to go with the gesture. They sat for 15 minutes in silence, each staring at their cups without drinking. Eventually Robert reached for the milk jug, and held it in a kind of disgusted wonder. The jug was nothing more than a small tin of evaporated milk onto which had been pressed a steel contraption with an uncomfortable handle and a combined spike and spout. When pressed onto the can, the spike made a hole and the milk would pour out through the spout. There must be a second hole thought Robert, to let the air in, and sure enough, there was a second spike under the handle. It was hard to see because the sugary milk had oozed out and dried in a brown scum around the hole. He decided to drink his coffee black. It was just as well, because the first mouthful revealed the coffee to be lukewarm. Robert, as usual, made to drink the cup dry in a single gulp and took a mouthful that was nearly all sludge. Filter coffee without the filters. Robert grimaced and put the coffee aside, looking Ursula directly in the eye, but still without speaking.

'How are you?' It was Ursula who finally broke the tension of the silence.

'I'm fine. And you?'

'I'm fine as well. Why are you here?' She meant Dresden and not the café.

'I came to see you. I just had to. There are so many unanswered questions. So many answers without a question.'

More silence.

'How did it come to this? I thought we were unshakeable. I thought we would last forever.'

'Me too. It just happened.'

'What happened?'

'You were never here. And he was so persuasive. And Oma approved of him.'

'You! The toughest sweetest cookie I have ever met in my life. An officer in the German Democratic Army and you run your life according to your grandmother's approval! Don't give me that. Of course your grandmother approved of him, he was German and maybe he could prise out the foreigner. I loved you. I still do. Tell me why? Tell me really why?'

For a minute they looked at each other, a mixture of hopelessness and residual longing, hanging on to yesterday. Both of them were sitting with brimming eyes. Neither could speak and neither would, because neither trusted their ability to speak without tears.

'Never here?' Robert eventually broke through the new barrier.

'I came over more often than I should. It's not easy to get into your damned country. Why is it so difficult? What have you to hide? But it's the same for you and me. To have come for good means one word and one word only, defection. It's a nasty word and it doesn't matter that it is done for love, for life, for you, it is still a nasty word to describe an act of loving. The German word is no better. Could you have lived with me in England as an Abtrünnige?'

'It's been three months.' Ursula changed the subject. 'You must have a new life by now. A new girl friend? They must be queuing up. You'll be quite a catch.'

Robert felt a wave of anger from the patronising tone. He reacted in style.

'I have a good way to deal with this. I think I told you of it once. I've done it before in cases like this and I know it works. There is no perfect woman so there is safety in numbers, one for each mood and season. So yes, I do have a number of girl friends now. Yes, three even. One who looks nice, one who cooks nice and one who fucks nice.'

It was meant to be a joke but Robert failed to realise that Ursula would take it as a comment on her deficiency in all three departments. She froze, turned black and got up to go, furious. As she stood there, in that instant, her coat, which she had been hugging tightly around her, fell open. Her thin flowered dress, a present from England in happier times, that fitted her whole body like a glove, was now distended from just below her rib cage, stretched by six months of pregnancy. Robert's jaw, face and body fell and the hairs prickled at the nape of his neck. First, there was a silence as both stared at each other. No motion. No words.

'You ... You ... You ...' The words would not emerge.

Ursula sank back into the chair, put her head in her hands and started to weep. And shake. Robert was no expert but he had a lot of cousins and he had seen his auntie pregnant many times. Ursula was at least a half way through her pregnancy, perhaps more. With someone as fit and active as her, it would not be noticeable before four months except to a gynaecologist or midwife.

'What's his name?'

'His name? Whose name?' Ursula thought he meant the baby.

'The big blonde bugger?' Robert instantly regretted his retort. 'I'm sorry, that's nasty. It's difficult. It's awful. I can't imagine. I've never known. Nothing prepared me for this.' Robert swallowed, again and again. He needed another drink. There was a long silence before composure returned.

'It must, it must be mine. It just has to be. Ours.'

Ursula looked at him without replying. She did not need to. It could not be denied and she did not want to deny it.

'What are you going to do?'

'Marry Otto.'

'Marry him? How can you do that? Like that?'

'He has asked me and I have said yes. We are Germans. You are not and you don't understand.'

'But the baby. My baby. Our baby.'

'Otto knows. He accepts it. He is very German and he knows that what happened before he met me could not be changed. The baby is from a time before he met me and he accepts it as a statement of my past. He loves me and therefore he must love my past; they are inseparable. It would be illogical to love only part of me and expect me to accept that. He says it could have been his and the next one will be his. He will accept this baby as his and be a father to it as if it were his. Because he loves me and must love my past, he will love this baby because it is part of me and my past.'

'But he can't do that. It's not his. It's mine. It's ours.' Robert was now sobbing.

Valkyrie came over. 'Excuse me, but you must behave yourselves. We have other guests.'

Robert turned to swear but remembered, in time, that he was in Germany and not even in the West. He turned to look at the single dismal figure at the far side of the café, slouched over a grubby newspaper, probably rescued from a public waste bin.

'Please apologise to him for the disturbance. On second thoughts, I'll do it myself. That would be the polite thing to do.'

Robert had learnt the German formalities and nothing of the over-familiarity of an English village would work here. He half got up.

'No matter. I will do it.' Valkyrie frowned and scowled.

Everything added up neatly. A pregnant German. No wedding rings. A foreigner. The tears were only to be expected. Guilt was assigned and the German Democratic Republic triumphed again. Superior, as always, under the oppression of the decadent West.

'Another coffee please, and a tea.' The order given in German.

'Excuse me, my man.' The response came in German because Valkyrie knew no other language. She drew herself up to her full height and prepared to deliver the body blow.

'You are not a democratic German. You should be paying in West Marks.'

Ursula darkened, hesitated briefly and then snapped.

'He is not paying. He did not pay and will not pay. And if he would pay, he could pay in our money if he wishes. But I already paid and I will pay again. Do you understand? And if you are thinking of making any phone calls you ought to know that you will probably get my secretary. Tell her you have Colonel Strasser and an Englishman for coffee and see what happens.'

Ursula used her street name. Valkyrie changed from her natural shade of puce to slug-white in the blink of an eye. Officers from the Stasi, whose building was three blocks away, often came to her

149

café to exchange meaningful looks and few words. Why wasn't this one wearing the right clothes?

Ursula got up herself and went behind the counter, pushed aside a saucepan of over-boiled cabbage, the source of the fetid atmosphere and found two cups; they should have been white but were pale brown from inadequate washing. She decanted a coffee from the jug on the stove and poured some hot water into her teapot.

'I don't need more tea-leaf. Just water.'

'Jawohl. Indeed.' Valkyrie was now wringing her hands with anxiety.

Ursula had wanted to put space between Valkyrie and the new drinks. She feared that the monster would have been able to take revenge by stirring Robert's lukewarm coffee with her grubby finger, or even worse, probably sticking it somewhere unspeakably and personally filthy first.

'Eine Mark bitte.' Money always brought peace to Valkyrie. The East Germans had an ambiguous pride in their country and currency. It was always the Democratic Republic and it was always the Eastmark. But when it came to actually asking for payment, the prefix "East" was usually left out on the off chance they would be paid in the western variety which was worth anything from ten to a hundred times more. The official rate of exchange was one to one although any valuation of prices suggested that the higher rate of a hundred would be more appropriate. The local currency was supported by a number of State enforced crutches. Foreigners essentially had to pay for everything with Westmarks. They were forbidden to import and export Eastmarks and if they needed any local currency, they had to accept the State theft of their western money in return for a stack of grubby tired paper and a few aluminium disks. On leaving the wretched country, any unspent Eastmarks were stolen by the border control guards by order of the State. These tedious thoughts ground through Robert's mind as he sat, unable to think beyond the trivia of the artificial sick currency of a sick, artificial country.

Ursula now tossed a flimsy aluminium mark onto the table. It fluttered like a piece of paper before making a feeble noise on the table. No tip. Tipping was frowned on in the democracy. Two dark, greasy, rectally contaminated digits plucked it off the table.

150

Robert poured a level teaspoon of sugar from the sugar jar. The central spout was encrusted with brown sugar even though the contents were white. Someone had dipped the spout into their drink in their attempt to raise its carbohydrate level. The sugar dispenser had been cleverly designed to dispense one teaspoon per tilt, more if shaken. He flicked the brown granules off the spoon before sliding the off white remnants into his cup. It would need a lot of stirring to dissolve the sugar in the tepid coffee. The tears had stopped and Ursula had regained her control and composure.

'We have to talk, Ursula. We have to sort this out. You cannot expect me to go through life knowing that you and Otto are raising our child. I love you. I always have and I always will. I can't help that and I can't change it. I don't know Otto and I can't judge him. I have nothing against him but you can't do this to me for the rest of my life.'

'What do you propose to do then, Robert? Here I am and here I will always be. You know that if I come over they will never leave me alone and we will spend the rest of our lives looking over our shoulders for the devil, until the devil comes.'

'You think this will last for ever? An empire for a thousand years?'

'We are not an empire. We are a single State. You had your Empire and lost it all even though you thought you had won the war.'

Ursula had never gone deeply into Anglo-German politics. The door swung open and a small grey woman swept in, grey hair, grey face, grey raincoat, all glistening wet grey, flapping a gust of cold air and raindrops over their table.

'The Otto comes.' Frau Grey had translated, poorly and literally into English.

'Now? Here?'

Ursula sharpened and her training took control.

'You must go Robert. Now. Please understand. Otto knows of you. Not who you are, but of you. He would not expect to find you here. Go to your hotel and I will find you there. Later. Please.'

It was more than an hour later before Robert, having wandered through the dark drizzle, approached the cul-de-sac in which his hotel *Gasthof Zur Adler*, The Eagle Guesthouse, was located. He had walked mindlessly through the streets of the damp, drab, dismal suburb of Dresden till he finally realised he was only two streets from his hotel. Hotel was an exaggeration; this was a seedy guesthouse run by seedy owners, usually for seedy visitors. But they knew how to make decent coffee out of the wretched available raw materials. Robert perked up and started to look forward to a hot brew even if it meant an hour talking about the West with the owner, Lothar.

At the corner of the cul-de-sac, almost invisible against a backdrop of wet shiny cobbles, a small person wrapped in a Klepper raincoat, wet, shiny and grey, pulled the collar higher up her neck, pulled her face deeper into the rim and glided into the darkness of an adjacent doorway. Only someone who had noticed the slinky movement would have known she had been there, and now had gone. Inside the cul-de-sac, a Trabant stopped shuddering as the engine was switched off. It was silent for only a second before it shuddered once more. The over-heated, under-cooled engine ran hot and didn't even need a spark to ignite the last drops of low octane petrol that gave the impression that the engine went through death throes every time it was switched off. As if responding to a signal, it gave up its contents, spewing with difficulty, two tall grey men, dry and smart, out onto the pavement. One of them, the driver, scratched and rubbed his rear end, tugging his trousers out of the fat crease of his buttocks. This Trabant, like all of its breed, was well known to East Germans as the "haemorrhoid maker" on account of its harsh, abrasive suspension. The two giants smoothed down their suits and moved to the front of a shop next to the guesthouse staring intently into the window. They were looking with inexplicable interest at the shop display, which consisted of a stack of tins of carrots. The colours on the labels had long since faded, the carrots were white, not red, and the kitchen table was blue, the only surviving colour. "Feinkost" it said challengingly in pre-war lettering on the wooden panels at the side of the window. It had been many years since foods normally expected in a delicatessen had graced this shop.

Robert walked briskly up the middle of the street, stepping deftly aside to pass the two missing cobbles, the holes now filled with rainwater. He flipped down the soaking collar of his mac in preparation for entering the hotel and reached the pavement just before the shop.

'Abend!' in Sachsen, from one of the dry suits. 'S'limmes Wetter nit?'

'Guten Abend.' in Englisch Deutsch, from Robert. 'I would also say.'

Robert hurried past and at the very instant that it registered with him that the dry suits should be wet, he was pinned on each side by two fierce grips, three fierce commands and a statement.

'Halt. Stay. Relax. You are coming with us.'

'Why? Who the hell are you? Let me go or I'll call the police.'

'We are the police, you Dummkopf. Let me introduce you to officer Wilhelm Pohl of the State Security Police.' All was spoken with a heavy Sachsen accent.

Robert turned to the voice on his right and stared up into the grim, lightly pocked, but otherwise handsome face of a giant. Almost immediately the same voice broke in from the left. 'And let me introduce you to officer Helmut Pohl, also of the State Security Police.'

Robert whirled to his left and saw a mirror of the giant on his right. Identical twins. Identically grim. Identically pocked. They had probably on the same day thirty years ago, both scratched a chickenpox scab on the end of their noses, thus providing the two of them with a third nostril for the rest of their lives.

Back at the Trabant, Left Pock released his grip on Robert and pulled out his car keys and a hand-gun from his inside pocket. He gave the keys to Right Pock and stepped backwards out of arms range as his colleague fumbled with the keys before trying to open the car door. They had not locked the car because there was no need to, but the excitement of the arrest had pushed such temporal details out of their mind and they dealt with cars by instinct. State property must be locked when the intention is to leave it for more than one minute. Although the door was not locked, it was stiff and would not open. Therefore Left Pock naturally turned the key in the lock and tried again. It still wouldn't open because he had now just locked it. He had been through this routine a hundred times before and now jerked the door in an attempt to force it open. It wouldn't budge. That meant it was locked, so he turned the key again and snatched once more, violently. The door now jerked open and Left Pock almost fell over. Right Pock sniggered, forgetting that they should be impressing their new prisoner. He climbed into the rear seat with considerable difficulty. A Trabant is not really built for rear passengers. Left Pock gestured to Robert to sit in the front passenger seat, where Rear Pock could keep an eye and a gun on him. He then slammed the door three times with no apparent success, before moving round the front of the car to the driver's side. By this time, Rear Pock had extricated his handgun from his inside pocket and noisily slid the safety catch off and on a few times to pass the message to Robert. After the fifth click, he held the gun up to the light, looked at its status and slid the catch once more into the off position. He wished he had practised the manoeuvre so that he would know without looking whether the catch was on or off but this was the first time he had ever pulled the thing out of his pocket on duty and he was shivering with excitement.

The excitement was even better than terrorising innocent foreign motorists on the transit autobahn between Brunswick and Berlin. Flash them to stop. Wait a minute before getting out of the car. It feels like ten to them. Walk slowly over and by then they had their wallets out, fingering their Westmarks for the on the spot fine. They always paid with a smile, having feared for their freedom or even worse, their lives. Speeding was the ace card. The limit was 100 kph and the idiots just didn't know how to drive on an autobahn at that low speed. Especially the Wessies in their BMWs and Porsches. Can you speed English? Run Englishman, run. There is nowhere to go. I'll have you before you reach the end of the street. Twenty marks won't save you this time. He overlooked the fact that it would take him five minutes to get out of the car and he would be unable to run because he had not yet recuperated from his haemorrhoid operation. Sitting down again caused a sear of pain in his anus and he leaned back to relieve the pressure. He sought consolation in the thought that his brother, his dear twin, bastard Wilhelm, was having his haemorrhoid operation next week. Damn these Trabants.

Wilhelm threw open the door and hurled himself into the front seat in the nonchalant style of his hero, Jack Webb in Dragnet, of whom he was an avid fan. Dragnet, an American police series, was shown on East German TV, dubbed into German and bought from the State West German TV company, who did the dubbing. It cost them aluminium peanuts. He had practised the move countless times in his off duty hours with little success. The fundamental problem was that Jack Webb had a small and lithe frame, whereas Wilhelm had the size and suppleness of a mature whale. Moreover, a Trabant was no larger than the boot of an American car. He landed firmly and awkwardly on his own un-operated haemorrhoid, red and ripe, a cherry ready to split and drip juice. Which it did.

'Aaaa ...' began Front Pock, ready to follow this with 'Scheiss'. But the second word remained un-shouted as his training took over and he converted the exclamation. 'Aaaalles was Sie wissen, holen wir 'raus. Warte du.' 'We'll get everything you know. Just wait, you.' The familiar version "du" for "you" is used for children, loved ones, animals and prisoners.

Most of the tragi-comedy-farce passed Robert by, unaware as he was, of the two haemorrhoids. He had been simply transported to a state of panic by the events of the last few seconds. Under these circumstances, the human pituitary gland secretes adrenaline, which in its turn, provokes the body into instinctive defence. He never knew what made him do it because it was pure instinct, induced by adrenaline. Front Pock had not shut the door properly. It had probably needed lifting, pushing and twisting to shut properly. He rolled through the door, pushed himself back onto his feet and set off for the far corner of the street, slipping, sliding. He was a wing three-quarter slipping under the grasp of slow moving tacklers, slipping over the slithery Yorkshire mud towards the try line. He was bound to score. When he got going, he always scored. No one could ever stop him when he got up to speed. The studs of his rugby boots would bite into the mud. But here there was no mud, just grey, hard, wet slippery unforgiving Dresden cobbles. And he had no studs. Front Pock swore, threw himself out of the car, wincing with haemorrhoidal pain as he staggered round the front of the car in pursuit.

By the corner, in the shop doorway, Stasi superior Ilse swore under her breath. She had watched the two buffoons making their first and last snatch. It would be her last as well, she thought, unaware how emphatically right her thought was.

She had argued for their one chance and now they were letting her down. Talent was in short supply as it drained to the West. Ilse pulled out the standard issue hand-gun from her voluminous coat pocket and stepped out of the shadows to intercept Robert. She raised her gun, holding it in two hands and steadied her aim. She opened her mouth to order him to stop. At that moment, Rear Pock, having leaned forward and pushed aside the flapping door, also took aim. He couldn't miss. It was too easy. Robert had barely slithered 10 metres. It was easier than someone stuck halfway up the Berlin wall. He would be a hero. As he squeezed the trigger, the decrepit car door swung back, deflecting his aim as the detonation sent the bullet on its way at more than one thousand feet per second, one foot per millisecond. Thirty feet away, a thirtieth of a second later, the bullet passed almost a yard away from Robert's left elbow, rising. It was now on a head-on collision course with Ilse's right clavicle, her collar bone. In engineering terms, the collar bone is a tie-rod, holding in the arms and side of the body, much like the roof rafters and purlins prevent the weight of the roof from pushing the walls apart. German student duellers avoid striking this bone with their swords because it is not covered by muscle and is intensely painful when struck. They don't want the same done to them in return. A bullet has high momentum. In physics terms, momentum is the mass (which is modest for a bullet) multiplied by its velocity (which is huge). Also in physics terms, when the momentum of something changes, it exerts a force, the force being bigger when the change in momentum happens faster. The bullet struck Ilse's collar bone about halfway along its length. The bullet was deflected in an instant, changing its momentum by a large amount, thus exerting a massive force on the bone, causing it to snap. In the half a millisecond that it took the nerve signals to reach the brain, wanting to tell Ilse that she was in agony, albeit not mortal, the flattened bullet travelled a further six inches. It had recoiled upwards and diagonally, passing and slicing through the jugular vein before destroying the lower cortex of her brain and passing out of the skull. Ilse was dead before her forehead smacked into the cobbles, crushing her skull and rimless spectacles into a mash of bone, glass and blood. Before Ilse even started to fall, her finger, held lightly against the trigger, jerked involuntarily as the body took the impact of the bullet and launched into spasm. She would never know that she had fired her own hand-gun, nor the consequences. This bullet set off, also travelling at more than one thousand feet per second and missed Robert by three feet. It struck Front Pock, who had just appeared round the front of the car in the centre of his lower stomach. It shredded five loops of Pohl's intestine before exiting through his lower back. Death from stomach wounds is rarely quick and it was four weeks and two fruitless operations later before Wilhelm Pohl died. His haemorrhoid operation was deemed unnecessary.

156

Robert, on his hands and knees, staring at carnage, could taste the blood. It had sprayed from the severed jugular as if from a garden hose, his face, his neck, his hands were all stained and dripping with the colour of Ilse's death.

Rear Pock had scrambled out of the car in terror and was making to execute Robert when the groans of his brother from behind gave him time to come to his senses. He clubbed Robert unconscious with a single blow and pulled out his radio.

Fifteen minutes later, Robert was being bundled through the rear entrance of the Dresden Stasi headquarters. As he was half rotated, half pulled through the door, he caught a blurred red glimpse of the sheeting rain, the wet cobbles and his last sight of the outside world for two years. Half way down the street, the last thing he thought he saw of this world was a small figure, grey, wet and shiny, head deep in her collar. The café, the shadows. Ilse Kresser. What was she doing here? He blinked and the figure was gone from his imagination, along with his illogical hope that the events of the last quarter of an hour had all been a dream. Inside the building, half crouching, almost on his knees, and still dripping with Stasi blood, he was bundled in front of a small prim figure who either shaved with a triple blade or had never grown a whisker in his life. Two black eyes, beady and unblinking surveyed Robert with menace, like a smooth white shark.

'Welcome Mr. White. I have been waiting for you for some time. Why on earth didn't you come quietly, it would have saved two lives.' Robert's last thought as the hypodermic needle was slipped into his arm, was 'Two lives? Who else has died? Oh Christ, they are going to kill me. This is it.'

Wolfgang Steuer now turned his attention to Helmut Pohl, white and shivering with fear.

'You will pay for this Pohl. Your brother already has. What happens to this specimen is nothing compared to what will happen to you. Take him away. Take them both away. I'll see them tomorrow.'

~   ~   ~

157

Chapter 14

Harrogate 1964

Robert's back was aching, his head was aching, everything was aching. He was thirsty and had not slept for 20 hours. His new tormentor turned sharply and placed his unusually cherubic face six inches away from Robert's.

'Names. You must have heard some names. We won't let you sleep till you give us names. And we have ways of keeping you awake even when you are screaming for sleep.'

'You have asked me that already. Many times.'

'And I'm asking you again. Because I don't believe you. Why should I believe you? Just because you are English? Well, aren't we just the honest race? The master race on one side and the honest race on the other. Which of these is true?'

Cherub turned the lamp away from Robert's face, walked to the corner and took out a packet of cigarettes, removing one and tamping the tipped end on the packet. Robert noticed the pink paper and gold tip. Out of place. Why the tamping? Robert was also intrigued by the caricature of the lamp being turned away every time the Cherub stopped talking to take a rest and then being swung into his eyes every time the questioning resumed. He half expected Cherub to say he had ways of making Robert talk. Cherub had only been in the room for twenty minutes, he was new and Robert found him laughably naïve compared to all the others, the experts.

'Do you smoke?' Cherub offered the packet.

'Never. Never have, never will. Thank you. Nice try.'

The politeness was added like a postscript. Richard would not desert the moral high ground.

'Really. We'll see about that. Do you know we also have ways of making you smoke? You'll be begging for one before I'm through with you.'

Robert pretended a chuckle. But he did not find Cherub in the least bit funny and he wasn't sure if it was meant as a joke or if Cherub really meant it. Cherub took out a cigarette himself and flicked open his Zippo, one of his proudest possessions, stolen off an American, such a valuable one that he rarely risked using it. But this was his first real job and he wanted to make an impression, on White, and on the Commander.

'Do you have to smoke? I mean there are no windows and there is something quite offensive about your exhaled tobacco smoke combined with your rampant halitosis. Haven't you clocked that once in a lifetime of smoking? Or are you just doing it to pretend you are the boss?'

Robert surprised himself with his boldness. He immediately felt the fear of having gone too far. Cherub stopped in astonishment, the Zippo flame flickering. This was not supposed to happen. The hunted should not go hunting. Cherub made to flick his Zippo shut but paid the price of having selected a prop that he had rarely used and had not learned how to use. The cap sprang back instead of closing and Cherub found his finger in the flame. He dropped his toy. Check suit, who had been standing at the back of the room, wordless and motionless, now leapt forward and retrieved the lighter from the floor. He closed it and put it in his own pocket. Cherub wanted to leave the room to nurse his charred finger. He looked down at the packet of Balkan Sobranie, a present from his maiden aunt who knew he was a hopelessly addicted smoker. He had been looking forward to this moment, flashing off the foil tipped fancy cigarettes, intimidating the prisoner. He had made the mistake of assuming that a non-smoker would be impressed by a glittering cigarette. But he had also made the mistake of clumsiness before the first strategic mistake could take effect. Robert looked on with mild amusement. The menace of the moment had passed and Cherub was looking like one half of a comedy act. Grey suit looked like the serious half. He decided to move on to distract attention from Cherub's recovery.

'Start at the beginning, tell us everything and the names will come out.'

Robert looked at Check suit, then back at Cherub and decided to lower his resistance for the moment. He was about to say "at the beginning again!" but he was frightened of Cherub. He reminded him of Whitaker at school who used the front row of the rugby scrum as a smokescreen to throw punches. Fancy finding a Whitaker here. Rugby at grammar school was an arena where you could learn how to be a man, so any complaints would earn retribution, not only from the games teacher in charge, but also from the perpetrator of the punch. Grow up. Robert admonished himself. Stay cool. Don't get involved. The Whitakers of this world become bank managers, building society bosses, local council officers, prison warders or inquisitors. They always end up in charge. They always control destiny in a trivial but influential way. Money or freedom.

'The two who arrested me were twins. One of them was called Helmut, the other Wilhelm. Both Pohl. I've never heard of police using their Christian names before. Inside, I never heard a name. Even I was called just "England". Not even "Englander" or "der Englander". They never used the word "the" even when they were talking about me. It was always – "Was machen wir heute mit England?" What shall we do with England today?'

'You've got to do better than that.' Cherub interrupted him. 'It cost us a lot to get you back. Somebody up there likes you. But we had to give them Wolff and that was far too soon. He had done us more damage than fucking Fuchs and we had to give him back for you. Now why? Why are you so important? We don't know. We in the block don't know why you are god. No one seems to know why you are god. Even God does not know why you are god but he has told me to find out.'

Cherub was referring the head of the Harrogate Block, Sir Godfrey Ffyffe, commander, or God as he was known.

'Do you realise that we can send you back?'

Robert did not break the long silence that followed the ominous question.

'If we think you are doubling on us, then they can have you back, today. Even your own mother doesn't know you are back. No one knows but us.'

'My mother is dead. She died in a bombing raid in 1944. I was four.'

It was a sentence that Robert emitted automatically, almost as a defence whenever his mother cropped up. It did not work on Cherub.

'Why were you in Dresden? It wasn't the first time. Why did you stay two years? No one at the University there knows you, not in physics anyway. We've checked. Strangely enough, they know your father. Why is that?'

'He's also a physicist. He's well known. I have … I had just qualified. I haven't done anything yet.'

160

'Oh haven't you England! I'm not so sure about that.'

Robert almost wished he were back in Dresden. He almost admired the intellectual skill of his Ossi interrogators, how they always won, like chess-masters playing schoolboys. He had learned a lot from them and now Cherub was behaving like a pompous sixth former. He was Whitaker all over. Yet he wasn't in the same league. He wasn't even playing the same game. No subtlety, no style, no *je-ne-sais-quoi*, or as Robert had tired of telling the Germans, you have the *je-ne-sais-quoi*; but I have the *ich-weiss-nichts*. It had taken a week to explain to Wolfgang that it was a joke. Wolfgang did not find anything funny.

'Wolfgang. I'm sorry. There was Wolfgang. We spent a lot of time together. He was my mentor.'

'Your bloody mentor? What were they training you for England?'

The use of the German inspired nickname hurt. Cherub had no right to use it. He had not earned the right. He was a buffoon. He was bottom of the class and dunces don't call Robert "England".

'Steady on. They used all words like that in a different sense. I'm just repeating them in the context they used them. He wasn't a mentor in the sense that you or I know it. But they called him that.'

'Came from Mars did he? What other kind of titles did they use? Mother?'

'Yes! I did have a mother, Mutti. She came at the end of the week, on Fridays. At least they said they were Fridays but I never knew. I had no idea of the days and I lost track of time.'

'No scratches on the wall to keep track?'

'I tried that but they filled them with grout or wiped them off, polished them off and painted them off as fast as I could scratch them, each time they moved me to a different room. Mutti would say she had come to prepare me for Saturday, or Sonnabend, the eve of Sunday as they call it. Sunday starts at midday on Saturday in Germany and there were no questions on Sundays. At least not from Paul.'

'Jesus Christ, now we have a fucking Paul. I thought you said you didn't hear or remember any names?'

The face of Cherub had turned vermilion, his lips were swollen from anger and there were small white flecks at the corner of his mouth, either foaming saliva, un-rinsed toothpaste or Rennies.

161

As he expleted the Anglo-Saxon word, he spat involuntarily into Robert's eyes. Robert got up, went to the wash-basin in the corner of the room and rinsed his face. His voice was low.

'You really are a bit of a toad Sir, if you don't mind me saying. And if it matters to you, it is virtually impossible to think when you are spitting at me from a distance of centimetres.'

'Centimetres! Oh, lah de dah. What's wrong with fucking inches? They've got into your mind haven't they? Brainwashed you into using poncy German centimetres have they?'

'I'm a scientist. We all use centimetres, not inches. And it was Napoleon, not the Germans who started them off. Nobody knows the velocity of light in inches per second but we all know it is three times ten to the ten centimetres per second.'

'I don't care if you remember it as fucking furlongs per fucking fortnight you ponce, I don't fucking believe you.'

'Two trillion. Nearly.'

'What?'

'Nearly two trillion furlongs per fortnight, the velocity of light. It's easy to work out when you know the number of seconds in a week and you know light goes at 186 thousand miles a second.'

Robert never got to the end of the sentence. Cherub's scream of rage was heard all over the building and everyone came running. Guns were drawn, expecting that Robert had somehow pulled a weapon on Cherub and hurt him. The door burst open and the first guard entered the room followed by the Commander, only to find Robert sitting calmly behind a desk and Cherub banging his head against the mirror above the sink. There was a pause.

'Are you all OK? What on earth is happening?'

Cherub's voice responded in a quivering, vibrating hum. 'He just told me that the velocity of light was two fucking million fucking furlongs per fucking fortnight. This fucking guy is fucking mad. How did the fucking Germans fucking stand him for two fucking years? I've had him for twenty fucking minutes and I'd swap him for fucking Burgess and fucking Maclean and fucking Philby and God only knows who fucking else.'

Cherub seized control of his vocabulary with reluctance.

'No wonder they are swapping him for Wolff. It's the fucking bargain of the century.'

The commander took out his little notebook and wrote "M G→14F/1": his shorthand code for "Major Groves used the F-word fourteen times in a single utterance".

Cherub, more formally known as Major Groves, stopped and a manic stare crept into his eyes. He turned to Robert and his voice had an edge of potential harm.

'White you wanker, if you could do a swap to save yourself. For Burgess, Maclean, Philby and God knows who else, who else would you choose? Who'd be your fourth man?'

'You've lost me Sir. Who are you talking about?'

'Never mind, it was just a thought. Why, . . . why do you say you know no names and then every two minutes another name pops out like one of the seven dwarfs?'

'It's your style Sir. You are worse than my geography teacher. He used to snap whenever he caught Spencer fiddling with his penis in class. I'm not even doing that. If you just let me talk it through, slowly and calmly, I'll tell you all I know and even all I think I don't know. It will all come out, I just know it.'

'What'll come out? Your fucking dick? Do you envy Spencer? Is that what you want? Two years locked up with cameras on you day and night? Daren't even have a quiet wank? Christ, you must be frustrated.'

'Let's have some tea, I think.' It was the Commander who finally spoke. The Commander was intensely embarrassed by any mention of masturbation. He belonged firmly to the Victorian school, holding the belief that productivity of all kinds was severely impaired by such activities.

That evening, Cherub was debriefed in the Commander's office. The Commander slapped the stop-button of the Telefunken tape recorder, still working seventeen years after it had been confiscated from the defeated Germans, thus bringing the playback to a close just before Robert related his experiences in geography class.

'Groves, I'm very disappointed, I counted twenty-one F-words within a minute. Twenty-two actually, there was another one coming when I switched off the tape recorder. You know that is completely against standing orders. You are allowed one for effect and that only after four hours. You had only been going twenty minutes and you snapped worse than White's geography teacher and he wasn't even playing with his, erm erm, he was just talking, using words. The Germans have had him for two years. I don't

163

think you are in the same division when it comes to getting stuff out of him. You make him either clam up or get aggressive or even worse, smart. I thought you were one of the best graduates from the Purley school? What on earth is going on there if you are the best of the class?'

'I don't know Sir. It's the style we are taught, try the fast stuff early on. Disorientate them with speed. Catch them before they can catch their breath. It's not my fault that the fucking Ossies got to him first.'

Godfrey blinked at the continued obscenities, uttered obliviously.

'The East Germans will always have got to them first. That's what you are supposed to be doing. Finding out what the East Germans have been doing to him as well as what he knows.'

The Commander did not like the slang forms Ossie and Wessie for the Eastern and Western variety of German. He drew a deep breath.

'And furthermore, that's nine. That's more than enough for today.'

'Enough what?' 'Sir.'

The Commander pondered if the gap between "what" and "Sir" was deliberate or because Cherub had become disorientated by his own speed.

'Enough F-words, enough interrogation. Let him sleep.'

'Sleep! Sir! We'll have him in two hours, Sir. He'll tell us everything for the sake of a five minute kip. And I'll tell you what Sir, he'd tell us even faster if we offered him a woman.'

'What! No, Groves. No! You just don't get it. The East Germans have effectively trained him to be an insomniac. After two years of being questioned, you can get to a state of not needing sleep and you can even have your questioners themselves begging to be let off to have a rest. He had you frothing at the mouth after twenty minutes. We need to think again. I think we need Geoffrey.'

'Geoffrey? Who's Geoffrey?'

'Never mind, he's in Hong Kong anyway, but we might have to bring him back for this one.'

~ ~ ~

164

Geoffrey was sixty but looked forty. When he was twenty, he also looked forty. He had already looked forty the day he was born. He would probably look forty when he was eighty. Slim, Scottish, sly, softly spoken, superior, suave, sixty and single, Geoffrey specialised in the psychology of criminology and young female students. They found him irresistible. Most of them started off by regarding him as a father figure, substitute or real, but he invariably ended up tucking them up in bed, and getting in himself. His particular speciality was all women who were not British. His young women had been French, Thai, Finnish, Albanian, Japanese and currently Greek. They all came the same way, a by-product of his criminal psychology lectures at the University of Dundee. Aspiring criminologists flocked from all over the world to listen to his genius, and in many cases, although they did not know it as they set off for Dundee, to be fucked by him. The curious thing was that he actually loved them in his own way. He loved easily and fell into and out of love as often as the trains passed back and forth over the Tay Bridge, bringing a fresh load of lovers from Edinburgh airport and taking the old batch back. Aphrodite had arrived a month ago. It wasn't her real name but he called her that, gently and lovingly, as he stroked her waist-length hair before, during and after lovemaking. He serially loved Aphrodite, especially as he had experienced for the first time, at the age of sixty, what it was like to make love to a multi-orgasmic nymphomaniac. With Aphrodite, Geoffrey was beginning to show signs of flagging for the first time in his life. Even though he had only been back from Hong Kong for a day when the phone call came from the Harrogate Block, he had to control his enthusiasm to get away, lest Aphrodite should sense that there was something else in his life that he liked more than her. He need not have worried. Criminal psychology lectures were an allowed passion. That was how she had met him and she wanted to be a top criminal psychologist. There was no better place to learn criminal psychology than in bed. She could stay in bed all weekend between lectures, mixing love-making with tutorials and tea. This was her plan for the next six months of the course after which Geoffrey could jump into the Tay for all she cared. She was unaware that statistically, she had a lot to lose since four weeks was the average length of Geoffrey's affairs, with the longest of them rarely exceeding two months.

'Geoffrouley, where are you going and why?'

'I'm going to London to see the Queen. A long weekend.'

'Geoffraki, is it possible that you have a boyfriend in London?'

Aphrodite was direct and she thought that she understood Geoffrey's oblique humour.

'A boyfriend! Whatever brings such an idea into your head, O gorgeous one.' Geoffrey could never contemplate the possibility of a boyfriend, now or ever. He was the epitome of heterosexuality.

'You weigh every word. And I know what Queen means. I thought you were being, hmmm, I don't know the word, like clever. If I thought you had another woman, I promise you I will keel you and you will be found floating in the river. You are a creeminologist of psychology and the Greeks invented the word, so I think you understand what I mean. Yes?'

Geoffrey fell in love all over again, with the flashing black eyes, the mild but unique accent, the breasts, especially the breasts as they heaved up and down in time with the lilt of Aphrodite's threats.

'Let's go back to bed now, please. I don't have to go till tomorrow and it will only take two days. I'd like to take you with me and let you watch. It's an interrogation (that's a Latin word by the way), a very special one, but the military are involved and I couldn't possibly get you in, not even as a student and you're not British either. But I will teach you what it is all about when I come back. It's very special and you will be the only one in the class to know. These are things that I do not teach in my class because they are very, very special and our military pays me to provide it to them and only to them.'

'So if you teach me, you are being unfaithful to the British army. I like that. Then I can go and do it for the Greek army. Waaah. It's superb, just like being an unfaithful lover.'

'I beg your pardon! Who's an unfaithful lover? I don't like the sound of that.'

'You know what I mean, penakis!'

Geoffrey didn't like being called little penis and the rest of his body stiffened. In any case, it was a Latin word with a Cretan diminutive ending and that violated etymological purity in Geoffrey's book. Geoffrey was a purist. He also knew that Aphrodite had made up the hybrid because she knew he wouldn't know the Greek word for penis. 'And you know I don't like that little name. Otherwise I'll make one up for you. A Scottish one.'

Geoffrey took a taxi to Edinburgh Waverley. He did not run a car, having worked out that a taxi a day at an average of £2 cost a fraction of the depreciation of a Jaguar, the only car he could have driven, if he drove. He could charge the expense of the Dundee to Edinburgh taxi run to the Block. He had been careful to get that in writing when he first got the commission. Taxis between Dundee and Edinburgh, taxis between York and Harrogate. After about a year, a new-broom admin officer, Osborne, had rejected his expense claim with a supercilious, pencilled comment in the margin about the need for prior permission for taxi fares over £1. Geoffrey had walked into Osborne's office without knocking or saying a word. He had laid his rejected claim form down on Osborne's desk with a copy of his blanket permission, pushed them both towards the blinking clerk with the tip of his immaculate finger nail and walked out of the room. Osborne made the mistake of retaliating, questioning the price of the rail ticket to York, pointing out that a cheaper advance purchase ticket was available. Two mistakes in one move. Geoffrey was almost always hired by the Block at a days notice, precluding the purchase of a ticket a week in advance. The second mistake was to waste Geoffrey's time on administrative trivialities. He worked as a consultant, even for the Block, on the same basis that he took his lovers. Take me or leave me - on my terms. Osborne was moved to Swindon a week after the altercation, a disgrace for a Yorkshireman, even one from Hull. Geoffrey had achieved his aim without saying a single word.

~   ~   ~

'Cigarette?' offered Geoffrey, knowing full well, having listened to the astonishing tapes, what the answer would be. Geoffrey was determined to get a copy of that tape, to use in his lectures. Groves had provided enough material for a whole lecture course. It should only need a mild threat to take his services elsewhere to bypass the Official Secrets Act and get his hands on a copy.

'No thanks. Don't smoke. Never have, never will.'

'Thank goodness for that. Shall we have some coffee sent in?'

'Could it be something decent? They offer me coffee all the time, the blood rises in anticipation and then this grey stuff arrives. They must go to a lot of trouble to make it like that. I mean Nescafé isn't all that bad; the first spoonful out of a freshly opened tin I mean. But they manage to turn it into something dreadful.'

'I know what you mean. I know exactly what you mean.' In the pre-briefing, Geoffrey had picked up on the coffee addiction. It was one of the few useful things that the East Germans had included in the "agreed" exchange files on Robert and Wolff. Within a minute the door opened and a smartly dressed ash blonde woman brought in a tray containing a jug and two cups.

'Thank you Janine. Just what the doctor ordered.'

In fact Dr Geoffrey had ordered it yesterday as soon as he read the files. He'd been driven round to Taylor's of Harrogate to pick the most aromatic and tasty blend they had after a bout of tasting. He would have liked to stay an hour and try more, but other matters were more pressing. As already briefed by Geoffrey, Janine removed the lid for a few seconds, pretending to inspect the contents, but allowing the aroma to escape into the room. Geoffrey observed Robert out of the corner of his eyes and noticed to his satisfaction that his eyes were riveted to the jug. One-nil, thought Geoffrey.

Robert had eyes only for the jug and was completely ignoring Geoffrey's shapely attractive former mistress Janine. He'd been without decent coffee and access to a woman for two years and yet his eyes were on the jug and not Janine's mammaries. Robert's mind was rooted in the last two years of deprivation. It had been two years. Two years of drinking East German sludge. God only knows what it was made of. Toasted rye grains, chicory and pharmaceutical caffeine was his best guess. Now a cup of Colombian or even Kenyan was only seconds away. Cherub had jibed about needing a woman. If only he knew. Robert had prepared himself for this moment. He knew how he would cope. He was not going to gulp it down like a starving Magwitch, nor ask for more like an Oliver. He would take it slowly, push the empty cup away and wait for Geoffrey to offer him more. He noticed that Geoffrey had taken control of the tray, keeping it out of Robert's reach and so he played along with the game. If only there was somewhere else to look. A window to look out of. He contented himself with inspecting Geoffrey's tie.

Geoffrey noticed the shift of attention and thought ahah, the lad's got spirit. One-one.

'Right Robert. To business. Help yourself to another cup whenever you feel like it. There's plenty and there's more where that came from.'

He pushed the tray towards Robert. Robert nodded and wondered if he could time a leisurely five minutes between cups.

'You are going to tell me more than you think you know. Not only from the time you got arrested in Dresden, but why you were there in the first place. I want to know when you first went to Germany and why. You are going to tell me a long story and I am going to listen. The sooner you get through it, the sooner we will be out of here and back home. You too even if that's what you want.'

'And if I want to keep it to myself, what then? How are you keeping me here? I'm not under arrest am I? I haven't been charged.'

'Oh dear Robert. Dearey me.' Geoffrey dragged out the vowels with a Scottish swirl. 'You don't know where you are of course, do you?'

Geoffrey had been through the tapes six times to check whether the oaf Groves had given the game away. Fortunately Groves had lost control of the session within twenty minutes, before he had the chance to say anything damaging.

'You are in the process of being exchanged for Albrecht Wolff whom we picked up about three months after you defected. We have come to an arrangement with the German Democratic Republic and the People's Republic of China to do the mutual interrogations in the Summer Palace in Peking. It's not used at this time of the year. The cold winds off the mountains keep everyone away. There's more contact with the Chinese than you might imagine although to be honest, I'll be glad when we are all out of here.'

Preparing Robert's room and toilet facilities and the corridor to the interrogation room had taken two days of round-the-clock carpentry and plumbing by Gary and his gang. There could be no windows and it had to feel like it was in China. The toilet had been the most difficult. Gary had brought a plumber in from Cheshire who had been made to sign the Official Secrets Act before ripping out the conventional English porcelain toilet pedestal and replacing it with a tiled hole in the corner. Robert would have to learn how to shit Chinese style, standing and leaning against the walls in the corner. All the new fittings and workings had to be distressed so they looked like they had been used for a hundred years. The plumber was equally distressed to be told that the quality of his work was too high (Gary would select no one less) and he had to lay the tiles more unevenly and break a few. Then the grout had to be soiled, excrementally in some cases, and at this point the plumber had wanted to walk off the job in protest. He was eventually pacified by being told that he had to regard the job as a kind of film set and only a true artisan could achieve a realistic appearance of age and decay.

Finding a hard mattress had not been difficult. Firms were advertising them widely on commercial television although not describing them as such. A chance had been taken on the bed linen and towels. The only source of Chinese clothing and textiles had been in the Liverpool Chinatown and if Robert could read Chinese, he might spot that the towels had labels that read "The Happy Long Life Vest Company". Geoffrey had taken a few vests for himself. They were made from an unusually thin and fine cotton material. The seamstress who had removed the labels from the vests and stitched them to the towels, had done it quickly and had made sure the labels were pristinely intact, paying less attention to the vests, which were discarded. Geoffrey seized them all.

'When we are finished,' Geoffrey now fixed Robert in a deliberate stare, 'we will all fly back to Berlin. One of two things can happen then. Either you and Wolff will both board a U-bahn train and cross the border together - in opposite directions, or if things don't go well, you'll both stay on the wrong side of the border. Or will it be the right side Robert? Which side of the border do you want to be on?'

Robert had been trying to get a word in since Geoffrey had uttered the d-word.

'I didn't defect. I was arrested. You said that yourself. You said you wanted to hear about the arrest.'

'Ah yes. Well Robert, you had better be very clear about that. Very, very clear indeed because we think you did a bunk and the arrest was a set-up. That's why we are here now. To find out.'

'I want to go home. I desperately want to go home. I miss everything.'

'Had enough have we? Democracy East German style not quite what it's cracked up to be is it? OK. Let's keep calm. Tell me.

What were you doing in Dresden to get arrested? Why were you there in the first place? There's no record of you flying by any known airline so how did you get there? Military jet from Poland or Czecho-slovakia?'

'I went the usual way, for me. I took a train to London. Boat train from Victoria, across the channel to Ostende and then train to Cologne. Down the Rhine to Frankfurt and then back up to Brunswick to cross through Helmstedt.'

Geoffrey's one weakness on this job was a lack of detailed knowledge of the geography of Germany, so he accepted for the moment that one would naturally go from Cologne to Brunswick via Frankfurt. That evening he would pencil gently over his map and the eyebrows would raise as he realised the diversion.

'What about a visa?'

'I got through Helmstedt on transit to Berlin. We English have to travel through that crossing; we're not allowed on other routes that aren't autobahns. Then I would hang around in West Berlin till I got permission to enter the East and go to Dresden. It's easy when you know how. I have contacts at the Zeuthen Institute and they vouch for me to visit there and I add the trip to Dresden.'

Geoffrey noticed the switch from past to present tense. White had done this route more than once.

'What's Zeuthen?'

'A physics institute. They're in the same business as us and despite the cold war, physics goes on.'

'Nuclear?'

'Sort of.'

'Well it's either nuclear or it isn't, isn't it? Bombs.'

'Bombs are engineering. I do physics.'

'But bombs are nuclear physics, aren't they?'

'The nuclear physics part of bombs was sorted out long ago. You can get all the nuclear physics that you need for a bomb from any text book on nuclear physics in any bookshop. The engineering is somewhat more complex and I am not in that line of business.'

Robert was only partly telling the truth and there were many peripheral aspects of a bomb, the fine tuning, the attainment of high efficiency, neutron triggers, that still needed innovative nuclear physics. But he could always claim lack of knowledge of that. There was no formal training on bomb technology in University nuclear physics lectures, especially at Manchester where

171

Professor Brian Flowers, at the start of the course, had told everyone:

'I will not teach you how to make a bomb. Even though I could.'

'So you were also going to Dresden for nuclear physics?'

There was a long silence. Robert's mind was racing. The threat of what would happen was fresh in his mind but this was a path down which he did not want to go.

'What's so difficult about that question? You've already prepared me to disbelieve whatever you are going to say next. It had better be plausible.'

'It's personal.'

'Oh Christ, it's a bloody woman, isn't it? It's always a bloody woman. Come on laddie, tell me all about Mata Hari. It had better be good.'

'She's not a Mata Hari.'

Geoffrey noticed the instant defence. Two-one. Robert was plunging into despair. How could he get this across without mentioning the Stasi connection? Despite the betrayal, he still couldn't bring himself to take the path of mental revenge. The barrier between love and hate was leaking like a sieve but he couldn't go through it. After an hour, Janine came in to remove the empty jug and cups. Robert now noticed the tightly belted figure, the fresh face and smiling eyes. He even thought he detected an eyelid flutter. He was correct. Janine, initially incapable of eyelid fluttering had been taught how to do it by Tracy in the typing pool. The eyes, blue and smiling under the dark canopy of hair, reminded him of Ursula and his stomach lurched. He forced a smile. His forced his eyes to glide up and down and up again. Janine felt the friction of his gaze and turned to smile warmly as she had been ordered and trained to do. Geoffrey was watching like a starving osprey and thought he saw only the stirrings of lust. But then Geoffrey would. Three-one.

'You'd better tell me where you met, and how. Dresden? Zeuthen?'

'Hamburg. It was in Hamburg, three years ago.'

'Hamburg!' Geoffrey knew that was in the West. In the North of the West of Germany.

'What were you both doing there?'

'I was working there for a year at the Hamburg Physics Institute, a bit like Zeuthen. I was living there and we got to know each other.'

'Not so fast laddie. Take it slowly. I want to know every detail, how, where, when, what. I'm afraid you are going to tell me every little detail, no matter how small, personal and painful. I will even need to the brand of contraceptive. I will have to know or else, you know where you are heading. Let's take a break shall we? More coffee?'

~   ~   ~

Later that day, Emil looked down at the thick file on the desk in front of him, glanced across at his victim and allowed himself a warm glow of satisfaction. There is a moment of sheer ecstasy for the hunter when the prey is transfixed, the unsuspecting deer caught in the cross wires, the petrified refugee caught in the searchlight half way up the Berlin wall. For Emil, this was the culmination of two years painstaking work and only a German could have pulled it off. Only Deutsche Ordnung, German order, could have done this. Only the son of Emil Schaeffler, the unappreciated customs officer of the German Reich could have done this, in honour of his father.

He had painstakingly studied hundreds of phone number logs, hundreds of snooping neighbour reports, passenger lists, hotel registration slips, every little contribution and squirrel's hoard that built up the paraphernalia of a neurotically ill, psychologically ill and terminally ill state. It was not even a nation. A rotting carbuncle trapped between the inner thighs of Western Germany and Poland, fatally conceived, fatally born and born to perish. Yet Emil was proud, conditioned as he was within his narrow world, within an East Germany that still, just, lived. And Emil, the epitome of East Germany, had played the data like a chessboard. He had drawn up huge multidimensional grids on large sheets of paper made by joining sixteen sheets of standard paper together with sticky tape. Emil thought, with pride, that it needed one square metre of paper to hold one of his charts. It needed a piece of paper four folds up from A4. The number sixteen is two multiplied by itself four times, thought Emil, mathematically. Four folds of his chart would bring it exactly back to standard paper size, A4.

Then it could be filed in a standard box. 'God in Heaven, you can be cruel,' thought Emil. 'Had I been the one with opportunity, I would have invented the paper size standard, German DIN A4. Fold, fold, fold and fold again. Then it is a normal piece of paper.'

The chart had grids with crosses and ticks and names. With luck, this would become known as the 'Emil chart' and his future would be assured. Perhaps even a new flat. He looked across the table:

'I suppose men find you attractive.'

It usually disconcerts a woman to be told this, because for most of them, there is no answer. They could neither agree nor deny it without degrading their image, either by being conceited or lacking self-esteem. Emil toyed with his thoughts, from well within the boundaries of his suppressed alter ego. No one will trap me in the same way I have trapped you, because there isn't another me to catch me. Ursula was shocked and nervous, unable to construct the reasons for her arrest. Why now at all times? The trouble with Robert was surely over. He had gone back two years ago, so she thought. He had vanished and she would never hear from him again. There was the problem of Ilse, who had disappeared without trace at the same time and there were times when she thought she must have gone back with Robert, unlikely as it seemed. Unless Ilse had defected and had used Robert to achieve it. She glared back across at Emil with undisguised hostility. If she only knew the contents of Emil's charts, what he had irrefutably demonstrated, she would have been conciliatory. Emil had all of her activities for the year leading up to the fiasco mapped out in undeniable detail. She would eventually, as a conditioned East German, be compelled to accept the painstaking truth of East German Emil. Emil in turn, picked up his notepad, a spiral bound pad of recycled paper. He could almost read last month's newspaper. He scribbled a few words and gave it to the Grey suit, standing inside the door. He had just had a flash of inspiration, as he had prepared to start his interrogation, to suggest a pause before handing over the Englishman for Wolff. This is going to take a week he thought. Maybe longer.

~   ~   ~

'I remember everything about that day. It was September the 12th, hot and sunny in Hamburg. I had been living in that apartment block for three months and had passed that flat several times and often heard music. That day, the door was open and Bruch's violin concerto drifted out. It had a purity, a cleanliness, that I had never heard before. I thought the violinist must be inside. It couldn't have been a record because it was so clean, no scratches. It couldn't have been the radio, it was too clear. Then she came out. She must have been going out and had then gone back inside to get something, leaving the door open. I had stopped and was listening enthralled. When she came out, I could not believe what I saw. The smiling eyes, the perfect teeth, the dark flowing hair, the whole. At first she did not speak either. We just stared at each other. She told me later of her thoughts when she first saw me and it was word for word what I had thought when I saw her. Eventually it was she who spoke.

'Can I help you?'

'I was just listening, sorry, I'm being rude. Who is that playing?'

'I think that one is Kreisler.'

'Chrysler?'

'Yes, I think that recording is Fritz Kreisler. He made it before the war.'

'Oh, that Chrysler.'

'Bist du auch Romantiker?' She smiled with eyes and mouth.

She told me later that she could not believe that she had used the familiar address "du", but it had come naturally because I did not seem to be a stranger. At least if it had been written, she later excused, it would have been "du" and not the very close familiar "Du". Geoffrey made a quick note to himself to ask a native German lecturer he knew at the University to explain the subtle difference between "du" and "Du". Till then, he had only been aware of the two forms of "you"; "Sie" for strangers and formal use, "du" for friends, family, children and animals and prisoners.

'I told her "Yes, I am a bit of a romanticist. And you?" Of course, she had already answered that in her first question with the word "auch", also, and I had not noticed. "Are you also a romantic?", she had said. My German was not so good then. I hadn't noticed. She actually explained it to me later. At that moment, Kreisler and Bruch climbed the scales of purity and tone and we both turned to listen before they descended again.'

'Oma likes this music on the classic programme. She always listens on a Friday.'

'It's on the radio! How can it be radio, it sound like real?'

'Ah yes, that is one of the few advantages of being the vanquished. We had all our wavelengths taken away by the Allies at the end of the war so we have had to develop VHF FM radio on the higher frequencies. It's much better quality.'

'Yes, I've heard about that. And it's true, it does sound really good. I'd like to listen to it carefully. Oh I'm sorry, I don't mean that, I mean I don't want to come in and listen. I do but I don't!' Robert flustered.

'That's all right! I'm going out anyway. I'm going to a concert by the Alster. It's Brahms tonight. Why don't you come?'

'I don't have a ticket and there is not much time to get one.'

'Don't be silly.' She laughed and her voice was now more beautiful than Bruch and Kreisler.

'It's open air and free. Anyway, we shouldn't have to pay to hear our own Hamburger composer. If we get a move on, we should be able to sit on the grass not too far away. It hasn't rained all summer so it's going to be dry to sit on. Parched even.'

~   ~   ~

'I have never experienced an evening of such sheer joy. It was total perfection. The weather, the lake, the music. We did not speak during the music and only exchanged pleasantries in between the pieces. It got dark long before the end and we walked back to our apartment block in Altona. It took about an hour but I did not want the evening to end and I thought if we took a bus we would be back in ten minutes and I would be saying goodbye and never see him again. As it happened, I need not have worried. At my door, he asked if he could see me tomorrow and I said "Yes" before he had finished the sentence, before I could stop myself. We saw each other every night thereafter, becoming closer and closer until finally, in his flat upstairs, we became lovers. It took less than a month but it felt like a year. He was my first man and I was his first woman. It was natural, it was pure and it was beautiful. The expression of the love I felt for him and still do, in between the hate.'

'The hate? Why do you hate him now, Fräulein Masur?' Emil drew out the word "Fräulein, Miss", to emphasise the lack of a formal marriage.

'No, him. He must hate me, after what happened.'

Emil was content to let Ursula tell the story. He had all the fixed points. He knew where she had been and when she had been there. He knew the times of contacts with Ilse, He knew the times of all telephone calls made from Ilse's office. Ilse had telephone privileges according to her rank, she was a thorough professional and would never have used the Democratic Republic's electricity to make personal calls to the apartment in Hamburg. If the call was over a minute, Ursula was definitely there. If they lasted only a few seconds, it was possible, but by now means certain, that Ursula was out. The calls to Luneburg placed Ursula there, at that time, on that day. Ursula's travel file contained the times and dates of all journeys. A week spent in the local offices of Aeroflot revealed two journeys booked and paid for privately by Ursula; Dresden to Prague. There was no record of an official visit in the official files. Now Ursula was filling in the blanks in between the fixed grid points. Soon he would have a road map of her life for two years. Any lies, any contradictions would be pinned like a dead butterfly in a display cabinet. Emil looked across at Ursula and did not see the attractive woman with a bright personality, whose only negative point was to have drawn the lottery ticket of East German birth. Emil saw a brightly coloured butterfly that would soon occupy position number one in his new display cabinet.

'Hate you for what happened? What happened to make him hate you?'

~   ~   ~

'Don't run ahead. We have plenty of time. You are doing OK. Just fine. Go back to Hamburg. September plus a month plus a bit, it must be coming up to Christmas, the end of 1959?'

'Yes, 1959, Christmas. We started to talk about what we would do over Christmas. Oma, grandma, was the priority of course. It had to revolve round her. I had originally planned to go back to spend Christmas with my father. He had never married again and I have no brothers and sisters. So it wasn't easy. But he had been saying for a few years that I had to find my own life and not to hang on him. Even so, I didn't want to leave him alone. His own father had died in the first war, leaving him an only child, like me, and so he would probably go to stay with his mother, Nana, in Yorkshire and all his female cousins who showed up like bees round a honey pot every Christmas, fawning for their inheritance. He was never too keen on that, too many women. Anyway, I was getting on quite well with grandma, Oma, and spent a lot of time in their flat, especially for meals. Oma did most of the cooking. Ursula and I would talk and listen to music and sometimes walk down to the river in Ottensen. We went upstairs to sleep in my place. I suppose Oma knew what was going on.'

'It all sounds so idyllic. Go on.'

~   ~   ~

'It was only to be expected that Oma would not approve. He was not German and she always hoped that I would like and love Otto, the grandson of her school friend. I found it hard to accept that I should marry someone on the basis of a school friendship between two women fifty years ago, long before I was born. But I do think that Oma liked him as a person. He was kind and considerate to her and always bought her favourite magazine. And he would talk to her, improving his German and learning. He would read the magazine to her, especially the romantic women's stories. At first he was almost comical, struggling with the strange words. Although he could speak good German, every little corner of life has its own special vocabulary and Robert soon picked up the special words from the romantic side. What I really liked once was him using the word "Spatz" "sparrow" on me in a way that he had constructed. We were watching a little flock of sparrows in the garden and the new baby sparrows were fluttering their wings in front of mama so they would be fed. He said he wanted me to be his Mama Spatz for our children. He was good with words, both English and German and used them to good effect. I also remember him once telling Oma that the Anglo-Saxons came from the region round the River Schlei, especially where the river was narrow or "eng" in German. So they were known as the Englanders. She wouldn't have it. She was almost angry. She telephoned a history teacher friend at the University in Freiburg and he told her it was probably true. She sulked for a week, but

I know she admired him for it, knowing details of his own history like that, even though he did not belong to the real Fatherland. Oma was always going to be a problem almost as much as home, the East. I knew I had to come back, especially with the plans for the wall being so far advanced. I knew I ought to have reported my relationship with him, but nothing prepares you for the real thing. Oma actually wanted to return home especially as things got worse and worse and we knew the wall would go up eventually, some kind of wall or control. Her only sister lived in Cottbus and I think she needed her more than she needed me. And Otto was in Dresden. Everything looked like it had a neat solution if only Robert did not exist.'

Emil Schaeffler was writing slowly, almost with a lack of interest. Men, women, babies, ugh. He suddenly snapped to attention as he realised the lack of professionalism in allowing his inner feelings on heterosexuality to cloud his judgement. No judgements he told himself. No judgements. This woman will judge herself with her own words. Let her do it herself.

~   ~   ~

'She suddenly started talking about Dresden as if it were home. Dresden was never home at the start but slowly it became home. Then she went there for a visit and disappeared for two months. We never heard from her. The telephones did not work. Oma, still in the flat below, became more and more anxious and then one day, the anxiety fell off her like an overcoat in the sun. I don't know why but she obviously knew something I didn't. And then, that day in November, Repentance Day it was, a public holiday in Germany but nowhere else. It was grey and white, foggy and misty like it only can be in North Germany. You can go to the coast, the coast at Travemünde on the East or Büsum on the West and it will be grey, white fog. You can go into the Heide at Lüneburg and it will be grey, white fog. Ursula returned without warning and I knew at once it was no longer the same. She would not talk about anything and she would not sleep with me, at least not at first. It was as if she was wrapped inside a grey, white fog. Eventually we had it out. We went to a small village on the heath, near Lüneburg. It actually turned into magic, the two of us and no one else, walking through the Heide landscape with only the

179

sheep for company. Sticking to the footpaths because it would be easy to get lost in the fog. Walking, talking and loving again.'

~   ~   ~

'I had to go to Dresden for instruction and then to the Lindow camp in the village near Berlin, for the field course where the future was mapped out for me. At the training centre in that village, it was like a prison. We were inside the complex most of the time and the village was tiny. In fact the complex was bigger than the village. There was a phone box in the little Gaststube, but early on another girl had tried to phone her boyfriend and the operator was part of the system, asking for her name and saying he could see her on the phone anyway and she would have some explaining to do. It was true, that evening, the girl, Gabi, was hauled in and asked what she was doing, making contact with the outside when the rule-book said no contact. She said she didn't make contact but had only tried unsuccessfully, and that saved her. The ability to apply cool, German logic to the situation. I could not see a way out of the impending dilemma and I resolved on my return to say goodbye to Robert forever. It was easier said than done. I switched on the ice machine as we are trained to do. But it was Robert. They don't teach you how to overcome love. They just tell you and that's not the same. We went off to the Heide, the Lüneburger Heide, for a weekend and it was just like old times. Hopeless. I wanted to go away with him, forever, anywhere. Anywhere but Dresden or the East.'

'So Fräulein Masur, why didn't you?'

Emil had a weakness born of his homosexuality in that he could not understand a woman's mentality. He thought they would think about a man like he did.

~   ~   ~

'I suppose it was because she is German. I don't think I will ever understand it because either she loved like I did or she didn't. I am sure she did, so what stopped her? Only being German could have stopped her.'

'But Robert. What about you? There were two of you. What should work for her should work for you. Weren't you prepared to give up something for her? To follow her to Dresden.'

'But that is East Germany.' Robert almost shouted. 'I'm English.'

'Well, you've just answered that one, haven't you laddie?' Four-one. There followed a long silence during which Robert poured yet another coffee, pulling a face as the familiarity of the Columbian began to bore his palate.

'Do you think you could get them to buy some Kenyan? A peaberry?'

Geoffrey sighed. Five-one. It was becoming a rout.

'Of course.' Geoffrey thought it was worth reminding Robert where he was supposed to be. 'We'll get a pound or two from Fortnum and Masons and have it flown out. We might as well have a grinder sent as well to save Hong Mo the trouble. He chopped up that Columbian with a Chinese chopper. I've never seen anything like it. There was a pile of beans, a whirl of a machete and the next thing a heap of ground coffee. Why don't you try some tea if you want a change? They've got an awful lot of it here. Very refreshing.'

Robert had been pondering his gaffe, yet not a gaffe, about not even allowing Dresden to be a possibility in his life. Up till that moment, he had regarded his love for Ursula as being infinite, without bounds. With a half a dozen words, Geoffrey had ruthlessly exposed the limitations of his feelings. He actually loved England more. Or so it seemed. He needed to philosophise on this. To talk it through to a different conclusion.

'I know what you mean and that actually sums it up. There was an insurmountable barrier between us. Whichever way we thought about what to do, it was just one of us, or both of us defecting.'

'So far you haven't mentioned anything about what she did. What she did for a living. Shall we talk about that now?'

'I told her all about my work. There was nothing secret. Now that I think about it, she was always a bit vague. It was something to do with science and for a while I thought she was in government in some scientific role. But for that she'd surely need to have been in Bonn, if only some of the time. And she never went to Bonn. If she went anywhere, it was always Dresden. And then there were times when the woman, Ilse, came to see her. I think Ilse came from Dresden but I never socialised with her. When Ilse came, and stayed a few days, I got shunted into the background.'

'Tell me about Ilse then. We need to know much more about Ilse Kresser.'

There was a long pause. Robert had only said the name "Ilse". He never called her "Ilse Kresser". He realised that Geoffrey knew a lot more than he was letting on.

'I never really met her as such. I saw her once, small and grey, but I don't think she was that old. Just prematurely grey, dressed in grey. Apart from the hair, she reminded me of one of my cousins, an older one, I mean about forty.'

'Tall? Build?'

'She was small, not much over five foot. I think if she had done her hair a bit better and got some decent clothes, she could have looked quite attractive. But she came across all drab. She wore the same coat all the time, a raincoat, one of those grey shiny things, older Germans wear. Rain or shine hot or cold, always the same grey. She said it was a genuine Klepper. I guess she couldn't get one in the East, but I mean, you might boast about a genuine Burberry but not one of those. And then of course I saw her that night. She came into that stinking café. Grey, grey and more grey. And then she was running at me out of the shadows and then and then. Oh, you can't imagine what it is like when a person dies in front of you. Bang.'

'Let's not run ahead. We'll come to that. Go back now to Hamburg.' Geoffrey played his soft voice. Gentle, barely audible, reassuring. 'What did Ursula have to say about her in Hamburg? What did she say she was?'

'Not much actually. Really not much. She said that she, Ursula that is, was still a trainee and Ilse was her boss. She came to check how she was doing and advise her and to report back her assessments.'

'Assessments of what?'

'Industry assessments. Reading the Frankfurter Allgemeine. Talking to people. Getting the picture of German Industry for the Easterners. I suppose if it was all in the newspapers, it wasn't spying.'

'What about the grandmother? Did she ever have anything to say about Ilse?'

'Oh yes, they must have got on all right. If it were not for the fact that she wasn't, you could have said she was a daughter, from the way Oma spoke about her. I'd say they hadn't just met for the first time in Hamburg. They really were like relatives, close ones even. Of course Ursula's mother had died in the war and she had been brought up by her grandmother and aunties. Four adult woman and Ursula, brought up as a beautiful princess. I think Ilse bridged the generation gap for the occasions when Ursula came across with too modern a mentality. Ilse was very conservative.'

~   ~   ~

Chapter 15

Dresden 1964

'It is a lie, although not altogether universally accepted as such, that you English are especially good at sport and war. Ask any Australian about sport and, if they were still alive, any 19th century Afghan about war. But you English have your pride and you also have your prejudice which will not allow you to admit it.'

Robert had looked up at his tormentor in amazement and saw the smirk of superiority, held for nearly two seconds until Wolfgang Steuer was certain that Robert had taken it in and understood its meaning. Relating the episode now to Geoffrey, the words retained their clarity as Robert began to play both parts, interrogator and interrogated.

"Come on England; let us see you pull out a snappy remark about Goethe or Schiller." The words, unspoken, were written into every crease of Wolfgang Steuer's face. He took a long drawn out pull on his cigarette, drawing the nicotine deep into his lungs.

"Keep calm," thought Robert to himself. "this is just a mind game. You know enough Goethe to strike back."

Robert had responded in style, alternating lines from Goethe and Schiller into a truly mongrel poem.

'Freude schöner Gotterfunken
Du mußt herrschen und gewinnen
Töchter aus Elysium
Amboss oder Hammer sein.'

He had lilted the words to the music of Beethoven's Ode to Joy. Two raised eyebrows put creases into the creases on the forehead. Steuer moved his head a grudging millimetre towards Robert in acknowledgement. 'That was really awful England, wirklich schrecklich. It doesn't even rhyme or scan. It is almost worse than your English National Anthem. Why did you visit the Brocken?'

'I had to. I wanted to see the spectre. I know now that it was stupid because there are only about thirty days in a year when there is no fog.'

The creases in Wolfgang's creases frowned, but Robert was not aware of such minutiae.

'Tell me about the spectre.'

'I only know it from one of our famous physicists, Wilson. He was on the top of one of our mountains in the early morning. The sun was behind him and below was the covering of cloud. He was above the clouds. Normally you would see a shadow of yourself if the sun is behind. But Wilson saw an enormous shadow, because the clouds have no substance and the shadow spreads all the way to the ground, getting bigger and bigger. Also, for reasons that Wilson did not understand, because he was still a student, there were colours mixed in with the shadows. A myriad of coloured fringes of spectacular beauty.'

'What has this to do with Brocken?'

'There are only a few places on earth where this phenomenon happens. Our mountain Ben Nevis is one; that is where Wilson saw it. Brocken is another.'

'You said "one of our mountains" England. Ben Nevis is in Scotland.'

Robert groaned.

'Scotland voluntarily joined the United Kingdom in 1707. Not like parts of Czechoslovakia "joining" Germany in 1938. But that is not important. The thing is, Wilson was determined to re-create the phenomenon in the laboratory. He did so and along the way, invented the cloud chamber.'

'I thought that was done by our Herr Doktor Geiger.'

Robert could not believe the carelessness, giving him such an opportunity on a plate.

'Firstly, Herr Doktor Geiger is renowned for inventing the Geiger counter in Manchester, even though he didn't really, his boss Rutherford did. And he didn't invent the Wilson cloud chamber either. Secondly, Herr Doktor Geiger was Herr Doktor when he worked in Manchester and Herr Professor when he worked in Kiel, later. You also said "our Doktor Geiger", he is actually West German, not one of yours.'

Angry, Steuer got to his feet, burning with rage. How could a pathetic Englander trap him like that? If he conceded that Geiger was Western he would have to admit that the young Englander knew more than he did about famous German scientists. If he claimed West and East were the same country, he would deny the legitimacy of the East. The length of a cigarette later, he sat and faced Robert again.

'I don't believe that anyone, even a scientist, or even an Englishman obsessed with weather, would go to the top of a cold mountain to look at the sun, shining on fog.'

'Goethe did. Everything on the Brocken is named after him. Goethe's path, Goethe's hut, Goethe's rock. He went up there to see the spectre. He walked all the way up and all the way down. Just like I did. Except I didn't have a guide like he did. He went with a crowd and did not wander lonely as a cloud.'

Steuer became uncomfortable. He wasn't sure what the bit about wandering lonely as a cloud meant in the context of Goethe, but he would look it up. It was already a sensitive issue about the Englishman, who had walked onto the forbidden peak after materialising out of the fog and then disappeared back into it before he could be arrested. It had been a catalogue of stupidities. Why hadn't they used the dogs to round him up? Dogs' noses worked in fog. Dogs' noses are used to find buried truffles, not that Steuer had ever tasted one in the deprived East Germany where any truffles unerringly found their way to tables of the State leaders. He had screamed down the phone at the station commandant and asked why the dogs had not been used.

'They were all sick Herr Steuer.'

'All five of them?'

'Yes. One of them had caught a sick rabbit and they had all had eaten bits of it. God knows what was wrong with the rabbit but all the dogs vomited for a day. They are fine now.'

'I am pleased to hear that Herr Gruber.'

Wolfgang knew exactly what was wrong with the rabbits and the dogs. They had a tendency to set off the booby-trap land mines near the security fence, blowing holes in the fence. There had been a covert eradication programme using a cyanide based powder rabbit control product. The powder, spooned down and around the rabbit holes, reacts with water producing cyanide, and the rabbits are gassed. Obviously some rabbits had brushed against the powder and poisoned the dogs.

"Why this stupid secrecy?" thought Wolfgang. If everyone had been told, the dogs would have been kept in and the Englishman would have been caught. He had to close his eyes as the details of the whole fiasco flooded back. Normally, supernumerary rabbits were dealt with by the Jägermeister, the master hunter. But they could not risk him blowing his legs off, chasing after rabbits. So they had tracked down a product used by English farmers to control rabbits: "Cymag". A German firm offered an agricultural product "Zymag" which simply had to be the same. Logic. The German for cyanide is Zyanid; Zymag and Cymag must be the same. But too late, they had found out that Zymag was a high-technology fertiliser and not the poison Cymag. Wolfgang shuddered to think of the highly trained Stasi officers, dressed in plastic suits and respirators, sprinkling fertiliser around rabbit holes. It took them a year to realise that they had the best shrubbery on the Harz mountains and four times the normal rabbit population, feeding on lush vegetation. They had swallowed their pride and ordered Cymag from England. Now Wolfgang remembered why they had to keep it secret, to hide the shame. Robert seemed a good target on whom to extract his revenge.

Yet Robert had walked up the Brocken, had come within a few metres of the security fence around the radio communication listening post and walked off into the fog. No one does that. The Brocken was where the East listened in to every word that the Chancellor of Germany, Konrad Adenauer, ever spoke into his office telephone in Bonn. The pick-up coil buried behind the skirting board in Adenauer's office, beamed the conversations up at 600 megahertz to a device behind the guttering. The frequency was within the television band, but cunningly slotted precisely between two TV channels so no one thought of looking. From there, it was relayed onwards to the Brocken listening station.

Wolfgang had not known that Robert knew nothing; but he had taken a long time to find it out. It was their own woman who had been stupid. So Wolfgang had filed Robert away as being of little immediate resource, but probably useful some time in the future. Trading him for Wolff was a good bargain. But first, the essential insurance policy needed to be put in place. Wolfgang opened the drawer of his desk and pulled out a sheaf of papers.

'What would you say to a professorship at Dresden University?' Wolfgang let it sink in and before Robert could reply he disorientated him further, 'and your own research institute thrown in – with an additional salary of course as Herr Direktor.'

'What on earth are you talking about?' Robert's brain had become almost unhinged.

'Part of the responsibilities of the professorship and being Direktor, of course would mean that you would have to become the President of the Dresden Bezirks Committee for Democratic Science, a bit of a boring chore, but you'd get paid extra for that.'

Wolfgang let it sink in and just when Robert thought that he could not be stunned further, Wolfgang stunned him even more:

'And the fifty thousand Deutsche Mark that you have stashed away in the Commerzbank in Hamburg, we'd let you bring that over legally and we'd give you a far better rate of exchange than the official one to one. How does ten to one strike you? You'd have half a million Ostmark. Oh, and the contents of your safety deposit box as well.'

It struck Robert dumb. How could they possibly know about his stash of gold sovereigns in his private box?

'All you have to do is sign here and it can all be yours.'

~ ~ ~

At the debriefing meeting, Geoffrey wasted no time in telling the rest of the team what they did not want to hear.

'He is not a criminal. He does not have a criminal mind. He does not have criminal thoughts and therefore he cannot knowingly carry out criminal acts and has not, in my opinion, ever done so. Moreover he is not a traitor and in my opinion would not work for a foreign power against the interests of his country.'

'Is that what we are paying you for?' Groves was burly in body and burly in thought. A burly bully. He had wanted to take part in the interrogation but Geoffrey had refused, on account of previous experiences.

'It's either him or me.' Geoffrey had been adamant on the first day. It was always the new raw idiot interrogator, a Groves or a Thompson wreaking almost irreparable havoc and then Geoffrey brought in to mend the breakages.

'His style is counter-productive. If you let him loose for even five minutes, it will take me days to repair the damage. It's happened before and I'm not prepared to be pulled in to these kinds of fiasco any more. There's no end product and then I get associated with the blame for the failure to get a result. He has absolutely no skills in this department. He is as much good here as I would be in a trench. So why isn't he in the trenches where he would be more useful. I know we don't have a war but you could still dig a trench and put him in it.'

Geoffrey did not rise to Groves' bait. He did not even look at Groves. Others would deal with Groves and he was not prepared to get into even a conversation with Groves, let alone an argument. Don't argue with fools.

'I'm talking to you.' Groves persisted. 'I want answers.'

Although coffee had been available for a quarter of an hour before the meeting, and everyone had taken advantage of the exceptional quality, Geoffrey got up and with cool deliberation, walked over to the back of the room, poured himself a slow cup and went to the window, looking out across the Nidd valley. He always enjoyed needling bullies like Groves. It was so easy, you didn't even have to say a word. If it had been the school playground, Groves would have hit him by now, smashed him to a pulp and showed the class that bullies win. But Groves could not use his fists on the criminal psychologist in front of the senior members of the non-combative wing of the British army.

'So where do we go from here?' The Commander spoke, snapping and yapping like a bad-tempered little dog.

Geoffrey wanted to reply that he could walk out, go back to Dundee and they could do what they liked with their prey. But they were holding a British civilian for no legal reason and they couldn't expect that he would keep his mouth shut, even with a 'D'-notice. But saying that would alienate people like the Commander, whom he respected, almost liked.

'There are a few ways forward. It depends what you want out of this. I assume that the interests of national security far outweigh any personal matters. This is serious. He has not committed any offence. We have not even caught him smoking behind the bicycle shed.' Geoffrey looked hard at Groves as he made his schoolboy analogy. He was playing pure psychological games. Groves caught the look and thought that he, for reasons unfathomable to himself, was being accused of something, which in his time, he had considered manly when he had done it. The others caught the real meaning that if Geoffrey walked, Groves would physically assault White for simply being at school while others smoked behind the shed.

The Commander had learnt to recognise when Geoffrey had a pearl or diamond in the offing. He leaned forward. 'Go on.'

'You could just let him go and hope he won't say or do anything. Does he have anything of interest to the general public, to the newspapers?'

Groves turned purple.

'Then of course you could charge him with something. The whole country hates a spy. I've signed the OSA, but if his defence calls me and trots out the truth and I stand there and hide behind the Act and say no comment a hundred times then it's obvious what has been going on. I'm just a civilian. If I say no comment it means that what is being said is true. End of story.' For reasons as unfathomable as his "logic", Groves liked the sound of that, "End of story," failing to see the disadvantages.

'Or?'

'I have to tell you that this person has information, intelligence, as you call it. I'd also say he has intelligence, as I call it, a lot of it and the advantage would be to merge his intelligence into the intelligence you want. I don't think he understands the significance of some of the things he knows. He does not talk about it naturally because it has been buried. He has just spent two years being squeezed like a lemon by the East. He is nothing more than skin and pulp and fibres. But it is the fibres you want. They are the key. They still contain everything you want. If he worked for you, with you, there is possibly no limit to what you might get out of it, pearls, nuggets, perhaps a whole gold mine.'

'Over my dead body.' Groves was in a rage that knew no bounds.

The Commander got up. Excuse me a moment. 'Too much tea for breakfast.' He left the room and charged his secretary like a bull.

'Janine, I want you to write out a rail warrant for Major Groves to travel on the next train from York to London. There's one every hour. Then you write out one of those messages on your pad as if it came from somewhere in London, use your imagination, the better the imagination, the better the promotion and that is not an idle promise. Then bring it in to the meeting, grovel, and whisper in his ear so we all know it's secret. Then get him to the station on time. Oh, and while he's away, I want his name unscrewed off his office door, the contents of his office put into a packing case and the lock on his office door changed.'

'Anything else, Sir?

'Make him feel like he's important.'

Back in the meeting everyone had broken for coffee and Groves already had his mouth crammed full of digestive biscuit, with a further two in his hand.

'You don't like him do you?'

Groves sprayed moist, half chewed digestive crumbs over the Commander in his attempt to say the 'The bastard deserves it.' It was the "b" of "bastard" that did it. The digestive spray, that is.

The Commander took Geoffrey's elbow in a soft grip. 'Geoffrey, a quiet word.'

The meeting re-convened and it was clear from his posture that Groves was expecting the usual wordy, mindy, twaddle from Geoffrey. But it was Godfrey who started up.

'Geoffrey has to leave us in half an hour so I'd just like to change the agenda and talk about the running order for tomorrow. With Geoffrey away for two days, meeting his obligations to his millions of admirers in Dundee, we need to establish a strategy that will conjoin continuity until Geoffrey returns. Let's go round the table. Major, what would you do if you were given the candidate all to yourself.'

Groves couldn't believe it. He only took in the last sentence. He'd never been given an offer like this before. He wanted to say, 'Ram the bastard on a skewer and get his dying confession.' The problem was that this was truly the limit of his innovative skill and his brain went into seizure.

'While the Major is gathering his thoughts, what about you Thomas? As our secretary you haven't been involved but maybe you have a detached view.' By a perversity born of a combination of crude ambition and lack of erudition, Groves actually thought he had won.

'They are giving me the show.' He thought. 'The bastard is all mine. I'll shaft him good and proper.'

Janine walked into the room and inflated his ego almost, but not quite, to bursting point. She whispered the words into his ear but modulated her voice so that everyone heard 'Cabinet Office'. He had no need to repeat it louder, but he did.

'Cabinet Office!?'

Groves got up and vanished.

'What on earth does the Cabinet Office want with him?' asked Geoffrey, half an hour later when the meeting had ended.

'I don't know,' offered Godfrey, 'but I have about three hours to think of something. The Cabinet Office staff not only have the ear of the P.M. but also the ears of the toilet cleaners. I am sure we can think of something in between'.

~ ~ ~

Chapter 16

Harrogate 1964

'T his is not an interrogation any more.' Geoffrey looked at Robert but was also speaking to Harry. 'You both know what this is about and you've both agreed. Harry and I have seen each other's certificates, and now Robert has also signed the OSA form so we can talk freely about anything. Both your Universities have agreed and so has mine. That doesn't mean we can take for ever but we have to strike the right balance between our usual academic freedom and discipline.'

Harry wanted to tell Geoffrey not to be so bloody patronising. He wasn't the only one who could be professional.

'I've been here before. I wouldn't be here now if I hadn't been here before. I'm not here because I'm his father.'

Geoffrey had the decency to blush. 'I'm sorry, I didn't mean it like that. I agree, I am damned arrogant sometimes. It's my job to twist people round my finger. I will make a special effort not to do it here. Please bark if it looks like I've lost the thread.'

'OK. Woof's the word!'

'Harry, I think you should start and lay out what you know from Bletchley. Then, eventually, we will have to discuss Beethoven the musician. We will have to try and relate it to everything else we know. At the moment we don't know enough background to relate to. We know it, but we don't recognise it well enough. Now, Robert, I also have a "shopping list" of things I wrote down during your interrogation. We'll do that next.'

'OK. That's fine by me.'

'Beethoven cropped up on the fringes as it were. It was never mainstream. I was given it as a kind of spare time job, to give my brain something different to look at while I was mainly working on the naval intercepts. This is how we worked in our team, one big task but a sideline that might grow into something. If it grew, it might need someone to take it over full time. Beethoven never grew like that. Then the war finished and a lot of us went home. Thereafter, I don't know if anything came of it. The messages weren't even encrypted. But the language was obscure. The source appeared to move around inside Germany. There was probably more than one source. It's all filed away. Are you getting the files?'

'The word "Beethoven" had produced the same effect as throwing a fox into a henhouse. It has produced a lot of flapping and clucking down Cambridge Circus way. They are sending up the files. No one ever understood them. They'll be here in about an hour so we can get things started before they arrive.'

'I can outline all the headings, there are some things that can be laid out now and maybe they will strike a resonance when we get on to the other stuff. I am pretty sure that Beethoven then and Beethoven now are one and the same. There was a British connection then and there is a British connection now. Maybe even the same connection. There's no knowing where it will lead. It's quite frightening.'

~   ~   ~

'The word "Beethoven", where did you hear it in Germany? I mean from Ursula and Ilse, not from the usual musical environment.'

'That's just it, the only time I heard the word in a way that surprised me was when I stumbled in on a conversation between Ilse and Ursula and I heard the word Beethoven twice before they realised I was there and then they clammed up. It was odd because I was always included in conversations about music. It was the way they looked at each other and at me that made me not pursue the subject. It wasn't like there was a concert coming up. It was like when you surprise people who are talking about you and they don't know where to look.'

'And then there was that incident in Dresden. At the station. When you met Blackmore.'

'I didn't meet him. I saw him and he saw me. I knew who he was and I saw him. He did not know who I was and yet he saw me.'

'Can you explain more what you mean please. No codes.' Geoffrey was taking notes frantically. It was not his usual style.

'He is a Nobel prizewinner. A British one. There aren't many of them alive and in physics, you know them. He looks very characteristic. And anyway, I was at a lecture he gave in Manchester when I was a research student. But I have never met him face to face. I saw him once from a crowded auditorium. I was one of a crowd of a hundred and fifty. He never looked at me, nor saw me. And yet in Dresden, he was walking across the concourse with another man, straight towards me and as I looked at him, he stared at me. He stopped and stared at me so intensely. I felt it.'

'How did he look?'

'Shocked. He looked as if he had seen a ghost. I have never felt so uncomfortable. I thought I must have done something wrong.'

'So he recognised you. He could have seen you anywhere. You are both physicists.'

'No, when you see someone you know, you don't look like that. I could see shock and feel hate. Seriously.'

'Well, either you had done something to annoy him in the past, or ...'

'Or?'

'He thought you were someone else.'

'Possibly. But then the whole episode is meaningless without knowing who that someone is.'

'I think I know.'

Geoffrey and Robert turned on Harry. There was a long pause.

'You know who he looks like?'

'Yes. Yes, I do. His grandmother, my mother, almost cries every time she sees him.'

'Go on.'

'He looks like his grandfather. I don't. But he does. His grandmother says he looks the spitting image.'

'And why should that make her cry? Although I have a feeling I know what is coming.'

'Robert's grandfather went to war, 1916, and never came back. The Somme. He wasn't much older than Robert is now.'

'Go on. There's more isn't there. That hasn't explained Blackmore's reaction.'

'Robert's grandfather, my father, was in a team of scientists tracking German artillery using the sound of their guns. There was Bragg, Darwin and other scientists, you wouldn't know them. Except. . . .'

'Except who, Harry?'

'Except Blackmore. He was also in the team. He knew my father. He worked closely with him. So I feel sure he thought he was seeing my father on Dresden station.'

There was another long pause.

'Is there more? I have a feeling there is more.' He looked at Harry, then Robert and back to Harry. 'He doesn't know, does he? There's something Robert doesn't know, isn't there? Do you two want to do this alone?'

'No.' Both Harry and Robert said it together.

'Go on Dad. Whatever it is, if you've lived with it. I can.'

'Blackmore and my Dad went out on some mission towards the German trenches. The mission was not entirely authorised, as far as I can tell. The section leader, Bragg, Captain Bragg as he was then, later Major, was away, back at the central control. Anyway, they came under fire. My father was killed. Blackmore came back.'

'You never told me he was involved! You never mentioned Blackmore.'

'What was the point? It was bad enough. By the time you were born and old enough to understand, your mother was dead as well and what would it have done to rake over what could never be put back together.'

'That probably explains Blackmore's reaction on Dresden station. He really did think he was seeing a ghost. But you thought you saw hostility – hate; as well as shock. That is strange. Shock yes, but hate, that is most curious. It can only be related to the death. Or did they know each other before that?'

'They were in the department together before that, in Manchester, for about four years.'

'Hmmm, that gives plenty of opportunity for things to cook up. Was there anything between them? What do people remember from that time? Have you ever asked them?'

Harry looked down without speaking. Robert stared at him.

'Didn't you ever think of asking Rutherford? Or Darwin? Or Chadwick? Or even Bragg? You can't ask Rutherford now but you can still ask the others. Can't you?'

'What will it achieve?'

'We may have to go down that route, Harry. We may get to the stage where we have to start lifting some very old stones. I will be honest with you, I would do anything right now to have Mr. Blackmore in for a couple of days questioning. We may have to pull him in anyway.'

'Why? For being present at my father's death nearly fifty years ago?'

'Not at all, Harry. But you are losing sight of our objectives. Quite apart from what happened in 1916, which may or may not be relevant, we have placed Blackmore in Dresden. We shall have to investigate his business connections in the East. You said he was not alone. What did the other man look like?'

'Tall, English. I could tell that from his clothes. All right, Irish, Scottish or Welsh as well, the smart set. I got to recognise English walking around in Germany, even before they spoke. But he was stylish and distinguished. Tall and slightly gaunt. At first, from a distance, I thought it was Blackett. But then, somehow, he was less, oh, less handsome I suppose, less imposing. Even though it wasn't Blackett, there was something familiar about him. I've seen him somewhere before. But I don't think he is a scientist.'

'How old was he?'

'Compared to Blackmore, he looked young. Blackmore looks ninety even though he's probably about seventy. This man looked about fifty-ish. Younger than Blackett even.'

'This Blackett chap. Describe him.'

'I can do that.' Harry cut in. 'And then Robert can add anything he wants. Blackett was my boss in Manchester during the war.'

Harry and Robert completed the description of the man, his stern angular, film star looks with two deep lines in the cheeks. His dominating demeanour. Aged early sixties, indeed born in 1897, memorable, since the electron was discovered that year. Nobel prize for physics in 1948, although that did not affect his appearance.

'There's no shortage of these Nobel Prize chaps is there? I thought you said there weren't many of them?'

'There aren't many physicists actually. Compared to, say, bank managers or civil servants.'

'I'm not a civil servant. I'm a consultant and a don, like you. I think we ought to take a look at your Blackett. I'll have a picture wired up by the agency in London. They are bound to have one of a Nobel Prize winner on file, especially an English one.'

'But it wasn't him. I only said I thought it looked like him.'

'Good, so we can have a picture on the table that looks like the person you saw.'

Geoffrey opened a pad with a brown cover. "Requisitions" was printed in heavy block on the cover. He took the thin aluminium plate from the back of the pad, inserted it under the second page and wrote his wishes in the wide central field. In the cost column he wrote "Under £50." He then took out his diary and copied his new project account number into the relevant cost code field. He signed it, tore off the top two sheets and left the room.

An hour later, Geoffrey laid the wired picture he had received down on the table and asked: 'Is that a good likeness of your Blackett?'

Harry and Robert needed only a short glance. Blackett was unmistakable. Anyone would say that no one looked like Blackett. Except someone apparently did: an Englishman in Dresden.

'Yes, that's a pretty good picture of him. Very good.'

Geoffrey said nothing, smiling the grimmest of smiles. He reached for the pad again and repeated the identical procedure except for the details of his wishes. Half an hour later, he returned and laid a second picture on the table in front of Robert.

'Is that him, Robert? Is that the person you saw in Dresden?'

Robert rotated the picture on the table and stared.

'Yes. It is. I'm pretty sure of that. Yes. The face is striking isn't it. You only see people like that once and you recognise them instantly, for ever. Who is it?'

'Who is it, Robert? Mr. Blackmore is going tell us that. We are going to show him the picture, ask him to identify this person so we can see his reaction, and then ask him what the two of them were doing in Dresden on, on . . . you will have to remember the date Robert. You can do that can't you?'

'I think I will be able to work it out. It won't take long. But we are not going to wait for Blackmore to tell us who he is. You know already. Stop playing us along.'

'I'm sorry. It's me again. Just enjoying the moment. Gentlemen, you are looking at Sir Anthony Blunt, Surveyor of Her Majesty the Queen's pictures, Soviet Spy and Traitor to his nation. We are in business. 1-0 to us.'

'Who are we playing against? A team or a country or a bunch of disorganised idealists?'

'Well put, Harry. Well put. Probably all three.'

Geoffrey picked up the photograph of Blunt together with a crisp, new, red folder. The photograph went into the folder as the first entry.

Let's concentrate on Beethoven for a while. It may only be a codeword. Nobody's daft enough to give the game away in the codeword.'

Harry smiled. He had just been given an opportunity to patronise Geoffrey.

'It's a German codeword. The Germans have a tendency to give the game away with their codewords. Knickerbein, the name of the bent radar beam. The German word means cross-legged. Wotan, the one eyed god, gave his name to the single beam directing bombers on Coventry. Oh, and while we're at it, Overlord was not all that obscure.'

'What's wrong with Overlord?'

'Hmmm, it's English history before 1707. You probably weren't taught it up there in Dundee. French invasion, dominate the enemy. Henry V. Agincourt.'

'I take the point. Let us start with Beethoven. There must be a lot of information about him. Where do we start?'

'I would start with the symphonies. They are his most important works and there aren't all that many of them.'

'Did you get this from Ursula, or did you know it already?'

'I thought I knew about classical music till I met her. But her knowledge was profound. For days before any concert I would get tutorial after tutorial.'

'Phew, laddie, didn't you feel a bit put upon?'

'No. I loved it. It was better than reading two thousand year old German poetry.'

'So. Start us off. Let's have the titles, on the wall there.'

The papers on which they were taking notes were beginning to build up. Searching for key points was taking longer and longer. It was getting untidy, so Geoffrey took control. He got the block to prepare a whole wall in the discussion room. It was a wall without windows or doors and it had been re-plastered and buffed until it shone like a mirror. Then it had been painted dark green. Geoffrey had then tested it with a piece of chalk and found parts that were too rough. It was sanded, buffed and painted again. The whole wall was a green "blackboard", thirty five feet long and seven feet high. It was their working "Ops" room. No cleaners were allowed in. The windows were shuttered.

Robert started in the top left corner, as a physicist would if starting off a lecture, but he was brought up quickly by Geoffrey.

'Put this in the middle. I have a feeling everything may fan out from this and probably converge back again.'

Robert wrote a column of numbers, 1 to 9. Nine symphonies. Against the number 3, he wrote "Eroica". Against number 6, he wrote "Pastoral". Finally, at the bottom, against the 9, he wrote "Choral". He then stood back, moving to the far wall to check that he had written the column in a straight vertical line.

'What about the other names?' Geoffrey didn't know Robert had finished.

'You Philistine! The others don't have names, just numbers.'

'Ah, and I thought you would be providing just the science! I'm going to have to pull my socks up. What does a list like that mean to a scientist, a logician?'

'Symmetry.' Harry and Robert said the word together.

Robert went to the board and chalked a copy of the list. But instead of the names, he just wrote the word "name". He drew a box round the nine entries and then three smaller boxes around the first, second and third group of three.

'Symmetry. Symmetry means that I can move any box, shuffle it, re-order it, swap with any other box and you cannot tell the difference by looking at it. Only when I replace the word "name" by an actual name, is the symmetry broken. Even then the symmetry breaking is only weak.'

'Weak? I'll take your word for it.'

'Weak broken symmetry.'

Geoffrey strode to the green-board and wrote his newly acquired word "symmetry" in the top right hand corner.

'Is that enough? Or do you want the weak broken stuff as well?' he smirked.

'That will do.'

Geoffrey drew a single vertical line on the board from the top to the bottom, just to the left of the word "symmetry". He then drew a line under the word to put it in a box.

'Here we shall write things of significance. I think symmetry is significant. We ought to write Burgess, Mclean and Philby here as well. And Blunt.'

'Blackmore as well?'

'Of course.' Geoffrey frowned again, but warmed, feeling able to rise to any challenge offered by the two scientists.

The next part the discussion covered the keys in which the symphonies were written. Symphony Number 1 in C major. Number 2 in D major. Number 3 in E flat major. Number 4 in B flat major. Number 5 in C minor. Number 6 in F major. Number 7 in A major. Number 8 in F major and finally, number 9 in D minor. After an hour they got nowhere. If there was a pattern, they couldn't see it.

'Let's bring in a musician to help us.' Geoffrey was looking for straws to grasp.

'No, definitely not. A musician will tell us something musical. I suspect that the key to solving this is not in the keys. Start a new column on the left side for things that are interesting but not yet significant. We might have to move them later from left to right or vice versa. Write the word "keys" up there. Probably not significant.'

'I was just going to do that. I think you have sussed out my method.' Geoffrey wasn't sure whether he was felt cross or full of admiration. Probably both.

Geoffrey started a new box. Burgess, Maclean and Philby. Three entries.

'Three names we think are linked to Beethoven. We have three Beethoven symphony boxes and three names. It fits doesn't it?'

'Not really. That would be very inelegant and I do think that the person who set this up was not inelegant. He was elegant. Or she.'

'Why is it inelegant as it stands?'

'Because if it were a physics theory, it would be ugly. If Nature has nine slots available, she uses them all, not just three. And if there are only three objects to fit, there is usually a very good reason, a selection rule, that deletes the unused six.'

'So why not find a reason to delete six? There are six symphonies with no names. Delete them. The selection rule is just that the symphony must have a name.'

'Not good enough. There would be no reason to set up and use Beethoven if you were going to remove most of it, two thirds, the moment you set it up. Anyway, I think you, or rather we, would have a bigger problem if we eliminated six slots. I think we really ought to be writing Blunt on your box of three. And Blackmore. But that would open a real can of worms.'

201

Geoffrey had caught up and knew what was coming. He was so sure he knew what was coming that he held up his hand to stop them speaking.

'That would mean, with five names on the board, we have to find another four.'

'Exactly. Somebody is not going to be very happy about that. Nine spies, nine moles in top places. We have three government officials, the Queen's art surveyor and adviser and a Nobel physics prize-winner who advises the government – already on the list. That is already dynamite. I wonder what sort of person we are going to turn up next. Forty per cent of them have knighthoods. Burgess, Maclean and Philby would all have got knighthoods if they hadn't been found out. That's the way the Foreign Office works.'

'Not so fast.' Geoffrey was enjoying the cut and thrust. He was usually in a dominant situation but suddenly realised what he was missing in his day-to-day work: sparring with equals.

'I think we should consolidate and examine. If this withstands everything we can throw at it, we can build up and out. Burgess, Maclean and Philby. They are all rather similar. Cambridge men and career civil servants. Blunt and Blackmore are different. Both Cambridge men, but more academic and scholarly. Do we put the three civil servants in one box of three symphonies or one in each of the three boxes?'

'We can try both hypotheses. One may work better than the other, one may not work at all. Do the three fit in any box? We have Eroica, Pastoral and Choral. It could be that we have a box of heroes. Would we want to put these three under such a banner of heroism? It sort of sticks in the craw.'

'That would be one reason for them using it. To us they are traitors, but to them, a bunch of top civil servants betraying their country from the heart of government would be heroes. They are telling us that they would decorate these traitors with honours.'

Geoffrey felt the lurch in the stomach that usually came when his probing turns up a truth, initially unpalatable but which unlocks the whole investigation.

'Let's write them in the first box for now. Let us try to call them "heroes" for the moment.'

'That clears the deck. If we can't find what to do with Blunt and Blackmore in the remaining spaces, we might have to take these heroes out again. Now we've got Pastoral and Choral. Where do Blunt and Blackmore fit?'

'Art and Science. If we had a university linguist or something like that, then we would have a good academic spread. Quite a pastoral scene. Can't we just drop them in the pastoral box? What's choral about either of them? What's heroic about them? To the other side I mean. I suspect a top intelligence person from the other side would not regard a Cambridge academic as a hero. Much more par for the course, don't you think? Any university come to that. There's nothing special about Cambridge in this regard, except that before the war, they were probably pulling in the best.'

'Ahem.' Harry brought Geoffrey to a quick stop. 'Not true for physics. Manchester has its share. Indeed, Manchester sent Blackmore to Cambridge, plus Rutherford, Chadwick and Bragg. It's hard to imagine someone less traitor-like than that crowd.'

'Apart from Blackmore!' Geoffrey beamed. Anyway, even if all boxes were empty, we'd be putting them in the pastoral.' Geoffrey's face was glowing.

'Where's the coffee? They said they would have coffee for us by now.' Robert was getting agitated.

'It will be outside the door. I can smell it. No one but us is allowed in here. Unless we authorise it.'

As if on cue, there was a knock on the door. Janine was there with two trolleys. One had the coffee and the other had a stack of box files, each one tied up with string and sealed with wax.

'Let's have a coffee first and then decide what to do about these boxes.'

It was over coffee that Robert suddenly blurted it out:

'It's obvious. It's very simple really. Three is the key. Three groups of three making up the nine. Each group of three has a special characteristic. Philby, Burgess and Maclean, all working for government. I'll bet they are the heroes. Risking their necks literally. Blackmore, Blunt and Cairncross all perceived as elite Cambridge intellectuals. They will be the pastorals. All we have to do is figure out what "Choral" signifies and then identify three people to fill the slot.'

'I'd rather we had at least one "Choral" then it would give us a clue.'

'Nah,' scoffed Robert, 'that would make it too easy. We need a challenge. Starting is never easy. Finishing is easy when you have everything on the table.'

Geoffrey tapped on the top-most box on the trolley.

'We are going to have to decide whether to start with our thoughts on this theory or go through these boxes with an open mind. I have a suggestion. We sit side by side at the long table there, with the boxes on the left. We start on the first box, one of us sits on the left and reads the first paper in the first box and then passes it to the next person in middle who passes it on to the one on the right. We work our way through the boxes that way and just make notes of anything of interest. We then have a discussion and compare notes. This may take some time. We don't want to miss anything. This has been going on for over twenty years, maybe thirty and an extra day won't matter. We do not work through the night exhausting our brains; we stop for the day when the first one feels mentally tired.'

'We don't have to restrict ourselves to people whose names are in the public domain. We can speculate here.' Geoffrey wanted to broaden the discussion. It would be easy to mark things as proven and the rest as speculation. 'I suggest we don't jump to conclusions. We can jump to conclusions and then read the box files and find we have blundered. In fact we should read the box files now. I have a scheme. We start with the oldest box. Turn it upside down and make a pile of paper, upside down, oldest will now be on top. We sit at the long table, side by side, A, B and C, with the box contents on the left. A reads the first paper and passes it to B who reads it and passes it on the C who reads it and puts it face upwards in its original box. Make any notes you need. We might need to take a break between boxes depending on the material but let's see how it goes.'

Three hours later, Geoffrey placed the last sheet in the last box and rushed to the door moments before Janine delivered a fresh consignment of coffee right on cue.

'How did you know?' Robert was astonished.

'I am very disappointed in you Robert. Didn't your Stasi interrogators have push buttons under the desk to summons people "unexpectedly"?'

Over coffee, they exchanged preliminary thoughts. All three thought the material was meagre and much of it seemed irrelevant, nothing more than a mysterious document stamped "Copy to Beethoven".

Harry had made most notes. He spoke first.

'I ignored names we already knew, Blackmore and Blunt, Burgess and Maclean and the rest. I looked for a common thread in the other names, some of which are very well known. I think I have a clue.'

'Go on.' Geoffrey was good at the live stuff and had already recognised that Harry and Robert were deeper thinkers of written material.

'There were three who cropped up more than once, indeed, I put my threshold at three mentions and I came up with three names. The three mentions is just a coincidence. I get the same three if I make the cut later to be four or five.'

'Go on.'

'William Joyce and Cecil Day Lewis and P G Wodehouse.'

'One's dead, executed. One's never coming back to this country and one is tipped to be the next Poet Laureate. Not much in common.'

'Not so fast. I am thinking of the "Choral" link. What do choristers do? They sing. All these three can write and they all wrote dodgy stuff during the war, especially Joyce and Wodehouse.'

'So you want the third grouping to be these three? Where does that get us?'

'It's just a suggestion. We should consider alternatives and hammer things out. If this is what we are left with then I don't think there is a lot to do. We could ask them to line up Cecil Day Lewis with Anthony Blunt and shoot them, but it wouldn't help us to learn more. They do say Blunt gives nothing away. You almost have to film and record him doing it before he will admit to anything. He doesn't leave tracks.'

The trio wrestled and grappled with their information, tearing it to pieces and then re-assembling it. Schemes were written on the blackboard and then rubbed off. They went round in circles and ellipses, and at one stage, Robert wanted to teach them the concept of real and imaginary numbers. But one scheme kept coming back and after three days, they accepted it as the best working hypothesis. Harry and Robert believed it to be inevitable. Geoffrey held doubts but eventually admitted inwardly that it might be because he hadn't thought of it himself.

Harry summarised their findings in a neat chart, having obliterated everything on the blackboard:

There are nine B symphonies, three with names. The names define the group of three. There are nine top potential spies or traitors in three groups of three. Each group has the name of a symphony.

The names are:

Choral for the group of choristers, spies or traitors who sing. They are top journalists or writers and they communicate with the East via their articles or radio broadcasts.

Pastoral for the group of university or cultural types, Blunt, Blackmore and Cairncross.

Heroic for the group of true heroes, in government service and the sort who historically would have been executed for treason.

An irritating feature was that eventually, they had more names than slots. Harry was not worried by this.

'Look, they devised this scheme and someone musical thought up the Beethoven wheeze because he had nine contacts who could be subdivided into three groups of three with the symphonic names to loosely describe them. But as time passed and more were recruited, there became more than nine. But the hard core remained and the code name remained. I am not completely happy with the people we have assigned to the Choral group because Wodehouse for instance was essentially useless living in France and slowly going mad. Yes he would give moral support and maybe at the start they had ideas for him, getting him to return to England and exploit the fact that British Prime Ministers historically had a weakness for him. I think we should write in our report that other journalists or writers, as yet unsuspected, might exist and that should be an open project.'

'So we advise that Blackmore and Blunt should be hauled in for "questioning"? For starters. That should concentrate their minds.

'Done!'

~   ~   ~

Chapter 17

London 1964

'**H**ave you ever been to Dresden?'
The same question was asked of Clive Blackmore and Anthony Blunt at the same instant in separate rooms. Each was shown a picture of the other and each was told, not entirely truthfully, that they had been observed together.

'What have an art surveyor and physics professor got in common, that they need to go for a stroll on Dresden station? Were you at the same conference? What kind of conference would that have been?'

Although rooms apart, Blackmore and Blunt might have been connected by a stiff rod. In unison, they leant back, looked scornfully at their questioners and said nothing.

'This is not something you can ignore and make go away. If you choose to sit there and say nothing, then eventually you will be arrested and charged. Would you like a solicitor present now?'

For Blunt, this was not his first interrogation on shady matters. He easily stayed cool and maintained an appearance of aloof superiority. The threat of arrest held no fears. He was keeper of the royal family's pictures and drawings and even related, albeit distantly, to the Queen. "Touch me if you can" was the challenge he threw at the buffoons who were clumsily interrogating him now. They seemed totally unaware that MI5 already knew about him. Blunt allowed his thoughts to wander to that duplicitous American, Michael Straight, one of his recruiting failures, who had ratted on him. Blunt already had immunity from prosecution and a promise of secrecy in return for information concerning everything he knew about the KGB. He had interpreted the word "everything" somewhat conservatively. The business couldn't be revealed now because those in government who had conspired to keep his secrets dark would themselves be revealed if his role hit the newspapers. The government would not allow that. Even if that idiot Blackmore blabbed, a D-notice would be slapped on the newspapers and the status quo would remain.

Blackmore was struggling not to blab. He could wrap University departments, faculties and senates around his middle finger, but these questioners did not seem to play by his rules. "Deny everything" was the order he had been given for such days and that is what he was trying to do.

'I don't know Sir Anthony Blunt. I know of him, who doesn't, but I don't know him. That's all I can say. If someone saw me with him on Dresden station then either it wasn't him or it wasn't me. I only go to Dresden to see people at the University there who are working on similar things to me.'

'Are you still working? I thought you would have retired by now.'

This allowed Clive to assume a position of superiority.

'Your brain might have stopped working already, but passing the age of 65 did not affect mine. I wouldn't be surprised if I was still writing scientific papers at the age of 100.'

'How much do they pay you?'

'Cambridge don't pay me any more. I have formally retired from employment, but I have not stopped working.'

'I meant the East Germans.'

'You mean Dresden University? Nothing. They refund my travel expenses and put me up when I visit.'

It was almost true. He had hardly received a pfennig from the East Germans, he had been pleased to offer them a disservice to his own country in return for not getting the Cavendish Chair. Just when he thought that Blunt was out of the discussion, Geoffrey bowled him a bouncer.

'You are a Fellow of Trinity College. Blunt is also a Fellow of Trinity College and yet you say you don't know him!'

Clive hooked the bouncer over the square leg boundary.

'Tsk, you don't understand Universities do you.'

Geoffrey thought he meant Universities, including Dundee. Clive meant Cambridge alone.

'I am a scientific Fellow of the College. Sir Anthony is art. We don't even dine on the same evenings. I live at my home, he lives at his and even if we happen by chance to be dining in Hall on the same day, we are unlikely to talk. I suppose someone you know saw us going into Formal Hall together one day. Just because you walk down the street at the same time as someone else, doesn't mean that you know them.'

'But you told us earlier that you didn't know him. Now you are saying you do.'

'Absolute rubbish. Don't you listen to what people are saying? I said earlier that I didn't know him, but I knew of him. I have just repeated that, consistently. Why don't you call the Master and ask him.'

Geoffrey was not sure who Clive meant by "the Master". For reasons he could not identify, he found the title intimidating. He was finding Clive to be one of the most slippery subjects he had ever questioned.

In the end, they had to let Blackmore and Blunt go. Blunt had eventually managed to call in his solicitor by some means unknown, since he had not been allowed to use a telephone and before the day was out, MI5 intervened and ordered his release. MI5 also strongly advised that Clive should also walk, "Lest the waters be muddied." Geoffrey shrugged his shoulders and got on a train to Edinburgh. File closed. He was even forbidden to tell Harry and Robert what had happened.

In ignorance, Robert took immediately to scanning the newspapers for news of Blunt and Blackmore's arrest. He waited. His initial excitement that it would happen within a week gave way to frustration as the week became a month. He watched every TV news bulletin, expecting to see the same two faces he saw in Dresden. Nothing happened. His daily excited phone calls to his father became less frequent. After six months, he was ready to burst with frustration. He called his father one more time.

'Why haven't they done anything, Dad? Shouldn't we go to the newspapers?'

'Have you forgotten Robert? You signed the Official Secrets Act. If you talk to anyone except me and Geoffrey, it will be you who gets arrested, not them.'

'But it's a disgrace. We know they are spies, traitors, and they are walking around with their knighthoods as if nothing had happened.'

'Wait. These wheels grind terribly slowly. But they will grind these two into dust. Just be patient. It may take a year or two.'

'I can't wait that long.'

'I have waited forty five years. I think you can manage one or two. Believe me. Get on with your work and put your energies into that. I thought you were making good progress on the plasmas.'

'I am. But I am not the same as you. I am less placid. Sometimes I get exasperated with you, so calm, after all that happened. I do not trust Blackmore an inch. He was there when granddad died. It's stupid, I know, to call him granddad; he was only twenty six when he died.'

~   ~   ~

Chapter 18

London 1964

R obert answered the call to the Prof's office. Professor Brian Flowers, head of the department and Jimmy Braddick, his right hand man, had architectural blue-prints laid out on every surface. Braddick was squinting over one of the prints in the corner and barely looked up. The irascible Braddick had been with Blackett in his student days in Cambridge, followed him to Birkbeck as his right hand man and optics expert, and followed him to Manchester. When Blackett had left for London, Braddick had stayed.

'White, good. We have a job for you. Two in fact. Some of the stuff in this building will be moved to the new one. Not much because we are having a complete refurbishment. People will take their own equipment and contents of their offices but that is not our concern. Down in the basement there is a room full of old stuff, maybe junk. Probably it needs throwing out. There are some old photographs from Rutherford's days and earlier and there are loads of old books. I'd like you and Douggie Broadbent to go through it and keep anything that is valuable. But try and throw out as much as possible. If in doubt, throw it. We don't have unlimited space in the new building.'

'Yes, Sir. You're talking about that room near the old Geiger-Marsden lab? I looked through some material back in there about two years ago. It had been used for that Rutherford Jubilee conference you organised in 1961 and never put back. There's a fair amount of stuff there, but it shouldn't take too long. What's the deadline?'

'We'd like it clear in two weeks so you had better drop what you are doing. Jimmy, anything to add?'

'No.'

Douggie and Robert worked out their plan over tea and got started that afternoon. The basement room had not been swept or dusted since the building had been built in 1900. Archeologists could probably work out the date that piles of books had been placed on other piles of books by studying the layer of dust between the two layers. In the corner of the room was a peculiar tank with ducts leading to the outside. There were electric fans embedded in the ducts and judging by the cloth covered cables, the fans were probably the oldest electric fans on earth.

'I know what that is! I read about in those old brochures that got displayed during the Jubilee conference.'

Douggie was grinning.

'That tank contained, maybe it still does, oil. They used to drag the air from outside in over the oil so that all the muck stuck to the oil instead of the apparatus. It needed changing twice a year and I remember Jimmy Nuttall saying the whole building stank of machine oil.'

'So what are we going to do about all this stuff. We can't shift it all over to the new building.'

'Let's get the cleaners in with their vacuums, maybe even borrow a machine. Then we can do it at leisure, layer by layer.'

The framed photographs were cleaned and cleared first. Pictures of groups of physicists, usually with Rutherford in the centre of the group, looking proud. Some pre-dated Rutherford's arrival and others were as recent as 1953, the year Blackett left. One gorgeous sepia print dated from 1861 and showed Wilhelm Bunsen, the Bunsen, who invented the burner together with his Heidelberg colleague Kirchhoff and the Manchester chemist Roscoe.

Piles of loose papers were dusted off and put into crates. That only left various pieces of apparatus, books and teaching aids. The apparatus was old, mahogany and brass with lenses and prisms and it looked like it might be interesting. They were packed in paper and crated. Douggie held up a piece of blackboard about 2 feet across.

'Hey, look at this. It's Einstein's signature in chalk! He must have done it when he gave that lecture, when was it? Not long after the 1919 eclipse. Wow. I'm going to take care of this. We don't want to lose this, it's precious. We can't even risk the chalk being wiped off.'

Robert smiled. He had just found another photograph, unframed, undated, cracked and faded in one corner where the sun had once bleached it. It was an informal group, standing outside the workshop. There were hand-written names in the margin above and below the men. Some were familiar without the names, Schuster, Beattie and Lees. One young man, a boy almost since he looked about twelve, looked out across the years with an expression of optimism and hope for the future; his future.

'Look, it's Dibblee. I often wondered what he looked like.'

'Dibblee? Who's he?' Douggie had never met Dibblee.

'It's a long story. I'll tell you over tea one day when we've finished this lot. Well, well, Dibblee. Who would have thought it? You look like an urchin almost!'

'I'm going to get this crate of pictures out into our empty lab. It will give us more space down here. You'll see to those books won't you Robert?'

'Yes, they need cleaning carefully along the edges before they are opened. They are simply grimy. John in the University library told me to get some artist's putty to roll over the edges with the book closed. Then we can see what's in them. I'll take them upstairs to my office. I'm ready for some tea to wash this stuff out of my throat.'

In the tea room, it suddenly occurred to Robert that the Prof had said he had two jobs for him and he had run off into the basement before he had found out about the second.

'What was the other thing you wanted me to do, Sir?'

Flowers frowned.

'I can't remember!'

Nuclear physicist Eric Paul sauntered in for tea. Although Canadian, he looked like a prairie cowboy. He had the drawl.

'Ah, now I remember. Eric thinks it's time you went to a conference. He'll sort it out.'

~   ~   ~

213

Chapter 19

Bologna 1966

'Have you ever been to Bologna?' Professor Eric Paul, now settled in Manchester and hired to drive the nuclear research on the new linear accelerator, loved encouraging the young scientists. He had suggested to Flowers and the conference organisers that Robert would be a good choice of speaker and the committee had gone along with the suggestion.

'I've never been to Italy!'

'You'll enjoy it. Bologna is a lovely city. Compact. Neat, clean. Super cafés and restaurants and shops. There's plenty to do between the conference sessions. You'll be flying to Milan and then taking the train. Italian trains are an experience in themselves! Keep all your receipts and see Mrs. Crosby in the office about your tickets and an advance. Make sure you give them a good talk. I'm sure you will.'

The conference was everything that Eric Paul said it would be. Robert loved Bologna the moment he stepped off the train from Milan. He smelt the air and loved it. He loved the old hotel with its noisy brass plumbing and the gorgeous breakfast coffee. He loved the way he could walk with no jacket from the hotel to the conference centre in five minutes, taking in the smells of the cafés.

The first session of the conference was pure post-war Italy. The building and conference rooms were majestic and historic. Over a hundred physicists assembled for the opening session as the first speaker gave his slides to the projectionist. The room had been used for every historic event imaginable but had never entertained physicists with projectors and screens before. By ten o'clock, the sun burnt in through the windows at the top of the atrium and bleached the projected image on the white painted wall that was being used as a screen. The Italian sun was more powerful than the projector lamp, much more powerful. The poor speaker was denied all his visual aids and could not show the results of his research. The session was temporarily abandoned. The conference organiser, Professor Antonio Zichichi, powerful in Sicily, spreading his influence throughout Italy, took control. He unfolded several large denomination lira notes from a roll the size of wallpaper. The assistant was ordered to go and buy a few tablecloths from the market to use as a replacement screen, that could be hung against the dark oak panelling. Half an hour later, two beautiful white bleached linen tablecloths were unfurled and pinned to the wall.

It was a compromise between science and art. The tablecloths were of lace and all the subsequent speakers had to tolerate the fact that their science was overlaid onto an ornate pattern. It looked nice.

Robert had watched as the delegates had floundered, one after the other. He took it in his stride. He always used bold lines and large lettering in his slides and was confident he would dominate the lace. He had noticed that virtually all scientists had no graphic skills and crammed too much information into their slides. The lines were too thin, the lettering was too small and their science became wrecked on the soft fabric of Bologna lace. They wouldn't even have shown up on a decent projector and he wondered if they ever looked at them, projected, before they left home. To be sure, Robert sacrificed one of the two possible coffees that the morning break provided. With the help of the assistant, he loaded the slides for his talk that was scheduled for the next day and had a preview. With a smile of near smugness, Robert knew that his slides would triumph over the lace. Even if Zichichi brought in some Emperor sized bed linen, his slides would emerge triumphant.

Robert also took the city in his stride, strolling through the colonnades out of the burning sun. He paused at the windows of the restaurants, with red lobsters, crayfish and langoustines, laid out on trays of ice, dressed with tomatoes and asparagus. He popped in an out of the cafes, an espresso here, a ristretto there. What a life. Manchester must be on another planet. Science and Italy were a good marriage. Galileo, Galvano, Volta, Fermi. No wonder they had thrived.

Robert stepped out of the café, the astringency of the coffee washed away with a glass of cold water. He was about to return to the conference building but had to step to one side. The trio were striding through the colonnade, almost as a unit. In the centre, the tall woman could have been painted by Michelangelo. Her hair streamed out in a perfect equilateral triangle. Robert later remembered thinking of that triangle, a myriad of curls descending on curls to form a swathe that fell and extended from the top of her head to below her shoulders. Her red coat, totally superfluous in the heat, spread out in a further triangle that started at her shoulders and ended by her ankles in a wide flare that embraced her companions. Her blouse was white, her trousers were white and her belt was red, shiny red to match her coat. Her lipstick was a perfect match.

Robert White looked, saw and was vanquished. He barely noticed the two young women who were framed by the burning flame of the coat. The two acolytes were pretty, attractive, pert, animated and smiling and were the sort of woman most men would die for. But Robert saw only the spectacle in the centre. He moved to one side to let the entourage pass. For his trouble, he was impaled on a stare of derision and haughty dismissal.

"Get out of our way!" The words were flashed by the eyes, unspoken.

Even though he was being deferential, he felt crushed like an ant. "Bologna certainly makes you think", he thought.

The incident made him need another coffee – a double espresso to calm the nerves. Sometimes his crave for coffee led him to understand the craving of others for tobacco, even though he did not share it. He went back to the café he had just left. His table by the window was still free and the waitress was brushing his grissini crumbs to the floor. The waitress and he smiled at each other and she said something he did not understand.

'Expresso doublee.' He said, holding up one finger and not knowing what language he had just spoken, if any.

The waitress stared.

'Do you want a double or two single espressos?'

The voice was clean and intimidating, coming from the next table. Robert turned to look at the spectacle and entourage, already looking too large at a table for four.

Robert found it hard to collect his thoughts, let alone speak.

'You spoke in English. But you're not! How did you know I was English?'

'Your clothes I'm afraid!'

'My clothes? Afraid?' Robert was on the verge of panic.

'Yes, your clothes! You must be English. Where do you get them from? Do you have to send away for them? Or does England make them?'

The acolytes were giggling, until silenced by an icy stare.

'It's not always warm in Manchester. You're rather lucky living here. If I lived here, I'd wear different clothes.'

'Are you here for the conference? All these scientists?'

'Yes. I'm afraid it's my first conference and my talk is tomorrow. My slides are going to be projected on to a lace tablecloth. I hope they will look right. We are not good at clothes in Manchester, but Bologna is not very good at projector screens.'

The spectacle laughed. Her teeth were large, white and perfect.

'I am not a scientist but I come from science!' The spectacle held out her hand.

'I don't understand.'

'Of course not. I am being devious. I'm sorry.' Her English was perfect. 'My great-great-great grandfather was a scientist. You may even had heard of him.'

'Try me. I do know a lot about the history.'

'Volta. Alessandro Volta. That thing, the "volt" is named after him. I am Alessandra. Alessandra Volta. I am named for him, even though I am a woman! He was handsome. I am proud of him. I am proud to be his great-great-great grand daughter.'

'Oh my goodness. Oh yes. Everyone has heard of him. Oh my goodness. You are a volt. I can't believe it.'

Suddenly, Robert realised that the acolytes were no longer there. He was alone with the spectacle. Alone with Alessandra. Bologna was getting better and better. They had a glass of cold water each. They had a lemon ice. He had another double espresso which made Alessandra frown. She had tea. Then they had delicate crisp thin lemon flavoured biscuits with more tea. Then they had more water. Robert had no more coffee because he did not want to see another frown. Would he have to choose between coffee and Alessandra?

'I've missed the whole afternoon session. I should have gone back and listened to Dalitz. Now I will have to get a copy of the notes to find out what he said.'

'Does it matter?'

'Not today. Not to me. But when I get back I will have to tell the whole department what went on here. I must give a summary lecture about the conference. Dalitz is very famous and very clever. If he has talked about something new and exciting, I could not possibly go back and not mention it. I would turn out to be a fool and I would never live it down.'

'So you are sorry you missed the conference? That you missed this ... who did you say, Dalitz?'

'There are different levels of sorry, just like there are millivolts and megavolts! I am slightly sorry that I missed Dalitz but I am not in the least bit sorry I missed the conference.'

Robert was as good as his father when it came to logic. And he was a better physicist.

'Who is speaking tomorrow afternoon? Will you miss him? Will you be here?'

Robert hardly dared answer.

'I am speaking tomorrow afternoon. For half an hour. Then I shall come here.' He thought and hoped he knew what she meant. He hoped his answer was adequate.

~   ~   ~

Robert soon got into his stride. He had stripped the details of his talk to the bare essentials. Too many scientists droned on and on, covering every tiny detail, afraid that if they missed a dot over an "i" no one would understand what they had done. Half the talks at the conference had been like that. One hour lectures gabbled into twenty and thirty minutes with the result that no one understood a word. This morning, everyone had been talking about Dick Dalitz and he had been embarrassed, hoping no one would notice that he had nothing to say about the subject. Now he was in his comfortable zone, talking about the concept of quark-gluon plasmas and Fermi-Boson hybrid statistics. It was early days, but he was making progress. The four o'clock slot at a conference in Italy was never easy, with the delegates returning from siestas and long lunches. Several came in late and one by one, the latecomers drifted into the back of the hall. Robert didn't mind. He could see from the faces that he had the audience in his grip. Until, that is, the red coat entered the hall.

It was not fair to disorientate him like that. But then, how could she have known what happened inside Robert when she walked in to see him, to listen to his voice. He noticed, looked, hesitated, stuttered, paused. He looked down, closed his eyes, picked up his notes and looked up to the atrium, catching the afternoon sun coming from the opposite direction than it did on the first morning. Then he continued, calmly, without looking again at the back of the hall. For the rest of his lecture, he fixed his attention on the second row. He spoke personally to the German, Behrends, on the left, then to Weber and to Froissart, to the Danish American Bjorken and finally to Zichichi himself. Each one received his undivided attention as he blotted out the red coat. At the end of his talk, he heard for the first time in his life, but not the last, the sound of applause from an appreciative audience. It shook him. It felt better than a double espresso. After Dalitz, it was only the second talk that the delegates had understood and enjoyed.

Robert walked with some trepidation along the colonnade. There in the café, at the same table, was the red coat together with her two acolytes. He entered nervously. Somehow, in this heat, he thought that everything from yesterday would have evaporated. These thoughts had preceded his talk and hence the intoxication induced by the anticipation of speaking to a hundred physicists had probably clouded his memory.

Yet she had come to listen to him. She had taken that trouble. Why?

'I think you were good! I did not understand a word, but they did. All the ones who had come in out of the heat to have a quiet nap stayed awake and nodded their agreement at everything you were saying. Yes, you were very good. Do you feel good? I don't feel completely good because you did not look at me even once. Why was that?'

Robert had no answer he dared utter.

The acolytes got up, kissed their leader goodbye and left. Robert had two hours before he had to leave and get ready for the conference reception and dinner. He wished he could take her to the dinner but knew no way to achieve it. The two hours passed in two minutes and they arranged to meet, same time, same place tomorrow, Friday, the last day of the conference.

Friday came and ended almost before Robert and Alessandra could catch their breaths. Time was running out and Robert at least did not know where he was heading. They exchanged addresses. They would write. They would meet, soon. Robert wondered when, but did nothing to ensure that they would.

~   ~   ~

At Linate, Milan airport, Robert was astonished to find he was not actually on the direct flight back to Manchester.

'You see. The status printed on your ticket is "R" for Request and not "OK".

Why did Italian women turn a mini crisis into a Verdi opera?

'You only have a request reservation and not confirmed. The flight was already full when you booked. Didn't they tell you?'

The check-in girl was singing an aria. Robert noticed she was much fatter than the average Italian woman of her age.

'But don't worry! This is Italy. Most people will not show up for the flight – unless they are all English returning to Manchester! I will just type in your details into this new computer and it will put you on the waiting list and tell us when I can check you in. These new computers are very good. It's an Olivetti!'

Robert thought he would prefer a Manchester built ATLAS computer to get him home, failing that, an IBM. He had heard of Olivetti but thought they were scooters.

'Oh, look at that. You are already in. How did that happen? You have to go to that desk there, the first class one. You are upgraded. Somebody up there likes you.'

Robert walked, bewildered, across to the first class counter. There was already someone there, a queue of one. He found himself staring, gazing, stunned, into the smiling face of Alessandra.

'What are you doing here?'

'I've just checked in! Now it's your turn.'

'But how did you get on? I booked two weeks ago and I am on the waiting list. When did you book?'

'Just now. I decided to fly to Manchester this morning since you didn't invite me.'

'Didn't invite you? I, I, I . . . '

'Are you going to say "I am English?" The English could not do such a thing, could they? What would you do? Go away forever? You were going away forever, weren't you? You were leaving me. You did not want to see me again.'

'Yes I did. I did not sleep last night. I have thought of you every second since I met you.'

'Oh yes? Do you expect me to believe that? And here you are running away! Flying away! Well, thank goodness I am Italian. I will not let you. We are flying together, first class, to Manchester.

220

My father has paid. He is a director of Alitalia, so it did not cost him much. But he would have paid more.'

In years to come, Robert would often think of this moment, how his life had been rescued by a woman of passion who had known her own destiny and his and had seized them both, in the moment. His inability to be decisive in matters of the heart had cost him Ursula. Ursula had not had the passion to secure him so they lost each other. He had no passion to take her. He did not deserve Alessandra and now here she was, his life and his wife.

On the plane, flying over the Alps into Switzerland, looking down on Lake Geneva, they had drunk an orange juice and then a champagne, to the future. Alessandra leaned over and rested her head on his shoulder. Robert realised that they had not even kissed and yet he was sure, they would be married.

'I shall need to find somewhere to stay in Manchester.'

'What?'

'Well, I don't think I shall be staying with you, Robert! If your clothes are anything to go by, I can't imagine what your flat is like. But that will all change. We shall sort everything out and then we shall go back to Italy to see my father. And my mother. You had better see what I will look like in 25 years. Don't look alarmed, she is beautiful beyond words.'

'Why does that not surprise me?'

~   ~   ~

Chapter 20

Panorama 1967

T he suddenness of his marriage and the complete change in his lifestyle swept all thoughts of Blackmore from Robert's mind for six months. Setting up home in Alderley Edge kept them out for another six. Eventually, he remembered the books and papers he had found in the basement of the old building and had moved across to the new building in a tea chest. The tea chest was still where he had moved it six months ago.

He started on the two log books that had belonged to his grandfather. Opening the pages, he felt a surge of excitement, reaching back more than fifty years. The entries were dated from 1912. The work was detailed and thorough and some, but not all of the work was familiar to him. He was no science historian but he kept returning to page 50 in book 1; something wasn't right and he needed to go to the library. Every Nobel prizewinner gives a speech on the work that led to the prize. Usually, they referred to all the great papers they had written. Clive was no exception. In his speech, recorded for posterity in the records of the Nobel Foundation, there were all his papers, published in the journal, *Philosophical Transactions of the Royal Society*. The full copy of the *Transactions* was on another shelf and it did not take long to find the papers in them. There, in 1925, Clive was publishing the equations from Robert's grandfather's notebook and their derivation, in the journal. He got the credit. This in itself was nothing unusual. It would not have been the first time that someone failed to publish their results for whatever reason, in Robert's grandfather's case, death. It is a truism in science that someone eventually will make the breakthrough or discovery and so, a scientist wanting the credit, should publish quickly, or else someone else will. Robert White senior had not been able to publish his results before he died. The question that occupied Robert junior's mind was whether Clive had worked it out independently or had come across the information in some other way. By the time he got to the end of the second log book, he was in no doubt. Most of the meticulous measurements and the underlying theory were there as plain as one could see. All the equations and formulae were identical to those previously published by Clive just before his Nobel Prize.

The birth of little Robert Harry and then Alessandra left no room outside his scientific research for further action. Then, one day, in a documentary on the new BBC2 television channel, Robert saw Anthony Blunt, preening and fawning before the Queen. At the end of the programme, he had written down the name of the producer and director and telephoned the BBC the following day to establish when the footage had been taken.

'We shot that about a month ago. What's the interest?' The producer, Tristram Baldercock, was wily enough to recognise a hidden agenda.

'It's difficult for me to say, but I know a thing or two about Sir Anthony Blunt that you don't.'

'Don't count on it. I know things about Sir Anthony Blunt that we are not able to broadcast. When are you next in London?'

At Broadcasting House, a month later, Robert and Tristram sat in the BBC canteen with a cup of foul coffee each.

Robert kicked off. 'I have to be honest with you. It has to be off the record. I have signed the Official Secrets Act and this covers some, most, but not all of my knowledge of Blunt. It may take time to build up my confidence to tell everything. Have you got one of those new radio microphones under your shirt?'

Tristram smiled. He spread his arms wide to reveal two sweat patches under his arms, extending almost to his waistline.

'Are there any Turkish baths near here? Where we can talk in privacy? All you need to do is to have set someone up here to film me from a hidden camera. You don't even need a microphone, you just call in a professional lip-reader and transcribe it to paper.'

'Goodness me. You do have a story to tell, don't you. Why don't we go to the men's toilets where you can do a body search and then we can go for a walk in St James' Park where we can chat in privacy?'

It was the look of keen anticipation when Tristram mentioned the body search that led Robert to say. 'Let's go for the walk. I trust you.'

A week after his visit to the BBC, Robert had a return visit from Tristram in Manchester. Tristram had an assignment with BBC North West and they were able to talk on and off for three days. Robert had kept most of the details of Beethoven to himself. He had not even mentioned the code name, Beethoven, and if ever it cropped up, it would be from Tristram. Tristram never mentioned it. At the end of three days, Tristram was adamant that Clive Blackmore was a key element in any story and quite simply, not enough was known about him. The connection with Robert's grandfather's death sounded too much of a coincidence to be true.

'If you die in suspicious circumstances,' observed Tristram, 'and the nearest person turns out to be a spy and a traitor to the country, you can bet your bottom dollar it was not an accident. I feel it in my water.'

'So what can we do about it?'

'Two things. Firstly, I'm amazed you never spoke to those people who are still around. Bragg, Darwin, Marsden and James. They won't live forever and then the trail, already cold, will freeze over. That's something you can do. You know them. But secondly, there is bound to be a German angle. If the English never found a body, then the Germans probably dealt with it. It was war, but in that war, the Germans and the English respected each other's dead unless it was physically impossible. I have connections in German television. We can start something. Germany is not unknown to you, so it might need a visit or two from you.'

Robert went to Cambridge to see Bragg. He went to London to see Darwin. He wrote to Sir Ernest Marsden, now Chief Education Officer to the New Zealand government and to Professor James, now Vice Chancellor of Cape Town University. Bragg spoke kindly and with obvious affection for Robert's father. Despite the military experience and having firmly directed two outstanding Physics departments in Manchester and Cambridge, he became emotional when the conversation touched on the day after Robert White's death. His memory of all members of his team, Marsden, James, Blackmore, White, Perkins and the rest was incisive. Robert wrote notes, copiously and left with over ten pages of a detailed transcript of what Bragg had said.

Darwin was equally helpful and genial. He recalled the wartime interview with Robert's father, mentioning the General, now dead. As with Bragg, Robert led the conversation, but did not force it towards the relationship between his grandfather and other members of his team. The friendship and camaraderie of the team was paramount; they pulled together. There had been some abrasion between Clive and Robert in the early days, but Captain Bragg was having none of it and had stripped them both down in public. He had handled them both equally, apportioning no blame. They had behaved themselves thereafter as Bragg had also said.

From Marsden came a fifteen page handwritten letter of reminiscences. They were written so clearly, with conversations recalled verbatim, it might have been a recollection of the most recent war and not the Great one.

James' letter, almost twenty typewritten pages, flowed with humanity and fact. He likened the trenches to paradise after seeing his transport home from Shackleton's expedition crushed by the Antarctic ice and spending months in a small boat that should not have survived the storms. He had not been able to believe that God would have spared him from Antarctic ice, only to let him perish in the Belgian mud. James had corroborated the others and had added his own dimension.

The four transcripts taken together, gave a picture of a scientific team working almost as if in a laboratory. There had been no friction. There had been an atmosphere between Robert White and Clive and when this was combined with the statement of two of the four that Robert had never a hard word to say of anyone, but that somehow, everyone thought that Clive, for whatever reason, did not like him. But Bragg had kept it in check. Whatever happened between Clive and Robert, and assuming it had some connection with Robert's death, probably started in Manchester.

Robert wrote a "Geoffrey" scheme on his blackboard. As a scientist, he had to say that his first effort looked pathetic. He had a probably unknown event in Manchester, a hint of animosity in the trenches, which a few people had seen, but which had been extinguished. Then there was his grandfather's death. There were no facts from the Manchester days and few facts about the death. But Robert felt sure that a breakthrough on either of these two would link to the other. What happened in between, in the trenches, was a neutral interlude. It was a meagre conclusion. But it gave him focus. Then he returned to the blackboard with an inspired thought. In the box labelled "death of gf", he wrote a short sentence, "The only known facts are supplied by B." The sentence looked so significant, that he gave it a double outline. He doubted if anyone from the British side could supply anything into the box. He doubted if anyone could. Except Blackmore.

Blackmore knew and if he had lied, he would continue to lie unless he could be proved to be lying. The task looked impossible.

There was still one line to follow up. Bragg had told him that Chadwick, who was in Cambridge with Bragg before the second war, in the 1930s, had once spoken of a German whom he had known in the Berlin Institute just before the first war and with whom he had corresponded after the armistice. The German had been in the first war and been in action in the Somme. It was a long shot, almost all the men in Europe had been concentrated into a few square miles in the Somme in 1916. But this German had once mentioned Bragg's team. Bragg's team had been famous and the Germans knew of it.

Robert drove to North Wales where Chadwick lived in retirement. They sat and talked in a dark sitting room with Welsh rain slanting out of a grey Welsh sky, lashing, relentlessly against grey, glistening Welsh slate. Everything was dark, wet and shining grey. Chadwick still wrote to his former colleague about once a year. Eberhardt Geisler, Kantstrasse 190, Ratzeburg, Schleswig Holstein, West Germany. Robert had been struck by the extreme apparent nervousness of Chadwick. His hands had writhed and entwined. He had only relaxed briefly whenever he was pulling on his pipe.

'You really need to speak to Eberhardt. He spends most of his time at home now; like me, we are both getting on. But he says he's in the pink of health and stays at home because he likes it. Write to him. Go and see him. He will talk to you with the greatest of pleasure. He can talk for days about the Great War. If you want to know it all from the German side, talk to Eberhardt. I'll write and tell him you will be in touch if you like. Give me a few days head-start to write to him first.'

'Do you remember the department before that war? You were there with my grandfather and Dr. Blackmore as he was then.'

'Yes. I was just a research student doing an MSc. Your grandfather and Blackmore shared an office if I remember rightly. In those days, Blackmore was always making a fool of himself and we thought he wouldn't make the grade. There was that almost embarrassing business when he thought your grandfather was married to Miss White, Margaret the kite woman.'

'Did they get on together? My grandfather and Blackmore?'

'It's very hard to say from this distance of time. I always put it down to my memory after the war, but for a while, I was confused between the two of them. I always thought it was your grandfather working on the solid-state stuff, the semi-conductors, but it turned out it was Blackmore all the time. And look what he made of it. You can't ignore a Nobel Prize.'

Nobel prizewinner Chadwick allowed himself a wry smile. His fingers entwined and writhed. 'It's always easy to have the last word on something but it's much more difficult to have the first word. That's where the credit is due.'

'So you don't know what my grandfather was working on, in the department?'

'It must have been alpha particles. If you didn't come up with a good idea of your own, PROF Rutherford would give you something to work on concerning alpha particles. He liked them. They were his friends.'

'Who else do you know from those days? I've spoken to Bragg and Darwin and written to Marsden and James.'

'Hmmm, you've certainly done your homework. Kay died a few years ago. Jimmy Nuttall too. What about Dibblee, the little technician who went to Berlin with me. He came back eventually didn't he. Yes, Dibblee. He worked with Geiger again after the war after I returned home from Ruhleben. That's where I first met Eberhardt. He was the medical orderly at the internment camp at Ruhleben. He used to cackle when I said I missed a beer more than anything. Then Dibblee came back didn't he, soon after Hitler took over. That's right, I remember now. He married Miss Bauer of all people. She was a like a schoolmistress with him, always telling him what to do. I suppose she told him to marry her.'

'Dibblee. Yes, I heard of him and I have seen an old photo. Where is he now?'

'He's no chicken any more but he came in to see everyone during the Rutherford Jubilee Conference in 1961. Didn't you go to that?'

'Er no, I was in Germany at the time and I couldn't get away. What about Dibblee?'

'I remember, he was all smart and businesslike. He was running a jewellers shop in the city centre. He was an accredited goldsmith, no less.'

'What will he know about what happened before the Great War?'

'He seemed to know everything. If anyone wanted to know anything, they went to the pub and asked Dibblee.'

Robert found the jewellers, "Bauer and Dibblee", in an arcade between King Street and St Anne's Square in the centre of Manchester. Dr. Dibblee and Mrs. Natasha only came in on Saturday mornings. After a strenuous term as City Mayor, Cllr Dibblee was taking a rest from meeting people.

'Dr. White?' The distinguished, grey-haired almost military looking owner of "Bauer and Dibblee" extended a hand in greeting and ushered Robert into the inner sanctum where coffee was waiting. The aroma was heavy, almost a Germanic coffee house in its richness. An equally distinguished, grey-haired, almost military woman poured the coffee with a smile. Robert looked past them at the wall. There were certificates and photographs, in frames. There was a certificate announcing a doctorate at the Berlin Institute for Herr Doktor Thomas Alfred Dibblee. Next to it was another certificate naming Dr. T A Dibblee as the recipient of a degree from Göttingen University "Honoris Causa".

There was a photograph of a distinguished looking Dibblee, head bowed, receiving a blessing from the Pope. The centre piece was a journalist's award winning photograph of Dibblee, grinning from ear to ear in the winner's enclosure at Epsom with his horse "Swift Gold". The horse's upper lip was curled back to reveal a smile bigger than Dibblee's. In the background, walking past the enclosure, the Queen was looking back over her shoulder at the victory parade with a scowl.

Dr. and Mrs. Dibblee stared at Robert with a curious look of distant recognition.

'Have we met? I'm sure we have met.' Natasha was the first to speak.

'So am I.' Dibblee picked up the theme. 'Where was it? It feels as if it ought to have been Berlin, but that's a long time ago and it couldn't have been you, you're too young.'

'I think you knew my grandfather. My grandmother says I look exactly like him.'

'Your grandfather? Also called White? Not the Mr. Robert from the department before the war?' For Dibblee, like many others, there would only ever be one war.'

'Dr. White. I remember him. He was so handsome. He died didn't he, in the war.' Natasha's memory was also working hard.

'So what can we do for you, Mr. White? I'm sorry to call you Mr., but we called everyone Mr. in those days, and it seems so right, even now.'

'How well do you remember from then? Particularly my grandfather and Mr. Blackmore. Do you remember him?'

'Mr. Blackmore! I'll say. He was hard work. He married Brenda Wilkins. She could also be a bit difficult. She took a shine to your grandfather, I remember that. But he was already promised to that chemistry lady.' Dibblee failed to conceal a blush.

'Thomas, what is the matter with you?'

'Nothing, my dearest. The chemistry lady must be your grandmother, mustn't she? Well, when she couldn't have your grandfather, Brenda Wilkins snapped up Mr. Blackmore. It had never been good between your grandpa and Mr. Blackmore but after that, there were times when I knew things were far from right. I used to do the post every day and had to sort it in the back room. He'd come to talk to his missus, Mr. Blackmore that is, and your grandpa was often mentioned. She was always egging him on and using Mr. White, your grandpa, as a kind of stick. PROF, that's Mr. Rutherford, was very pleased with your grandfather's attitude and was always bellowing Mr. Blackmore out of his office. Mr. Blackmore and your grandfather shared an office on the top floor. I remember now. I used to go into the pub, the Nelsons and we would talk about it, the two Mr. Kays and me and the Polish gentlemen. Oh, those were the days. Mr. Geiger and Mr. Marsden were as thick as thieves, but you could not say that about your grandfather and Mr. Slimy as we used to call him.'

Robert wanted to take notes, it was flowing so fast.

'Look, Mr. White. It is nice to talk about those times. I think we should do it more comfortable surroundings. Shall we have lunch at the Midland? Café de Paris?'

Robert smiled in agreement. 'But only if you will agree to be my guests.'

'It started the day your grandfather and Mr. Blackmore arrived. They were both new. There was a big row between the Prof and Mr. Blackmore on the first day and it took some time for him, Mr. Blackmore that is, to settle after that. He got told to work on alpha particles while your grandfather got on measuring very small electric currents. I remember going round to Mr. Cook, that's Mr. Chas Cook, the instrument maker. He had a new gadget for measuring the small currents. Everyone else was only interested in volts. Big sparks. But your grandfather wanted to measure small currents, the smaller the better. You know the difference between volts and amps?'

'Oh yes! I married a volt.'

Robert knew he ought to stop teasing people like that, but he only had to think of Alessandra, to be reminded of her by a chance remark such as Dibblee's, and he swelled with pride. He explained.

'I know how you feel Mr. White. I married a bottle of carbon dioxide. If it weren't for that bottle . . .'

'Stop that Thomas. People aren't interested in how we met.'

'Oh yes they are Mrs. Dibblee. Without being rude and nosey, it's what being human is all about. Do go on about the carbon dioxide, Mr. Dibblee, if you don't mind Natasha!'

Lunch lasted three hours. Dibblee and Robert chose turtle soup, poached sole and chateaubriand. Natasha maintained her prim waistline with a prawn cocktail without mayonnaise and a portion of fillet of plaice. With the fish, they drank a Sancerre but as soon as the chateaubriand arrived, so did a bottle of Margaux, quickly followed by another as Natasha joined in.

'What I like best of all about a good Margaux,' Dibblee leaned back expansively, 'is that if you get started on it with the fillet steak, it takes you right through to the Roquefort. I hope you like Roquefort.'

The history of human and scientific relations in the department between 1912 and 1914 was unpeeled, layer after layer. From Dibblee's point of view, his input and knowledge ended when he left with Chadwick to go to Berlin. Robert was left with a dilemma, a growing mystery. Everything that Dibblee remembered seemed a contradiction. At one point Robert had interjected after Dibblee had recalled one measurement, or a claim by Robert's grandfather of a measurement.

'He came up to tea and said that he had cut a small cube of this stuff he was working on. Some sort of coke or coal, would you believe. I don't know what it was except that he was measuring this small electric current when he sent it from one side of the cube and picked it up on the other. He said it shouldn't matter which two faces you passed the current between, you could rotate the cube as much as you wanted, but the current ought to be the same. If it was a piece of metal, it was the same. And the currents were large with metals. But if it was this stuff, there were always two faces that were special. If you passed the current one way, it would be quite high, he said. But if you flipped the cube over and passed the current in the opposite direction, it was small.'

'But that must have been Blackmore who did that. That's what he became famous for.'

'I never got those two mixed up. There was no mistaking that Mr. Blackmore. He looked like a toad. I remember that day. I have good reason to remember it. Mr. White had just told us about it in the tea room. There was only me, Natasha and Mr. Kay. Then there was the business with the carbon dioxide bottle and not long after that, PROF insisted we all helped on one of his experiments counting scintillations. I left soon after and I don't know if there was any more work done on that. I don't know who else you could ask from those times. Darwin stayed on a bit, and Marsden or Andrade of course. Little Marsden and little Andrade. I haven't seen or heard of them since then.'

'I've spoken to some of them already. They told me about you. I think I may have to talk to them again. Something you said has got me very worried. I don't understand it at all. My grandfather should not have been measuring small electric currents, it had to be Blackmore. Surely the PROF didn't get them confused.'

'You'd think not, I agree. PROF never missed anything. But it was all happening just before the war and PROF and Geiger and Marsden had just done the nucleus stuff so they would have been a bit focussed on what they were doing and maybe distracted on your grandfather and Blackmore. Then everyone went away before it was cleared up and your grandfather never came back. Sorry, I didn't mean it like that.'

'That's all right. I wasn't alive then.'

'Of course, you could always go and talk to Mr. Blackmore. I saw his photograph in the paper the other day. He hasn't changed much has he?'

'I don't know! I never saw him in those days.'

'Of course. It's just sometimes I think of you as old Mr. Robert. You do look alike.'

Eberhardt Geisler was next on the list. Robert flew into Hamburg, one of his favourite cities and the place where he had been working when he had been intercepted by the East. He had called Klaus, a friend from work days whom he had met in the local Sportverein he had joined to be able to play football. Klaus had been the club football coach and although about 10 years older than Robert, the two had got on like bosom pals. He had an open invitation to stay with Klaus and his wife Anka, whenever he visited Hamburg. More relevant to Robert's immediate needs, Klaus' job was taxi-driver and he was needed for the journey to see Geisler in Ratzeburg.

Geisler had replied to Robert's letter within a week; he had produced three pages of handwritten German gothic script which had taken all of Robert's skills to first transliterate into familiar letters and then to translate. Geisler had said he would be happy to meet Robert and talk about those days in the Great War that he remembered so well. They now sat in the full blast of a hot August afternoon, made tolerable by the breeze coming off the Ratzeburg lake that formed the panorama in front of Geisler's terrace. Eberhardt Geisler was proud of his view and wanted everyone to share his pride. His wife Martha had come like a waitress to enquire what they would like to drink,

'Kaffee? Tee?'

Geisler waved her away.

'Two ice cold beers, Martha. You should know by now.'

Martha, as usual, wanted to enquire what the gentleman visitor would like, instead of being ordered to drink a beer by the boss. Robert sensed the situation and knew he could not undermine Geisler's order but he was sure that Frau Geisler would be proud of her tea assortments and was anxious to show them off.

'A tea later would be nice.' Robert compromised.

'Tea on beer will make you queer.

Beer on tea I counsel thee!'

Geisler's paraphrasing of the standard German aphorism about wine and beer into English caught Robert by surprise. He knew he was in for an interesting session and old though Geisler was, he cut through the situation like a razor.

The beer was perfect. Frau Geisler might prefer to serve tea, but she knew how to prepare a perfect pilsner from the bottle. The head was stiff and creamy and held up as the liquid was drunk over the next ten minutes. A second appeared without asking and with the immediate thirst quenched, was sipped more leisurely.

'Thiepval. Ah yes. No one there will ever forget it. It doesn't matter what you did, how trivial, everything becomes etched into the memory for ever. It is like yesterday.'

Robert was writing as fast as he could.

'You have one problem. All the reports sent back daily, which included the official details of what happened that day, were destroyed by the bombs on Berlin. I checked that for you yesterday. I called the offices in Berlin. They have perfect records of all the things they no longer have. That is German Order, Deutsche Ordnung. Most people don't know what they haven't got, but we Germans do.'

'So you can't help me after all?'

'Not so fast, young man. I would not let you waste your time if I had nothing for you. The official records may be lost, but I have my diary. I wrote it every day during that war. I thought I would write a book, but somehow, I never found the time.'

'Maybe this is the time, if something interesting crops up.'

'We'll see. Now you did not tell me the date that your father died. That may not be necessary.'

Eberhardt held up his hand to stop Robert telling him. He wanted the drama. He reached to the floor hidden from Robert's view by the table and picked up a worn leather bound and well-thumbed volume. There was a bookmark half way through and Eberhardt gently opened the book at the place. Robert could not resist looking over at the tight, economical script, the hand-writing almost unchanged from the style he had read from the letter. Except it was half the size, to save pencil and paper. Eberhardt pushed the volume across the table.

'Do you want to read it yourself?'

'I could, but it would take me too long. I was able to read your letter, on my own, eventually, but that looks very small writing.'

Eberhardt screwed a monocle into his left eye, a glass golf ball. He turned to look at Robert, the pupil filling the whole aperture of the eye-glass. His eyes were still the cleanest of blues.

'My suspicion is that your father died during the night of the twenty-third and twenty-fourth of September, 1916. Near Thiepval Wood, in the Somme.'

In that moment, Robert knew that Eberhardt had in his possession, everything that he needed to know about his grandfather's death. He possibly knew as much as Blackmore, who was unlikely to tell the true side of his story.

'I was then, as I told you in the letter, a medical orderly. I had many duties. Treating minor wounds, deciding on those that were likely to become serious if the person was not moved to the field hospital and of course, most important in order to save all the resources, those who would die within hours no matter what. During that night, there was little bombardment. I was awake and on duty, dealing with minor complications of previous wounds and of course, checking that everyone was taking appropriate precautions against trench foot. Trench foot could wipe out more men in a day than your English guns.'

Robert wanted to correct him and say "British guns" but knew from years of experience that to the Germans, the British were "English".

'Suddenly, there was a flash and a bang, not one hundred meters far from our trench. The experts said later that it must have been a grenade because they saw no distant gun flash and they heard no whistling of a shell. And of course, the real experts said that the sound was a grenade, an English one. I confirmed it was a grenade, an English one and I wrote it in my diary.'

Robert was writing. He did not need to ask how Eberhardt knew it was a grenade, a British grenade, because he knew that Eberhardt was meticulous and everything would be in the diary and the diary would tell him everything. Then Eberhardt would inevitably explain why it was not only a grenade, but an English one, a British one.

'We did nothing until daylight. Even then we looked cautiously. Eventually, I was taken to the place of the incident to make a report on the deceased, an English soldier.'

There was a long silence. Robert did not wish to hurry Eberhardt unless his memory became erratic. After half a century, there was no rush.

'You know, in war, when someone dies, someone you know, a colleague, you may not cry. You have to look and accept it as a consequence of war. People, individual men, fathers, sons, brothers, they become a continuum. You talk of how many were lost but only later, who. So when I see the body of an enemy, I must be neutral. It would be someone who could kill me if they had the opportunity. But still, they will be someone's husband, father or son or brother. So one must be human and respectful. Your grandfather had died within a fraction of a second and he would have known absolutely nothing about it. I can promise you that. He was killed by the force of an explosion behind him, that removed most of his spinal column and the lower part of his body. It was a clean death in the sense that the dying would have had no duration. There was part of an identification disk, the centre, because the edges were melted. The digits 491 were still readable. You will want to check it against the number that your government war department will be able to tell you.'

Robert already knew his grandfather's number. There was a match. The number alone was almost confirmation in itself, unless everyone at the Somme that day had 491 in the middle of their number.

'From his facial appearance, which was peaceful, I would put his age in the middle twenties. His hair was black. His teeth were good; every one, including all of the wisdom teeth, were in place. He wore the uniform of an English captain in your Royal Engineers. I knew all the uniforms. There were no personal belongings in the pockets that remained. Now for the artefacts. There was a wire, twenty meters in length nearby. The end nearest the body had melted. The other end was cut sharp as if with a knife. The remains of an English grenade were impacted in the body and the ground nearby.'

Robert could contain himself no longer.

'How could you be so sure that it was English, British, when it had exploded?'

'Not difficult. There were fragments that I collected and I needed only five minutes later on to put them together. The casing was one of yours and the number was one of yours.'

'The number? You have German grenade numbers and English ones? Surely not.'

'Essentially yes. The number seven in German is the normal one with the strich, the stroke across. You English don't write it like that. You write it almost like a German "one", and as for the number ones, when you write them, you make a simple stroke without the rising serif. This grenade had an English seven on it. But I didn't need that, it was already English from the shape.'

'And then, the body? What happened to my grandfather's body?'

'He received a decent burial, there, where he had fallen. We buried him as deeply as we could, said a prayer and placed a small cross of wood. He has rested in peace for over fifty years.'

The sun had lowered across the lake and Robert now had both the direct sun and its reflection off the mirror surface of the lake directly in his eyes. It was a hot sultry German August evening without a trace of wind. Eberhardt knew his home well enough to be sensitive to Robert's sudden discomfort.

'Come, sit round the opposite side of the table. You've seen enough of our lake. Now you can look into my garden.' He turned himself to look into the house. 'Martha! Noch zwei Bierchen für uns beide!'

Martha had been as sensitive to her husband's pending discomfort as he had been to Robert's. The bottles were already out of the special beer fridge in the cellar and were ready to pour. She used clean glasses and took the old ones away to wash immediately.

'Take a pause, young man. Enjoy your beer and think over what you have heard for a few minutes. You need to make sure that you collect everything you need into your head and your notebook. I have just read you my notes from that day and I can tell you, I remember the events as if they were yesterday. They were so unusual.'

Robert sipped the beer in silence, enjoying the cold dry bitterness of the Friesian pilsener. He turned over the information he had received. By now he had become efficiently analytic when talking to these memories of the past. It was best to let them do most of the talking, with an occasional nudge. It was a mistake to make suggestions; the old minds had a tendency to agree with the suggestion whether it were right or wrong, just to move on the conversation.

'Did you know what they were doing? The team that my father belonged to?'

'Oh yes. We knew they were working on something involving microphones and the sound of our guns. We both used flash spotters to see the direction of the guns, but we knew they were up to something else. Chadwick told me all about it later. He wasn't there of course. He found himself in Berlin when the war began, lucky man.'

'Lucky?'

'Well I think it was lucky to start that war with almost a 100% chance of living through it. If your grandfather had gone to Berlin with Chadwick, he might be alive today even.'

Robert stayed another half an hour, to clarify some details and to probe what he had already heard in case Eberhardt's memory was letting him down. All he established was that old Eberhardt was still as sharp as a cut-throat razor.

Klaus was waiting where he had left him an hour and a half ago. There was a pile of eleven cigarette ends in the gutter on the side of the road. Klaus was well into the twelfth. On the way back to Hamburg, Robert used Klaus as a foil to check his understanding of the events in Thiepval. Everything was now in place.

'That night, my grandfather and this guy Blackmore set out on an unauthorised mission to measure the distance to enemy trenches.'

'Unauthorised? So who suggested it?'

'Don't know, and in any case, only one survived and he isn't telling the truth. The two of them carry a roll of wire, unroll it eventually, someone rolled it back in. No one checked the length or even the condition of the end. A piece of that wire got left behind. Why? Because the far end was trapped under rubble from the explosion and Blackmore cut it off.'

'OK, that doesn't mean much. You can't match up the two ends of the wire, the one that the Germans got and the one that came back.'

'No. There is an explosion. Blackmore scampers back unharmed but my grandfather has half his body blown off. The German evidence is very strong; it was an English grenade. Blackmore came back and said they were fired on and he never saw his colleague again in the dark. That is a very big lie. The Germans were having a nap and knew nothing till the grenade went off. Whose grenade was it? How could Blackmore have a grenade? Could my grandfather have had one and it went off by accident? They weren't issued with grenades. I think I am going to talk to the one remaining person from those days I haven't spoken to yet. That's if he is still alive. I've got to find him. Sergeant Perkins. Bragg told me about him. He thinks he still lives in Aldershot where he grew up. He might not be easy to find, an army man amongst all the army men in Aldershot, but there can only be a limited number of army Perkins, even in Aldershot.

It was the fourteenth phone call to a Perkins that did it.

'I'm sorry to bother you at home, Mr. Perkins, but I am trying to find Sergeant Wilbert Perkins who was at Thiepval in 1916.'

'You've found him. What can I do for you?' The voice sounded like mud.

Perkins was able to do a lot.

'I never did like him, far too smug. He wasn't insubordinate, but his whole manner showed that if it wasn't a war, he would be.'

'What do you think about my grandfather being killed by a British grenade?'

'I'd say impossible from what I recall of that night; unless one of them had it with them. The whole job that night was botched. They had no authority to do what they were doing.'

'Do you have any notes? A diary?'

'Notes lad? A diary? No, I had no time to write things down for my own use; too many official reports to send in. But I've got a very good memory for things like that. You see, that Blackmore said it was your grandpa's idea for the night sortie. That makes him a blaggard as well. If it was his own idea and his mate got killed, a real soldier would own up to it. If it was your mate's idea, then you'd take the cop if anything went wrong. So there's only one conclusion and I always thought it. It was Blackmore's idea and he is a liar.'

Robert waited three seconds before gently demolishing Perkins' logic. 'Or else he was telling the truth and he is a swine.'

After another pause of three seconds, Perkins fought back.

'What are you defending him for? I thought you'd want to bring him down.'

'I do want to bring him down, but I want to do it with the truth. I must get at the truth if it is there to be got at. Where could the grenade have come from? Were they issued with them?'

'No. They had no access. They had no need. We didn't have grenades, working on the sound ranging. The only time they came near any grenades was when those two and me were sweeping the MacFadzean trench.'

'What was that about?'

'There was a trench where there had been an accident. A box of grenades had fallen into the trench and Private MacFadzean had got blown to bits. Some of the ordnance got scattered in the blast and they'd had to leave in a hurry before they'd had a chance to find them all. That Blackmore found one. I was sure there must be more.'

'So he did have a grenade.'

'No, no. He wasn't allowed to keep it! I took charge of that. But he was on his own when he found it and he could have found two or more and kept one. Dammit. I should have searched them both after that exercise. Trouble is, these officer toffs kick up a fuss if their honesty is questioned. You can't search a toff.'

'He wasn't a toff. Neither was my grandad.'

'No, but the other one behaved like a toff, even if your grandpa didn't.'

'Everything fits into place now. I think I have everything. I wonder if he has the guts to admit it when it's all laid before him.'

'It's a bit late for a court martial isn't it? The army doesn't like dragging things up from wars that are long since gone. It's over fifty years. They'll say no one can remember.'

'You just said you can remember everything.'

'I can, but when they say no one can remember it's because they don't want them to.'

'Anyway, it won't be a court martial. I have other ideas. Sergeant Major Perkins, you've been a huge help. I will be straight with you. I won't do anything or use the information without letting you know and clear it first. I might need you again.'

~ ~ ~

Over a long lunch, Tristram found it hard to contain his excitement.

'I feel like a dog with three tails and I want to wag them all! I've already put it to Richard and he is ready for action. After what Richard did to Savundra, it seems to have given him a taste for blood as well. We had thought we would get both Blackmore and Blunt in for a discussion on art and science through the ages, from their Cambridge days. No holds barred. But Blunt won't co-operate. He's adamant. No matter, we are making it a pilot for a series on Nobel prize-winners. We'll have your Eberhardt chap flown over from Germany and the Sergeant Perkins brought up from Aldershot if we can persuade him. Richard will have everything at his fingertips. He will be more thorough than any judge. He won't let them wriggle out.'

Chapter 21

Saffron Walden 1967

Sir Clive took down the well-thumbed copy of 'Who's Who' from his bookshelf. There was a dark line showing where the book had been perpetually opened at the same place, half way through the Bs. Despite its girth, the tome fell open at the usual page, the spine almost split at Blackmore.

> **BLACKMORE, Sir Clive Samuel,** Kt., cr. 1936. M.A. Ph.D. D.Sc. F.R.S. 1929; Professor of Physics, University of Cambridge 1936–62; Hon. D.Sc. (Bristol, Aberdeen, and Lisbon); *b.* 29 Feb. 1895; *s.* of late Silas Blackmore; *m.* 1922, Brenda Wilkins, *er. d.* of Albert Wilkins, 6 Gas Street, Wigan. *Educ:* Queen Eliz Grammar School Blackburn; University of London. Harling Fellow, University of Manchester; Lecturer in Physics, University of London. Nobel Prize for Physics 1934. Technical advisor on Sound Ranging to Map Section G.H.Q., France 1915–19. (promoted lieutenant). Member Sci War Advis Comm 1940–45. Dir. D.S.I.R, 1945–50. Chief Sci Adv to H.M.G. 1955–60. *Recreation:* tennis. *Address:* The Hollies, Rowcroft Lane, Saffron Walden. *Club:* Athenaeum.

Clive had looked as his entry almost every day since getting his Nobel Prize, and then his knighthood and chair at Cambridge in 1936. Brenda kept a copy at home and wouldn't let Clive touch it with his sweaty fingers. She dusted it every day, bringing it out from time to time at one of her tea parties to cluck over Lady or Dame Doo-dah. Clive had to make do with an old copy and looking at the stripe of grime marking the location of his entry, he thought it was time to get a new one for Brenda. He could then have hers. As usual, he pursed his lips at the details of Brenda's father. When the letter from Who's Who first arrived, soon after he won the Nobel prize, Brenda had gone to the local library to read through the typical entries. She had written out his biography and had indicated the strong possibility of a resumption of conjugal rights if her father could get a mention, as many fathers clearly did. Thirty years later, he was still waiting. He had checked up himself and had indeed found many fathers. But they were invariably former or present entries in Who's Who with titles, ranks or achievements.

Albert had none of these. In the words of Ecclesiasticus, apart from leaving behind Brenda and an entry in Who's Who, Albert had perished as if he had never been. Sir Clive then turned to the letter he had received from the private secretary at the palace.

```
Dear Sir Clive,
    Her Majesty is mindful to address
questions concerning the recognition of
those whose contribution to the war effort
has become more and more appreciated in
recent years, especially where reasons
of National Security have precluded their
earlier recognition.
```

Clive's little remaining hair above his ears stood up in anticipation. Was this the long awaited call to the peerage? Her Majesty's agent continued, and Clive's few hairs fell limply in acute disappointment.

```
        Highly respected sources close to Her
Majesty have mentioned, on more than one
occasion, the name of Professor Harold
White of Oxford University, who was
engaged on highly secret work at Bletchley
during the regrettable hostilities.  Her
Majesty would be pleased to receive your
valued opinion about the intention to
reward the Professor's contribution with
the due process.  Your confidentiality in
handling this enquiry is expected by Her
Majesty.
```

Clive allowed the letter to flutter to the carpet. He looked down at it with the annoyance, irritation and almost anger that the thought of another White catching up with him in the honours race had induced in him. He couldn't help speaking out loud.

'Damn you young White. I can't let this happen. Not before my peerage.'

Clive still lived easily with evil thoughts. He turned his attention to the procedures required to diminish Harry White's chances, without appearing to be visibly out on a limb. White had his admirers, and undermining his support would need all the skills that years of scheming had brought to Blackmore. He mopped his brow with the towel kept in his study for that purpose and reached for the phone.

'Good morning, Anthony. You owe me a favour, remember? You still have the ear of the Queen, I suppose. Despite everything?'

'Sir Anthony! What is it? We ought to keep our contact to a minimum. I'm not too happy about that TV programme with Dimbleby next week. What happens if it goes out of control?'

'Why should it go out of control? It's just a debate about science and art.'

'Art and science. They said there would be others there and yet I haven't been able to find out who the others are. I don't like it.'

'Well, I'm sure they can find someone else if you are not up for it. But I thought a nice polished performance would do your image no harm at all, especially given current rumours about you. Anyway, that's not why I called. I wonder if you can make sure that the right people know the truth about a person who is being considered for a minor gong. It wouldn't be right if he got it. It would make everything wrong and send out the wrong messages.'

'The Queen doesn't decide these things. She doesn't even sign the letter. There is a committee that makes the decisions, but stop worrying. The chairman is a member of my club.'

Then Sir Anthony decided to be blunt. 'OK, what's his name? One of your rivals I assume. What's he done to you? Shagged Brenda?'

~   ~   ~

Chapter 22

Panorama 1967

Tristram now turned his full attention onto Clive and was displaying all his skills, making the potential victim feel proud, secure and overconfident.

'I'll come to Cambridge to see you. We can talk through the details.'

'Will Mr. Dimbleby be coming with you as well?'

'Oh no Sir Clive, Richard doesn't get involved until much later and I need to get the full picture from you so that I can appraise him.'

'Sir Anthony isn't going to take part is he?' Clive whined.

Clive knew Blunt well enough to know that he would have spun a story to cover his reluctance to appear on the show and wanted to know what he had said.

'No, he's not going to be on the show, but that isn't really a problem because we really wanted to focus on you and use Sir Anthony as a kind of artistic foil to your science. You weren't contemporaries of course, but you are both Cambridge men, aren't you?'

'Yes, yes, true blue; light blue of course.'

'Look, Sir Clive, we've had a thought. You have known your wife since the very early days haven't you? Since the early days in Manchester even. We'd very much like her on the show, adding the family touch, as it were, to your scientific achievements.'

Although Clive felt a surge of comfort at the thought of being accompanied into the lion's den of television with someone he knew, he wasn't sure he could trust her. He knew Brenda too well and doubted her ability to cope with live television.

'Can we discuss that when we meet? When are you coming?'

'I was hoping for early next week, Sir Clive, if that is OK with you.'

Robert had already done his preparation. He had to condense all the discussions with Bragg, Chadwick, Dibblee, Perkins and Geisler into a series of headings. He was not going to mention any of these names on Panorama because it would betray the confidence of his discussions with them. Eberhardt Geisler himself would appear. Perkins would not. The golden rule was that anything Robert said on the programme had to be backed up with provable truth or a reliable witness. He had an hour-long discussion with BBC lawyers where the laws of libel and the consequences of a lawsuit were spelled out to him. Anything he said on the night that went beyond what he was saying now, would be his total responsibility, no matter what the legal cost. Robert had no wish to face financial ruin.

Robert was ushered in to the Green Room where Tristram was sitting with Eberhardt and a stranger. Tristram was listening as the other two were talking in German. He waved Robert over and whispered into his ear.

'Prof. Bancroft from Oxford is just getting the tone of Eberhardt's accent. He is going to do the live translations. It would be better of course with a professional translator, but using an Oxford don gives us more gravitas, don't you think?'

Robert nodded. Eberhardt paused and stood up to click heels and shake Robert's hand.

'Schön – nochmal zu treffen, Junge!'

Bancroft started to translate but Eberhardt cut him short.

'Er spricht gut Deutsch.'

'Good to see you here, Eberhardt!'

Bancroft wandered off for a coffee and Eberhardt began to eye up the beer, fumbling with the unfamiliar can and wondering how cold beer could possibly find itself inside a warm canister. He inserted his monocle and peered at the label.

'What is this Wort'ington E? Is it a beer? Why is it so hot?'

'Ah, I'll get some ice to cool the stuff down, Eberhardt. They always forget the ice because the English like warm beer. It will be nice and cold by the end of the show. We're on in 30 minutes, so best to wait.'

Eberhardt frowned and watched Tristram as he left the room. Tristram was not going for ice; he needed to hold Clive and Brenda's hands during the minutes leading up to the start of the programme. They were being kept in a small room near the studio floor.

'All ready, Sir Clive? And Lady Blackmore? Looking forward to your television debut? You will have plenty to talk about with your friends tomorrow. Not many people get to be interviewed by Richard Dimbleby on Panorama.'

'3, 2, 1, roll.'

The characteristic rhythmic opening music of Panorama caused Brenda to look around in panic, wondering where the music was coming from. The floor manager, who had placed himself in Brenda's line of sight, made gentle pacifying gestures with his hands and gave her an encouraging smile. Eyes and teeth.

'Calm down.' He mouthed. He also put two fingers into the sides of his mouth and pulled his face into a smile. Brenda rarely smiled and so she did not know what to do. The vision mixer cut to a close-up of Dimbleby who ran through the programme's contents. The camera pulled back to a mid shot as he started to talk about the Nobel Prizes of science and then there was a cut to a close-up of Clive and Brenda as their names were mentioned. Back to Dimbleby, who started the interview.

'Did the Nobel Prize change your life?'

It was a simple question but it caught Clive unawares. He had been told the questioning would start with him being asked to confirm the year he won the prize and when he got his knighthood. The prize had changed his life, but the fact that the prize never led to his greatest unfulfilled prize, the Cavendish Chair, was something he did not want to talk about. Yet there it was at the front of his thoughts, blocking out a coherent answer.

'Well, it got me a lot of invitations to dinner.' It was possibly the first joke that Clive had ever cracked in his life, although he was completely unaware of doing it.

'What about you, Lady Blackmore, did it change your life?'

All Brenda could think of was vacuum cleaners, carpets and the house in Saffron Walden. So that is what she said. It was not a good start from both of them. The nation was tittering in front of their 13 inch black and white television screens. After a minute of sparring about the scientific content of Clive's work, which Dimbleby had no intention of following up, the first blow landed on Clive's chin.

'Sir Clive, to what extent did you build on the early work of your Manchester colleague, Dr. Robert White. Didn't he start the work off on these semi-conductors before the first world war?'

The camera had already been instructed to close tightly on Clive before Dimbleby had finished posing the question. Three million viewers saw Clive's mouth open briefly, his eyes protrude and a swathe of sweat form on his forehead. It was as if a switch had been thrown and once again, Clive's endocrinology was about to let him down. He started to reach for his handkerchief, but Brenda, alert to Clive's normal response to his malfunctioning sweat glands, restrained his hand. He turned, annoyed and only stopped himself with difficulty from asking her what she thought she was doing; it was his normal response.

'None of my colleagues in Manchester published any work on that subject before I did and they were all working on other things. At that time, only Manchester and Cambridge were doing any effective physics research in Universities in this country and I was not aware of anything at Cambridge in those pioneering days. Of course, I took my research with me when I moved to London in 1926.'

'But you are aware of the *White files* aren't you? The notebooks recently discovered in Manchester?'

Clive, of course, knew of no such thing. Nor did he expect this line of questioning. The first coalescing drop of sweat gathered on the tip of his nose, swelled until the force of gravity overcame the cohesive force of surface tension that had allowed the droplet to cling to Clive's skin. Around the country, millions put down their newspapers, books, football pool coupons, knitting and cocoa, sensing the drama.

'I remember clearly when I came back from the war. I had shared an office with Robert White and I was given the job of returning his books and things to his widow. There were notebooks among them. She was given them then and I don't know what she did with them. They will show clearly what he was working on. I did not read them but I know for a fact they could not contain anything about semi-conductors because Dr. White was working on other things.'

Clive thought it best not to say he had read them, even though he had written the ones given to the widow Mary himself; it would have sounded like an intrusion into the personal effects of a dead colleague. Dimbleby moved on, but not before he delivered a blow to the solar plexus. He reached out and touched two notebooks on the desk in front of him, on the far side of Clive. They were too far away for Clive to read the covers, but near enough for him to recognise the dark blue covers, the green spine and the University crest.

'Yes, we have the books that were returned to Dr. White's widow; they are currently being examined by hand-writing experts. But the discovery I mentioned relates to two earlier books that were found recently in the cellar when a building was being cleared. I suppose someone will sort this out; we can't do it here.'

Clive's mind was racing out of control. He stared at the books and wanted to grab them. He was on the edge of panic and was trapped in the glare of millions of British television viewers. Brenda was blinking, unaware of the awesome significance of what had just been said and shown. Two more drops of sweat dropped off Clive's forehead, joined by another from his nose. The camera moved in to pick up the splashes on the table in front of Clive and then slowly moved up and in to fill the screen with his forehead, awash with a deluge of sweat. Tristram had agonised about the ethics of withholding from Clive, the make-up aids like powder that stopped Dimbleby's bald head from shining under the lights. He had wondered if Hitler would ever have been allowed his barber to trim his moustache and slick his hair if ever he had stood trial after the war. Tristram decided that Hitler would have, or else he would not have looked like Hitler. Therefore he should not take steps to make Clive not look like Clive. Let him sweat.

'Camera 3, stay back and switch to your long lens. Stay focussed on that forehead and the sweat puddle. Camera 2, don't get too close, don't crowd him. Good. Cut to 3.'

The director, Hugh Baldercock was quietly using talkback to his camera crew to get the dramatic pictures. The vision mixer on his left was cutting to his instruction. The trainee director, Jenny, was taking everything in and waiting for her promised two minutes of real directing during a quiet period.

'Sir Clive. It is true, isn't it, that you were with Dr. White the night he died. That night in the Somme, near Thiepval.'

'Yes it is. That is well known. What's that . . .'

Dimbleby cut in before Clive could ask about the relevance of the question.

'So you know how he died. You were there.'

'No. It was dark. There was a flash and a bang and mud everywhere. When that happens, you have to run if you can.

Anyway, it was a long time ago. You're lucky I can remember anything.'

'Most of us would remember the moment a colleague was killed right under our nose, wouldn't they? For the rest of their lives. So you didn't stay to find out if anything had happened to your colleague. Did you call out? Medals are awarded for bravery when a soldier stops to check out his wounded or dead colleague. Didn't you fancy a Victoria Cross, or even the eighth medal in order of precedence, a Conspicuous Gallantry Medal ahead of the Nobel medal?' Dimbleby's researcher had done her job well.

'We were yards from the enemy trenches. If we had spoken they would have got us.'

'So you don't know how he died?

'No. It was never established. He was declared "Missing in Action" and later officially and legally presumed dead.'

'But I know how he died. Or at least the German army does. He died as a result of injuries sustained from the explosion of a British hand grenade. A few yards from the enemy trenches, as you say. What was a British hand grenade doing a few yards from enemy trenches? Were you issued with them.'

'Of course not. It sounds to me as if he had one. Sometimes people found them and stashed them away; a kind of extra security. I never saw any. Possibly he had one and it went off. It's a very sad way to go and I hope his family can cope with your wild speculations.'

'If he did have one, then it is curious that German records show that the explosion took place behind him and severely injured his back.'

The mention of the phrase "German records" was a punch to the side of Clive's head. He was rocking from side to side and shaking the sweat off his brow.

'What German records? There aren't any German records.'

Dimbleby did not answer. He reached out again and picked up Eberhardt's notebook, turning the cover so that viewers could see the eagle embossed on the front cover.

'And what has all this got to do with my Nobel Prize? That's what we came to talk about.'

'Why don't you tell us what it has to do with your Nobel Prize. It is all part and parcel of the lead up to your prize isn't it?'

'I suggest we stick to the point.'

Dimbleby switched tack and once again, stunned Clive and this time, Brenda too.

'We shall move on. In the years after the award of your prize, the German, Ilse Kresser played an increasingly important role in your life. Where did you first meet.'

For the first time, Dimbleby unknowingly had lost control of the line of questioning. His brief was that Ilse Kresser would be the lead into Clive's espionage. He had no way of knowing what would happen next and what he had just triggered.

'I don't know anyone called Ilse Kresser. Where do you get that from?'

Brenda had turned to face Clive, to confront him as she always did when he annoyed her. It was as if Clive were answering her and not Dimbleby with his denial of Ilse.

'What do you mean you don't know her?' she screeched. 'Do you think I am stupid? You were always on the phone to her, in German, and having it off whenever you were away. Don't lie to me.'

Clive could not handle the sudden attack from Brenda. His mind was racing in several directions at once and he could not keep up with any. He briefly wondered how Brenda knew about the telephone conversations and what she could have gathered listening to one side of a conversation outside his study door. His mouth switched into the opening and shutting mode, a startled fish. Sweat was now dripping from the sides of his forehead. The splashes on the table had become a small pool. He strove to recover a single train of thought.

'Shut up woman, you don't know what you are talking about.'

Clive wanted the interview to end. But he also wanted to fight back and end it on his terms. His thoughts on the notebooks and grenade had finally caught up with him.

'I have to say, and make it very clear tonight, I had nothing to do with Dr. White's death, except that we both happened to be on a mission that went horribly wrong. It happens in war. You have come here with a cock and bull story about notebooks and British grenades after a period of more than 50 years. It is unfair to expect me to disprove that in front of you. It is unprovable and in any case, I have nothing to disprove. The fact that I can't disprove a speculation does not make it true.'

On cue, Dimbleby looked over to his left. Two BBC floormen, wearing khaki dust coats walked awkwardly onto the set and slid away the screen that was next to Clive and Brenda. Clive and Brenda found themselves staring at Robert and the old German World War I veteran medical orderly Eberhardt. Brenda stared at the face of Robert White in shock. She had not seen it since 1914. Clive had not seen it since that night in 1916 at Thiepval, apart from once on Dresden station.

'Sir Clive and Lady Blackmore, I think we have some proof. May I introduce ...'

Dimbleby never finished his sentence. Clive got to his feet and hissed. 'I did not agree to this! Never. How dare you?'

Dimbleby heard instructions from an unfamiliar female voice in his ear and turned to face camera 1. Jenny was starting her two minutes. Hugh had thought everything was going to plan and he could relax and enjoy a quick cigarette in the corridor.

'Tonight, ladies and gentlemen, we may find out that we have seen the lies fall like drops of sweat. Now it seems, he is not prepared to face the cold arrow of truth and its consequences.'

First Brenda and then Clive lost control. Brenda picked up the tumbler of water in front of her and threw the lot at Dimbleby. The glass bounced off his broad forehead, leaving behind a small cut. Blood began to flow. Even a small cut can produce a lot of blood. On camera 1, it looked like a lot of blood. More blood than Clive's sweat and much more than Brenda's tears. Clive seized Brenda to restrain her and she turned to slap him in the face, screaming.

'Leave me alone you vile creature! How many times do I have to tell you not to touch me?'

Dimbleby moved round his desk and tried to separate them. Suddenly all three were grappling and shouting. It looked like a fight, but wasn't. At this moment, the BBC resembled a submarine when a depth charge had gone off nearby, water pouring in through the hatches, klaxons going off and everyone panicking. At such a moment, it is the captain who counts. He is the only one who can save the ship by asserting his authority and control. But who was the captain at the BBC at this decisive moment? It should have been the director, Hubert, in control of the gallery, who was directing what going out from the studio. He was in charge of the gallery. Unfortunately for the BBC, the vague demarcation lines between director and producer played a decisive role. The best producers sit at the back of the gallery, if they are there at all, and let the director get on with directing the show. Tristram could not resist leaping to his feet and asserting his authority. The argument between Hubert and Tristram started as the debacle began and it continued for weeks. The vision mixer, young Val, was having an affair with the director and would do anything that he told her. But no instructions came. In any case, the vision mixer does what the director says, even if he is not sleeping with her and has no role of captaincy. In the absence of directions, Val left the feed on a mid shot with Clive, Brenda and Dimbleby grabbing and pushing each other. The trainee director Jenny, seizing her two minutes and the moment, and seeing the lack of direction from the director, kept up a quiet and authoritative talk-back to camera and crew. With the vision mixer at her elbow, she became the captain of the submarine, directing it, the BBC, into uncharted waters.

'Keep rolling!' she told the cameramen. 'Keep rolling. Camera 2, go in close on Richard, pull tight focus on the blood. Val, cut to 2. Sound, don't pull any plugs, we want to hear everything.'

Val, the cameramen and the sound engineers all did as they were told and TV history was made.

The Director General of the BBC was sitting at home in Kensington on his leather studded chesterfield. It was a full minute of shock before he took control of his quivering hands and picked up the telephone. He could not get through on the direct line to his own office. It was permanently engaged.

'Who the devil is in there, on my phone?' He demanded of himself.

His office was empty anyway and its phone was engaged because it was ringing continuously as all the top brass called the DG, who of course, was not there to answer. Six months later, he was unable to offer the internal BBC enquiry a good reason why his first action when things went wrong was to telephone himself. He also was unable to contact the gallery because he had to go through the main BBC switchboard, which was also jammed. Like a retired admiral in his deck chair on the cliffs of Dover on D-day, the DG was impotent and emasculated, a nobody of the moment. Both the transmission controller and the continuity announcer had difficulties at the enquiry. They could have saved the day. They could have been acting captains of the ship. But with twenty five minutes of the scheduled programme still to count down, they had both slunk out into the stairwell to have a quick cigarette. When Tristram had finally seized the talkback microphone off Jenny, and shouting for the transmission controller to cut to the caption 'Normal service will be resumed as soon as possible', there was no one there to do it. He had yelled into a vacuum.

With hindsight, Tristram realised that the presence of Robert and the German veteran, Geisler, on the programme, had only complicated and clouded the issue, so Clive had done himself a disservice to blow up the programme just then. The following day, the newspapers were full of the incident. The BBC quickly arranged a special follow-up edition of Panorama the next day and it attracted the biggest viewing figures in its history. To an estimated audience of 15 million, Dimbleby, with a conspicuous cross patch of sticking plaster on his forehead, carefully powdered, introduced Robert and Eberhardt. They told all they knew of the plagiarised notebooks, the suggestion and strong hint of a stolen Nobel Prize, the dead English soldier with his lower half blown away, the embedded pieces of shrapnel which were extracted and reconstructed into a quarter of a British army hand grenade.

Professor Bancroft did his live translation as the veteran related his tale and excelled himself with gravitas. Fifteen years later, the BBC called him in to announce the Falklands War. Robert did not need to name any names but all the members of the physics department in 1912 were shown on an old photograph. The camera zoomed in on Robert's dead grandfather, and panned across to the unmistakable face of a young clammy Clive. Robert also produced an old photo of the Bragg sound ranging team in France. The camera moved slowly in on the unmistakable froggy face of Clive, bald at 22 and now even balder at 75 and panned across to Robert the elder. Clive was being dismantled and hung out to fry. Dimbleby himself summarised the details of Ilse Kresser and by 10 o'clock, the nation knew that Blackmore was a murderer, a Nobel Physics plagiarist and a traitor to his country.

Blackmore himself had watched the follow-up programme with increasing horror but had stayed true to form to the end. As the credits rolled, he immediately called the Vice Chancellor of Manchester University to get Robert sacked.

'Vice Chancellor? This is Sir Clive Blackmore. I'd like a word with you about your libelist employee.'

252

There was a click as the Vice Chancellor hung up on his phone. The titular head of Manchester University, the Chancellor, was the eleventh Duke of Devonshire. Alas for Clive, the lines to Chatsworth House were permanently engaged. The Duke was discussing Robert and Clive on the Vice Chancellor's private line.

Clive spent a sleepless night, turning and, getting up every half an hour for a glass of water, churning and flushing the noisy toilet. At breakfast, Brenda complained bitterly.

'I don't see why I should be kept awake all night for something you have done.'

'What do you mean, woman? The whole reason for you having your own bedroom at the other end of the landing is so you can get your beauty sleep.'

Nothing more was said and shortly before nine o'clock, Clive wobbled down his driveway on his bicycle and set off on the 45 minute journey from his home in Saffron Walden to his college in Cambridge. To his chagrin, the Master of Trinity was in a meeting, which was expected to last at least a further two hours. The lengthy meeting concerned potential charitable donors who wished to set up a new research institute for classical languages.

Clive found a relatively sheltered spot behind the fountain in the Great Court of Trinity, out of the direct line of the biting North East wind. He dared not leave the courtyard, lest the meeting finished early and he should miss his Master. Eventually, after a chilly hour and a half, he saw the unmistakable tall figure of the Master, Sir Michael Ponticus and his confidant and right hand man, Cambridge's top classics scholar, Welshman Donald Dafyd Papia at the other side of the Great Court, emerging from the Master's lodge. They were in gowns for the occasion and the fabric flapped horizontally in the wind. Donald Papia was as small as Micky Ponticus was tall and they had learned over the years how to find the comfortable separation and angle of tilt of both heads so that they could see and hear each other efficiently. But Papia was excited and animated at the thought of being director of an Institute of Classical languages. He was darting more than usual in and out of range of his Master's line of sight. His high pitched, strangled voice drifted across the courtyard but due to the gusty wind, reached Clive only as a series of disconnected quacks, none of which carried any intelligence.

Clive waited for his moment and then scuttled across the courtyard to intercept the pair. What he did not know, nor anticipate, was that Sir Michael Ponticus, the Master, was in the right frame of mind to deal with him.

'Master, Sir Michael, I need your assistance.'

The Master of Trinity, to his credit, did not even blink. He had thought Blackmore would crop up before long and was ready for him, and spoke for the whole British nation.

'Non in caelum Magis Nigrum, quia Britones fuccabas. Nunc te fucca!'

Clive's Latin was not up to the task.

'You what?'

The Master's right hand man for most events and circumstances, Donald Dafyd Papia, had been flapping and darting back and forth in expectation of the circumstances of this event as soon as he had spotted Clive approaching. Donald's eyes gleamed with the ecstasy of anticipation as he listened to the brief exchange in Latin and he was ready with his own quacked stab, delivered as he peered over the top of his cold rimless glasses.

'Νον ερισ ιν χοελι Νερομπλιυσ, θυια Βριτονεσ φυχχασ. Νυνχ τε φυχχα! Does that help?'

'You what?'

The Trinity clock struck the hour twice as usual. A double toll of doom for Clive. Papia tugged at the sleeve of the Master's gown and, now acting as if Clive did not exist any more, urged haste.

'Michael, we are going to be late.'

The two gowns flapped away across the Great Court, through the Great Gate and out into Trinity Street.

'Why did you speak to him in pigeon modern dog-Greek and not classical Greek, Donald?'

'I thought he wouldn't understand classic Greek being a scientist; I was trying to be helpful. And it wasn't Greek, it was Latin with a Greek accent. I'm trying it out for a discussion on the Third Programme next week. Fancy a quick pint of Guinness before lunch Michael? It's venison stew today, very earthy; and the Stilton is reaching peak maturity.'

'Oooooh, we are good Donald. No wonder we are in charge.'

Clive watched as his last contact with English academia disappeared into the uniform blur of his imperfect long distance vision.

The bitter North East wind had intensified during Clive's vigil in the Great Court. Although he was able to cycle at twice the speed of his inward journey, he was blown into the centre of the road several times, wobbling back to the kerb as horns blared and headlights flashed. He swept up his driveway, crunching only lightly on the gravel and left his bicycle flat on the ground with its front wheel still spinning, like a small boy at a sweet shop. Except there was nothing sweet waiting for him. He was relieved to find a note from Brenda, saying she had gone out to see friends. He then chose to play his last card. In his study, with a cup of hot weak tea, he called his one remaining friend, the lugubrious, salubrious lawyer Cedric Smeggers, to enquire about starting libel proceedings against the BBC and Robert.

'Well, Sir Clive. It should be quite easy for you. You would succeed, unless they could prove that what they have said is the truth. They can't do that, can they? And in that case, you win and we become rich.'

~   ~   ~

Chapter 23

Saffron Walden 1967

Robert sat across the desk from Jason Sykes. Sykes was expansive in girth and confidence. In his mid fifties, his hair was still without a trace of grey, or covered up by a bottle, although he didn't look the type to waste time with hair dye bottles. An ex-cop, his matter of fact approach to policing, although highly successful, had brought his career to nothing more than a useful plateau. Further progression was deemed unlikely in the extreme, due to his lack of finer social skills. He had seized the first opportunity to take retirement and had used the pension lump sum to set himself up in business as a private detective. He was smart enough to avoid seedy associations and had cultivated contacts with his former colleagues in the force, who still liked and respected him. Surveillance of respondents and co-respondents in divorce cases provided him with a steady reliable income, supporting both his company accounts and waistline as he spent many sedentary hours in his car, eating sandwiches and take-away chicken and drinking highly sugared tea from his thermos flask. Spice was added by the occasional contract to spy on someone interesting.

Robert's business sounded duller than divorce but it had the merit of being a job he could safely hand to his trainee son Jonathan, whom he was paying £20 a week to learn the trade.

'It'll be £200 for the first week. Minimum. If you get what you want after a day, that's tough on you. But that covers all operational costs in this area. If you want me to travel, or make trunk calls, that will be extra. After the first week, it's £40 a day and you can stop me at an hour's notice. Working after 7 and at weekends is extra, 7 pounds 10 shillings an hour evenings and £60 a normal length day weekends. You can phone me each day for a de-briefing after 7 in the evening. OK?'

'Yes, I understand.' Robert had bought gold sovereigns at the historically low controlled price and also invested in shares during the time of his fellowship in Germany. His decision to leave the investment there had been a violation of English tax law but he had recently been able to repatriate the equivalent of a year's worth of his salary in gold coin from his safety deposit box, the coins now worth an uncontrolled amount and still have most of his wealth left in Germany. Paying Sykes his £200 would be a pin-prick; he would still have enough to buy the new house he had found in the Yorkshire hills, less than an hours drive from Manchester and half an hour from his grandmother. He and Alessandra had seen the property a month ago and had been captivated.

Sykes flipped open his receipt pad. 'Cash?'

'Yes, of course.' Robert counted out forty crisp new five pound notes and pushed them across the desk. Sykes folded the wad and was about to follow the habit of years and put in his inside pocket. Instead, he took out the red cash box from his desk drawer, opened it with a key and put the cash inside.

'Your first week starts tomorrow at 9, but I might make a few phone calls for you this afternoon.'

'It's all legal isn't it?'

'You bet it is. I'd be out of business if I stepped outside the law. And it would be even worse for you because with two of us involved, it would be a conspiracy. Then you could sue me for failure to exercise a duty of care to you. Oh, it's legal all right! Here's my card. That's the number to phone when you want an update. Of course, you get a full written report at the end.'

Robert got up to leave. 'Can I give you my number? I'm staying at the Saffron Arms till this is over. I think he might make a dash for it. Oh, and you might find a few others are interested in him as well, newspapers, police.'

'Righto. That's not unusual. I'll know most of them. We can help each other. And calm down, I'm not going to tell anyone about you.'

Robert took a taxi back to his hotel in Saffron Walden, went to the bar and ordered a glass of white wine. As soon as he saw the bottle of Lutomer Riesling, he wished he hadn't. He had long since moved on from sweet wines and now preferred something much dryer. The Yugoslavian Riesling would be even worse on his carefully trained palate than a German. Early in their life together, Alessandra had sniffed one of his Rhine wines, dipped a tongue into the glass and pulled a face.

'It's not even fit to cook with!' She had then poured it down the sink and next day had toured virtually all the Italian restaurants in the North of England, not to try their wines, but to find out where they got their Italian wines from. Their modest cellar at home now contained a selection of Piedmont, Frascati and Puglia.

'Large or small?'

'A small one please!' Robert looked at the grubby fingerprinted glass, closed his eyes and swallowed the wine in a single gulp. He grimaced as the warm sweet wine assaulted his taste buds. The barmaid looked on in astonishment; it was usually a double scotch or brandy that desperate men grabbed, downed and pulled a face. She'd never seen it done with a Riesling before and looked down at the label in case she had made a mistake. But her training set the automatic response in motion.

'Another?'

'No thanks, I have some phone calls to make. Can you put that, erm, wine on my bill please, Room 6.'

Across the road from the hotel, from a public phone box, Robert called first Alessandra and then his father.

'I know it's important to you, but you are important to me and to us. Please, please be careful. Don't do anything stupid Robert. We need you and we want you as you are. You will let me know what's happening won't you?'

'Alli, there has not been a day since we met that we haven't spoken to each other. Every single day of our lives since that day in Bologna. Have you forgotten?'

'No, of course I haven't forgotten. I know that as well as you do. I am just worried that this thing is so big for you that it might get in the way. You are the biggest thing in my life. Nothing comes close, except of course the children. I don't want this to come between us and change you.'

'Alessandra, you are the one and only. I think of you all the time, even when I am doing something else. I always have a level of consciousness going on you. I don't know what is going to happen here, I don't even know why I am here. It's a subconscious force that is driving me. It really is my Odyssey, just like Odysseus; he didn't know totally why or where although he knew he had to.'

'I see, well I really don't want to be your Penelope, standing on the quayside wondering when or if you will return. Don't just call me at the end of the day, please; call me in the morning and at midday also. I'd like to know where you are and how it is going. All the time.'

Alessandra could read Robert like an open book and if she spoke to him morning, afternoon and night, she knew that she would have a pretty good idea of his state of mind, motivation and evolution. They spoke for half an hour till Robert said he needed to call his father. The call to Harry took no more than five minutes. Harry was shocked to find that his son had followed Blackmore back to Cambridge and even more so when Robert couldn't explain why he had done it.

'Keep your head down, Robert. He's a vicious bastard. Do not tangle with him or you might live to regret it. He is wounded, perhaps fatally, and that makes him even more dangerous. He could easily take you down with him since he knows you are largely to blame for his current predicament. I have known him for a long time and I can assure you he has felled better men than you and that is me being a parent and not being disloyal. I want you to keep me informed and if I have the slightest reason to doubt what you are up to, I shall be there on the next train. I might come anyway.'

'Please don't Dad. I want to see this through myself. I do need your support and I need to talk to you every day. Please be there and understand.'

Outside the phone box, Robert toyed with the idea of buying a decent bottle of wine. The thought of drinking it on his own depressed him so he decided to go to his room and start writing the paper on the quark gluon plasma measurements he had completed. The hotel could at least manage a pot of coffee to keep him going and then he would have a look round Saffron Walden to see if there was anywhere interesting to eat – after he had phoned Sykes.

'It's been a nothing kind of day I am afraid. The media are camped on his doorstep, or rather in the road at the bottom of the drive. The missus came out and shrieked at them when they encroached on her land. She must have phoned the police because they came round five minutes later and chatted with the gang. Since then, they have stayed in the road and smirked on the two occasions when the ma'am came out and said they had nothing to say and would they all go away.'

'OK, thanks. Let's see how it goes. I don't think they will be able to put up with that for long. Something will have to give. Is there a way to deal with the media like that? I mean what should they be doing instead of calling the police?'

'Of course there is. You smile. You make them cups of tea and even scones. You give them an interview and then tell them that's it. There's then a 50:50 chance they will go away. Something else will crop up and they have to earn their living.'

Robert juggled with the idea of going to have a chat with the journalists but his father's cool advice would not go away. If he appeared on TV, giving interviews outside the Blackmores' house, that would be seen as a most provocative act. The Blackmores would be sure to see it. They were probably tuned in to every news bulletin on every available TV and radio channel.

Wednesday and Thursday proceeded with the predictability of the phases of the moon, each hour barely perceptibly different than the one before except to the keen eyed, a tiny but distinct motion in a distinct direction. There were indications that the media were getting bored. On Friday morning, they left abruptly as news came through of the assassination of the MP for Cambridge Central in the car park of Westminster. The field was clear. This was it. The moment the pressure was off, Blackmore could not wait a second. A damp white sphere, glistening in the late morning sun, sticking out of the huge collar of a Crombie woollen overcoat, perched on a majestic pre-war bicycle, swept down the drive and turned in the direction of the town centre. Sykes junior stubbed out his cigarette, started the car at the first try and waited till Blackmore had turned the corner before moving off. Following a bicycle was child's play. Without mirrors, cyclists rarely looked backwards and paid most of their attention on maintaining stability as vans and lorries passed by within inches. Young Sykes had no intention of overtaking his prey. He was enjoying himself like never before in his life and in that instant, knew the destiny of his life, to follow in his father's footsteps.

Robert had gone for a walk and taken a short lunch in the town before phoning Alessandra again. He was so wrapped up in the conversation that he failed to see Blackmore gliding past the phone box like a vulture on wheels, followed by a maroon Ford Escort. Blackmore himself paid scant attention to the phone box and would hardly have recognised Robert anyway, out of the context of the lecture theatre and TV studio. Robert saved the coffee till he got back to the Saffron Arms, ready for an afternoon's work.

'Ooh Mr. White, message for you.' The dumpy, titty young receptionist plucked Robert's key and a piece of paper from the pigeon hole of Room 6 and handed them over with an expansive smile.

'Thank you, Miss.' Robert scanned the message and rushed straight back to the phone booth. 'Yes?'

'Ah, Mr. White. News for you. The chickens look restless. Maybe they know there's a fox in the bushes. Have you been up to anything? Your Mr. Sir Clive Blackmore has just booked tickets for Hamburg. Him and his missus. They're on the early flight tomorrow. Odd actually, they are flying Pan Am from Heathrow. You wouldn't think an American airline would do the London-Hamburg run would you?'

'Yes, spoils of war.' Robert felt confident. 'The German airlines aren't allowed to fly from West Germany to Berlin so the Allies carve it up. Pan Am fly from Houston to Berlin and stop off in England and Hamburg. It's a lucrative business. That's why they snaffled it.'

'OK.' Jasper Sykes filed the information away for possible future use and immediately lost interest. 'But that's not all. They've booked on to Heligoland. Where the hell's that? Isn't it in the South Atlantic, near Argentina. Or is it in Denmark?'

'No Mr. Sykes, those are the Falkland Islands. Heligoland is not far from Hamburg. And you're thinking of Legoland in Denmark.' Robert explained needlessly. 'Are they going on to Heligoland tomorrow?'

'No. They had a bit of trouble getting the tickets. It's a local booking in Hamburg and it needed a few phone calls to Germany. They're on the ferry on Saturday.'

'Thank you. Well done. How on earth did you find that out?'

'Don't worry about that. That's what you pay me for.' Sykes thought he had better not mention that his daughter worked in the travel agent otherwise Robert might want some of his money back.

'I guess you won't be needing me next week.' Sykes, also needlessly.

'No, I shall be doing some travelling. Where's the travel agent in Saffron Walden?'

For a second, Sykes thought that Robert was on to his daughter but then his police training took over as he realised he was just chasing after Blackmore. It was difficult for policemen, even an ex, to imagine laymen behaving like policemen.

'There's Althorpe's in the High Street. They have some new fangled machine that allows them to make the booking without using the telephone, unless,' and Sykes could be heard grinning over the telephone, 'you want to book on to Heligoland.'

Robert didn't need a travel agent in Cambridgeshire to book him on a Hamburg ferry to Heligoland. He could do that himself when he got there.

'Thanks, Mr. Sykes. I might call in later this afternoon, in case you get anything else. I guess I have paid you up to the end of this week haven't I, and there is no need for anything next week since they will be in Germany.'

Less than an hour later, Robert emerged from Althorpe's clutching a Lufthansa open return ticket to Hamburg. His plane left half an hour before the Blackmores. The hunter was leading the prey. After an abortive discussion in the men's hairdresser, Robert plucked up courage and slunk into the ladies hair salon a few doors down from Althorpe's.

'I've got this audition in London and I want to look the part. Can you make me blonde with a crew cut? I don't trust the gents down the road.'

'You mean 'Cut Loose?' round the corner?' The receptionist was slender, smooth, sexy and smiling. She was also the proprietress. 'That's my Sebastian! He'll be amused when I tell him. But you're quite right not to trust them, they wouldn't know how to get your hair blonde; it would end up khaki! They wouldn't think of doing it three times. Twice is not enough for hair like yours.'

Sexy had taken the liberty of touching Robert's jet black hair, the hair that had burnt its way into the consciousness of Alessandra within seconds of their encounter on the streets of Bologna. With effort, Robert hid the feeling of violation and smiled.

'Khaki will not do! It has to be Nordic blonde.'

'Swede or Dane? I can manage both shades.'

'I'll settle for Swedish thank you. No make that Danish, it's next to Hamburg.'

'I think I had better do this myself. We don't want you messing up your audition. Now, why are you going for a crew cut? I can do you the very latest Danish men's style.'

Two hours and much head caressing later, Robert took his leave and felt the day had passed him by.

'You can come here again you know. We do men's hair just as easy as women's and your hair is really worth the special attention we can give it. If you need to go back to black, we can do that.'

Robert felt a sudden panic. 'But it will turn back on its own won't it?'

'Of course it will, silly. But from blonde to black is a big step. Growing naturally, you will look like a big wasp for a while, or a liquorice all-sort. We can make it look less striking for you.'

"I'm sure you can," thought Robert. "and another tenner in the bag." Still, it was a lot cheaper than Sykes, almost as important and he was beginning to like it.

Coming out of the salon, Robert realised he hadn't told the hotel he was leaving. He really should have done that before his hair changed. Now he might draw attention to himself. It shouldn't be a problem but the two involuntary years in East Germany has taught him to question every probability. He dashed back into the salon.

'I know this sounds odd, but is there an Army and Navy stores in the town?'

'It's not actually called Army and Navy as such, but they do that sort of stuff. Go right to the end of the road, turn left, left again and it's on the right. You can't miss it, they have all the stuff hanging up outside like a Victorian butchers.'

Sexy had locked a firm eye contact onto Robert. She couldn't help it. It wasn't because it was Robert, it was because he was a man, and a good looking one at that. Ten minutes later, Robert was walking out of the store, a navy knitted woollen hat covering his new locks and an ex-US marine navy winter coat with broad lapels inside a duffle bag over his shoulder. 'Lieut Williamson' was painted onto the lining of the coat with a kind of whitewash. Robert wondered who made them and if they had ever been to the United States. No matter, it was exactly what he needed. At the hotel, he told the dumpy receptionist he wanted to settle up and would be leaving early in the morning, very early. How could he get to Heathrow for 6.30? It would need a night taxi to Peterborough and then the Caledonian sleeper to Kings Cross. He paid up and then went back to the phone to make another call. This time to Hamburg, speaking German.

'Beautiful greetings Anka! How is it going with you two.'

'Wunderbar as usual, Robert! How are you? When will we see you again?'

'Tomorrow if that is all right with you. Can Klaus do a job for me in the morning?' He nearly said early in the morning but 9:30 is almost time for lunch in Hamburg. 'I might need him quite a while and of course I'll pay him.'

'No you won't! He's got Friday and Saturday off although he was hoping to go to the Volkspark and see the game against Bayern.'

'Firstly, if he won't take payment, I'll book someone else and second, there's a good chance I'll be through by Friday evening and maybe come to the match with him. Is he working right now?'

'Yes indeed, it's usually hectic on a Thursday afternoon and he does a lot of business.'

'I'd like him to meet me at the airport, please. I'm on the early Lufthansa flight from Heathrow tomorrow morning. Is he still driving the same car?'

'Lufthansa aus Heetro for Robert.' Anka repeated the instructions slowly as she wrote them on the pad. 'How long are you staying? And more important, where are you staying?'

'I'll sort that when I get there. It's all a bit of a rush and I'll explain everything when I arrive. You actually know most of it already, it's now just falling into place.'

Robert then paid a visit to his bank, just in time before it closed at three. He wanted five hundred pounds from his account and after a few minutes of pursed lips, a couple of phone calls to his branch in Manchester, he had the cash. He was about to use his passport as identification, realised the colour of his hair and chose his driving licence instead.

'You know, it's no problem if you book it in advance . . .'

The clerk wished to retain a modicum of authority after he had been overruled by the manager and coerced into giving this layabout five hundred pounds of the bank's money.

'I know. But there are things in one's life that sometimes happen without warning and this is mine.' Harry was about to say he had to leave the country urgently but something about the clerk's demeanour reminded him of East Germany and he could imagine him on the phone to the local constabulary, whispering his suspicions that a criminal was about to abscond with his loot.

He could do without a few hours in Saffron Walden police station, explaining why he had dyed his hair, bought clothing which had "nefarious" painted all over it and was about to flee the country with a "large" sum of money. After the bank, Robert called on Sykes. He waited five minutes, was about to be ushered into the office when Sykes appeared and told his secretary he had forgotten to call his latest client. 'Would Robert mind waiting five more minutes?' Robert had no choice in the matter. He needed a few minutes to cool down. The knitted hat which he was using to hide his new blonde hair was making his head itch.

'Goodness me, you've changed!' The secretary didn't miss much.

'Yes! I've got a new part in a play for German television. At least I hope I've got it. I've got an audition tomorrow.' Robert wanted to keep the same story going but was conscious of saying too much. Echoes of East Germany came back. Don't say more than necessary. The less you say, the easier you can remember it and say the same thing again without contradiction.

'How exciting! Can you speak German?'

'Yes. That's one of the reasons why I get offered these parts. I can speak English with an English accent, English with a German accent, German with an English accent and German with a German accent.'

'Ooooh, how clever. I can't even do the first of those properly. Excuse me a moment, I need to get some papers from the next room.'

All that remained was for Robert to receive copies of the hand-written reports. He could have typed ones tomorrow. Sykes looked up at the blonde hair and gave Robert a long hard look.

'Do you think that's wise Sir?'

'The hair? Oh, that's nothing to do with it. I've got an acting job lined up as well. I can combine business with business while I am in Hamburg.'

'Good for you, Mr. White. It'll help to cover the fee won't it?'

'Possibly. I've got to get through the audition first.'

~   ~   ~

Chapter 24

Hamburg 1967

Robert was at Heathrow by six and checked in for his flight. Lufthansa flew out of Terminal 2 whereas the Blackmore's Pan Am flight came in from Houston and would leave from Terminal 3. He had no way of knowing if the Blackmores would catch their flight. He had pondered how they might travel there and had kept a low profile on Peterborough station in case they had chosen the same route. Most likely they will use a driver. They were rich enough. The Nobel Prize had set them up for that.

On the flight, Robert toyed with the breakfast of cheese, raw cured ham and sausage. He wondered how it was that Germans were able to get up so early and start work almost at once with a breakfast of cold fat under their belts. The adrenaline suppressed his hunger, but he knew that it could wear off at any moment and leave him starving. He asked for a couple of extra bread rolls and forced himself to eat them. Two more coffees helped.

Sitting in the shuttle bus between the plane and the terminal building at Hamburg, Robert had a sudden panic when he realised that the Blackmores might have switched to the Lufthansa flight after making their booking. He had been behaving as if he were on the moors instead of among thieves. He scanned the passengers in the bus, slowly and out of the corner of his eye. One couple had given him a start, standing with their backs to him, but eventually the man had turned to look at the approaching terminal and spoken to his companion in German. Ten minutes later, Robert was through passport and customs control. "Nichts zu verzollern. Nothing to declare, or as the Germans put it: Nothing on which to pay duty. Declaring was taken for granted."

First thing through all the checks, Robert looked at the arrivals board. Pan Am from Houston and London was expected 20 minutes late. Still an hour before Blackmore would walk through. That is, if he was on the plane. Second thing, Robert went to the Hansa Bank opposite the arrivals barrier and changed £300 into Deutsche Marks. He looked wryly at the receipt and the bundle of notes. 1500 marks only compared to the 3000 he would have got five years ago. "What is happening to our money?" he thought. Then he thought of the two hundred thousand Marks he now had saved in a special account at the Commerzbank and felt better. It was comforting to know that whatever happened here, he could probably cope with it financially. Third thing, Robert went to the news stand and picked out a pair of sunglasses. He could have bought a pair in Saffron Walden but then they would have looked just that – bought in Saffron Walden – and Blackmore probably also had a pair like that anyway. In front of the mirror, Robert tried on the glasses and failed to recognise himself in knitted black hat and sailor jacket. He yanked off the hat and recognised himself even less. Perfect. He had only met Blackmore the once and the circumstances, although only a few days ago, were as far from Hamburg airport as one could imagine.

Outside the terminal, Robert looked to his left at the short line of taxis that were actively taking passengers. To the right was the stack, those waiting for the short line to empty. It shouldn't take too long to find Klaus even though all the taxis were identically cream. Towards the end of the line, one of them looked as if it were on fire, a plume of blue-grey smoke rising in the still morning air. It was an understatement to say that Klaus was a heavy smoker. He smoked seamlessly, every waking moment. If he could have found a way to smoke while he was asleep, he would have exploited it.

'Morgen, Klaus!'

'Robert! You it is? Beautiful to see you again. How goes it with you? What have you done with your hairs?'

Robert threw the duffle bag onto the back seat and slipped in beside Klaus. His attention was immediately caught by a large notice stuck to the dashboard. In English. "Passengers are kindly requested to refrain from asking the driver not to smoke."

'Ha ha. What's that? And why in English?'

'It's not in English, it's in American. It's this new wave of Californians who come and try to stop us Germans smoking the moment they off the plane step. I had one couple. They would not even with me travel when they saw my cigarette! But we drivers are a fraternity. As they out stepped, I give a special wave and instead of the drivers telling them that they would not them take, they all held a cigarette and the Californians walked to the end of the line and probably had to take the bus. Tscha! You never smoked Robert. But you seem to understand. Now. Let us get to the point. What is this all about?'

'It's a long story and most of it will have to wait till later on. Probably this evening. Right now I've got about an hour before my friend arrives on the Pan Am flight.'

'What is it that makes me think that this friend is not a friend? The way you twisted your mouth in an unpleasant smile as you the word expressed? Forgive me my very good friend, but that is exactly how the Ossies look when they are trying to justify their murders at the wall. Especially Honecker. But to the point Klaus, this is the man who murdered my grandfather, stole his work, his ideas, his discoveries and then got the Nobel Prize for it and a lifetime of honour. Well, the shit has finally hit the fan and he is running away. Naa jaa.' Klaus let the air and smoke curl out between his teeth in a quietly audible hiss. He stubbed out the half smoked Red Hand, tossed it out of the window and lit another. Like many smokers, the act of lighting a cigarette gave the hands something to do whenever the brain was required to increase its speed.

'We cannot here for an hour wait. This is for taxis in service to join the queue. We can go and wait over there where the drivers have their own little Kaffee Stube.'

'Look, his plane is listed as twenty minutes late but suppose it catches up and comes in earlier. I don't want to miss him. I really can't afford to miss him, not now.'

'Number one Robert. Remember you are back in Germany, not England. If the arrivals board at Hamburg airport says the plane will late be, it will late be. Number two, I have a way to know when the flight will land. But if you happy feel to wait inside, then wait inside.'

Klaus reached for his radio mic, a wedge of black plastic on the end of a tight black coil.

'Hallo Hilda! Pan Am aus London, sag bescheid bitte.'

Anywhere else in the world, radios crackle reluctantly into life. But in hi-tech Germany, radios purr into action. Hilda in the taxi control spoke like Marlene Dietrich with a Hamburg accent. But then all taxi control operators in Hamburg speak like Marlene Dietrich with a Hamburg accent.

'Na Klaus. Der Flug ist verspätet. Zwanzig Minuten. Wird erst in eine Stunde landen. Du kannst ruhig eine Kaffee holen.'

'How does she know that?'

'We need these things to know. It is our business.'

'Klaus!' Marlene again. 'Der Gerd wird jemand aus London abholen. Er wird sich melden, sobald es klappt.'

Robert stiffened with shock at the news that one of the drivers was picking someone up from London. 'Klaus, can you get a name, quietly, so they don't know we know?'

'Hilda, erstens, nur zwischen Du und mich, hast Du eine Name aus London?'

'Nanu Du. Wie geheim! Der Kerl heißt Blackmore - mit Begleiterin, seine Ehegattin. Ziemlich alt.'

Germans were taught spoken English in school so that the "a" of Blackmore was pronounced as an "e", just as the English upper class speak it. Together with the hard Hamburg "k" in place of the normally softer "ch" of high German, the sentence came across like Marlene Dietrich speaking to the accompaniment of a machine gun. The "ck" of Blackmore came across especially hard. Robert leaned forward in earnest.

'Tell her it's not a secret, well not really, just a big surprise. The Englishman is 80 today and we are planning a celebration. Even his wife with him doesn't know about it.'

The coffee at the drivers' rest hut was pungent and hot. Robert quickly adjusted to the taste of coffee with evaporated milk again, indeed, it made him feel comfortable to be recognisably back in Germany. Breakfast was sufficiently long ago that he managed a cheese filled bread roll, and then asked for another. After forty minutes, he got nervous and restless and took his leave of Klaus, determined to see the arrival of his prey in the arrivals hall. He had filled in Klaus as much as time allowed. Klaus had immediately fingered the same problem that Harry had pointed out.

'You don't know why you this do! What is your motor? What is your reason? What will you do?'

'When I know it, I will do it. But I will not do anything stupid, I know that. Have you any coins?'

'Of course, I have lots of coins, I am a German taxi driver. It is only the English taxi drivers who never have coins. Telephone?'

'Yes, and can I borrow your newspaper? And a couple of cigarettes.'

'Of course, I have it three times read already, here. And take a box of stroking woods.' Klaus had never needed to learn the word for a match.

Robert took the *Hamburger Morgenpost*, nodded to Klaus and they exchanged their special handshake, elbows fully bent and forearms vertical.

'Till equal.'

It had taken Robert a few years to figure out the German logic of language that used the same word for "soon" and "equal". When you have only one word for two meanings, it is easy to pick the wrong one in translation. Robert and Klaus had spent hours discussing language; Robert explaining that it was inevitable that the English language could sustain many different words for the same object or action. One for the Romans, one for the Saxons and one for the Normans. Throw in some Greek, Danish and more latterly, some from the Empire and the result was a language of flavour and spice. That was Robert's line.

'You are a country of mongrels!' retorted Klaus. 'You need something like our purity laws for beer to your language applied! Water, malt and hops. More not. Both your beer and your language are full of unknown shit. You need a thorough clean up!'

Close friendship allowed Robert to forgive what Robert perceived as excessive eugenics. It also allowed Klaus to forgive what he perceived as excessive laxity in things that mattered, beer and Germanity. Robert took a seat by the 'Treffpunkt', the meeting place for people who didn't know Hamburg airport. With the Morgenpost open, hat off to show the blonde crew cut, sailors jacket hanging open, cigarette hanging from the corner of his mouth, Robert felt sure his own grandmother wouldn't recognise him.

"Gelandet." The arrivals board changed for the Pan Am flight and Robert calculated 5 mins for the plane to taxi to its halt, 10 minutes to offload the passengers onto the bus, 10 minutes for slow Blackmore to creep through customs. No need to add on time for baggage, this was Hamburg; baggage was often there in the baggage hall before the passengers. Twenty four minutes later, Robert saw the unmistakable silhouette of his two creeping evil geriatrics, emerging through the customs barrier with a single suitcase on wheels. Robert quickly lit his Red Hand and took a drag. He coughed, spluttered and choked. "Keep the damn thing out of your mouth you idiot." He ordered himself. "Hold it in front of your face you clown." He suddenly felt awkward. He didn't even know how to hold a cigarette let alone smoke one. He felt he looked more conspicuous with one that he did without it, so he dropped it and stubbed it out beneath his foot.

'Die Aschenbecker sind dafur gemeint.' The middle aged woman with a prune complexion wagged her walking stick at him and jabbed the stick in the direction of the large ashtray. Ashtray was an understatement, it was more like a chrome plated dustbin and Robert felt another stab of uselessness at the careless mistake. 'Stick to things you know. Don't try to act. You may as well just call out to Blackmore and wish him "Good Morning" at this rate.' Robert bent down, picked up the flattened Red Hand and dropped it in the bin. He raised his hand to the woman in an acknowledgement of guilt. The woman nodded grimly. Everything was in order again. Guilt had been established and acknowledged. The silhouettes were getting larger and nearer. Creeping. The footsteps were so short that they hardly seemed to be moving. But they were getting nearer. Nearer to him. They were coming straight towards him. They had seen him. They were coming to find out what he was doing there, spying on them! His own grandmother might not have recognised him, but they had. Panic, sweat. "For chrissake, calm down. How can they possibly have recognised me"

'Entschuldigen Sie bitte! Blackmore in perfect German. Addressing Robert. 'Wo sind die Taxen? Wir sollen abgeholt werden. Sind Sie Taxifahrer?'

At this moment, Robert realised with certainty that he was no good at this. No good at all, even though they were only asking him the way to the taxi rank. He looked up at Blackmore, strayed his gaze across to Blackmore's wife and then noticed behind them, a taxi driver holding up a placard with the single word "Blakmore". He opened his mouth to say 'There you are. He's looking for you.' But how could he know their name and reply in English. He strangled the word 'There' half way between his brain and his tongue, swallowed and put on his best Hamburg accent.

'Ick empfehle Sie melden sick dort, beim Information ... or else look around for your driver. They usually hold up a sign with the passenger's name on it. There's a few over there waiting.' All in Platt German.

271

'Danke.'

Robert looked at them both through his glasses and realised that neither of them were actually looking at him. He was just part of the wallpaper of the airport. Someone to ask who wasn't even a someone. The Blackmores turned to creep away and immediately bumped into their driver.

'Ah, wir sind die Blackmores. Nehmen Sie unser Gepäck, bitte.'

The driver nodded, folded up the placard and took their luggage as ordered. Robert was out of the terminal a good minute before the creeping trio. The smoking chimney taxi was waiting out of the main line across the road and Robert ran across. Bouncing on to the front seat, he gasped, croaked.

'Here they are. They are the creeping oldies with the driver dragging their luggage.'

'What in heaven is with you loose?' Klaus stared at Robert, at the ashen sweating face. 'Are they ghosts?'

'Never mind. It's not easy. I was not made for this.'

'Have you smoked those cigarettes? I'm running low.'

Robert felt in his pocket and pulled out a handful of cigarette paper and tobacco shreds.

'Sorry, I smoked one and didn't look after the other.'

'Give it to me, I have some papers to remake it if necessary. Hold on, they are not wasting the time. We have to go.'

Two identical taxis left the forecourt of the arrivals hall. Nothing unusual in that, they left in ones, twos, threes and sometimes in convoys. It was all the statistics of chance arrivals and chance loading into taxis. Klaus tucked behind the taxi in front. There was no need to follow two or three cars behind in spy-craft fashion. Being in a taxi, following a taxi, it was the perfect cover.

'Hallo, Hilda. Bist du noch dran?'

Hilda was still on duty and her Marlene voice slid over the airwaves.

'Na Klaus. Was jetzt?'

'Der Gerd is unterwegs. Weisst du wohin?' Klaus was asking where his mate Gerd, driving the taxi ahead, was heading for,

'Naturlich! Hotel zum Adler, Altona.'

Knowing the name of the hotel was just insurance in case of red lights or other eventualities. Klaus did not want to use Hilda more than necessary. There were probably a dozen 'Eagle Hotels' in Hamburg but by pinning it to Altona, that meant only one, near the station, not far from the Ferry terminal.

'We could shoot ahead and get there first.'

The thought appealed to Robert, once more chasing the prey but being in front, but he preferred caution in case the wily old bird changed his mind. Fifteen minutes later both cars entered Hindenberg Allee. Klaus immediately turned right into a side street, turned round and positioned himself near the junction so that the main entrance of the hotel was in full view of both of them. Sir Clive peeled off a fifty Mark note and the habit of a lifetime led him to ask for a receipt. As the driver Gerd scribbled the details, Marlene came on the radio. Robert dived in.

'Please tell Gerd to greet your guest welcome to Hamburg and wish him Happy Birthday.'

Clive was staggered by the unexpected salutation, understanding it without comprehension. He allowed a deep frown to furrow his brow, extending to the top of his bald head.

'What birthday?' he queried, in German.

'Don't know, My Lord.' Gerd in English.

'Lord? Birthday, What Lord? Where do you get that from?'

Gerd had read Lord of the Rings, translated into German under the title "Herr der Ringe". So naturally, he translated the form of address "Mein Herr" as "My Lord".

'Mein Herr. My Lord. Nicht?'

Clive started to explain but decided that life, especially the rest of his, was too short. That cleared up the Lord business, but didn't explain the birthday. The thought niggled.

~ ~ ~

Clive and Brenda stuttered out of the hotel doorway. Brenda's heels were too high and she had difficulty crossing the cobbled street. They had no luggage so Robert reached his hand across and laid it on Klaus' sleeve as he was about to turn on the ignition.

'They're not going far. Not in those shoes and they have no luggage. I'll follow them on foot. You wait here . . . please.'

Along the Allee, left, and then a sharp right. At every junction Clive had studied the piece of paper in his hand, clearly a street map and compared the legend on the paper with the script on the street signs. Out onto Max Brauer Allee, they had a clear view up to the Altona station on the left. A relic of Bismarck. Straight ahead, Clive spotted his goal, nodded, and waited obediently for the green man until he crossed the street. The Kraftbank building now towered above the once dominant station building. Clive looked it up and down. But first, he and Brenda had immediate business in the adjacent arcade. Clive picked out his target shop, a comprehensive stationers. Stationery is a German expertise, like cream-cakes or beer and Clive had decided he was more likely to get what he needed here than in Saffron Walden. It only took him five minutes and he wasn't satisfied. The briefcase he had bought did not snap open briskly enough. It was almost as if the clasps had been damped with oil; they glided open silently with the speed of a motor driven antenna on a top of the range Mercedes instead of snapping noisily. German efficiency. Outside on the pavement, Brenda was transfixed by the display in the shop "Pelze und Moden". Furs and fashions.

'Do we have time to do it now?' Brenda had waited for this all her life. Clive simply did not understand the longing. He had never had to long for his prize; it had come too soon and too easy, if committing murder be discounted.

'It's not so much the time as the price, look at them, thousands of marks. I need to do this business first. The bank shuts at 3; your shop stays open later.'

Clive nodded towards the bank. Brenda pouted, but waited. Clive exchanged a few words with the receptionist cashier in the glass cage by the door of the bank. He was asked to wait. Five minutes later a prim smart woman with close-cropped hair and rimless glasses appeared from nowhere.

'Herr Blackmore? Kommen Sie mit.'

It was a board-room, oak panels and oil paintings of anonymous historic banking officials. There were no windows. A large flabby man shuffled towards Clive, offered a hand and a greeting and shuffled back to his seat at the end of the table. He gestured Clive to sit down. Clive had barely recovered from the shock of being clasped by a hand that was colder and clammier than his own. He shuddered. The flabby man introduced himself with brevity.

'Pfannkuch. Finanzdirektor . . .'

"What other kinds of directors were there in a bank?" thought Clive.

'... und Investitionsleiter,' almost as an afterthought. Clive nodded.

But I am taking money out thought Clive, fearing he was about to receive the banking equivalent of double glazing talk.

'Hier ist Herr Tischler, mein Assistant.' Pfannkuch nodded towards a dapper youth with black shiny hair, parted down the middle and flattened against the skull.

'Was zu trinken? Appolinaris? Gerolstein? Bismarckquelle?'

Clive was being offered a range of German mineral waters.

'Bismarck bitte!' Clive thought he had better stick with the local hero.

The water was warm, fizzy, slightly earthy and unappetising.

'So, the arrangements are all in place, Mr. Blackmore, as you requested.'

Pfannkuch had switched into English, heavily overlaid with Bavarian vowels.

'Three quarters of a million now and three quarters through our eastern channels. Five percent commission on the total transaction value.'

Pfannkuch was claiming a fee of seventy five thousand Deutschemark, about fifteen thousand pounds for writing a letter to his cousin at a bank in Dresden where the Commerzbank held credit. Clive was equal to it. He took a letter from his inside pocket. 'Three quarters of a million is a cash withdrawal. You don't charge your valued customers for withdrawing their money. And in this letter, signed by you, you state five percent to make another three quarters of a million available in the East as Westmarks.'

Pfannkuch just smiled and slowly extended his hands sideways.

'That is what I have said, Mr. Blackmore. Five percent on the total Eastern transaction.'

Little Tischler opened a file and fished out four pieces of paper. Two copies of two different contracts. The two that showed five percent on the whole deal were placed back in the folder. The other two were slid across the table to Pfannkuch.

'Here is the receipt. But first the money.'

Pfannkuch bent to his right to open a drawer. Clive bent to his left to pick up his briefcase. It was as if they were connected by a rod on a football pin-table. This was the moment the clasp was supposed to snap open. The clasps glided noiselessly and slowly away from their locks, controlled by a small damping mechanism.

Clive opened the case to a smell of suede and the sight of a mound of tissue paper filling the case. Damn, he should have opened it and cleaned it out before he came in the bank. He started to screw up the paper.

'No, do not discard the nice paper, you might need it.'

Pfannkuch placed two quarto sized manilla envelopes on the table, both thick, but not impressively so.

'Shall we watch Herr Tischler count it? He has a clean action.'

'But, but … '

Clive had imagined a stack of clean freshly minted and packed notes, pristine, stacked high. The stack should have been as wide as Pfannkuch and just as high.

'We have thousand mark denomination notes for you. You will be able to break them down in the East and they take up less room.'

'But, but … ' Clive was still struggling for his words. 'I thought, I wanted smaller ones. They would be easier for me.'

'Smaller ones? But of course Mr. Blackmore. How small?'

'Tens or twenties?'

'Tens or twenties? Hmmm, let me do a calculation Mr. Blackmore. If we get you tens, that is seventy five thousand banknotes. You will want to count them, or see them counted.'

Pfannkuch reached into his left hand drawer and took out ten banknotes.

'Time me Herr Tischler. Eins, zwei, drei, vier . . . acht, neun zehn.'

'Knapp fünf Sekunden, Herr Pfannkuch.' Almost five seconds.

So seventy five thousand notes, with no mistakes, is, let's be generous and say, thirty five thousand seconds. Almost nine hours. Yes, you can do it faster, but not at full pace for nine hours! Someone will have to work overtime or work in shift relays. We could make them twenties, that will bring it down to less than five hours. Oh, and we need to arrange a delivery from our central safe across the river. That will take about two hours as well. It is entirely up to you Mr. Blackmore. Your wish is our command. As ever.'

Clive, with mounting, but well concealed fury, had already decided. He was furious with himself for not having applied elementary numerology to his money. It was his mistake and his fault. He smiled.

276

'Of course.   We in physics never think of such things. Herr Tischler, please count. I assume I can change one or two at the counter?'

'Naturally, Mr. Blackmore.'

Unable to resist, Clive unpacked the notes again and tried to lay them side by side in a thin layer on top of the tissue paper. Now he was glad of the tissue, it filled the void. He frowned again. No matter how he shuffled them, they would not fit. Another dream vanished. Every time he had seen it in the movies, the briefcase had snapped open and it was always pristinely full, sideways, front to back and flush with the lid. The width and depth of a briefcase in the movies was always an integral multiple of the banknote dimensions. It was always a perfect stack of paper notes in the movies. Dollars or white five pound notes. But this was not the movies. Clive had never worked out the volume of a quarter of a million marks in the various denominations. So he simply did not know what he wanted.

'Ah, you are having trouble with the packing Mr. Blackmore. You should have told us.   Seven hundred and fifty thousand Deutschemark in notes to perfectly fit in a German Industry Standard briefcase! No problem. We would have worked it out and had it ready. We understand these things. Your briefcase is very nice, but it is not a German Industry Standard money case. Tja. What a pity.'

~   ~   ~

Out on the street, Brenda was nowhere to be seen. Clive peered inside the fur coat shop and caught sight of her pirouetting in front of a mirror in a silver grey arctic fox. He approached her and was about to speak when he noticed she had stopped, was hugging herself and appeared to be in trance. In truth, Brenda was experiencing the first orgasm of her life. It lasted two minutes.

'It has to be this one.'

'But what about a mink, a little less light coloured? I thought you always wanted a mink.'

'Yes I did, but I never saw an arctic fox before. Not in Saffron Walden.'

'Madame looks very fashionable.' The assistant recognised the symptoms and knew that if she did not intervene to tip the balance, the two might leave the shop unable to agree. Most men were flattered if they heard their wife being flattered.

'The mink is certainly warm, but it is definitely a coat for an older woman. The mink may make you look ten years older, more mature, but the fox will make you keep your youth.'

The fox it was and it consumed two of Clive's thousand mark notes. It didn't seem so expensive in exchange for just two banknotes.

'Please wrap my old coat, I will wear this.'

Out of the street, Brenda looked up to the sky, hugged herself and experienced her second orgasm. This time it lasted two seconds. The excited nerves from the first one were quickly laid to rest.

Robert followed them back to the hotel and slid into the seat next to Klaus.

'That's it. He just bought a briefcase and went into the bank. Then he bought her a fur coat. What now Klaus?'

'Not much. They are booked into this hotel for tonight and tonight only. I asked the desk man. I know him. They wanted a taxi for nine o'clock tomorrow morning booked. I told him I was from the "firm" and would I need to pick them up. He said they needed a taxi and hadn't booked it yet so would we do it. I might drop you at the jetty before I pick them up!'

Robert looked at Klaus with amazed respect.

'You wizard.'

'And if they change their minds, they will telephone the firm and we will know! I gave them our number. Now we can relax tonight, don't you think Robert? A good time will be had by us and Anka.'

~   ~   ~

At 8:30 am, Robert waved Klaus off from the ferry terminal and strolled up to Pier 2. The 9:45 to Heligoland via Cuxhaven was already in position, but not yet taking on passengers. Robert bought a coffee and a newspaper from the kiosk and settled down where he could see anyone on the wooden duckboards, approaching the ticket check for the ferry. The newspaper, the *Hamburger Morgenpost*, did not last long. The headlines showed a football score 1-0. But it was a prediction for the game ahead that afternoon, Hamburg versus Bayern Munich. North versus South. If there was a North-South divide in Germany, the North thought they had the edge with their subdued culture; Hamburg, the city of Brahms and Mendelsohn, the industrial powerhouse of Germany with its biggest port, the gateway to the world. If there were such a divide, the South thought they had the edge with their flamboyant culture, worn on sleeves, lederhosen, town halls, large beer mugs with lots of froth and motor car badges.

It was a repeat of yesterday. The hunter was once again ahead of his prey, hunting from the front and not the rear.

All Robert could do was sit and wait for the Blackmores to arrive. At ten minutes past nine, there they were, once again stuttering along like a pair of birds. This time, Brenda was not in black so only Clive looked like a wizened vulture with his scrawny neck protruding out the neck of his Crombie. Brenda looked more like an Ostrich, thin legs sticking out of the furry fox. Her hat was black, brimless and close fitting. It looked more like a black skull cap than a hat and sat uneasily above the fox. A matching fur hat would have been a good investment but she had been so overwhelmed by the experience that she had overlooked the need for matching accessories. The surprise was that Klaus was carrying their big suitcase. Clive was clutching the briefcase to his bosom while Brenda had a small black leather handbag over her arm: another clash with the silver fur. Klaus came within a foot of the almost shaking Robert and tipped a wink as he passed by. Robert caught a whiff of the naphthalene of mothballs as Clive's Crombie overcoat flapped past him. At the top of the gang plank, by the ticket check, Klaus put the suitcase down and tipped the peak of his hat. Clive poked a hand into his pocket, peered at the pile of unfamiliar coins and plucked one out, giving it to Klaus. A fifty pfennig mite. Half a mark and yet he had seven hundred and forty eight thousand of them in his briefcase, with more to come. Half way down the gang-plank, Clive skimmed the coin into the river Elbe. It didn't even bounce once. He looked back to see the couple disappearing into the ferry and paused a moment to wish Robert a pleasant journey and to hope they would meet tomorrow.

Two minutes later, Robert was on board and looking for a suitably sheltered place to sit. October in the Elbe estuary and the North Sea could be chilly. Brenda would be glad of her fur coat although she would soon be wishing it were six inches or more longer and not quite so girlie fashionable.

Robert was conscious that Clive had spoken to him at the airport on arrival, to ask about the taxi-driver. He did not wish to provoke the couple into any action until they were all on dry land. So he chose his place carefully where he could only be seen from one direction and where he could hide behind his newspaper if the two were pottering around on the deck. He was on a wooden slatted bench on the leeward side of the upper deck, under a canopy. What little wind reached him, was kept at bay by his US marine jacket. It was the usual slow pull out of Hamburg along the Elbe estuary towards Cuxhaven. Once out into the open sea, it was a quick dash across the Deutsche Bucht, the German Bight, to Heligoland or Helgoland. The wind was too sharp and it kept most of the passengers below in one or other of the many bars. The food as always on this boat was dreadful and with a substantial swell, much of it ended up over the side. Once again, Robert was feeding on adrenaline, having long digested the huge plate of scrambled egg provided by Anka.

Clive looked up from his pot of tea, already cold because the first cup had not passed his tea test. He could not drink it black, nor with lemon, and he had never, on his many visits to Germany, become accustomed to the taste of tea with evaporated milk.

'What on earth have you got there, woman?'

Brenda was standing before him holding two bright yellow duty free shopping bags, bulging with packets. She looked proud.

'Getting some butter.'

'Butter! Why on earth butter?'

'This is one of the butter boats. Butter is very expensive in Germany because of the tax and they sell it here without tax. You can buy as much as you like to take back.'

'But we're not going back. Butter is tuppence where we're going. Who's going to carry that lot and how are you going to keep it fresh?'

'It's been kept already for years in the refrigerated butter mountain. It will keep a bit longer in a fridge.'

'Well, let's hope the hotel has a big one for tonight. I thought you were going to buy some perfume. Did you get my whisky?'

Brenda delved into one of the bags and pulled out a bottle.

'Yes of course. This was on offer. A very good offer.'

Clive stared at the cheap printed glossy label. A Scotsman, in full kilted regalia, was playing bagpipes. "Carnaby Street Wiskey" was all it said. The liquid was pale yellow, the colour of a child's soft drink. A craggy German in the next seat, wearing the semi-naval clothes worn by most of his generation, leaned over and tapped the bottle with his finger nail.

'Japanisch! Sehr Gut! Sehr günstig!' His voice matched his face. Even the vowels cracked and grated. 'Japanese! Very good! Very cheap!'

To Clive, a Japanese attempt at whisky could never be good value, no matter what they called it, nor how little they charged. He suddenly thought of the three quarters of a million with more to come, his imminent new life, made the first extravagant gesture of his life and cracked his first joke. He stood up, walked to the side of the boat, unscrewed the cap and emptied the bottle over the side.

'No doubt the price of cod will rise sharply next week.'

The ferry anchored about a quarter of a mile off from the jetty and showed no sign of moving further. Everyone had gone out on deck to watch as Heligoland approached. Those who had not seen it before were, as all their predecessors, impressed by its smallness and the image of the red rock cliffs jutting vertically out of the ocean. The craggy North German sailor-type had explained to Brenda in faltering English that the ferry boats were not allowed to dock and that all the passengers would be taken off by small "taxi-boats", thus providing additional income for the local fishermen. A large square hole appeared in the side of the ship, cordoned off by a rope and three crew members. No one seemed to be in a hurry, so Brenda moved to the rope and peered out. The first taxi-boat, with seating for about a dozen, was bobbing up and down about twenty yards away, sideways on to the hole and bouncing a yard nearer with each vertical oscillation. It paused about two yards away as ropes were exchanged and two of the crew hauled it alongside. The cause of the reluctance of the experienced travellers to rush to the head of the queue, otherwise an almost genetic characteristic of Germans, was now revealed. As the boat came alongside, it squeezed a wave of water onto the deck, drenching Brenda from the waist downwards. Her new fox coat partially saved the day, taking the brunt of the splash and the water missed Clive. Half of her coat, her legs and butter were soaked and both her shoes and the butter bags filled with North Sea. She coughed and her false teeth flew out into the waves.

Robert had watched with mixed feelings. He was not happy that the couple were drawing so much attention to themselves. They had become noticed. He decided not to travel in the same taxi-boat as the Blackmores. He felt sure they could not get far on the Island even if he arrived five minutes later. In any case, his eyes were already in place on the jetty. When Robert stepped out onto the jetty, Clive and Brenda were still there, arguing about the butter. It was packed in a kind of greaseproof paper and not foil. It had not survived the onslaught of the ocean and paper was beginning to curl to reveal the bare pale yellow fat.

'How much did you pay for it?'

'Twenty packs at one mark each. It said it costs one mark eighty in the shops in Germany.'

Clive fished a note out of his wallet, a twenty.

'There, I've paid for it twice, now leave it here next to the bin and shut up.'

'How dare you. It was my money and it is my butter. I am keeping it.'

'What's happened to your mouth?'

'I lost my false teeth over the side when I got splashed. Will I be able to get some new ones where we are going?'

'Good grief, I didn't know you had false teeth. Yes, but I think they make them out of aluminium.' Clive ran his tongue along his sound teeth with a feeling of inner gratitude.

Robert had no difficulty in spotting his host. He scanned the few people waiting for passengers and immediately spotted the cigarette smoke torn almost horizontally away from the smoker by the wind. He walked over to Klaus. Except it wasn't Klaus but a slightly older version with a deeply lined weathered face.

'Manfred! You must be Manfred.'

'Good day to you Mr. Robert. I have heard a lot about you.'

Manfred's English, like his brother's, was uttered with Platt Deutsch overtones, but, unlike his brother's, was almost grammatically perfect, apart from an occasional lapse into literal translation.

~　　~　　~

Chapter 25

Heligoland 1967

From the moment they appeared round the corner, on the cliff path, fifty yards away, it was a full five minutes before the Blackmores struggled up the hill to become level with Robert. Up hill at the age of 80, it was difficult to achieve much more than a quarter of a mile per hour. Brenda was still a sprightly 75 but she was blowing even more.

'Schön guten Tag!' Good day to you and Happy Birthday! Robert started in German and unwittingly delivered a body punch with his spontaneous birthday greeting.

Clive's mouth fell open and then shut and opened in his usual fashion. His brain was unable to function.

To add to his confusion, Robert now switched to English, exaggerating his Manchester accent. 'What brings you here then? It's a long way from Saffron Walden at your age. And it is your birthday isn't it?'

Brenda's eyes narrowed and widened, unable to comprehend the vision of a local German talking to her in perfect English, apart from the accent. Something took her back to the distant days in the office in Manchester where she had been surrounded by such accents. Her mouth opened and stayed open, the usual dark figure of eight, wider at the edges than in the middle. She was still overburdened with the fact that for the first time in her life, she was without teeth. She had almost forgotten them, leaving at such an ungodly hour the day before, and she had got into the taxi to the airport before realising they were still on her bedside table. She had taken to not sleeping in her teeth during the last month because her jaw had gone through a further cycle of shrinkage since her last teeth were produced. Now they were on the bottom of the North Sea. Robert saw the shiny gums and felt a brief pang of pity before burying it firmly below his anger, his rage as he faced the focus of a lifetime of grief and frustration.

'You murdered my grandfather. You stole his life, his future, his work and his recognition. You built your cosy life and your fame on that. My grandfather should have lived and got that

283

recognition. He should have gone to Cambridge and then, most likely my mother would never have died in Manchester. You owe me a lot.'

Robert knew he had gone too far in his logical development but this was no debate in the University Union. All was fair in war. But still, had he thrown too much too soon?

'Then you went and betrayed your country. You vile traitor. How many more of your compatriots died because of you? And what for? Money? You contemptible little shite. And now you are running away? Where to? Shiteland?'

Although Robert knew he had gone too far he felt the pistol inside his pocket and wanted to finish the job there and then. But he would have to take Brenda out as well and that wasn't in his plan. Clive could not help the involuntary gesture to the two envelopes inside his overcoat pocket. Brenda was the first to break.

'Get me out of here.' Brenda's missing false teeth now left her with a black hole on her face, whenever she spoke. She then hissed through gritted gums and the words slithered their way out through her now ugly mouth. 'Get me home now.'

Clive raised a bony finger and drew on a lifetime of deceit. He wagged as he spoke. 'You ... you have made the biggest mistake of your life. You do not know what you are doing. This is Germany, I am at home here. This is my second home.'

'Correction Mr. Blackmore! This is West Germany. You are at home in the East. In this part of Germany, you are as much a traitor as if you were in England. The British Army of the Rhine could pick you up within an hour and the German police would be powerless to stop them. Oh, and by the way, you are plain Mister again. It was announced on the BBC this morning that the Queen has taken your knighthood away. I'm sorry Mrs. Blackmore, but you ain't no lady any more.' Robert mocked the last sentence in a passable American accent.

'How many times do I have to tell you Clive.' Brenda's voice was in a tremor, close to breaking down. 'Get me away from this horrible little man.'

She turned and started to wobble down the path. Clive pulled himself up to his tallest height and stuck out his chin, saying nothing, but barring the way. His eyes were those of a big white shark. Unemotional. Ready to cause death. Robert drew himself up, half an inch taller than Clive.

'Go on Blackmore. I want to hear you say it. I know how you did it. A grenade from the MacFadzean trench. Perkins told me about it. He always suspected something but had nothing to go on. When I brought back the vital information from the German medical orderly, Eberhardt Geisler, it all fell into place for Sergeant Perkins. He's been to the police, yesterday and there is a warrant out for your arrest – murder. There is no statute of limitations for murder in English law. You're sunk if you ever go back.' Robert was playing with the details. 'And I have the books; my grandfather's notebooks, the ones you didn't find and destroy. I found them in Manchester. You didn't. So what are you going to do now, Mr. Blackmore? You are a murderer. You are a wanted man. You are a wanted man in Manchester, a wanted man in Saffron Walden and you are a wanted man here. You can never go back.'

'I'll tell you what I will do. Follow us and I will have you killed.'

'I don't need to follow you physically, Blackmore. My spirit is behind your right shoulder. And if you look over your left one, you will see the ghost of my grandfather. In front of you are the ghosts of the dead Englishmen and women you have betrayed. What are you going to do about them? You cannot kill ghosts and spirits. They will stay with you for the rest of your life, however long that is. A day, a month, a year, who knows? Aufwiedersehen, Mr. Blackmore. Till I see you again. It will be soon.'

Robert leaned against the cliff wall and watched the two of them as they staggered down the path. Clive was tottering like a sick crow in his black Crombie and Brenda was lopsided with half the fur coat still matted from the drenching during the disembarking procedure. Once again, Robert felt the pangs of pity and had to crush them. It was made easier by the sound of Brenda, wailing about Clive's knighthood.

"Dammit," he thought, "I'm really not cut out for this cloak and dagger stuff at all."

As soon as the Blackmores had jerked out of sight down the path, curiously like clowns on stilts, Robert by-passed the corner by using the rough path and once more overtook the slow moving prey, arriving in the square a full ten minutes before they did. He bought himself a dark coffee from the Stube and stood in the street with his eyes on the hotel entrance. He didn't care if they saw him or not. He rather hoped they would. When they came round the corner, Brenda's mouth and tongue were in full flow and from Clive's demeanour and from the look on his face, he wasn't enjoying it. They paused briefly outside the little hotel, Clive hoping that Brenda would at least stop nagging while they walked past reception. Looking across the square, Robert saw Manfred leaning against a wall, smoking. He walked over to join him.

'Mr. Robert. You have the eyes of the island and yet you are not content? Since they left you on the cliff they were watched every centimetre of the way. They cannot leave the island without us knowing it will happen. You should be relaxing in the bar with a beer. Have you hunger? Come on, I know some good sausages. Or better, I know a great place that does a superb Labskaus, topped with a huge pile of spinach and a mirror egg.'

'Mirror egg.' thought Robert, translating it into German as Spiegelei and back into English as fried egg.

'Let's go and meet your sausages. Do they have a Nuremberg accent?'

'Ah yes, a plate of little fried Nürnbergers, Sauerkraut and a cold Pils Bier. Let's go to Annie's. She knows some good Nürnbergers. And her Pils is Jever!'

~   ~   ~

'He said "Happy Birthday". The taxi driver's radio said "Happy Birthday". It isn't your birthday and yet these two people who should be unconnected both told you it was your birthday.'

Brenda was not scientifically logical but in matters of false birthday greetings from unconnected strangers, she could not accept it as coincidence.

'They're on to us.'

'Who? That idiot? I can deal with him.'

'I don't know. it could be more than just him.'

Brenda was now snapping and hissing like an angry swan, pecking at anything that moved.

'You are the one with all the connections. You have friends in Germany. Here we are in this awful place, pursued by this awful man, yet he and other people like the taxi-driver are on to us. Where did the taxi come from?'

'It came with the hotel booking. It was part of their service.'

'Whose service? Who fixed that up? You told me you had never been to Hamburg before. You said you had been to almost every German city except Hamburg. Who did the hotel booking?'

'The travel agent in Saffron Walden. Althorpe's. We've been using them for years. They know us.'

'Exactly. They know us and thanks to you and your blithering performance on television they know even more.'

Brenda had never spoken like this before. Even as her words flowed, she scarcely recognised them herself. The adrenaline and stress were laying open the full range of her vocabulary, normally barely more than a thousand regular words. Now all the words she had learnt during her life and had never uttered, flowed, without inhibition, spoken with innocent, virginal enthusiasm as they met her tongue for the first time.

'But they are not going to start phoning up Heligoland.'

'Why not? They and only they knew we were going to Heligoland. No one else knew.'

'It was just the girl in the agents who knew. She did the booking all on her own. She was just a slip of a girl.'

'Give me the ticket wallet from the agent, I want to look at the itinerary.'

Clive fumbled and fished out a crumpled envelope from the side pocket of his cabin luggage. Sheepishly he handed it over to the suddenly, undisputed superior being.

'Susan ... Susan Sykes served you. It says it here. Typed at the bottom. "In case of enquiries, please contact your personal travel organiser Susan Sykes, Saffron Walden Office, Saffron Walden 0799 555123. Well, I'm going to make a travel enquiry and it won't be Miss Sykes I'm calling.'

It took Brenda fifteen minutes to persuade the receptionist of the hotel to call England. In the end the receptionist had come up to the room to collect a deposit of twenty Marks. After a further ten minutes of clicking and buzzing, she heard the characteristic double ring. The sound of the ringing tone in her ear, a familiar English ringing tone, gave Brenda sudden comfort. She felt close to home.

'Althorpe's. How can I help you?' The voice sounded as if it came from next door. It was a good line.

'Good afternoon. This is Mrs. Blackmore, one of your customers. I am on a visit that you have organised and I am in Heligoland. It is most important that I speak to Mr. Althorpe. Extremely important. In fact, it is a matter of life and death.'

It took Brenda a further ten minutes to manipulate the proprietor of the travel agent to her own ends. She threw in a few images of Sir Clive and the Rotary Club and he was soon ready to betray the confidence of one of his own employees. He accepted that a security leak could only have come from Miss Sykes or the newly hired computer expert who was still setting up their new system. But the Welsh youth, whom they knew as Tecwyn the Techno, had not been in since Wednesday and the booking had been made on Thursday. He could be eliminated as a suspect.

'I'm surprised at her. Her father was a former policeman, Jason Sykes. The travel agency knew him well because as a private detective now, he had advised on security, having, as he himself had said, a long and intimate knowledge of the criminal mind.'

'Right.' Brenda's mouth was now a curved slit as she turned on Clive. 'The girl's father is a private detective. His daughter knew we were going to Heligoland. That dreadful man also knew we were going to Heligoland because he was here waiting for us. You are the clever scientist Clive. You work out who is the link here. And when you've worked it out, you get on to your music men back in England and get it sorted out.'

'Music men?'

'Your Beethoven lot.'

'Beethoven?'

'Don't think I don't know all about that.'

For the second time in an hour, hearing the unspeakable, the look on Clive's face precluded any chance that he could deny convincingly. It was Brenda who kept up the pace.

'All those secret telephone calls you make in your study. Do you think I don't know what it was all about?'

Every thought that spluttered into Clive's mind was immediately demolished by whatever Brenda said next. Just as he was contemplating how much Brenda could have learnt by eavesdropping on one side of a conversation from outside his door, she struck him with rapier precision.

'You remember Scottie, your expert whiz kid who used to come round? We got very chatty. You remember how he fixed the TV aerial so you could get the London local news? Well he did another little job for me while you were off gallivanting to Dresden a few years back. He put some wires on your study telephone extension and ran them into my sewing room. If you had ever done any housework you would have spotted them. I don't know how those things work but Scottie was very clever. It was always on so you never heard a click when I picked it up. There was no mouth piece, just a listening piece that fixed to my ear so I could listen but you couldn't hear any noises from my room. The boy Scottie said he had put on some extra bits so that the echoes were cancelled, whatever that meant.'

'You tapped into a Post Office Telephone? Without permission? It's against the law!'

Clive's grip on reality was effectively at an end.

'Against the law? you silly little man!'

Both Brenda and Clive gasped at the unprecedented insult. Brenda recovered first.

'I thought you must have another woman, going off on your own and always so vague about what you had been doing. Then there was that woman Ilse and I was convinced you were having an affair with her, ever since Windermere. I still do. What about that hotel in Dresden? You both spent the night there, I know it. You were going with her. It was a surprise to find you were spying as well. It would have been better just spying than going with another woman. But spies can't resist foreign women, can they? I couldn't believe it at first. I thought no one would look at you. Do you think I married you for how you looked? You remember those shorthand lessons I took? You asked me what on earth I was doing it for, since I didn't need to work. Well, my little husband. I have news for you. It was my insurance policy. I took down every conversation you ever had on the telephone. What you said. What they said. There are now about sixty shorthand pads in a safe deposit box in my personal bank. There's even that time you phoned Blunt to get that knighthood squashed. Who was it? That White person wasn't it? The one you are always on about. I never knew why Blunt was so keen to help you. Was he your boyfriend?'

Brenda lied about the safety deposit box. But she discounted the possibility that now, Clive would ever rummage through her boudoir to find her stash of notebooks. And of course, sixty was an exaggeration.

Clive was in his fish mode, mouth opening and closing noiselessly.

'I did not "go" with Ilse Kresser. It was professional.' It sounded so feeble, so lame and so late.

'I am not interested in her now. So now, you go down there and pay that receptionist another twenty Marks and get on the phone to your Blunt or your hero or your chorister or whatever and get it done.'

'Get what done?'

'Get rid of that travel agent. And use your connexions to Germany to get rid of that pest we met on the path.'

'Get rid of the travel agent? Why?'

'Why? Revenge you idiot. Revenge. You killed someone already out of greed. Why don't you redeem yourself like a man and kill someone out of revenge.'

'But it doesn't achieve anything. What he's done is done. We are not going back there so he doesn't matter.'

'I can go back.' Brenda was hissing. 'You can't. Now get on that phone and do it. I'm going to take a bath.'

The telephone lines to England were busy that afternoon.

'Sit down love. I went to Heligoland this morning. Everything is all right. I'm all right. I am not doing anything illegal or dangerous. Everything is under control.'

It was probably the first time that Robert had deliberately lied to Alessandra. He himself was beginning to feel the fear of not knowing. Everything was anything but under control. He looked over to Manfred across the clean tables of Annie's bar. Manfred pressed his thumb on the table. The German equivalent of crossed fingers. He could see Robert moving the telephone a centimetre or two away from his ear and knew from years of experience that poor Robert was on the receiving of an ear bashing. Ear bashings only came from women. If he had known that the woman on the other end of the line was a hot-blooded Italian of high birth, he would have ordered a stiff Schnapps for Robert to go with the tall half litre of Jever Pils waiting for his return. Robert had to withstand several minutes of pure undiluted rage before the volcano subsided and warmth and love remained.

'Bobbie, please, please do not do anything stupid. We need you.'

Robert took the subsequent personal intimacies as a welcome relief but was still pleased to end the conversation and get back to his beer. He put his hand on his chest and let out a long slow deep breath. Manfred smiled. He was enjoying seeing someone else in his least favourite position, on the receiving end of a wifely tirade.

'Here come the sausages. I've been smelling them for ten minutes.'

~   ~   ~

Jason Sykes stepped out of the fish and chip shop with his newspaper wrapped bundle. He paused briefly to watch a pigeon pecking hungrily at a pile of half chewed and vomited chips, still soaked in the beer that had caused the vomiting the night before. Queasily, he eased himself into the front seat of his Jaguar XJ6. His car was his sole indulgence. He had earned it. Sitting outside dark wet houses, down dark wet suburban streets, waiting for the miscreant husband to emerge after a two hour tryst with his mistress, had earned him the right to spend those two hours in a comfortable car. The smell of the hot vinegar wafted up from the newspaper wrapping. He was about to unwrap last weeks Saffron Walden Times, to shovel the contents of the pack into his mouth when there was a tap on his window. Winding the window down, he looked into the face of a pristine bank manager or surgeon or headmaster of a public school. The face had been exceedingly fine shaved so that the skin glowed. The glasses, rimless, looked un-English and expensive. The head was topped by a fine fedora. The black matte coat was of the finest leather. Leather coats on some men look sinister. This one just looked expensive.

'Excuse me, Sir.'

The voice was curiously and simultaneously English and foreign. It was the type of voice that reads the English news on foreign radio stations, droning on with immaculate grammar about the productivity and five year forward look of some failing Eastern European economy.

'I've lost my way. I should be back in Saffron Walden, meeting a client at the Saffron Arms. I came by train, asked the way and here I am! Can you help me?'

Jason had no way of knowing the lie. He was on his way to watch the unfaithful husband and not his own back. When private detectives or ex-policemen or even active policemen have a contemptuous suspect in their sights, they rarely watch their backs. Leather Coat's Mercedes van was parked round the corner, having followed Jason the short distance from his office. The back of Leather Coat was being watched with meticulous professionalism by a supportive craftsman. Jason's back was open and vulnerable. Jason looked at his watch. He had allowed half an hour before his husband-watch was due to start and he had locked up and left the office to allow Hilda, his secretary-receptionist, to go home. Hilda was not good at locking up.

'Hop in. I'll drop you off. You'll have to excuse the fish and chips but I haven't eaten since breakfast. I've got a job starting in half an hour.'

'Ah, are you sure? I thank you. You are most kind. Perhaps while you eat, I will telephone the hotel. How long will it take to get there?'

'Five, ten minutes at the most, after I've finished this.'

Leather Coat strode to the red telephone kiosk outside the take-away and pulled open the stiff door with difficulty. He recoiled at the stink of urine and recoiled again at the equally offensive stink of the mouthpiece, irradiating the odour of years of stale tobacco, fish and chips and spittle. A number was dialled, not in Saffron Walden. A pause, the rapid pips and after much effort, a shilling was forced into the coin slot. It was as if the English didn't want you to use their public phones, he thought. The door is stiff, the coin slot is stiff and the phone booth stinks. And who wants to hold this instrument next to a cleanly shaven face, dappled with Etienne Aigner Number 2.

'Gleich geht's los.'

The Queen of England had nodded sagely when the President of Germany had translated the words into English for her at the start of a horse race. "Equal goes it loose." he had uttered. The Queen had probably translated it directly back into German and then correctly back into English to get "It's starting", or more colloquially "They're off", and in the case of Leather Coat, "We're off."

'Let's say 15 minutes.'

Nothing was said in return. Leather Coat hung up and got out into the fresh air. Unexpected as it was, Jason knew exactly what was happening when the wrong end of a silencer was pressed deep into the side of his neck, the moment he had got the car moving. He had been accosted by "injured" parties before and knew how to keep calm. All this experience allowed him to get the first words in, almost seizing the initiative, except for the gun.

'OK Sir, keep calm. I'm not going to run away. By the time I've stopped the car to get out, you could do your worst. What do you want me to do? Stop?'

'Bend right here.' Leather Coat's accent was perfect, his vocabulary and grammar less so. He would have read the news perfectly only if someone had written it for him.

'What? Bend? Turn in there you mean?'

'Yes turn, turn now, where the road bends.'

The side road was heavily tree-lined and the street lamps were obscured.

'Stop in the dark there.'

'Look, I am still not going to run. I can't run. If I run I won't get far. So take that out of my neck, please. I'm a professional and with your gun, I think you are a professional too. Just tell me what you want. Normally people pay me for information but your currency is very persuasive.'

'You will tell me about a client. A client who is in Helgoland. Right now. You know who I mean?'

'Yes, of course. I have only one client in Heligoland. You mean Heligoland don't you? Helgoland?' After the Legoland jibe, Jason had brushed up his geography and read all about the island - Heligoland. Now here was a well informed, well groomed potential assassin calling it Helgoland.

'I can tell you something, I don't know why he is in Heligoland. He's gone after someone and I don't know a thing, just that he has gone.'

'You don't need to know why. We know it already.'

'We.' Thought Jason. There's even more of them.

'I want his name. Who is he?'

This was not Brenda's plot at all. Brenda's plot would have had Sykes dead by now. But in working out the source of the leak, Brenda had exhausted her total reserve of logical deduction. The death of Sykes would immediately draw his daughter Susan into police enquiries. Brenda's phone call to the agency from Heligoland and Jason's file on Robert and the Blackmores, now both in Heligoland would be an easy case for the Cambridgeshire police. In any case, Leather Coat and his associates only killed for need. Here, there was no need. Yet. They had other immediate needs. They needed to know who had followed Blackmore, and why. But Jason did not know that.

'His name is White. Robert White. It's his proper name, I checked.'

'You checked? Why? Did his real name matter to you?'

'No. But I once was a policeman. I can't help it. He works at Manchester University. His father did patriotic things for the government during the war.'

Jason was saying far more than he needed to. It was only the second time a gun had been pulled on him and he was finding it much more persuasive than money.

'I need a description. A full description.'

'I can do better than that. I've got a photograph. Two photographs in fact. He looked so different on the second visit so I got my secretary to take another.'

'You take pictures of all your clients?'

'If I can. I had one disappear owing me two grand. And a few owed me hundreds, till the photograph passed to the police made them change their minds. It's good insurance.'

'They sit there and let you photograph them?'

'No, she, Hilda, takes it through one of those see through mirrors.'

'And this one, of Mr. White, is already developed and printed or still on the film?'

'Don't need to. They're Polaroids.'

'And these ... Polaroids, where are they.'

'In the office. Where else?'

'Then we are going to your office, Mr. Sykes. Is anyone else there?'

'Not at this time. No. Of course not.'

'So do you know what you are going to do now? Tell me Mr. Sykes. You are a professional. So you said.'

'I am going to drive us to my office and we are going to go inside and get the photographs. And then ... ?'

'And then Mr. Sykes, it depends on how well you behave.'

It took no more than Sykes' estimate of five minutes to reach the office and a further minute to enter the office. Leather Coat took up a position near the door, away from the window. He jabbed the gun at Sykes.

'Where are the photographs kept?'

'In that filing cabinet there.'

'And how do you mark them with the name?'

Leather Coat could smell the fear, even the fear of death. Fifteen times he had smelt the fear of death in his prey – when death had followed and his prey had known that death would follow. But creatures facing death often panicked and did stupid things. People had died who were not meant to die. Sykes was not meant to die and Leather Coat was taking no chances.

'How will I know it is the right photograph?'

'Each one is in the customer file, with the name on the file. This one will say "Mr. Robert White" and there should be two polaroids inside.'

'Should?'

'Will. I saw them yesterday and no one else goes into that file.'

'Then Mr. Sykes, open the box and get out the file. Slowly.'

Sykes needed no bidding to go slowly. He pushed up his sleeves and with the tips of his fingers, opened the cabinet, standing behind the extended tray in order to face his master. Slowly a hand was inserted and emerged with an orange file. Sykes laid it down slowly on the desk, turning it round so that the title could be read.

'Open it. Fish out the photographs for me.'

Sykes, using only his finger tips, indeed, the tips of his nails, flipped open the file. There were about 10 sheets of handwritten reports and two polaroids.

'Shut the file. Move into the corner.'

Sykes backed into the corner and shut his eyes.

'You think you are going to die, Mr. Sykes? Why? You will only die if you have managed to fool me with these photographs. I won't come back. It won't be me. I am not the killer.' He lied.

'But if you do anything to interfere with what happens now, you will die, soon, somewhere.'

'So why not now? I have seen your face?'

'I thought you were a professional Mr. Sykes. But of course you are not. A professional would know that yours would be a messy killing. Not just blood on the carpet. But your daughter would get drawn in and everything else, and I can't afford to leave a track.'

At the mention of his daughter being "drawn in", Sykes' turned a paler shade of puce.

'You can choose to live or die. Talk to your daughter, talk to anyone and it will spread and then Mr. Sykes, if you do that, you should visit the undertaker and have both you and your daughter measured for coffins. Very few healthy people get the opportunity to decide whether to live or die like you have. Make the most of it.'

In the time it took Sykes to slither to the floor in the corner of the room, Leather Coat was out of the office and half way across the square where he was met by the black Mercedes van that had followed them from the fish and chip shop. Forty five minutes later, Leather Coat was driving the van past the North Circular Road up the A11. His companion had transferred to the motor cycle that was kept in the back of the van and was already at work in an upstairs flat in Islington, having shot ahead at bike speed.

Rolf had got everything ready in the dark room before Siggi, the motorcyclist, ran through the door. The two polaroids were copied to sheet film in two minutes, developed and fixed using rapid chemicals in three minutes, printed from wet negatives onto A4 and put into the drum scanner for onward transmission. Ten minutes after the polaroids entered the flat to be placed under the rostrum camera, the images were arriving in Germany and were relayed from the receiving office in Bonn onwards to Dresden without having to be printed off in Bonn. It was barely three minutes longer than it took the barmaid to pull a cold Pils for Robert in the Blue Angel.

In Dresden, Emil picked up the prints, pushed his glasses up on to his forehead, pursed his lips and turned to Wolfgang Steuer.

'He's back. Mr. Robert White is back.'

Steuer took the prints, stared for three seconds without a trace of emotion.

'The fly has tangled with the web again.'

He passed the pictures back to Emil.

'Herr Konrad Spinner, he is our best in Helgoland. Use him. Use him now. I do not want Mr. White back in Dresden. But I do wish to close the file. The file is very untidy.'

'I agree, Herr Steuer. Very untidy. And I can close his chart too.'

Five minutes after Leather Coat had left, Sykes pulled himself to his feet, flopped into the chair of his office, picked up the phone, looked at it, saw death, and put it down again. He unwrapped his pack of fish and chips, looked briefly at the cold congealed chips and vomited over them. He opened the bottom drawer of his desk and took out a flat quarter bottle of scotch, his emergency supply for medicinal purposes. He was in dire need of medicinal attention.

~ ~ ~

'Ich bin von Kopf bis Fuss
auf Liebe eingestellt . . . '

After the welcome sausages and sauerkraut, Robert had moved on to *Die Blaue Engel* bar, waiting for Manfred. Manfred was not allowed to miss Abendbrot with his wife, Jutta, and he had gone home for an hour. He would join Robert in the bar later. Robert was cradling a beer and listening to Marlene who had just started her nightly act. It sounded like the taxi-Marlene from Hamburg but since all taxi controllers talked like Marlene, there was no reason why this one shouldn't do the same. Across the blue smoky atmosphere in the Blue Angel, Robert could just make out the figure behind the microphone. Robert himself was in the far corner of the bar, invisible except to his nearest neighbours. He could just make out the accordionist: North German peaked cap, sailor jacket and striped shirt. It would have been a caricature except that most of the other men in the bar were dressed like that. With a striped shirt, Robert would have looked the same, so he did not look especially out of place. And when he had told Hilda in Sykes' office that he could speak German with a German accent, that, at least had not been a lie. Marlene slunk over. Putting a thigh-booted foot on Robert's chair, she switched to English. One arm was outstretched with the hand opened to frame Robert's head, the other hand palm face-upwards, imploring.

'Fallink in loff again
Neffer vanted to
Vat am I to do
Can't 'elp eet'

Robert thought hard; did she always sing in English? The other people in the bar were taking no notice. Marlene was wallpaper as far as they were concerned. There was nothing unusual today; it was just another German visitor from Hamburg, Bremen or Cuxhaven, having a beer in their bar.

'Loff's alvays been my game
Play eet as I may
I vas born zat vay
Can't 'elp eet'

Marlene was flirting, almost caressing. From the reaction of the others, she always did this and nowadays, stuck to strangers. The locals had long since had enough of being flirted at by Marlene and when there were no strangers, she didn't bother. But tonight she had Robert.

'Men flokk around me
Like motts around ze flame
And if zeir vings burn
I know I'm not to blame'

But it was Marlene who was flocking around Robert. Paying a lot of attention. Too much attention.

'Fallink in loff again
Neffer vanted to
Vat am I to do
Can't 'elp eet.'

Marlene concluded, to spasmodic applause and a few sarcastic jeers. Robert joined in the clapping.

'Komm. Komm tanzen mit mir.'

The male voice was a shock and Robert looked "her" straight in the eyes, which he had avoided so far. Marlene had not had time to shave that evening, having slept in.

'Come, ve dance ein tango togezer.'

Robert knew the song from over 10 years previously, when he had been researching physics in Hamburg. It was a kind of stand-alone Kurt Weil Thruppeny Opera, Drei Groschen Opern type of song without an opera to support the ambiguous lyrics.

'In der Taverne
Dunkle Gestalten
Rote Laterne
Abend für Abend ...
Und sie tanzten einen Tango
Jacky Brown und Baby Miller'

It was a tango, but not quite a tango.

'Down in the tavern
They're dancing a tango
Night after night ...
By the light of the lanterns
Nobody knows
What happened that night
And why they're now dancing
The criminal tango.'

That was as much of the song plot that Marlene bothered with and Robert knew it anyway. What followed was more interesting, drawled into his ear in German, compressing the syllables to a rhythm into which they did not fit. Each sentence was hurried as their faces converged in the tango, with gaps of silence as their faces turned away.

'Your Jacky Brown and Baby Miller
They leave tonight from beyond quay three.
Don't speak a word, it will be heard.
Manfred, quay two at eleven, watch out.'

'Hör auf Marli.' A deep gravelly crackle, born of a lifetime of smoking in smoky bars came from the throat of a sailor near the dancers. 'Give up Marlene. He's not your type. You won't talk him into your bed tonight!'

The few that heard the heckling, crackled their own gravel with supportive guffaws. At the end of the tango, Robert and Marlene received rapturous applause and more heckling. Money was thrown. Robert was in the process of returning to his table, but Marlene grabbed his arm.

'No, no, you must pick up the money, thank them and put it in collection box on the bar. It's for the families of fishermen who don't come home. And then you must escort me back to the band.'

Robert scooped up the coins, bowed formally to Marlene and then to the other guests. The money went in the pinewood box on the bar, to the smiles from Annie who always closed her little café when things livened up next door in the Blue Angel. She owned both.

'Do you like our atmosphere? Dark with the red lights?'

'The atmosphere is good. But red lights are not my favourite. Nor red hands. Thank you.'

Robert declined the "Red hand" cigarette that Annie offered him with a smile. 'I don't smoke.'

'Wise man. It's too late for me.'

Annie's voice was as deep as the heckling sailor's.

'Look, there's Manfred here. His spouse has let him out. I'd better tap him a beer. Another for you?'

'Please. Yes.'

Robert couldn't wait to tell Manfred his news. He got no further than the first two words.

'I just ...'

'Of course you did. You will have to tell me later. Let's have a drink, chat casually for an hour and then we can have a stroll down by the quayside to get a breath of fresh air before turning in. You have a busy day tomorrow.'

'But I ...' The penny still hadn't dropped.

'No if. No but. This time you will do as you are told. Jutta says so!' Manfred was saying everything with a big grin on his face, not daring to wink or tap the side of his nose. Just hoping and waiting for Robert to catch on that they shouldn't talk in the bar about what might happen later on.

~   ~   ~

Chapter 26

Heligoland 1967

I n the fisherman's cottage up the hill, overlooking the quay, a phone rang once, before the newspaper photo transmission machine clicked into life and started to scan an image onto the drum, line by line. Konrad Spinner could hardly wait for it to finish. Once, in sheer exasperation, he had switched the machine off to peel the image off the drum. On that occasion, all the cogs had jammed and he'd had to call in the service. It had been out of action for a week. He nearly got fired, but one of the problems with his employers was that they could not afford to have disgruntled former employees flapping around Heligoland. They would have had to extinguish him and just jamming a cog wheel was not quite a capital offence. Yet.

He had been waiting for this transmission since the call came in an hour ago: his orders for the night. He could hardly wait. This was his big one. The whirring stopped and five seconds later, Konrad was holding the new image in one hand and fitting a fresh sheet with the other. Standing orders, after receiving an image, always put in a clean sheet for the next one. Konrad took the picture into his kitchen where the lights were brighter. Using a pair of magnifying glasses mounted on a head-band, he scrutinised the picture of Robert. It looked like it had been taken in a doctor's waiting room. The doctor has some bad news for you Mr. England. You are not going to live.

In the corner of the kitchen, Konrad opened the door of the cooker, grasped both sides in his hands and rolled it out from between the work-tops. He swivelled the cooker to one side and then pulled up the small trapdoor in the empty gap. Out came a smooth rounded briefcase. Reaching down into the void, Konrad groped further and felt the sharp edges of the box containing his favourite toy, his crossbow. He wasn't allowed to play with it in public; his bosses in Dresden didn't understand how effective it was, nor how it struck terror into those that witnessed the execution. One day. One day he would be allowed a field test where the bosses would finally, grudgingly concede that it couldn't fail under these specific circumstances and he would start an epoch that would go down in history. He patted the box and muttered,

'See you soon, friend.'

Konrad closed the trapdoor, placed his tool box over the hatch and left a spanner and screwdriver by the tool box on the floor. If things didn't go to plan and he did not come back alone, there would be cover; he'd been fixing a leak. He poured a jug of water over the trapdoor for verisimilitude. He would need every second when he got back, so anything he could do now, would save time. He snapped open the case and looked longingly at the disassembled rifle. It was a prototype of the soon to be announced SSG-72 "Scharfschutzengewehr." Konrad had personally modified the sporting rifle on which it was based, improving its balance and stability. He closed his eyes and drew in a deep breath. It was the first stage of a careful physiological preparation. With his eyes still closed, Konrad worked on the retained image and in less than a minute he had gone through the assembly in his mind. He could do it in the dark. He would do it in the dark.

Konrad changed his clothes for action. Two vests, a black close-knitted pullover, black moleskin trousers. Thick black socks. Into his pocket he folded his pride and joy, bought on a training visit to China, one of his two black silk balaclava-like face masks. The edges of the eye and ear holes were woven selvedges. They never frayed. Whenever he was on a mission, the act of pulling on the silk mask over his facial skin caused a surge of excited anticipation. The response was so fierce, as he gave in to an adrenalin fuelled intoxication, he always had to allow himself an extra five minutes to recover. He had sifted the libraries to seek a medical explanation for his reaction. He half wanted to conquer it, his other half wanted to wallow in the ecstasy. The nearest thing he could find to match his feelings was an obscure psychiatric report that some English judges had experienced a similar response whenever they placed a black silk cloth, the black cap, over their wig before passing sentence of execution. Some of them even kept a spare silk cap under the judges' bench, to fiddle with as they anticipated the death penalty. Konrad liked the thought of being a judge, passing a sentence of death. He knew exactly what it would feel like. The power. The unassailable power to cause death, supported by the State. The moment. The exquisite moment when law and justice had decreed that this person must die and the judge became the sole articulator of death.

With his case ready by the back door, Konrad slid out into the lane behind the cottages. He needed to check that his elderly neighbour, Mattheus, had completed his nightly routine of taking his dog for a walk, locking up and had gone to bed. The next door cottage was in darkness which meant Matti was back and was now almost certainly sleeping. Konrad slipped his own door onto the latch, took his case and left his cottage with lights on.

From his long prepared "fox-hole", Konrad could see the whole of the eastern wharf. Through the telescope, he could almost read the label on the cigarette packet, discarded on the quayside. It was an empty packet of Lords. There was a small taxi-boat tied up at the quay. He could see movement but the figures were crouched. Scanning the quayside and water, he noticed ripples coming from the far unlit corner of the quay. He could just make out a second small boat, tight under the edge of the quayside. At eleven o'clock precisely, a beige taxi pulled up on the quay and discharged two small frail figures. A woman in a fur coat and a man in a large, black overcoat and an equally oversized homburg hat. The two looked around as if dazed and then, as if startled, hopped, turned and made their way to the taxi-boat.

The man took off his hat, running his hand over his white bald head. Even from that distance, the head could be seen glistening with sweat, even on this cool evening. Within a minute the boat was on its way, heading for open sea. Within a second minute, the second boat, up till then dark and empty, sprouted two occupants, started up and moved off, initially on a bearing that would take it to the other side of the quay. Eventually, the second taxi-boat swung round and followed the first boat out through the harbour gate into the open sea. Using his night glasses, Konrad picked up the trawler. It was on the move. Nearer shore, the second taxi boat had caught up with the first and was on a parallel bearing. From its wake, Konrad noticed the steer to the left, not more than a degree but enough to close the gap. It was some time before the first boat carrying the two passengers responded. It made a two degree shift to the left. Now Konrad, with his glasses on zoom, mounted on a tripod for stability, could pick out the trawler. It had no lights.

On the taxi-boat, Clive and Brenda were having one of their bitterest of arguments. Few marriages would have survived the sort of venom that Brenda saved for her days of anger. This was the day of anger that surpassed all days of anger in their half a century of marriage. Like all the previous furious arguments, this one had trivial origins.

'I can't believe you still have that butter. I even gave you the money to buy it. Actually, I gave you money to buy perfume but you chose to fritter it away on butter. Butter! I can't believe that you could buy anything under these circumstances that would be of so little use.'

The argument raged and the boatman, hired for twice the usual fee, was perplexed. He assumed that the argument must have deep significance but it was laced with confusion. "Butter", the word, was the same in English and German and he thought he recognised it. He could only assume that some business deal, involving unimaginable quantities of butter, had gone wrong. He was actually right. But he was wrong to pay them so much attention as the trawler approached.

On the other taxi-boat, Manfred pointed the trawler out to Robert. The first taxi-boat continued as if it had not seen it. Indeed, it had not. The boatman was transfixed by the heated conversation. For the first time in his life, he was watching a man being filleted with more precision than his beloved Edeltraut carved him into slivers for staying too long in the bar. He and Edeltraut would then end up padlocked in a ferocious embrace of copulation that wiped the slate clean. He could not see how these two people could ever find a way to wipe the slate clean. In the dark, he could not even see the trawler as it bore down on his vessel.

It clipped the stern, lifted the taxi completely out of the water and sent the small vessel flying through the air. A dozen limbs flayed the air before the boat and its former occupants responded to the inexorable pull of gravity and splashed back into the sea. The trawler disappeared into the darkness. Manfred swung his boat round in a tight arc and returned to the floating wreck. The hull was upside down and was floating only due to air trapped inside. Manfred had been involved in a rescue a few years previously and knew what to do. By the time the coastguards scrambled a rescue, these people would drown or perish from shock and cold if they were not pulled out of the water now. He switched on his main light and told Robert to sweep it over the surface. Someone was clinging to the hull, calling out. A young male. He could wait five minutes. Keep looking. Ten yards away, an unusual sight was caught in the beam of the small head-light. A woman, Brenda, was still in her fur coat, which was flayed out in all directions on the surface of the water. She was still alive. Manfred steered to her and despite her total lack of co-operation, he and Robert managed eventually to haul her back on board. At one stage, she screeched at Robert to let go of her leg. Manfred barked at her in German and asked if she wanted to die. It did not shut her up for the simple reason that even if she had understood it, she would not have obeyed an order in German. Brenda was tossed into the rear of the boat like a landed fish.

'Save my butter!' she screamed shrilly.

Manfred assumed she was talking about her man, despite it sounding an odd term of endearment. He preferred to call his wife Schnucki. He now turned his attention to the survivor on the hull. It took only a minute to rescue the professional sailor who could have got himself on board without the help of Manfred or Robert.

'Where is he? You have to find him. You're in trouble if you don't find him.' Brenda was in hysterics. 'There! There! Can't you see him?'

A small white sphere bobbed up and down on the waves.

'Get him. Go on!'

Manfred had never had a hysterical Englishwoman on board before, and so he treated her as a logical German.

'That is nobody. That is a marker buoy.'

'It's my husband. He is bald. He was always bald. That's his head. Save him!'

After fifty years of marriage, Brenda could not distinguish between her husband's head and a white plastic marker buoy. Manfred swept round in a tight curve, jabbed at the buoy with an oar and pulled away, expecting Brenda to have taken it all in. But as the boat pulled away, Brenda panicked. Casting off her coat she threw herself over the side, splayed her arms wide twice and went under.

It is a common and general misbelief that humans, being lighter than water, will always float. They do initially, but the Principle of Archimedes then dictates that only about 5% of the volume of the body is above the surface. The second exposure of Brenda's feeble body to the cold North Sea caused a massive exhalation. Her body sank slightly and she swallowed water, causing her to sink further beneath the surface. Pressure increases with depth and this forced the last breath of oxygen out through her nose. Water rushed in to take its place. She sank further, tried to breathe, her last mortal effort and took in more water. The pressure increased as she sank. The process was relentless until Brenda's cold, airless and lifeless body reached a drifting equilibrium depth, two hundred yards below the surface. Brenda became a smorgasbord for the fish life of the North Sea. Curiously, or rather not curiously, if its density is taken into account, 911 grammes per litre, the packs of butter that Brenda had been carrying in her yellow duty free bags when she was tossed into the water, now floated to the surface and bobbed around as marker buoys to her North Sea grave.

After the pilot had been rescued off the taxi-boat hull, Clive, who had been struggling to increase his finger-hold on the far side of the boat, slowly, relentlessly, pulled himself onto the upturned boat. He was there, sitting, shivering, but with an almost nonchalant demeanour, when the rescue dinghy from the trawler picked him up. The trawler captain, looking at his radar, did not hesitate as he ordered full steam ahead; race to Rostock with the cargo.

Clive started to speak. He wanted to say "Where's my wife?" But he could not bring himself to say it. He thus embarked upon the last years of his life, in a miserable communist State. At first, he felt irate that he had lost the money he had withdrawn from his account, but when the other portion was eventually transmitted, minus 5% commission, he discovered that there was nothing to spend it on. He couldn't even fly back to England for nostalgic trips or else he would be arrested.

Back in the other boat, Robert and Manfred were still staring at the sea into which Brenda had disappeared. Their rescued pilot was retching into the bottom of the boat. Manfred picked up the sodden fur coat.

'What about this? It's had a soaking. Over the side?'

'I suppose it's evidence that we had her. We'd better just dump it.'

Manfred felt inside the squelching pockets of the fox fur and pulled out two sodden envelopes. There was an inside pocket with a zip that held a ring with two keys.

'They're yours, I think, Mr. Robert. They are no use to me. Whatever it is, if they belong to anyone, they belong to you. Let's get back home. It's all over.'

Robert stuffed the envelopes and the key into his duffle bag. The coat went over the side.

'What are we going to say to the police. They will be there by now. We weren't out on a pleasure cruise.'

'Police? At this time of night? You must be joking. This is Heligoland. If they do come, we were night fishing. If you know nothing of night fishing keep your mouth shut. Speak no German. We saw the splashing and we went to help. We saved someone. We are heroes.'

'What about the pilot?'

'He's not going to hang around and talk to the police. I'm pretty sure he has no right to be on Heligoland. He's from the East. Now, when I put you on the quayside, I'm going to put my boat away. Get yourself to my place as quick as you can. I'll meet you there. Jutta will still be up.'

On the quayside, Robert and the pilot paused, side by side. The pilot stooped, still struggling to overcome the seawater in his bronchial tubes. Konrad scanned them from left to right, from right to left. Which one? They looked the same, both wearing black woollen hats. It was Robert himself who decided his own immediate fate. He snatched off the hat, now soaked and irritating his scalp. His blonde hair bristled in the quayside lights. Konrad saw it all through the telescopic sights, switched aim, whispering 'Got you, England.' and squeezed the trigger with the feather touch of his finger.

There on the quayside, Robert saw the flash, up on the hillside. The ten millimetre diameter bullet, over an inch long, traveling faster than the speed of sound, arrived at its target before the crack of the rifle. Robert heard the whistle of the bullet through the air, the slap, the peculiar slewing noise as the bullet severed both jugular veins, and even the splashing noise as blood poured from the hose pipe that once was a neck. He felt nothing. The body fell backwards into the water, its arms and legs performing the back stroke through the air. It slowly sank, the seawater eventually masking all trace of what was once a living being.

Almost before the body had hit the water, Konrad had removed his rifle from the tripod, dismantled it and put the pieces in the carrying case. With a small towel, he wiped the dusty ground beneath his feet, walking backwards, wiping, till he reached the grass and then the path. Less than a minute later he was passing Mattheus' cottage. There was now a light on upstairs and the dog was barking inside. He slipped inside his own back door and with haste but no speed, stashed his equipment and special clothing away in the void under the cooker. He took off his trousers, throwing them onto the chair where they normally spent the night and put on his grey night vest, his normal sleeping attire. Behind the kitchen door hung his shiny black raincoat, which he pulled on, as he would when investigating strange noises in the middle of the night. Ever since a colleague had run his fingers down the wide collar of his coat and remarked that he looked like Hermann Goering, he had taken to not wearing it in the daytime. On dark nights, his coat didn't shine because there was no light to shine off it.

'Goering!' he had snorted later. 'It's my hero, Goebbels, I'm trying to emulate.'

Konrad made to take his storm lamp, kept by the back door, but thought better of wafting its strong beam from the hilltop, from the same direction that someone might have seen the rifle flash. He took a small torch and went round to see Mattheus, who was now in his own kitchen, peering out through the window.

'Matti! Did you hear anything?'

It was a smart move. If Mattheus said he heard the shot, he could confirm it. If Mattheus said the dog had woken him up, he could say the same. Either way, he would know.

'Don't know. I was asleep and then I was awake and then Dobi was barking. I suppose he woke me.'

'Same here. Exactly the same. It was probably Dobi that woke us up. I haven't heard him bark like that before. I'll have a look around. It might have been a rat. I saw one the other day.'

'Dobi doesn't bark at rats; he just bites their heads off.'

Mattheus was now outside in his thick winter coat, hugging himself.

'Come on, let's have a look around.'

308

Five minutes peering into the darkness was enough to persuade a shivering Mattheus that there was nothing to see.

'Back to bed!'

'I think so! See you in the morning, Matti.'

Back in his cottage, calmer, Konrad could now put the lights on. He poured himself a small glass of Korn, a cheap but enjoyable Schnapps, and went to his snug room. Sinking into his soft chair, he closed his eyes and relived the hit, once, twice and again, burning it into his memory of unforgettable experiences. He dozed off, for almost a quarter of an hour until he was wrenched from slumber by a sharp knock at the door.

'Hey Konrad, It's me, Matti. Can't sleep. You coming for a nightcap? Cocoa and grog?'

Konrad had to say yes. The cocoa and grog turned into a second grog and a third and eventually into the second bottle. At four in the morning both of them leaned back, opened their mouths and began to snore.

Robert had also stared open-mouthed as the taxi-boat pilot had fallen in a flailing curve into the sea. It was a full five seconds before he recovered some measure of composure and ran towards some trees by a shed at the end of the quay. His haste was redundant; Konrad had already dismantled his rifle. Manfred was already in the shadow of the trees.

'Go to my home, separate. I will see you there.'

Manfred disappeared into the darkness behind the shed. Robert expected waves of police cars, pouring onto the quayside with sirens wailing and blue lights flashing. All he heard was a dog barking, far off. Robert was about to melt into his share of the darkness when the barking of the dog became louder. He froze against the side of the shed and then slithered round the corner. Looking back from his sanctuary of darkness, he saw a BGS uniform, a German border guard, emerging from the customs shed at the far end of the quay, with a dog. The two of them strolled, each in their own way, along the waterfront, in no apparent hurry. Fifty yards away, where the carnage had taken place, the dog stopped, refusing to respond to the handler's tugging and started licking a smear of dark liquid.

'Now what Fritz? You're always licking the quayside you disgusting hound. That's enough!'

The officer turned away, thought, pulled out a packet of cigarettes and lit one, pausing to enjoy the inhalation while Fritz licked up the remaining drops of blood, removing the last traces of the crime from the crime scene.

'Come now. You and me, Fritz! Let's finish the patrol. We make a fine team. No one tries anything on while we are around!'

Three minutes later, cigarette consumed, Fritz and his handler headed back to the warmth of their shed. The handler looked at his watch. Time for the football highlights on the second channel.

Fifteen minutes later, Robert had skirted the main street and found his way back to Manfred's, waiting five minutes in a dark alley until Manfred himself half walked, half jogged up the hill to his front door.

'Manni! I'm here.'

'Komm 'rein, schnell.'

Jutta already had the coffee going. They sat at the kitchen table staring at nothing.

'Why him? Who was after him?'

'No one. They were after you. I think they made a mistake. It won't be long until they realise that and then they will come looking. You have to get off the island as quick as you can. I don't think the ferry tomorrow is a good idea, too open, even though it will be full of tourists. Do you have to go back to Hamburg?'

'No. I just want to get back to England.'

'Hmmm. I think a special trip to the Friesian islands needs to be arranged. We can do that tomorrow. Right now I need something stronger than a coffee. Jutta!'

It was almost midday when Konrad was woken by a strange rasping sound. Someone was sandpapering the bristles of a wire brush. He looked, not knowing where he was, seeing the Doberman slowly licking his master's cheek with slow strokes that rasped against the stubble. Dobi was hungry.

'O Mein Gott, look at the time! I have work to do. See you later Matti, that was a good night.'

Back in his own cottage, Konrad went round opening the curtains and noticed with a start, a fresh picture on the drum scanner.

'Damn, when did that come in?'

The timestamp was ten minutes later than the one he had already received the previous evening. It got worse. Taking the image off the drum, the blood drained successively from his stomach, face and then the extremities of his limbs. He tingled with shock and he saw his career starting to unfold before his eyes. It was the same man and yet it wasn't. This one had blonde hair. The location was the same; the posture was the same. He placed the two pictures side by side. The first one, of a dark haired young man, had a date written on by hand. The second, the same man blond, was dated two days later. In a different hand was some handwriting in German:

'Haare gefärbet.' Hair dyed.

Konrad tingled more as the blood returned to his extremities. He snapped to attention, remembering who he was, the great Konrad. He took a pen, wrote the single word "Eledigt" "accomplished" on a single piece of paper and fed it into the machine, dialled a number in Frankfurt and let the machine do his talking. Two minutes later, Robert's plane took off for Wangeroode, one of the easterly Friesian islands.

The hop from Heligoland to Wangeroode was notable only for Robert's anxiety. The Dornier made the journey to the little Friesian island in half an hour, most of the time taken in climbing and descending. He was sick all the way, using up most of the plane's small supply of sick bags. He worried about the bumpy flight. He worried about the previous evening. But if he had known that Manfred Steuer, at that moment, was smiling as he placed what he believed to be the last entry into Robert's file in Dresden, his sickness would have been the more bearable.

He had stepped off the plane before he realised that he had not only left his duffle bag behind, but also still had not looked at the packages extracted from Brenda's pocket. The stewardess retrieved it with a smile. The packages were still there inside, with his still damp woollen hat. Two hours later, he had flown from Wangeroode to Bremen and was booking himself on the evening flight to London. He had already phoned Alessandra soon after midnight before talking through the night with Manfred.

'It's all over, love. I'm on my way home and I think I will see you Tuesday sometime, depending on the trains. I'll phone you to let you know when and where I'm landing.'

Alessandra had said little. This was not "all over" until he walked through the door. And even then, who could ever be sure? As soon as he had bought his ticket at Bremen, he called again.

'I'll be in London tonight, late. I need to pick something up from Cambridge and then I'll be on the train from there. I can't wait to see you.'

'Neither can we. We've missed you terribly.'

After he hung up on Alessandra, Robert dialled again.

'Felsby 205.' His grandmother never answered in any other way. She had looked with disdain when the post office engineer arrived two years ago with a paper label for her phone, 0SK6 9205, telling her this was her new number on the new subscriber trunk dialling exchange. He had wanted to change her big black heavy telephone for a slim red one, but she was having none of it.

'Young man, my number is Felsby 205 and always will be.'

'Nana, it's me, Robert. I want to come and see you as soon as I get home. I have some things to tell you.'

'Where have you been you naughty boy? I have had your wife and your father on to me complaining about you.'

'It's about Grandad, I have found something out.'

Mary White née Ramsbottom did not speak.

'Nana! Are you still there?'

'Yes. I hope you can handle what you have found out Robert. And I hope I can. I will see you soon. Look after yourself and hurry home. Bye bye.'

That night, in his overnight room in the seedy hotel near Liverpool Street station, alone and finally feeling safe, Robert laid out the two packages on his bed. They were identical. The two stiff manilla paper envelopes were now almost dry. The adhesive had not fully re-bonded and he was able to peel back the flaps. The money was inside polythene bags inside the envelopes. His throat dried out completely, yet he did not dare count it. That could come later. It looked a lot, high denomination notes. The Nobel booty. The prize had come home. At the bottom of the duffle bag, he located some keys. There were two, a Yale house key and a Chubb mortice. There was only one house they would fit and he knew which one.

From Liverpool Street Station in London, Robert took a train to Cambridge and then a taxi to Saffron Walden. Sykes looked as if he was seeing a ghost.

'I have one more small job for you, Mr. Sykes. I need you to accompany me while I look through this house for something important.'

Sykes had not yet got over the previous Friday evening.

'I'm not going in that house. It would be daft anyway, both of us inside if anyone should turn up.'

'So you will watch my back while I go in?'

There was a long pause while Sykes considered the options.

'Five hundred.'

'That's an awful lot for an hours work.'

'Take it or leave it.'

It meant another visit to the bank, the same cashier. Robert couldn't help wondering that if the police ever did start enquiring, he had left a huge trail. Sykes wanted to distance himself from the operation as much as possible so he gave Robert a walkie-talkie and told him that he had to make his own way there; Sykes would be strategically hidden and keeping an eye out for any visitors. He suggested that Robert should unlock the back door the moment he arrived in case he needed to slip out. Try to manage without switching on any lights. He gave him a torch. He gave him a pair of surgical gloves. Do not leave a fingerprint anywhere. When he'd finished, he had to leave quietly and never come back. Not to Saffron Walden, not even to Cambridgeshire.

'Please do not come back here. This was a peaceful little place until you showed up.'

When Robert had got what he wanted, he should put the walkie-talkie, the torch and the gloves in the bag provided and drop them in the litter bin at the end of the street. Sykes knew the location of all the litter bins in Saffron Walden and when they were emptied.

Once inside, Robert did a quick tour of the house and established the locations of rooms he would avoid – for now. He could miss out the bedrooms, bathrooms, dining room, reception rooms and kitchen. There was a study and a kind of dressing room with two sewing machines and lots of baskets of wool. It all looked as if Brenda had not intended to be away too long. There was only one chest of drawers. Under some fabric in the bottom drawer, there were fifteen notepads. Each one had dates on the cover, 1953, 1954, right up to 1967. Full of shorthand. They all went into the duffle bag. A job for later. There was a key but no obvious place where it fitted. He slipped it into his pocket.

In the study, there was much more to do. So many books and filing cabinets. He was half way through the filing cabinet when the phone rang. He reached for it instinctively, even putting his hand on the receiver until common sense prevailed. It rang eleven times. When it rang again five minutes later, he ignored it and accelerated his search. The filing cabinet had little of interest, domestic finances, letters to his bank and stock-broker, nothing scientific. The desk drawers were also dull. Pencils, paper clips and all the paraphernalia of the obsessively tidy. The bottom drawer was locked. There were no keys that fit, even on the spare bunch in the top drawer that appeared to be a spare set for the house. The key in his pocket fitted and there they were: four old Manchester University log books, six red exercise books and some torn out pages. The log books were the same as the ones he had found in the basement in Manchester. Robert's hands trembled more as he held the books than they had when he had held the money. The duffle bag was now full. Time to go. The phone rang for the fifth time as he was leaving. Sooner or later, someone, a friend or another traitor, or both, was going to get curious and phone the police instead. They might be doing it right now. The last call rang eleven times, probably the same person as before. Methodical people always let the phone ring the same number of times. Clive mixed with some very methodical people.

Robert checked the piece of paper in his pocket. He had two hours before the train from Cambridge would take him to Crewe and thence to home. He had one more appointment in Saffron Walden.

'Can you put my hair back to more or less what it was?'

It seemed that the sexy hairdresser needed to stroke his head a few times before she could decide.

'Hmmm. Of course. I wouldn't be a hairdresser if I couldn't. I dress hair.'

'But I haven't got two hours. I need to get the 3 o'clock train from Cambridge.'

'An hour is enough and we will call you a taxi. My, you do look tired. Have you been up all night with those actresses you were auditioning with?'

'Yes.'

'Naughty boy! I suppose the blonde hair did it. You'll have to get used to being dark again. Did you get the part?'

'I got everything I wanted, thank you. Everything.'

At Crewe, Robert took a taxi to the family home in Alderley Edge and was met in the courtyard by Alessandra, Robert Harry and Alexandra.

'Just look at you, the mess you're in. Those horrible clothes and your hair? What have you done with your hair? It looks like a floor brush.'

'I need to come in and change, love. I have such a lot to tell you.'

~　　~　　~

Chapter 27

Alderley Edge 1967 onwards

The next day, with the two children at school, Robert laid the two packages out on the kitchen table and finished off the story. Alessandra looked on the pile of banknotes with disdain.

'It's not ours. It's not yours. It's tainted.'

'I agree. It is tainted by the death of my grandfather. It should have been his.'

'That's a rather convoluted little argument. What would you spend it on? Not me I hope.'

'I can send it back. Though whom do I send it to? The bank, in Germany? They'll either keep it as commission or just dole it out to their shareholders. All those industrialists. I don't think Blackmore has any relatives. They certainly didn't have any children.'

There was a long silence. Alessandra got up and made Robert an espresso with a fine crema head, using their favourite Gaggia machine in the corner of the kitchen.

'When did you last have one of these?' She murmured, stroking his head, the hair now smoother and softer after several shampoos in the soft Manchester water. Robert leaned into the caress and shuddered at the thought of another haircut and colouring in Saffron Walden.

'I have an idea. I don't suppose it would be immoral if this money went into science. Build a new laboratory and allow human knowledge to progress. Perhaps it will give an opportunity to a new little Volta to contribute something to the understanding of our world.' Alessandra combined passion with pragmatism.

'It would look a little suspicious if I suddenly poured large amounts of money into a laboratory. Someone might ask where it came from. I'm not known to be a millionaire.'

'That's easy. An anonymous foundation will feed the money in. My father can arrange that. It will be done discreetly. Future young scientists will benefit. I can almost believe that Mr. Blackmore would approve.'

'I'm not sure he would. But that sounds a terrific idea. We don't benefit personally, not even with the credit of doing it. I just go on as if nothing had happened.'

'Except of course, you will have a nice new laboratory to work in, and young clever researchers to work with you! Can you cope with that spin-off?'

'I'll try!'

With the weight of the conspiracy off his mind and the injustice no longer gnawing at his stomach, Robert threw all his energies, undiluted, into research. The new laboratory in Manchester was furbished to cutting edge standards and became the envy of other scientists in the country and overseas. Alessandra had implemented another of her good ideas and part of the money had gone to endow a research fellowship that was available to give young foreign scientists the chance to come and work in Manchester and develop their careers. Robert had been surprised at the amount that had been achieved with three quarters of a million Deutsche marks. It was a fair amount of money but scientific installations were not cheap. One day, Alessandra would have to tell him that her multi-millionaire father, who had administered the foundation trust fund, had quietly doubled the money.

Robert resumed his work on quarks and gluons with massive energy. Under normal conditions, quarks and gluons, the apparent bricks and mortar of the Universe, writhed and squirmed and interacted with each other. The interaction was virtually maximal; they could not ignore each other even for an instant. But under very cold conditions, they behaved like oil and water. A population of quarks were described by statistical laws laid down by famous scientists – and Nobel prizewinners – Enrico Fermi and Paul Dirac. Large groups of gluons on the other hand obeyed laws worked out by Satyendra Bose and Albert Einstein. Bose never got a Nobel prize for any of his work. Putting the two together into a common scheme became Robert's goal. On the one hand, he was making all the measurements and building up a clear picture of how it all worked. But he was missing a believable theory of why it worked like that. Blending Fermi-Dirac with Bose-Einstein seemed beyond his grasp. He simply wasn't a theorist.

The months slid by; they became years. The children left school and went to University. Robert Harry broke the mould of the male

White line and studied medicine. It was Alexandra who went into physics, exploiting the merging of the genes of her Italian scientific ancestors with those of the physicist Whites. She was good. She was very good. She swept through her Tripos and PhD at Cambridge, attending the same college, Trinity, to which many generations of top scientists had added their lustre over the years. Blackmore was never mentioned over dinner. It was as if he had never existed.

'I know we said I would make my own career, but everyone says that the best place I can work at to further my career and do the things I want to is at your laboratory in Manchester.'

'It's not my laboratory, Alli. It's very much not my laboratory although I pop in now and then.'

'Oh, and another thing, and this will show that I am independent of you, you need to know that I have changed my name. I am now Alexandra Volta.'

Robert and Alessandra stared, mouths sagging.

'Why? Don't you respect your father? Aren't you proud of his name?' Despite her protests, Alessandra Senior was secretly proud.

'That's not the point. I'm proud of both of you. I love you both, massively. But you, Mama, were Volta, and I am extremely proud of that name. You Papa, are White, and I am proud of that. I think I should have the right to choose. Anyway, I have done it.'

'Done it? What do you mean? You were born White. We still have your birth certificate. How did you change?'

'I changed my name legally, by deed poll. Oh, and I also have a copy of my own birth certificate. Yours is a copy anyway. The government keeps the original in a book, people only get copies and yet they all think they have the original.'

Manchester 1992

Sue, the secretary bustled into the basement laboratory and interrupted Robert, Alexandra and Otto who were deep in conversation in the corner coffee area.

'There you are. Why don't you answer the phone?'

'We've pulled the cable out, it interferes with the apparatus when it rings, sorry.'

'You're wanted on the phone, urgently.'

'Who?'

318

'All of you. It's someone from Sweden, Stockholm. Nobel, she said her name was. She wants to talk to all of you and she's hanging on waiting. Hurry, it must be costing them a lot.'

'Professor White?' The voice was faint and might have been coming from the moon.

'Congratulations. It is my delightful duty to inform you that you have been awarded the Nobel Prize. You need to know that you will share the prize with Dr. Alexandra Volta and Dr. Otto Schmoeger. Are they available to speak to in your laboratory?'

'Oh yes. They are very much available. Thank you very much! Here they are!'

'That's enough work for today! I think we should pop across and see if the Nelsons has a bottle of champagne.'

'Or two!'

'And we can arrange the party while we are there.'

'First I think we should call Alessandra. Alli, you do it. And then Otto, I think you should call Ursula ... erm ... your mother in Dresden.'

Otto was too excited to notice the slip.

~ ~ ~

Chapter 28

Stockholm 1992

On the bench, overlooking the lake, Robert and Ursula pulled their coats tight around themselves on a bitterly cold Stockholm December afternoon. The sun was already dipping into the horizon at 2 pm, providing an appropriate backdrop as they exchanged forty years of hurt and hate. Old Otto should have chosen between his two girl friends but instead had married Ursula and kept Bibe as a mistress. Ursula soon found out and yet the two had stayed together to bring up young Otto. They never had children of their own. When young Otto went to work in Manchester, he had told his mother that his boss, Robert was married to an Italian, a beautiful Italian, Alessandra. She had been jealous and still was. She seemed disappointed to hear that the two were happy and always had been. She had tried to convince Robert twice over the recent years that she should pay a visit and she had been rejected twice. She now tried one last time.

'Du hättest fuer mich mehr kämpfen sollen.' She told Robert. 'You should have fought more for me.'

'Fought? So you could choose between the two knights who wanted your hand. Why didn't you choose the one whom you loved instead of the one you thought that loved you the most? It sounds to me like you just wanted to be flattered.'

'Then how do you feel now?'

'I don't love you any more Ursula,' said Robert. 'to be honest, I am not sure I ever did.'

'And young Otto?' snapped Ursula, 'Where did he come from?'

'From our love. I'm sorry. Yes. We loved. But that is it. We loved then. But now it is now.'

'What about your young Alexandra and my young Otto, should they know? Need they know? That they have the same father?'

'Does young Otto think that old Otto is his father?'

'Otto died before we could tell him. Now it doesn't seem to matter.'

'Then why add a complication? Alexandra is here because she also won the prize. She has worked with Otto but that's all she knows about him. It was difficult enough to receive him into our laboratory. I had to see them every day, half brother and half sister. I was in dread that they might fall for each other and then have to be told. It was dangerous. You kept your bargain by staying away. Why mess up an occasion like this with skeletons?'

'Yes, you are right.'

Robert got up.

'Let's go back to the hotel. This isn't working.'

His mobile rang.

'Is that you Robert?' It was Geoffrey.

'I have just come from a special meeting of the Cabinet Office's post German unification committee. Did you know the Stasi had a file on you?'

'It was a safe assumption that they did. Why?'

'We have just acquired it. I have it in front of me. It has some, how shall I put it, extraordinary information about you; all the details of the job they had lined up for you. Not just a job, three jobs. Professor at the University in Dresden, Director of the Research Institute and President of the Dresden Bezirks Committee for Democratic Science. And the Schloss in the mountains, not to mention the large luxury flat in the middle of Dresden. Luxury in the DDR!'

'They made that kind of offer to everyone.'

'And did "everyone" receive a letter that started "Further to our recent discussions, we are pleased to confirm our offer ..." '

'Well, I didn't receive an offer like that.'

'But it's in the file. You will be met off the plane from Sweden. I just thought I'd let you prepare for it, then it doesn't come as a shock.'

'Thank you, Geoffrey. I always knew I could rely on you. See you in Harrogate.'

That evening, with courage, Robert introduced Ursula to Alessandra; the one small and still attractive but showing the signs of too much sun; the other tall, still strikingly beautiful and, despite her sixty years, looking like a forty year old Sophia Loren. That night, Robert and Alessandra stayed up till 4 am as Robert told the story as it was and had been. Alessandra felt a mixture of intense relief and pride but with just a hint of sadness that she had not already been told this secret by the only man she ever loved.

"At least," she thought, "I now don't feel so bad about never telling you about the extra trust fund money from my father."

The next day, the enormity of what Robert had done came home to him as he heard the King of Sweden speak, not only his own name, but also the names of his lawful daughter and his illegitimate son.

~ ~ ~

25322594R00182

Printed in Great Britain
by Amazon